S0-ARN-006

HONEY DUST

"SIZZLING!"
—*Los Angeles Daily News*

❧

HONEY DUST

"I ALWAYS KNEW SUE COULD WRITE.
HONEY DUST KNOCKED MY SENSUOUS
SOCKS OFF!"
—**Angie Dickinson**

❧

HONEY DUST

"I COULDN'T PUT IT DOWN!"
—**Marlo Thomas**

❧

*Turn this page for more raves for HONEY
DUST.*

HONEY DUST

"A SHOCKER FULL OF SEXUAL DOUBLE STANDARDS, SECRET INNUENDOS, BETRAYALS, AND DEVIATE SEXUAL APPETITES. THE SETTINGS ARE REAL PLACES. . . AS ARE THE NAMES OF SOME VERY FAMOUS STARS. KUDOS TO MS. CAMERON—HER FIRST NOVEL IS INCREDIBLE, EXPLOSIVE READING."
—*Rendezvous*

෯

HONEY DUST

"A SEXY, SCINTILLATING READ. . .REVEALS THE INSIDE SCOOP OF HOW TINSELTOWN REALLY OPERATES."
—*American Woman*

෯

HONEY DUST

"SEXY. . .A PAGE-TURNER."
—*Beverly Hills* **magazine**

HONEY DUST

" THE SEX SCENES. . .ARE CAMERON'S
LONG SUIT."
—*Library Journal*

❧

HONEY DUST

"VERY INSIDE HOLLYWOOD. . .SEX FROLICS
OF MANY KINDS? THEY'RE HERE. REAL-
NAME-DROPPING? YES, AND A GOOD
GUESSING GAME AS TO WHICH CHARAC-
TERS ARE COMBOS OF REAL HOLLYWOOD
MOVERS, MALE AND FEMALE."
—**Jeannie Williams,** *USA Today*

❧

HONEY DUST

"CLEARLY THE WORK OF SOMEONE
WHO KNOWS WHERE THE BODIES
ARE BURIED. . . "
—***Movieline*** **magazine**

❧

SUE CAMERON

HONEY DUST

WARNER BOOKS

A Time Warner Company

WARNER BOOKS EDITION

Cover design by Diane Luger
Cover photograph by Herman Estevez

Warner Books, Inc.
1271 Avenue of the Americas
New York, NY 10020

W A Time Warner Company

Printed in the United States of America

Originally published in hardcover by Warner Books.
First Printed in Paperback: November, 1994

10 9 8 7 6 5 4 3 2 1

To Grace Metalious for Peyton Place,
the book that started my young fantasies on their way;
to Jackie Susann, who told me many years ago that I
would be a novelist one day;
and to my mother, Beryl,
who told me I could be anything I wanted to be.

ACKNOWLEDGMENTS

First and foremost, to Nanscy Neiman of Warner Books, who gave me back my life by putting the paint brush in my hand; to "Sister" Sandra Lee Alpert Frankel Seltzer Pressman for always being there, especially because I'm younger; to Lynda Carter for her special friendship and attention to every page, and for telling me, "Don't write down what you think should be in a book, write down what you think . . . and it will BE a book"; to Stan Zeigler for helping me get rid of paper bags forever; to Nancy Coffey for her encouragement and guidance, and for "getting it"; to Jim Jorgensen, Larry Rogers, and Susan Allen for taking care of me so well, and to so many of my friends . . . Marlo, Joan, Melissa, Lyn, Angie, Jessica, Valerie, Rona, Robert, Douglas, Helen, Andrea, Kate, Elaine, Elpida and Omorphia, Beverly, Ellen, Lynn, The Two Edgars, and Howard and Pookie. To Rocky's Kim. And to all my fathers . . . Paul, Eugene, and Murray.

PROLOGUE

Honey King couldn't help but watch her reflection in the glass covering the towering King Pictures' movie posters lining the halls on the way to her office. She knew her home looked like a shrine, but she didn't care. Her blonde Rita Hayworth–styled hair cascaded over her shoulders to the exact point where the front wave swooped to end right where the collar of her pink Chanel suit began. Honey had always pretended that she didn't know how "hot" she was . . . that the sophistication of Chanel suited her. In fact, she loved Chanel because of the visual contrast, knowing it was a combination that deliberately knocked any quarry senseless.

"Good evening, Mrs. King," said her assistant, looking up as Honey walked through her outer office door and kept going. Miss Williams got up and followed her, notebook in hand.

"What's my schedule tomorrow, Judith?" asked Honey, sitting behind her Louis XIV desk.

"You're all set for Mr. and Mrs. Stromberg's party tonight at eight, Mrs. King. At nine A.M. tomorrow morning, Mrs. Gallery and Mrs. Fields will be here to go over the decorations for the Angels' cocktail party. At one P.M. you and Mrs. Begelman will be at The Bistro. Three-thirty back at the house I booked Carl, that new masseur you liked, and then at five your hair and makeup people arrive. Saks is delivering your gown, and Mr. Diller is picking you up at seven-fifteen. The concert at the Music Center starts at eight. For tonight, I told Lupe to take out the navy blue St. Laurent and the short black Chanel dress in case you wish to wear either one of them.''

"Thank you, Judith. I'll see you in the morning." Honey watched her close the double French doors and then glanced at her desk. The thought of reading more mail annoyed her, and reluctantly she opened the thick correspondence folder. She looked quickly through the usual engraved invitations and then noticed an unopened airmail letter marked "Confidential." Her fingers quickly released the contents. As she read, her eyes focused more intently, then eagerly, devouring the information. A huge, almost frightening smile broke out on her face. She sat back in her chair triumphantly. "Well, well, my daughter," she whispered. "You've managed to keep the secret for years . . . but now I have it, and now I will use it to destroy you."

HONEY

* CHAPTER 1 *

No, Mommy, please, it's too dark in there. I can't breathe.''

Emmaline grabbed Honey's hand and pushed her into the closet, slamming the door. There was no handle on the inside. Honey was trapped. She was in the Black Forest again.

Five years earlier, when her mother first locked her in, she was so terrified she just kept screaming. When the blackness didn't go away, her child's imagination took over. As she lay on the floor she imagined she could feel the dampness of the earth. She could smell last year's leaves rotting. She cloistered herself in the tall trees of the forest, and they protected her. Even if she heard sounds of wild animals in the bedroom, she knew she would be safe. Sometimes she would close her eyes tightly and squeeze them until she almost had a headache. When she opened them the ''forest'' allowed in ''light.'' If she felt stifled by the stagnant air, she would put her face on the floor near the crack in the door to get fresh air, and then she'd fall asleep dreaming of a prince to take her away.

As she began to get a little older, she knew to keep a

"stash" of goodies in the closet so she would be prepared. She had a coloring book and crayons, her favorite bear named "Buddy," and some sticks that she used to build things. Today she was going to color. She was glad that it was a Saturday so she didn't have to miss school. Honey liked school. She was smart, and everybody looked up to her. She felt more like a worthwhile person there than at home, where she was treated like a trapped rat. She could hear her mother "straightening" the house now. The sounds were almost always the same. Today must have been the day for the bookshelves.

Honey vowed this would be the last time her mother was going to lock her in the closet. She was getting used to the smell of the shoe leather and the feel of the rough-hewn wood against her body, but it really bothered her that this happened to her again so close to her birthday. She thought when she turned ten that her mother would treat her more like a "grown-up." Honey didn't understand what she could have done to upset her mother so. She tried so hard to keep her room clean and help with the dishes. There were times when her mother would fly off into a rage for no reason and Honey had to pay the price. Her survival instinct made her study the signs, and soon she was getting good at predicting when these moments would come. She wanted to be prepared for the punishment ahead of time. That way she could tell herself that she was in control of it. She didn't want her mother to have that power over her. The signs had been apparent early that morning when she heard her parents arguing. Honey always felt her mother didn't want her. Her parents were always fighting about children. She tried to put herself to sleep, but she kept feeling the tears slide down the side of her face into her ear, making a deafening sound. It hurt not to be wanted.

Emmaline had been born in Honolulu, unusual for a Caucasian family in the 1900s. Her father ran a country store and her mother worked at home, or rather Emmaline worked for her mother at home, caring for her six sisters. Her days were filled with laundry, ironing, cooking, and cleaning. When she turned sixteen she shyly confronted her father one night and asked if she could work at his store after school each day.

"The other girls are old enough to help Mother, and I would really like to work with you."

Her father was taken aback by the suggestion, but he agreed, and from that day on she went to school, worked in the store, and went home. She lived a sheltered life, preferring to get out of the way of her sisters and spending as much time as she could in the store.

A year later World War I broke out, and suddenly thousands of soldiers were stationed in Hawaii, and there was a steady stream of young men in and out of the store all day.

"Excuse me, miss, do you have the new *Photoplay*?"

Emmaline was counting yellow hard candies as she looked up into the bluest eyes she had ever seen. He looked about twenty-five, and he had very fair hair with a friendly face.

"We do carry it," said she, "but we're out of it. The new shipment comes in on Friday."

"Thank you very much," said the navy man, almost bowing to her as he left.

When Friday came around she looked up each time the door opened until he arrived shortly after four P.M.

"Hello, again, miss. It's nice to see you. Have the magazines arrived?"

"Yes, they have, and the one you want is right on top in the center," she answered with a smile. He was wearing a traditional navy blue uniform and hat, but on him it looked jaunty. Emmaline watched him as he picked up the magazine, then diverted her eyes.

He put the money on the counter, saying, "I'll see you next Friday—that is, if you'll be here."

"I'm here every afternoon, sir. I'm glad you got your magazine."

As Everett Perry left that day he knew he couldn't wait to get back.

The son of a U.S. senator, Everett had run off to join the

navy rather than follow the predestined medical career his father had planned for him. Emmaline seemed to be the first natural thing that had happened to him. Up until the day they got married he only kissed her on the cheek. After the wedding night she knew what "wifely duty" meant, and to her that's all it was. When she found herself pregnant in the fall of 1917 she did not take it very well, but she pretended to be ecstatic. Everett was genuinely thrilled. Emmaline was upset that her peace and quiet was gone.

"Hold it right there, my little one," said Everett, focusing the camera. Honey was modeling this year's birthday dress from her Perry grandparents in South Dakota, posing for photographs that looked like Hollywood "stills." Everywhere she looked in her room were pictures of herself taken by her father. He was making her into his own little star.

"Look how pretty she looks, Emmie. I'm deliberately posing her against the blue sky, which matches the blue of the dress. Look at that blonde hair shining. It looks like honey. I was right in having us name her that. How perfect." But Emmaline could not share in Everett's enthusiasm about Hollywood or Hollywood things. It was a world that was foreign to her, and it made her nervous. She thought it was Hollywood, but actually she resented attention given to anyone other than her. She had been starved for attention as a child and was not thrilled with how she and Honey vied for Everett's attention.

Hours went by, and Honey turned off the flashlight that she was using in the closet to read the latest movie magazine. She had picked up the habit from her father, who left the magazines all over the house. She heard his key in the lock and knew that her mother would be by to unlock the closet any second. Honey quickly hid the flashlight and magazines and waited for the hurried footsteps. Honey soon caught on as a young child that she was supposed to emerge from her "prison," comb her hair, and then run into the living room to greet her father.

"How's my baby today?" asked Everett, picking her up

in his arms. She could smell the oil from the ship on him, and she loved it. He handed her a new movie magazine.

"Oh, Daddy, thank you. Read to me, please." Honey looked into her father's eyes as he carried her to the couch, where he read aloud to her all his Hollywood dreams.

"Dinner will be ready in ten minutes," announced Emmaline as she turned to go into the kitchen. "Then no more magazines, please."

Everett looked at Honey and winked as he started to read. Even at her young age Honey knew she was smarter than Emmaline and could manipulate her.

"Honey, look at Pearl White," said Everett as he showed her a picture of a young woman in her early twenties dressed in organza. "She was a little girl like you with beautiful hair, and look who she grew up to be. You could do that, you know. It's good to dream, because sometimes dreams come true if you believe hard enough. You can always do what you want if you believe in yourself."

By the time Honey was fifteen she did believe in herself, and she knew exactly what she wanted out of life. She knew her father was very sweet, and she loved his dreams, but she knew he was just that—a dreamer. She was going to be a doer. She was making her bed as her mother walked in the room. Honey looked her straight in the eye and said, "I'm going to the library. I have no intention of doing my reading in the closet anymore. You will no longer have the pleasure of locking me into anything."

Emmaline was stunned. "What I did I did for your own good. That's the only way a child learns discipline," she said.

"No, Mother. That's the only way you thought you could get any peace. I know you never wanted me. You think I didn't hear any of the arguments? Why don't I lock you in the closet and see if you can hear me telling my father about what you have done to me all these years?" countered Honey. Emmaline started to shake.

"No, I guess you wouldn't like me to do that, would you.

Remember, Mother,'' said Honey as she headed toward the door, "each time you look at me, know that the truth is just a breath away.''

By the time she was a junior in high school, Honey was the featured soloist of her high school's glee club, and Emmaline and Everett were trying to cope with the changes they were seeing in their "little girl."

One year for Christmas Everett gave Emmaline a mirror with an image of Rudolph Valentino painted on the top. She hung it by the front hall and rarely looked at it. Now it was one of Honey's favorite places in the house.

Her father caught her studying herself in the mirror early one evening. "What do you see, my darling?" he asked.

"Nothing, Dad.''

"It's all right to dream. You know I taught you that.''

"I was dreaming I was starring in a movie, and please don't laugh.''

"I'm not laughing. I believe you are going to do it. I told you that dreams come true. Don't ever stop believing.'' Just then there was a knock at the door. Everett opened it and saw a young man about six feet tall with dark hair.

"Hi, my name is Alii Brock. I sing with Honey in the glee club. I'm supposed to meet her here to take her to rehearsal.''

He was eighteen years old and the son of a British father and a native Hawaiian mother. He got the darker coloring of his skin and the jet black hair from her, but his features were strictly aquiline and almost "royal." He had very straight white teeth and a strong body. He also was a runner. He felt it helped him build up lung power for singing.

"It's okay, Daddy,'' Honey said. "He's supposed to bring me. We're doing a duet at the next assembly. Let him in and I'll be right back.''

Everett did as he was asked while Honey went to her room.

"And what do you think you're doing?'' said Emmaline as she saw Honey putting on lipstick for the first time.

"I'm going to rehearsals, Mother.''

"You look like a Hollywood tramp, and you're not leaving the house like that."

Honey turned and said quietly, "You have a very short memory, Mother. You can't stop me from doing anything I want, and you know it. Now why don't you just go into the kitchen and start to fix one of Daddy's favorite meals. That's definitely what you should do." She continued to stare into her mother's eyes until she felt her mother's body relax. "Good," said Honey. "I'll be back later."

Alii soon began coming to pick her up three times a week, and one day he announced to her, "We're not going to practice today. We're going to do something really special. It's a surprise."

"What kind of surprise?" asked Honey.

"It's something I want to share with you."

After an hour on the bus and then walking for thirty minutes, they were deep into the jungle on the uninhabited side of Oahu. They came to a shed that housed a railroad flatcar. Honey and Alii got on and started down the tracks that appeared from nowhere. After fifteen minutes Alii stopped pumping and the flatcar slowed down. Honey looked around and saw nothing.

"Okay, now I want you to close your eyes and not open them until I tell you to," said Alii. Honey obliged. "It will only be a couple of minutes until we get around this turn."

"Now!" said Alii as the flatcar stopped for the second time.

Honey opened her eyes, and before her stood a huge greenhouse that looked like a Victorian dollhouse sitting in the middle of a jungle. It was made of white wood and glass, with spires and leaded windows. "What is this?" Honey asked breathlessly.

"Isn't it wonderful?" said Alii. "Some of the first settlers on this island in the early 1900s built it and then deserted it. My grandfather found it about twenty years ago, and he and I have been keeping it up ever since I was a boy. When he died I had a hard time coming back here alone, but I did because I didn't want it to die, too." Honey was touched by his sensitivity. He took her hand and walked her to the entrance. He took out a pen knife from his pocket and flipped the latch on the front door. "Nobody knows about this. We never needed a lock," he explained.

Honey found herself standing in the middle of a jungle inside the house. The trees and ferns were almost two stories high. The ceiling of the building was glass so the sun could help the plants grow. The many smells of the flowers were intoxicating. As they went from flower to flower, Alii explained the different species to her. Because of the multitude of plants in an enclosed area there was a lack of oxygen in the building, but it made the closeness electric. Alii led her to a second room to the left of the main one. This one had a gazebo in the middle surrounded by tropical flowers. In this room there were no plants that were just green. Everything was in brilliant colors. "This is just like a giant Easter basket," exclaimed Honey. "I love it here. I don't ever want to go home."

"Wait until you see the next room," said Alii. He took her into a room that was a giant pond with lilies and big rocks for sunning. Honey could see the steam rising off the pond and the moisture trickling off the rocks. "Let's find a dry one to sit on," said Alii as he took off his jacket and spread it out on the biggest, flattest rock. He then took off his shoes and socks. "It's really warm here. I hope you don't mind," he said. He then took off his brown-and-white cotton print shirt and threw it on another rock. "You must be very warm, too. Let me help you," he said to Honey.

She was wearing a pink cotton dress that buttoned up the back, beige flat shoes, and her white lace socks. She began wondering exactly what he was going to help her do. He reached down and took off one shoe at a time and then each sock. His hands lingered on her right foot as he began to stroke it very gently, timing his strokes with the momentum of the water swishing around them. Soothed by his touch, Honey involuntarily reclined on the rock. While still stroking her right foot, Alii started on the left in matching strokes with his other hand. She jumped a little when she felt his mouth on her toes. His tongue darted in between each toe just before his mouth enveloped it. Honey had sensed nothing like this in his regular kisses. He was always the perfect gentleman. His tongue was now traveling up her leg. "Alii, don't! I don't know what we're doing," cried Honey.

"Yes, you do," said he. "You showed me pictures yourself of all those movie stars. You told me how much you loved Rudolph Valentino. You're as beautiful as any of those stars. I thought that's what you wanted to be." He moved his head between her thighs.

Alii had pushed up her dress above her hips and unzipped his pants. Honey was concentrating on the drops of steam as they condensed and flowed down the leaves over her head. She knew she wasn't supposed to be doing what she was doing, but she also had a sense that it was the right thing to do to prepare her for her life ahead. It was her destiny.

But she was also very much a little girl. She was frightened as well as excited. She worried about the pain. If this was what her parents did, she had a hard time imagining her mother in this position. She was filled with insecurities as she felt his hands groping her breasts. They were squeezing and rubbing. It hurt her a little bit at first, but then she started to really like it. She wanted him to do it more. There wasn't time now to take off her dress. He opened his mouth wide and placed it on hers, his tongue teasing her by slowly going in and out of her mouth. He took his hands and moved them under her knees as he raised them up. He pulled his upper body away from her. His left hand was on her knee, keeping her legs apart, and she saw his right hand go to hold himself. His eyes bored into her with an intensity that almost stopped her breathing. "Put your legs around me," he said throatily, never taking his eyes off her.

She knew to do exactly as she was told. He guided himself into her slowly, only partway, just as he did with his tongue . . . a little ways in and slowly out . . . until Honey thought she was going to scream. She hated the fact that he was just out of reach of her arms, but that only made her want him more. Just at the second that she could stand it no more, he went into her quickly and repeatedly, covering her whole body with his. He grabbed her hands and pushed them over her head as she learned to move with him, rising to a peak when she heard him moan and then stop. Her body was still shaking and wondering, but he was already putting on his pants. She sat up, and something on her legs felt funny. She looked down and saw some red. Alii reached into the pond and rinsed her off. She wasn't in pain. Her body was still vibrating from the experience. She knew then that she was going to love Alii Brock forever, and she couldn't wait to have him all over again. She knew that there was even more in store for her.

When she went home she was still shaking. She felt that her parents would know what she'd done just by looking at her. She felt so different inside. It was as if a part of her had died and a new person was reborn. She didn't feel dirty. She felt accomplished and proud. When she opened the door her father was sitting on his chair reading.

"Did my little girl have a good time?" he asked.

I'm not your little girl anymore, thought Honey, but, "Yes, Daddy," is what she answered. She was afraid to go near him in case he could smell Alii. She could definitely smell him. "I'm going to go get ready for bed. I already had dinner," said she as she waved and ran to her room. Once inside she carefully took off all her clothes. She held them up to her nose and inhaled the passion. These are never being washed, she thought as she put them in a shoebox way up high on the shelf of her closet. She put on a robe and made her way to the bathroom. She could hear her mother in the kitchen, so she knew it was safe. She shut and locked the door behind her. Part of her didn't want to take a bath and wash off her adventure, but she knew she would have to. She took off the robe and looked in the mirror at her breasts. Just the thought of Alii made her nipples harden. Her whole body felt different. She felt alive for the first time. Her senses weren't blocked, and she couldn't stop experiencing what had just happened.

She couldn't wait to go to school in the morning, took extra care to find exactly the right dress. She ran out of the house without breakfast, hoping to see Alii first thing in the morning. Sure enough, she spotted him on the playground playing basketball. She started to walk toward him, hoping he would stop playing and walk toward her, too, but he didn't. He simply shouted hello to her in the middle of a move.

"Alii, can I talk to you a second?"

"Can't we talk at lunch?" he called.

"Okay, I'll see you then." Disappointed, she lifted her hand in a half wave and walked toward her classroom. Suddenly whistles and screams erupted, and she turned around to see the guys on the court patting Alii on the back. No, she thought. Not Alii.

The three hours until lunch crawled by. She didn't hear the teacher call on her, she didn't talk to her friends. Finally it was lunch, and when she saw Alii sitting at their usual table outside, she asked if they could be by themselves.

"Sure," he said, picking up his lunch bag and walking toward a tree.

"I really wanted to talk to you," started Honey. ". . . about yesterday."

"Yeah, wasn't it great?" said Alii. "You're really something. Let me know when you want to meet me again. You're my kind of girl."

"Just what kind of girl is that, Alii?" asked Honey. "I need to know what you're thinking. Yesterday was very important to me. You're important to me." She was trembling now.

"Look," said Alii, "you're cute and I have fun with you. I don't want to get into anything deep. I just want to have a good time, and boy, are you it!" He put his arms around her and lifted her up to his face, where he planted a monster kiss on her right in front of everybody. She knew then what he was doing and what he had told his friends. She struggled to get down, filled with shame and anger. How could she have been so stupid?

He lost interest in her when he couldn't get what he wanted. He let her down just the way her father had let her down all these years. I can't trust men, thought Honey. I will never trust them. I was better off in the closet not allowing anyone in. The next time any man ever wanted her again, she was going to come out the winner.

She wondered how her father treated her mother in the beginning, wondered whether or not her mother might be disappointed in her father. Without Alii school was unbearable, and so was her life. She just wanted to get away, but she couldn't figure out how to do it.

One day, as she was reading about Greta Garbo in one of her father's magazines, she heard her parents call her into the living room. Honey obliged, but when she entered the room her eyes fell on her mother's nose. Honey knew that it expanded every time something significant was about to happen. The nose was in the "fresh kill" position, so Honey knew something was up.

Her father got up and began to pace. "Honey, we have something to tell you that is very important. It's going to mean a lot of changes in your life." Honey was at rapt attention. "I loved the navy all of my life, and I love this island. I spent the happiest years of my life here. It's been home to your mother for her whole life. Something has come up recently that your mother and I have discussed. We think it is important for you to experience more of life than just this island. It's time for all of us to have new experiences. I have been offered a job as an assistant manager of the Bank of San Francisco."

"You mean you're going to take it?" exclaimed Honey.

"Yes, I am. We are going to leave here in three weeks."

"Oh, Daddy, I'm so happy," said Honey as she flew to him and hugged him. "We're going to be near Hollywood!"

They arrived in San Francisco one month later in August of 1937.

San Francisco was a hustling place, and most of the kids Honey met at school were eager to go out and work, to become something in the world. For the first time she was meeting people her own age who shared her dreams. Honey adored San Francisco, but she noticed that her mother did not. There was only one occasion that Emmaline even traveled to the city, and then it was with Everett to go to a bank dinner. Honey saw that Emmaline was insecure and uncomfortable in her new surroundings, and it gave her a sense of power to see that she had overtaken her mother. It was a position from which she would never retreat. She loved her school and made friends easily. The gorgeous blonde with the beautiful voice had a very easy time. She joined the drama class and auditioned for and got the lead in the school's holiday musical, *Angel Wings*, which earned her the right to stay after school and rehearse. What else could her parents say? Rehearsals put Honey in the city during the late afternoon and early evening, and her sense of adventure was too strong to be ignored. One day after rehearsal, instead of getting on the number three bus back to Brisbane, the little town on the outskirts south of the city where she lived, she boarded the bus for Chinatown. She was used to seeing Chinese in Hawaii, but she had heard that Chinatown in San Francisco was really special. The bus let her off in front of an ancient gate on Grant Street that beckoned you up a hill. The minute Honey walked through that gate it seemed as though people stopped speaking English. The street was made out of cobblestones, and all along the way there were dark, crooked alleys with people lurking in them wearing brightly colored silk shirts, black pants, and little hats. She saw doors that led to God knew where. Honey was thrilled by the mysteries. She wasn't afraid at all. The sweet smell of incense permeated the streets, along with smells of fried foods being sold from carts. She looked up and saw crude shades covering windows and laundry hanging from rooftops. She remembered a treat that her father always brought her called *char sui bow,* a sticky bun filled with roast pork. She saw some being sold and bought one to eat as she continued her stroll. It was getting quite dark as she neared the top of the hill, and when she reached the top the view of San Francisco Bay hit her right in the face. She literally felt on top of the world. She knew she could do anything. She was no longer a prisoner on an island.

Everett could feel the audience in the high school auditorium sense the magic. Honey's beauty on stage was luminescent. She was really going to be a star. Her singing voice pealed off the rafters. When the show was over he was the one who started the standing ovation, but the whole audience joined in. He stared at her bow with tears in his eyes, and when he looked over at Emmaline, she was in tears, too. He was glad that she finally was about to show how proud she was, too. He was sure that was it. Yes, he was.

The show ran for three weekends. Honey was hardly ever home, so caught up was she in the whirlwind of the production. The Sunday morning after closing night Honey woke up filled with mixed emotions. She was devastated that the show was over, yet she knew she had turned another corner. She looked up on her wall where she had tacked up her reviews. Not only did the high school paper review it and give her a rave, but both the *San Francisco Chronicle* and the *Post* sent people to the show. In each case she was singled out as the best part of the show. She had been mulling something over in her mind, and now that the show was over it might be the right time to act on it. She thought it would be better if she put on a dress and heels. It was very important for her parents to start to accept her as a grown-up.

"Wow!" exclaimed Everett. "Who is this that showed up for breakfast?"

"Good morning, Dad," said Honey. "Would you please call Mother in here so we can talk a little?"

"Emmie? Turn off that stove and come in here. Our star has something to say to us," yelled Everett.

Honey looked at her parents. "You know I love singing and acting. It's the most important thing in the world to me. It's more important than marriage or children, or anything that you might think would be on my mind for my future. I believe that I have something . . . special, and from this moment on I'm going to pursue it. I have only a few months to go before I graduate, and I'll stick with that, but I'm also going to go out on auditions and do everything I can to get my career started. As of now I'm out in the world and on my way. My childhood is over." Her parents were too stunned to speak. Honey knew the balance had shifted.

* CHAPTER 2 *

It was tough being the only Jew on the University of Southern California football team, but Pinky Cohen was going to show them. He had done it in high school in San Diego, and he could do it now. It didn't matter that the cleat marks on his instep still stung from today's latest wound in practice. One day everyone would know his name.

Pinky had been born in Bayonne, New Jersey, to Russian immigrant parents who quickly moved their growing family to Arizona and then to California. He'd had a very religious upbringing and was extremely proud of his heritage. Excelling in academics as well as sports, Pinky was named "Jewish Athlete of the Year" by a local paper and was spotted by USC scouts and given a football scholarship. As a minority Pinky's view of the world made him aware of how things should be changed. He knew that lawyers and judges could do that, and he wanted to be one. USC had the best law school in the country, and he was a very ambitious young man. That, coupled with his size, was an interesting combination and one that could lead a determined man very far.

USC in 1935 was like a thriving city unto itself. It was the largest place Pinky had ever seen. From the moment he stepped on the campus he felt the pulse. Each step seemed like a run down the football field. He just knew he was going to be successful. He got into Zeta Beta Tau, the best Jewish fraternity, was well liked by his professors, and loved playing football. But he was always aware that he was a little bit different from most of the students outside of his fraternity. An occasional anti-Semitic remark was thrown his way, but he just ignored it and kept on going. He was not prepared, however, for the viciousness of a player from Wisconsin who smashed him so hard in the back during a game that he passed out on the field. The last thing he heard was "kike bastard!"

When the healing period was over after the precarious back surgery, he was left with one leg slightly shorter than the other. He was extremely relieved when USC decided to honor his scholarship. But now he really needed to make money, and he had to come up with a plan. One day at the frat house his eyes fell upon a desk blotter that was given away to each student at the beginning of the semester by the student bookstore. As a border around the work space, several university departments and service organizations placed advertising on the blotter so all year you had a phone number easily and were reminded of the existence of these organizations. And then it came to him. That blotter came out only once a semester. Whoever advertised on it only had one shot at imparting information. He devised the idea of an ad sheet that would fit on the wall around the phone in each fraternity, sorority, dorm, school building, and store. These could be plastered everywhere with ads from movie theaters showing what was playing to give the kids a guide on where to go.

He soon had a mock-up design and started selling the ads by soliciting theater owners. The idea caught on like wildfire, and he soon was making $500–$800 a week. He also made a new friend, Sam Lewis, Jr., son of the owner of the Metropolitan Theatre chain. Sam was the manager of the theater near the school on Figueroa Street. Although Sam was a little older than Pinky, he was immediately taken with his enthusiasm. Sam and Pinky would spend hours on a Saturday night sitting in Sam's office discussing show business, and Pinky got hooked. Pinky really wanted to meet Sam Lewis, Sr.

Pinky and Sam had been friends for four years when one day Pinky picked up the phone and heard Sam say, "Pink? I'm picking you up for lunch today. We're going to Hillcrest." Pinky had waited four years to hear those words. Hillcrest Country Club was a private club where all the studio heads and big stars had lunch on Saturdays. When they drove up along Pico Boulevard Pinky could only see a high hedge made of ivy and two brick columns holding up a gate. Sam drove in and waved at the guard. A parking attendant took his car, and he and Pinky walked into the club. The walls were painted celadon green with white molding. The floor was stained hardwood. Straight ahead was a large room for dining with windows that overlooked the golf course. When they walked in the room Sam turned left.

"This is the way to the Men's Grill. Women are never allowed in here."

Pinky followed along and saw two round tables in the middle of the room. Seated at the first one were Eddie Cantor, Al Jolson, Jack Benny, George Burns, and a newcomer he had heard about called Milton Berle. At the next table he saw a bunch of men smoking cigars, but he didn't recognize any of them.

"Follow me," said Sam. "There's my father." He pointed to the other round table. Seated with Sam Lewis, Sr., were Sam Goldwyn, Jack Warner, Louis B. Mayer, and Barney Balaban of Paramount.

Pinky had heard about these famous Saturday lunches. He also knew that after lunch each table would start up a gin game, and then the winners would play each other. There was no more powerful place in Hollywood than this Men's Grill. Pinky had wanted to get here for quite a while. In fact, it was only in the last two years that Sam's father had allowed Sam to stop by. He was never allowed to stay for gin, though.

He had to leave immediately after lunch. Sam Sr. had been listening to his son talk about Pinky for some time. He was impressed with the stories of the kid from San Diego. The other studio heads also began to hear about him through their field representatives. The studios owned all the theaters, and when grosses went up dramatically in certain areas, they wanted to know why. Areas near colleges were test markets for pictures, and although Pinky had no way of knowing it, he was working in an area the big studios kept their eyes on. They soon found out that Pinky's advertising scheme was worth a great deal of money to them.

Pinky was wearing his blue suit, which made him feel a little more confident. He was glad he had worn it as he approached the table. The cigar smoke was overwhelming, and he tried hard not to choke.

"My boy," said Sam Sr., rising to greet his son.

He stuck out his hand, and Pinky went to shake it. Pinky was embarrassed when he realized the outstretched hand was for Sam. In Pinky's family fathers and sons hugged each other, so this stiffness was new to him. Sam Sr. then turned his attention to Pinky.

"And here you are, the one-man band for the movie industry."

Pinky extended his hand and said, "It's an honor, sir." Just then a roar of laughter erupted from the comics' table, and Pinky turned.

"Oh, ignore them, son. They always laugh at their own jokes. They work for us, anyway."

Pinky got the message quickly about the power pecking order in Hollywood. Obviously being a star was secondary; it was the man who signed the check who had the power. He was now being introduced to the other men. Mayer didn't even look up. Goldwyn nodded, and Balaban shook his hand. Pinky was so in awe that he had to concentrate not to pass out. He felt like a speck in the presence of these men, but at least he was a speck in the right place.

"So, Louis," said Goldwyn. "I hear that Garbo dame is

holding you up for a lot of money." Mayer looked as though he wanted to kill.

"At least people go see her pictures, not like your Anna Sten, Goldfish," replied Mayer.

A chill went down Pinky's back. Everyone knew that Goldwyn's wandering eye had made him lose control over his pocketbook and fall for Sten, an actress who could barely speak English, who bombed in everything Goldwyn put her in. Pinky knew not to speak unless spoken to.

To release the tension, Sam Sr. asked him, "What are you going to do after you graduate from law school next month?"

"I'm going to rent an office downtown and start my own practice. I like relying on myself," answered Pinky.

"That may be, boy," countered Sam Sr., "but I'm going to keep an eye on you anyway."

"Thank you, sir," said Pinky, almost disbelieving what was happening. He was very flattered that at least someone at the table had bothered to speak to him. He was too naive in business to know that the silence of the others was not disinterest, but meaningful observation.

The world that Pinky graduated into was a tough one. The Depression was the worst time for anyone to start a solo business, especially a young man fresh out of USC Law School. He was still living in his fraternity house because they gave him a great deal on room and board, and it was near his office. Pinky had $10,000 in the bank, which he had saved from his ad business. He bought a beat-up Ford and rented the office, one room at the corner of Eighth and Flower. He was making a living doing divorces for $75 each, but his heart was with the movie industry, and he was determined to figure out a way to get in it for real.

On Monday morning at 8:00 A.M. Pinky's phone rang in the fraternity house.

"Mr. Cohen, you don't know me, but you got a divorce for my daughter. My name is Violette Greener."

Pinky recognized the name of the famous evangelist with a church of her own in downtown Los Angeles.

"I'm sorry to bother you at this hour, but a friend of mine is in trouble, and you were the only lawyer I could remember. Could you please come to the church right away?"

The door to the private apartment behind the church was opened by a pretty brunette in her early fifties.

"Thank you for coming, Mr. Cohen. Please come with me."

Pinky followed her to a Victorian parlor with burgundy velvet furniture with hand-crocheted white lace doilies all over everything.

"I'd like you to meet Mr. Giles Clifton, a friend of mine from England. He has a story to tell you."

"Mr. Cohen, this is very difficult for me," started Clifton, pausing to wipe sweat from his brow. "I am in terrible trouble. I have been bilked out of a hundred and fifty thousand dollars, and I don't know what to do."

Pinky couldn't believe that someone could have that much money during these bad times, let alone to be able to lose it and still have something to live on. "Just start from the beginning," he said as they all sat down. And then Clifton started to relax a bit and speak.

"I am from England, and I make periodic trips to the United States for various reasons. I like to gamble, too much, I'm afraid." Clifton paused to take sip of water from the crystal goblet on the coffee table before him. "Each time I come here," he continued, "I go to the Trocadero on the Sunset Strip to the back room and play cards. This last time I lost, and I lost big. I don't welsh on my bets, so I gave the winner, Lou Brice, a check for fifty thousand dollars and a letter to my stockbroker in New York ordering him to release the hundred thousand. I felt a little funny about all this, and then I came to Violette's. She told me she was sure the game was fixed. What can I do, Mr. Cohen?"

"What bank did you write the check on?" Pinky asked, trying to buy time to think.

"Bank of America," answered Clifton.

"Of course." He rose and asked Violette if he could use a phone in the other room. Once out of earshot of Violette and Clifton, he called a former fraternity brother who was a management trainee at the Bank of America Wilshire branch. With one call, Pinky stopped the check. He also had it confirmed to him that Clifton was worth a great deal more than the $150,000.

"I just saved you fifty thousand dollars, Mr. Clifton," Pinky said as he returned to the living room. "I would like a retainer of ten thousand dollars to continue your case and save the other hundred thousand. Since your broker is in New York, we have a few days to work on that."

"It's a deal, Mr. Cohen. I thank you."

Back in his office, he pondered the problem at hand, realizing he needed the power to stop the $100,000 and also put the gambling ring out of business. Then he remembered the most powerful lawyer in town, Jerry Geisler, friend to the stars, and the best friend of District Attorney Buron Fitts. He put a call through to Geisler's office, saying, "This is Pinky Cohen, and I'm an attorney with an emergency." When the attorney came on the line, he said, "Mr. Geisler, I am a lawyer and I need your help urgently. I am holding a retainer fee for ten thousand dollars given me by a client a few minutes ago. I need to see you right away."

Geisler paused for a second before saying, "You'd better come right over."

Standing before Pinky was an overweight man with a large bald head and a very big cigar, impeccably dressed in a black silk suit.

"So what do you need me for?" Geisler asked after Pinky told him of Mr. Clifton's troubles.

"I need you to get to Buron Fitts, sir. Together the three

of us can stop this gambling ring, and we can save Mr. Clifton his one hundred thousand dollars.''

"Okay," said Geisler, realizing Fitts would love to have the gambling business feather in his cap just before election. "I'm sure you have a plan."

Precisely at 9:45 A.M. the next morning, Pinky and two policemen were waiting around the corner from the bank. At exactly 10:00 A.M. Brice showed up. The plan was to wait until Brice went into the bank and asked for the money. Brice entered the bank, and quietly the policemen followed. Brice approached the manager's office. The policemen moved closer to him, but Brice was so interested in the money that he didn't notice them. "What do you mean there's no money?" Brice shouted at the man.

"Hold it right there," said one of the policemen as they both stepped into the office. "Come with us, sir."

Just then Fitts walked in. "Hello, Mr. Brice, I'm Buron Fitts."

"I know who you are," Brice said cautiously.

"I want you to sign this release of the one hundred thousand dollars, Mr. Brice, or you're going to jail," said Fitts. "I also want the names of your partners in this sham, and the location of the next game."

Brice was shaking. "I need a few minutes to think," he said.

"You'll have more time than you know what to do with if you don't sign it," said Fitts as he left him alone with guards at the door.

After a few minutes, when Pinky walked in, Brice beamed with surprise.

"Thank God. Someone who at least looks familiar. You can help me. But wait a second. What are you doing here?" said Brice.

"Never mind," answered Pinky. "Just sign the release. Sign it and go home and don't breathe a word of this to anyone." Brice knew he was serious, and he signed the paper.

Pinky was exhilarated as he drove to Geisler's office to fill him in.

"Well, kid"—Geisler chuckled—"you got ten thousand dollars for saving fifty thousand. Let's get twenty-five thousand for saving the one hundred thousand. You keep the original ten thousand dollars, and I'll keep ten thousand of the twenty-five thousand.

"Now listen, kid, you've got something that makes people trust you. You're ambitious, but I've got a feeling that you can be trusted. I've seen you hanging out at Hillcrest Country Club with the Lewises and Mayer and the guys. I know where you want to go. The movie industry, right? Well, I do big favors for them. . . . Together you and I can do even bigger ones. I don't want you to even go back to your office now. You're going to be spending more time here than there from now on. The first thing I want you to do for me is go to the airport and pick up Mickey Cohen. I know you probably think he's the new Al Capone, but just do as I tell you and you'll be fine. Introduce yourself as my man. Don't talk to him. Don't do anything. Just keep your eyes and ears open."

Pinky's mind was whirling.

"By the way," said Geisler, "what's your real first name? 'Pinky' sounds like a stripper."

"It's Philip," answered Pinky.

"Good," said Geisler. "That's much better. And don't call yourself Cohen. Mickey thinks he owns the name. Use Philip King."

* CHAPTER 3 *

W hat do you mean I can't go on the audition because my chores aren't done?" Honey screamed as Emmaline continued to iron. She had been auditioning for just about anything in the three months since she'd graduated from high school, and the competition was tough. There were many girls who had been doing it longer than she, and she hadn't learned the ropes yet. But she watched and she learned. "This is the one I'm going to get, Mother!" Honey was standing in the kitchen, holding her hairbrush. She always felt stronger with it in her hand. It gave her a feeling of power. She knew that her honey-blonde hair was her best asset, and just holding the brush made her more confident. "How much longer are we going to play these games, Mother? I know that you want me out of here, yet you pretend you want me tied to your perfect little apron strings."

Emmaline stopped ironing and looked up at Honey for the first time, her face flushed. "You know your father adores you. He must be kept happy."

Her passivity made Honey even madder.

"There you go again, Mother. You talk and say nothing. Why don't we talk about closets and lies?"

"If you aren't home tonight by nine P.M., I'm going to commit suicide. I mean it," said Emmaline.

"Don't tempt me, Mother," retorted Honey.

Emmaline looked up at Honey with hatred in her eyes but still said nothing. Honey walked out of the room before she could smell the burning shirt beneath Emmaline's iron.

Honey felt triumphant as she entered her room, determined not to play her mother's game anymore. After opening her closet, she found her favorite audition outfit, a turquoise-blue silk dress with matching pumps and a turquoise-and-pink bow that she felt contrasted beautifully with her hair.

The forty-five-minute bus ride into the city flew by. Every time Honey left Brisbane she got excited when the tall, multi-colored Victorian houses of San Francisco came into view. The high peaks and steep hills represented her life. She wanted more peaks and felt that today was her day. She got off the bus near the Wharf district and walked to Bimbo's 365, the most popular nightclub in the city. She'd read that they were looking for a singer to do a few numbers in between the headliner's sets so the customers wouldn't leave the club. When she walked into the club the first thing that hit her was the smell of smoke. To her the place reeked of show business, though the actual smell was garbage and grime. She didn't notice. She walked into the main room and looked around for someone, though it was very difficult to see because it was pitch black except for a small rehearsal light on the piano. Then she heard a rustling in back.

"Hurry up before the next one gets here," said a gruff voice still engulfed in darkness.

Honey couldn't see a thing until an overweight man in his sixties appeared in his shirtsleeves and khakis.

"Bring your music up here, sweetie," said another disembodied male voice.

"Can you play this in B flat?" asked Honey.

"Sure, let's get on with it."

Honey turned to face the darkened house and moved the one light to the side in front of her. "You go to my head, and you linger like a haunting refrain/And I find you spinning round in my brain/Like the bubbles in a glass of champagne. . . ." Her voice had a very clear, free tone. She kept on singing and finished the song, the first time in all her auditions that she hadn't been stopped before the end. She felt very good about this audition.

"You'll do," said the gruff voice from the back of the room. "You get fifty dollars a week to do three shows every Tuesday, Wednesday, and Sunday. You supply your own wardrobe and rehearse with the piano player on your own time. Be here next Tuesday night at eight."

"Thank you, thank you," Honey said a little too loudly into the mike. "This means a great—"

"Knock it off kid, you're just filler."

The piano player handed her music back and said, "I'll be here Tuesday from five to six. We'll rehearse then. You'll do fifteen-minute sets. Have three planned."

Honey flew out of Bimbo's three feet off the ground. She just had to celebrate, do something really special. Something that real grownups did. Before she knew it she was on a bus bound for Nob Hill and got off across from the Fairmont and Mark Hopkins hotels, the most elegant places in the city, filled with rich, successful people. This was where Honey longed to be. She had never been to either hotel, but she read about them all the time in the society section of the newspaper.

She stood in the giant motor court and watched a long black limousine pull in. The door was opened by a doorman wearing a long burgundy coat with brass buttons, black slacks, and a burgundy military-looking hat. The most beautiful couple she had ever seen emerged from the car.

She followed them into the lobby. As soon as she walked through the doors she was mesmerized by the beauty. The lobby was all burgundy, gold, and black with huge gold-and-black columns reaching up to the three-story-high ceiling.

Encircling the base of each column was a burgundy velvet couch. A gigantic staircase rose to mezzanine level. Straight ahead was a mahogany desk that appeared to be half the size of a football field. She could see the couple from the limousine heading to an elevator, their ten pieces of matching luggage trailing behind them. Throughout the lobby were men in burgundy uniforms, "The Fairmont" embroidered in gold on their jackets. She walked up to one standing in front of the flower shop and said, "Excuse me, sir. Where is the soda fountain?"

"Our Sweet Shoppe is behind me and to the right, miss."

No one has ever called me "miss," she thought smiling. She liked it. Walking into the Sweet Shoppe was like walking into a strawberry sundae. The walls were pink, the seats were pink, the floor was pink and gold, the fixtures were pink and gold, and the waitresses wore pink starched uniforms. She sat down at the counter and picked up a menu, trying to look as though she did that every day.

"This is a butterscotch sundae, and I've never tasted anything this good ever."

Honey turned to the young man seated to her left.

"Well, I really think I want a chocolate soda, but if I ever come back, I'll have a butterscotch and remember this day," she replied. She ordered her soda and could sense that the young man wanted to talk to her but was shy. She was so absorbed in her moment of triumph, plus the impending chocolate soda, that she didn't feel like talking. She was worrying about what she was going to sing. They'd asked for lots of songs.

"Enjoy your soda," said the young man as he paid his check and left.

"Hello, Mother. Still breathing, I see," said Honey when she arrived home at six P.M.

"What do you mean by that?" asked Everett, putting his paper down.

"Now, Daddy," Honey said, rubbing his head, "you

know that sometimes women have their secrets. Don't pay any attention to it.''

"Dinner will be ready in thirty minutes, Honey."

"Mother, Dad . . ." She took a deep breath. "I have a job singing in a real nightclub. I'm being paid and everything. It's finally starting."

Everett was the first to respond. "I'm so happy for you. I know you'll make us proud. But what kind of place is it?"

"It's Bimbo's 365 Club."

"What!" said her father. "I've read about that place. It's dangerous. You can't do it."

"But, Dad—"

"Everett, I think it's time for your daughter to grow up. She's not a child. We have to know when it's time to let her go."

Honey's dressing room was a converted linen closet next to the kitchen. There's a theme here, I know, and I don't like it, she thought to herself, but this time I've got the key. She actually had only thirty minutes in between the end of her first rehearsal to the beginning of her first show. She took a breath and, humming one of her songs, looked in the mirror and began to prepare for her new life. She applied as much eye makeup as she knew how and put jewelry clips at the sweetheart neckline of her simple black dress to make herself look older.

"You're on!"

The knock at her door startled her. She went to the door next to the kitchen as an announcer said, "Ladies and gentlemen, Honey Perry." There was no applause as she entered. The crowd didn't stop talking. She looked at the piano player and began. Even as she was singing, the crowd barely slowed down, which was very hard on her. During the second show the response was about the same, and Honey was dreading the third show. But going on was her job. Midway through it she finally got their attention with "How Deep Is the Ocean." Maybe it was the late hour and they were quiet, or maybe just some magic happened, but all she knew was that for that short time she experienced the power to make them want her.

On her way back to the "linen closet" she saw a slightly familiar face in the hall. As she passed him he said, "Hello," and smiled.

"Have we met?" She smiled.

"Not exactly," he replied, "but if I say 'butterscotch sundae,' you might remember."

"Oh . . . the soda fountain," Honey remembered.

"I think you're wonderful. You sing beautifully. My name is Sam Lewis." He extended his hand, and she took it.

"It's nice to meet you. My name is Honey Perry."

"I hope you don't mind if I tell you that your voice sounds like your name."

"I haven't heard it in a while, and I needed that tonight," said Honey. "Thank you, but, please, stay away from the 'Honey' jokes."

He nodded and then said, "The soda fountain at The Fairmont is closed now, but the bar at the Top of the Mark is still open. Have you ever had a grasshopper? It tastes like a mint chocolate sundae. Will you have one with me?"

Honey was unsure. She had never been picked up before, but how dangerous could he be if he hung out at soda fountains?

When the doors opened at the Top of the Mark Honey thought she was in heaven. The room was glass walls on all four sides with tables along each wall and a giant bar in the center. A piano player played Jerome Kern. It was all incredible.

"We'd like two grasshoppers, please," ordered Sam.

"Gee, that's super," she said, taking a sip, wishing she'd thought to say how "marvelous" it was. "I have a confession to make," she said. "When I saw you at the fountain I was celebrating this job. And tonight is the very first professional job I've ever done."

"To you," said Sam as he toasted her. "You look like you really love to sing."

"Oh, I do," replied Honey. "I really do."

"But you haven't been in the business very long," said Sam.

"No, but I'm going to make it. I know I am. And what about you?"

"I'm from Los Angeles, and I work in the movie business," he said matter-of-factly. "I was born into it, I didn't have a choice. But it's okay. I'm in San Francisco to survey the Metropolitan Theatre operation in the Bay Area."

"Are you the illegitimate son of Louis B. Mayer or something?"

Sam laughed. "No, but he's a good friend of the family. My father owns Metropolitan Studios."

Metropolitan Studios! Be calm. Be calm, Honey said to herself.

"Do you sing tomorrow night?"

"Yes, I do," she said, smiling.

"I'll be there," said Sam. "Now let's put you in a taxi. I don't want to keep you out so late that you hurt your voice." The doorman at the Mark whistled for one, and it immediately came around the corner. "Driver, take Miss Perry wherever she wants to go, please," said Sam as he put money into the driver's hand.

Honey thought she was in a dreamworld.

The pattern went on for two more weeks. Honey was being courted, and she loved it. One night after the show he met her outside the back entrance to Bimbo's, standing next to the longest, blackest limousine she had ever seen.

"Won't you get in, mademoiselle?" She did indeed, and before her was a bottle of champagne in a silver ice bucket. "Golden Gate Park, please," said Sam, pushing the button that closed off the passenger area from the driver's with a blackout screen. He opened the side windows and they sipped champagne, enjoying the beauty of the park at night. Sam took her hand, and she noticed it was shaking.

"I love you, Honey. Please don't say anything. Just let me talk. I've never felt this way before. I have such plans for us. I know you'll love Hollywood."

Honey was shocked by the suddenness of it all, but delighted. "Oh, Sam," she said as she leaned forward to kiss him. She opened her eyes and saw tears in his.

"I love you," he said again as he awkwardly pushed her down on the backseat. His hands pressed against her chest, just groping. She tried to pretend that she was excited, knowing it would mean a lot to him, but she just felt sorry for him. He stuck his tongue in her mouth and then didn't know what to do with it. All the while he was trying to slip her underpants down. She heard him unzip his pants and she parted her legs, then felt him on her as he started moving forward and back, but she realized he had not yet gotten hard. He continued to grind against her, and then after one huge attempt he just fell on her, sobbing. He obviously cared about her, but he didn't know how to show her properly.

"I hate this," he said angrily as he moved away from her. He opened the chauffeur screen a little bit so the driver could hear him bark, "Drop me off at the Mark and then take Miss Perry home."

Honey tried to comfort him. "It's all right, Sam. Don't worry," she said, attempting to hold him.

He pulled away again and then turned to ice. "Don't talk to me."

They sat in silence until the car pulled up to the hotel, and he got out without saying a word. Honey was upset and confused. She hadn't really had enough experience to fully understand. She was numb as she rode back to her house.

* CHAPTER 4 *

Hollywood in the early 1940s was the hottest town on earth. By day business got done on the screen, but at night the off-screen business was much more interesting. The area of the Sunset Strip from Schwab's Pharmacy on the east to the Beverly Hills Hotel in the west was like a combination of yet-to-be-born Las Vegas and New York City. By a fluke the land was part of Los Angeles County, as opposed to the city, and the county police simply looked the other way when it came to gambling. All of the studio heads put up money for different nightclubs, the Clover Club, the Colony Club, the Trocadero, and the Mocambo. Darryl Zanuck, Jack Warner, Joe Schenck, and Sam Lewis used these clubs as their playground, and each studio ordered their actors and actresses under contract to go there each night to be seen. Photographers stood outside each club, and some, who paid more money, were allowed inside to take pictures. Out front they had a glamorous restaurant with a dance band and a singer and perhaps a headliner. While the public thought the showroom was where the glamour and the action took place, it simply wasn't true. In the back of each club was a gambling room with slot machines, crap tables, and card games.

Each studio head would preside over his room, but they all visited each other, and frequently, after they were through gambling, they ended up down the road in a Strip club called Ball of Fire. Mickey Cohen was king of the Strip. One of his businesses was something called the "wire." It was the sound connection that horse rooms paid for to get horse race results as they happened. Whoever controlled the wire controlled the city.

Pinky's life changed the day he met Mickey Cohen at the airport. Even he thought of himself as "Philip King" now. The gangster and the kid. They hit it off right away. Mickey could see that Philip was smart and knew how to keep his mouth shut. The minute word got around that Philip was "Mickey's boy," doors opened for him all over town. Sam took him everywhere now, and even Sam Sr. perked up.

They had a routine. Philip, Mickey, Sam, an attorney named Monroe Goldstein, a gambler named Charlie Schwartz, and a private detective named Barney Ruditsky were the gang that hung out in off hours. They were inseparable. On Friday nights they would go to the fights at Hollywood Legion Stadium. Saturday afternoons you would find them in their reserved box at Gilmore Field for the Hollywood Stars baseball games. At both places Philip was aware of bets being placed and conferences with Mickey and different characters, but he just looked the other way. He loved the action. All the executives went to the fight, too, and he got to know the Hillcrest men better. At the baseball games the crowd was different. All the performers went there, Milton Berle, Phil Silvers, and Eddie Cantor. Philip again noticed that dividing line between the "talent" and the executives. They didn't even go to the same events. The only place they mixed was at the nightclubs.

Philip was late getting to the fights one Friday night because he and Jerry Geisler were working late on a divorce case. Geisler represented Lolita Leilani, one of 20th Century-Fox's starlets. Everybody knew she was Joe Schenck's girl and he wanted her to get a fast divorce. As soon as Philip was through proofing the affidavits, he raced to Hollywood Legion Stadium. Primo Carnera was fighting tonight. His uncle and manager, "Goodtime Charlie" Friedman, was going to join the boys in the box for the main event, and Philip didn't want to miss it. It was a very hot night at the stadium. Tickets were at a premium, and there were no empty seats. Philip charged through the crowd and almost knocked over Al Jolson and the two cuties on his arm.

"Hey, Philip, the police just picked up 'Goodtime,' " said Ruditsky, looking very dapper with a carnation in his lapel in honor of Primo. "You've got to do something right away."

"No jokes, kid. Right now!" Mickey spat out.

Where was he going to get a judge at nine o'clock on a Friday night to get a writ of habeas corpus?

"Where'd they take him?" asked Philip, his mind in overdrive.

"West L.A. Jail," came Ruditsky's reply.

As Philip rushed away he realized Judge Leo Freund was his best bet, and he headed for the nearest phone booth.

"Leo, It's Philip. I have an emergency. Meet me at your office right away, and please don't ask me why." Within twenty minutes Philip was standing face to face with Leo. "One of my friends was picked up tonight at Hollywood Legion Stadium and I have to get him out tonight. Just sign a writ and we can worry about the case later. Leo, this is crucial to me and to my friends."

Leo signed the writ, which was perfectly legal, and "Goodtime Charlie" was soon freed on his own recognizance.

"My God, how'd you do it, Philly Boy?" asked Charlie.

"Don't ask, Charlie. Mickey wants you in the booth so Primo's happy, and we'd better get there."

When Philip and Charlie walked into the stadium only an hour and fifteen minutes later, Mickey broke into a grin.

"That's my boy," he said proudly. He turned his attention back to the ring, but the people around him turned their attention to Philip.

* * *

The next day, when Philip walked into the baseball game, Ruditsky was not in his usual seat. In his place, next to Monroe, was a short man with a slightly hooked nose. There was nothing about him that said "California."

"Philip King, I'd like you to meet Dave of Dave's Blue Room in New York," said Monroe.

"It's a pleasure to meet you," said Philip. He remembered hearing that Dave's restaurant was closed by the mob because of his gambling debts. "I'm sorry about your restaurant. I hear it was a wonderful place," Philip said.

"Thank you," said Dave. "It's been tough. That room was my life."

"I wonder where Walter Winchell will eat from now on?" Philip said only half-jokingly.

"You're right. He's probably starving," joked Dave.

"I thought Dave should join us today, Philip, because he has a little business venture I thought we would be interested in. You know his restaurant, despite the problems of the back room, was very successful. He wants to open a Dave's in L.A. Can you handle everything for him?"

Dave's of L.A. was an immediate success, and the backers, including Frank Sinatra, were paid back within six weeks. Philip and Sam went there almost every night, welcomed by the doorman, who would open up the ropes and let the hundreds of people waiting to get in wonder who they were. Dave had everything painted blue. Even the booths were blue leather. The big hours were from one A.M. to three A.M. for the bar and the back room. The restaurant stayed open until four A.M., and there was always a new contact for Philip to make. Philip realized, of course, that Dave had gone back on his word about having a back room, but gambling was in Dave's blood, and Mickey wanted it that way as well. Philip saw that Sam was spending more and more time in the back room and losing more and more money, and nothing could stop him. Sam was usually surrounded by a woman or two, and Philip noticed that he was very hostile toward them.

"Hey, kid," said Mickey as Philip went into the back room one night. "Look who I have for you. Her name is Tondelayo." Tondelayo was a knockout all right. She was about five feet eight inches with flaming red hair. "She's your present from me, and you know what happens when someone doesn't like one of my presents," Mickey said.

Tondelayo put her arm through Philip's, and he knew he was trapped this time. She winked at Mickey and said, "I'll make him happy," and tossed her hair. She led Philip out the back door into the alley. "My place is just up the street. Let's go."

Philip didn't like to accept Mickey's girls, but often he had no choice because she was going to report back to Mickey. "Don't be so quiet, sweetie. I know your type," said Tondelayo. "You're all business and no fun. You have no idea what I have in store for you."

Philip wasn't frightened. He knew Mickey would never employ a girl who would do anything harmful—unless she was ordered to, of course.

Her apartment was all powder blue. "I work Dave's a lot, so I like to keep the same color theme going. Make yourself a drink and I'll be right back."

Philip decided he had better have a strong Scotch. He sat down on the slightly worn couch and put his drink on the serviceable wooden coffee table. Within five minutes she reappeared in a floral print sarong with a flower in her hair.

"You obviously take 'White Cargo' very seriously," said Philip.

"Not at all," said Tondelayo. "I use it only for fun." She sat down. "How come you don't have any fun?" she asked Philip.

"Don't be silly, I have a great time. I love the fights. I love to go to movies, and I love my work."

"Of course you do," she said, almost purring. She put her hand between his legs. "Is this fun, too?" she asked as she stroked him gently.

Between the Scotch and her hand, Philip was feeling much better. "How do you feel about fantasies?" she asked.

"I don't even know if I have any," Philip said honestly.

"Well, tonight I want you to open your mind and go on a little trip with me. Will you do that?" asked Tondelayo.

Philip nodded yes and moaned a bit at the same time.

"Then come with me," Tondelayo said as she led him into her bedroom.

Philip couldn't believe his eyes. The room was twice the size of the living room, and it was decorated like the South Seas. There were fishnets and colored lanterns hanging from the ceiling, and she even had a tropical fish tank on the wall.

"Did you work at Don the Beachcomber's before Dave's?" said Philip.

"How did you know?" asked Tondelayo, not seriously getting the joke.

Philip stifled a laugh, which she noticed.

"I'm Mickey's favorite," she said, putting her arms around his waist. "I'm going to do my specialty for you. Mickey says that nowhere in the world has he found someone who can do what I do. Lie down in that outrigger over there." How Philip could have missed an outrigger canoe in a bedroom he didn't know. The outrigger was definitely built for two. It had a mattress in it and was balanced on some sort of metal contraption. "Leave on all your clothes except for your pants and shorts," ordered Tondelayo.

Some part of Philip rather liked being told what to do as he climbed in the luxurious, silk-upholstered canoe.

"Very good, Philip," she said as she looked below his waist. "Mickey certainly shouldn't call you kid . . ." and then she sat on his thighs.

She reached out and flipped a switch, and within a second the canoe began a gentle rocking motion as if it were gliding through a lagoon. "Enjoy your trip, sweetie," he heard her say as he felt her slide her body toward his feet. "Shut your eyes," she ordered. He shut his eyes and felt the swaying motion of the boat, then her mouth on him. It was as if a liquid satin pillow had engulfed him. Nothing was sharp. She was working him from all angles, and all he felt was flesh against flesh. He almost jumped out of the canoe when it hit him. She had removed her teeth! They were plates! That was the secret! No wonder Mickey loved it. Suddenly he didn't care about Mickey or anybody. He was engulfed by the velvet receptacle, and he went to the moon.

The next night Philip got to Dave's about 9:00 P.M. A pattern had developed now. He and Sam would have dinner, and then Sam would go to the back room. Philip knew the gambling was affecting Sam's work, and he'd found out recently that Sam had been spending more time at the track during the day and less time at the office. Finally, Sam Sr. asked for Philip's help.

"I told you I don't want to discuss it," snapped Sam. "I'm just fine."

"You're not fine," said Philip, "and you don't even know it. You're so lucky to be working at the studio now instead of the theaters, and you're throwing it all away."

Sam bolted from the table.

At 11:30 P.M. Mickey and his bodyguards came in. "Kid, I want you and Sam to come with me at midnight to see a new club. Invite Sam for me, and meet us out front."

When Sam heard the invitation from Philip he was so engrossed in a card game that it barely penetrated, but he knew an invitation from Mickey was an order.

"You drive tonight, kid," said Mickey. Mickey got in the back with Sam, and Mickey's bodyguard, Dave "the Snake" Kitaen sat in the front next to Philip.

"Drive to 1200 Hoover Street," barked Kitaen.

Mickey had never been to Hoover Street . . . at least not with Philip, and there was no club anywhere near there. It was an area south of Los Angeles where Negroes lived. Who knows, thought Philip. Maybe it's a new jazz club.

When Philip pulled up to where 1200 should have been he was face to face with an empty lot.

"Drive on it," Mickey said ominously.

Philip tried to catch Sam's eye in the rearview mirror, but he couldn't find him. Just as he was searching for a glimpse of him Snake said, "Stop the car," and Philip felt a gun in his ribs. He did as he was told.

"What's happening?" Sam said in a terrified voice from the back seat.

No one answered him as Snake jumped out of the car, pulled open the back door, and yanked Sam out of the seat, dragging him in front of the car. Philip saw Snake twist wire around Sam's wrists as Sam yelled in pain.

Mickey stepped out of the car. "Don't you move, Phil," he said. "This ain't your problem, get it?"

Philip was frozen behind the wheel, suit soaked. He saw Mickey walk back to the street and Sam and Snake go to the other side of the lot, where Snake started to beat Sam with a blackjack. Sam went right to his knees. Snake raised a gun high in the air, and in an instant Philip hit the lights and horn and jammed his foot on the accelerator. He left the gear in drive and rolled out his door. The car barreled toward Sam and Snake, and they scattered.

"Enough!" screamed Philip. He turned to Mickey on the sidewalk and saw him getting into a car that just pulled up. "You made your point," Philip said.

Mickey was stunned. Mickey beckoned Snake to join him as Philip walked over to Sam, who was cowering on the ground, whimpering. "Hey, kid," shouted Mickey. "I don't like what you did, but I like you. Go home and clean up and take him with you. You both look terrible."

Within forty-eight hours after the incident, Philip King was a star, his phone ringing off the hook with potential clients. He didn't know what hit him. Even Geisler walked into his office and gave him a raise. At six P.M. of the second day after the incident, Sam's father called.

"Son, would you come over to the studio at seven P.M.? I want to talk to you."

Philip was there at six forty-five. He knew where Senior's office was because he had stood in front of that building many times. It was white with white columns. On pedestals on either side of the entrance there were identical carved stone eagles. He walked into the foyer, and the receptionist said, "Mr. Lewis is expecting you. Please follow me."

He entered an executive office wing consisting of another reception room, completely round. It looked like the Rotunda of the Capitol building in Washington, D.C. The curious thing was that there was no receptionist in this area. He took a seat on one of the rounded love seats. There were no chairs. Special curved love seats made a concentric circle. In the middle of the room was a working fountain. A couple of minutes later a conservative older woman walked in and beckoned Philip. He followed her through a smaller office into Sam Senior's. His office looked like the inside of a wooden cigar box. Everything was walnut-stained wood. There was a fire in the fireplace, and Sam motioned for him to sit on one of the leather chairs by the fire.

"Let's get right to the point, son," said Sam. "You saved my son's life. I owe you. But besides that, I've had my eye on you from the beginning. I was just waiting for you to mature. You certainly have, and in a very short time. I would like you to become vice-president of Metropolitan Pictures in charge of business affairs."

Philip could barely contain his excitement. The movie business at last!

"With your legal knowledge you'll be great with all our contracts," Sam continued. "You'll also be able to handle the unions, which are driving me crazy. You know a lot of people, and they seem to like you. You get things done, and I'm going to rely on you for a lot around here. Congratulations, Philip. You're one of us."

* CHAPTER 5 *

In the ensuing months Honey couldn't get Sam out of her mind, her thoughts centered more on the lost opportunity than her feelings. She was angry, but smart enough to channel that anger into her performances, and suddenly the audiences began to pay attention to her. They didn't talk through her songs now, and even the management noticed. When she asked for a raise they gave it to her. Honey wrote personal notes to all the members of the press in San Francisco to come to the club and review her. Even though it took most of her salary to pay for their covers, she knew she would benefit from it. "If I just keep concentrating on giving good performances and promoting myself," she half prayed, "something will happen."

"Play to table fifteen," whispered the piano player at the beginning of the second set.

Honey was fighting off a cold that night and really didn't feel like performing, but it was the first time that the piano player had ever said anything like that to her. She looked over and saw a man in his early fifties who looked very bored. When she launched into "All the Things You Are," she could see him perk up a little bit, and he paid attention to the rest of her set, not knowing she called upon all the willpower she had to finish. She was getting very hot and cold and wanted to lie down as fast as possible. She was sitting down with her head in her hands when she heard a knock on the dressing room door. She opened it to see the man standing there.

"Miss Perry, my name is Murray Wheeler. I work for 'The Meredith Willson Show' on NBC radio. Mr. Willson is auditioning singers for his show on Friday. Do you think you could make it at two P.M.?"

Honey thought her fever broke then and there. "How many songs do you want me to sing, Mr. Wheeler?"

"Pick two, an up-tempo and a ballad, and bring your music, of course. Do you know where NBC is?"

"Oh, yes," Honey said confidently, though she didn't have a clue.

"I sang 'I Can't Give You Anything but Love' and 'Hold Your Man,' and they loved me, Daddy!" Honey had met Everett at the soda fountain in the Fairmont. She now felt it was "her place," and she was giving him the good news that she was the new solo vocalist on the Willson show broadcast nationwide each week. "And I'm not going to quit Bimbo's, either, because I want to make as much money as I can."

"And what are you going to do with all this money you make?" asked Everett, smiling at his daughter's bubbling happiness after getting the job.

"I'm saving up because I want to be in the movies. I want to get out of the house. You know that, Daddy. Why don't you and Mother come down to NBC one time? You'd enjoy watching the show. Just let me know when you want to come. Oh, dear. I'm late. I've got to go to rehearsal now," said Honey. "Just stay here and finish your sundae. It's too fattening for me."

When Honey heard "Ladies and gentlemen, Honey Perry" for the first time she almost fainted, but a year later she was used to it, and she loved it. A few diehard fans of the show would sometimes wait at the stage entrance for Meredith Willson's autograph, and pretty soon they were asking her for hers, too. It was during a five-minute break in the rehearsal for the radio show that she spotted the item in the *San Francisco Chronicle*. "Lucille Ball has been signed by RKO Pictures to star in *Too Many Girls*, a singing, dancing extravaganza. The new Cuban import, singer Desi Arnaz, will make his acting debut in the picture." If it's a musical there must be something in it for me, Honey thought. That's the audition I want. She realized that she had no agent, didn't live in Los Angeles, and was generally in a tough spot. And then she thought of Sam.

Honey went right to the point when she got Sam on the phone. "Sam, I need your help with something. There's a movie about to shoot at RKO called *Too Many Girls*. I'll be happy with just a part in the chorus. I really want an audition. Do you know anyone who could set that up?" Honey could almost feel his relief when she didn't mention the incident in the limo or even acknowledge their courting at all.

Hearing Honey's voice again made Sam's shame and hurt come back, but he didn't let her know it. "Of course I can help you, Honey. The casting director will call you to set up an appointment."

There was a silence, which Honey broke by saying quickly, "Oh, thank you, Sam. I really appreciate this. I won't forget it. Thank you. Good-bye."

Honey was determined to get to Hollywood and stay. It was time she went after her real destiny. The owners of Bimbo's were only mildly upset that she was leaving. They still thought of her as "filler" even though now she was "good" filler.

Meredith Willson was another story. "You've been with us a little over a year. My audience loves you. Do you have to go? Can't you come up here each week?" he asked.

"You know how much I would like that," said Honey,

"but I can't afford the transportation. But thank you for everything, Mr. Willson."

"Good luck, kid."

Her parents went with her to the train station. "Here's an extra five hundred dollars that I saved up for you to have, darling. Consider that I'm investing in your future," said her father, tears in his eyes. Her mother, of course, was thrilled and couldn't say good-bye fast enough.

"I'm going to be at the Monteceito Hotel on Franklin right in the middle of Hollywood," said Honey.

Everett remembered reading about the hotel in movie magazines. "Isn't that where all the starlets stay when they come to town?" he asked.

"We're about to find out, aren't we?" said Honey. And with that she stepped onto the train, already aware that she had only enough money to stay there for one week, and something had better happen fast.

Her room was tiny and sparsely furnished, but it had a view of the Hollywood sign up on the hill, and that was all Honey cared about.

Twenty-four hours later she was standing at the gates of a movie studio for the first time. She was in awe, but she also felt as though she were coming home. She knew it was her destiny. As she gave the guard her name, she noted his: "Ken Hollywood." That was another sign to Honey. She got the directions to the stage and looked at the cracks on the walls and the signs as she went by. It was as if she had seen them all before. The smell of movies was intoxicating to her. She found herself slowing down as she passed a dressing room building, and she saw on the doors the names of people she had read about through the years. She wondered where the commissary was and hoped she could walk in there and be proud of who she was.

As she approached Stage 13, she saw a line of hundreds of young women streaming out the stage door, each one more energetic and cute than the next. Some were fixing their makeup. Some were doing leg stretches. For the first time Honey realized how small-time she was in San Francisco and how no previous experience could prepare her for what she was about to face. She just knew she'd have to be more creative and inventive than she'd ever been before. How could I possibly stand out among all these girls? she worried.

She walked up to the man holding the clipboard at the front of the line. "Sam Lewis sent me. I have an appointment."

"Everybody has an appointment, miss. Take your place at the end of the line, and fill out this form."

Honey was mortified. Couldn't Sam take better care of her? How dare he treat me like this! she thought as she went to the back of the line and started to fill out the vital statistics sheet. She saw that all the girls were holding eight-by-ten glossy photographs of themselves. She should have thought of that. She didn't have any pictures and was furious at her lack of experience. But as she stood on line she realized that one of the reasons she wasn't prepared properly was that she had expected a one-on-one meeting with someone. Sam will pay for this, she thought angrily.

It took two hours of standing in line in the sun before she got inside the building, and the only thing that kept her attention was watching the antics of the girls ahead of her. She couldn't keep her eyes off a couple of them who looked very much alike. They had brown hair and deep voices and pronounced everything the same way, as if they had gone to the same finishing school. The taller one of the two had some light streaks in her hair and hazel eyes. The shorter one had innocent blue eyes and slightly darker hair. Both were beautiful, but the shorter one was stronger-looking.

"Hey, Penny," said the tall one to the shorter one, "you need some more mascara."

"Thanks, Sheila," said Penny, "and don't you think you should darken your beauty mark?"

"What beauty mark?" said Sheila. "I don't have a beauty mark!"

"Maybe you should get one," Penny said, laughing.

"So what happened at the Troc last night?" asked Sheila. "I was asleep before you got home."

Honey couldn't believe how exciting their lives sounded. She was eavesdropping, hanging on their every word.

Suddenly Honey's section of the line was inside the stage, and everyone became quiet. Way on the other side of the stage was a table with three people sitting behind it—two guys and a girl. Next to the table was a big spotlight aimed right on the girl auditioning at the moment. There was an orange line painted on the floor that the girls were not allowed to cross until it was their turn. It was very cold on the cavernous stage, but Honey wasn't sure whether she was shivering from the temperature or nerves. As each actress went up to the table she handed them her résumé and picture and said her name. She then had to dance a few steps and sing "Happy Birthday" a cappella.

Well, they're not looking for the next Sarah Bernhardt here, thought Honey, taking a deep breath. She was frightened, but she hadn't come all the way from an island to fail now. She and Penny stood and watched Sheila audition, and when she was through Penny applauded and whistled. The producers didn't appreciate it, but Honey loved it. Penny turned at Honey's laughter and saw Honey smiling at her. "You and your friend are having a good time here. Aren't you nervous?" asked Honey.

"Are you kidding? Sometimes we have five of these a week. You have to keep your sense of humor if you're going to get through this. You look like this is your first time. Don't worry. Sheila and I will root for you."

It was Penny's turn as Honey turned her attention to what she was going to do. This wasn't going to be just an audition for her. What she accomplished today would determine her future in Hollywood. Some instinct in her told her she had to be clever, she had to think faster, be smarter, and surprise people. Always be ahead of the game. Never let them know where you're coming from, and dazzle them with your speed and power, thought Honey. Maybe in life all the skills, if applied properly, come down to the power you have . . . over yourself and others. Her mother had a power over her father that he never saw. She now had power over her mother, and she knew it. Seen and unseen power, but always used at exactly the right time.

"Next," said the women behind the table.

As Honey crossed the orange line she saw Sheila and Penny hanging around the exit to watch her. She walked right to the performing area, determined, yet so frightened that she could hardly hear. She stood in the spotlight, looked them right in the eye before they had a chance to ask for her picture and résumé, and sang a biographical song that she made up on the spot. She knew she'd stopped them cold. During a break in the verse she even did some dance steps. It was a smash, and everybody knew it. Sheila and Penny applauded from across the stage. Honey smiled at them gratefully.

"You've got the job," blurted out the director.

"Thank you," said Honey, and gave them her name and number.

Sheila and Penny were waiting for her when she came out. "Hi, Honey," they said in unison.

"She's Sheila," said Penny.

"And she's Penny," said Sheila. "Where did you come from? We haven't seen you before, and we know everybody. You must have just come into town."

"How do you know that?" asked Honey.

"Believe me," said Penny, "with your spunk and talent we would have noticed you before. Want to go get something to eat with us? We're starving."

"Are we allowed to go to the commissary?" asked Honey.

"Of course," answered Sheila. "What do you think—that you have to work here to eat? C'mon." Sheila and Penny let out a whoop, clasped hands, and motioned for Honey to follow along.

I got the job! I'm going to the commissary! I did it! screamed Honey inside her head as she was walking. Her heart was pounding. She felt proud and confident. Finally! She was on her way!

As those feelings of grandeur settled in, they were immediately overpowered by the view of the commissary. It was gigantic, and Honey felt like a speck. It was as big as a sound stage, and stretching in front of her was a sea of tables. As soon as she walked in with the girls she felt all eyes upon her, and she walked to a table as if she were parading in a beauty contest, hoping they wouldn't see that her legs were shaking. She decided to stare at them as they were staring at her as she passed by. The sight of a beautiful towhead blonde flanked by two brunettes was too much for everyone. The hush subsided as the girls sat down and were handed menus. Honey looked inside and began to laugh.

"What's so funny?" asked Sheila.

"I've never seen food named after people," said Honey. "I think I'll eat Howard Hughes. He's less fattening than George Brent. How come they do this?"

"It's all ego, honey," explained Sheila. "The minute you make it in Hollywood you get a sandwich named after you, but if your next picture bombs, you're off the menu. If you don't get back on the menu within four to six months, you know your contract isn't going to be renewed," said Sheila, very savvy in the ways of the business.

"My God," Honey said. "How could anybody ever digest anything here?"

"They can't," said Penny. "Do you see that room to your right? That's the private dining room where the executives eat. Every once in a while you'll see one of the really big stars invited to go in, and it's quite a scene."

Honey was observing and learning her position every second. At this early stage, she was aware that all she had was her brain and her talent, and no position, but that would change.

"You do have a job, don't you?" asked Sheila.

"Of course I do. You heard them tell me I got the part, didn't you?" asked Honey.

"No, no, that's not what I'm talking about. I'm talking about reality here. Movie jobs are sporadic. How are you going to pay your rent?"

"Oh, that. Well, I don't know yet," answered Honey. "I've only been here one day. I checked into the Monteceito, and I have enough money to stay there for one week. After that I'm not sure what I'll do, but I'll make it. I'll try to get a job singing in a club."

"Do you have a trust fund or something? Is somebody keeping you?" asked Penny.

"What?" asked Honey, surprised by Penny's question.

"Calm down," said Penny. "I didn't mean to insult you, but you're new here and you have to learn how things work. It's rare to get the first job you ever go out on, and you can't get a job singing unless you're somebody's girl. It's a closed business, and I don't think you're ready to hook up with the mob yet."

"Penny, are you thinking what I'm thinking?" asked Sheila.

"I usually am, doll," said Penny, smiling broadly. They both looked directly at Honey.

"We live just up the block from the Monteceito at the El Cerrito Apartments. They're cheap, clean, and run by a respectable couple. We have a one-bedroom apartment with a very big living room. Our roommate left to get married last week, and we have an opening if you want to sleep on the pull-out couch in the living room. It isn't bad, and that way we all can get by on fifteen dollars a month each for rent. What do you say?"

"You have a new roommate."

Their apartment was very cute. Sheila and Penny had painted it themselves. The walls were green with white trim, and the furniture had floral slipcovers, making for a "garden" effect that was very pleasant.

By the evening of their first night together both Sheila and Penny were also cast in *Too Many Girls*. Honey was having a wonderful time. She got up at four-thirty every morning and in the dark took the bus to work. Because she was in the chorus she had to go in a back entrance of the studio and had no dressing room. She and all the other chorus girls went into the hair and makeup building, into a large room with lockers and clothes racks. Her costume was among two hundred others, and each time she went to find it, someone had moved all the alphabetized pieces. The wardrobe department didn't clean it, and she wasn't allowed to take it home to wash it. All the chorus members had to stand in line at one of four areas that featured a makeup chair and mirror. They did their own hair at home, and it was just touched up and sprayed by the stylist at the studio. The makeup was slapped on, and after the first couple of days Honey had mastered putting it on herself. While she was shooting, the heat was unbearable, and the only rest area was a row of benches in the sun. There was water to drink, but that was it. It's my first step, thought Honey as she watched Lucille Ball with her own hair and makeup people following her around, her own huge dressing room with a kitchen, food delivered for her from the commissary. Someday I'll have all that, too, Honey thought.

At the end of the first week of work, Sheila and Penny decided to take Honey to Schwab's Pharmacy at Laurel Canyon and Sunset Blvd. It was a hangout for unemployed actors, who hung around at all hours of the day or night, discussing what parts were available. It was like a club with dark wood and goodies to buy, smelling of cigarettes, coffee, and newsprint. Just to the right of the front door was a magazine stand with anything you could want. Just in front of it, still on the right, was a soda fountain. To the left were all the racks with pharmaceuticals, candies, toothpaste, and other items. It was possible to sit at the counter and nurse a five-cent cup of coffee and see everyone you knew. Honey loved it there instantly and thought about approaching the manager for a job either behind the soda counter or selling products, but then she realized she didn't want to be seen by producers and directors "that way." Making a star out of a waitress was not interesting copy. Honey started to make the rounds of dress shops and retail stores when she wasn't shooting, and she soon was offered a job working behind the counter at Woolworth's five and dime on Hollywood Boulevard. They wanted her to work four nights a week, and she could start as soon as the movie was over. She was hardly thrilled, but she did want to eat.

"Excuse me, miss, I'm Nola Bernstein from the Bernstein Agency. May I talk to you?" Honey saw standing before her a woman in her fifties with flaming red hair and dressed in a business suit.

"All right," said Honey.

"I know you're on a break, so I'll make it fast. You're gorgeous, plus you have a look about you that I think might go far in this town. I haven't seen you before. I handle models and actresses. Do you have an agent?"

"No, I don't," said Honey, "but I'd like to know who else you handle if that's all right."

"You've got real guts, kid. I thought you'd be eating out of my hand," Nola said sternly.

"I've already had lunch today, thank you," said Honey with a smile. "What I don't have is an agent. Do you have a card? I'd like to call you tomorrow with my answer."

Nola doubled over laughing as she handed her the card. "I haven't met one like you in years! By the way, what's your name?"

"Honey," answered Honey.

"Of course it is," Nola said appreciatively, looking her up and down.

Honey immediately checked her out with some of the people on the set and found out she was a small but honest agent. Honey had nothing to lose. She needed someone to make the phone calls and set up the interviews, although she was going to do plenty of scouting herself to see what was available. She was going to really be on top of Nola.

* * *

On the last day of shooting, Honey walked in the commissary to wait for Sheila and Penny, almost feeling comfortable. Within a few minutes Desi Arnaz came in. Honey thought he was adorable and sexy. He was dark like Alii, and there was just something about him. Perhaps it was the way he moved. He was starting to walk toward her table. She looked up at him and smiled.

"You're in the movie, aren't you?"

Honey looked up at him. "Yes," she said. "My name is Honey Perry."

"Desi Arnaz, pleased to meet you." She could tell that he wanted to sit down, but she didn't feel right about asking him. Everybody knew that he and Lucille Ball were falling in love. Before anything was resolved, both Honey and Desi saw Lucy come in the front door. "It was nice meeting you," said Desi. "I hope you have a good time working in the movie."

Honey was a little disappointed, but she knew it would be meaningless for her in the grand scheme of things, anyway.

"Hon, where did you put the white blouse I had on last night?" asked Penny.

"Are you calling me?" asked Honey from the living room.

"No, I meant Sheila," shouted Penny from the bedroom, "but I guess I'd better find a better nickname for her since you're not about to change yours."

"I put it in the bag to go to the cleaners so you wouldn't forget it," replied Sheila, entering into the confusion.

From the living room Honey smiled. She thought it was really sweet the way Sheila and Penny took care of each other. At times it made her feel left out, but they'd known each other for years. "Hey, look at this, girls," yelled Honey into the bedroom. "Here's an ad saying that Earl Carroll is auditioning for new showgirls on Saturday. It's an open audition at ten A.M. Let's do it."

Penny and Sheila came rushing out of the bedroom.

"I'll never get this, I'm too short," said Penny. "But you guys go. You're perfect for it. I'm better off working in an office. I'll just keep calling in sick when I get an audition."

Honey desperately wanted to get the job at Earl Carroll's because it would make her more visible, and with the money she would earn there she could quit her job at Woolworth's. Earl Carroll had a theater on Sunset Boulevard near Vine Street in Hollywood. His showgirls were the most beautiful women in the world. Tourists as well as people in the industry flocked to the Hollywood showplace.

Sheila and Honey were so beautiful, and carried themselves off so well with such stage presence, that they were hired right away. Honey and Sheila soon learned that there were levels of chorus girls in the show: the line girls, who were always in the background and never featured, the principals, and the headliners themselves. Honey and Sheila were hired as line girls, but again, that was a first step. One night backstage the stage manager posted an audition notice. The girl in the dog act, "Bob Williams and Red Dust," had quit, and they needed a replacement. The climax of his act was when the light went out and a spot hit the top of the staircase, illuminating a gorgeous woman dressed in a flowing white gown wearing a red fox stole. Down the girl would come, step by step, moving to the music. When she reached the bottom of the stairs, Williams would clap his hands, and the "stole" would jump off her shoulders and run to him. It was a principal's part and billing, so Honey decided to go for it.

After almost ten months of acting as a pedestal for a dog, Honey was really getting restless. As was the pattern with an Earl Carroll show, a headlining act would join the revue for about six weeks and then move on. If Carroll really liked someone, he would extend the engagement a couple of times. It was three weeks into the act of vaudeville performer Eddie Foy, Jr., when his partner had to leave. Foy approached Honey after the last show on Saturday night to ask if she would work with him on Sunday to learn the routine and audition for Carroll on Tuesday to be the replacement. Honey jumped at the chance. She practically had everything memorized already. Foy was a smart guy. He was going to have Honey all ready before he told Carroll he needed to make a change. Foy knew that Carroll would be upset initially, but then be pleased that Foy had fixed it so that the act would not be interrupted. On Tuesday morning when Honey and Foy showed up, Foy kept her hidden backstage. When Carroll arrived, Foy walked out and said, "Are you ready?"

"Of course I am," shouted Carroll. "Get on with it!"

The lights went down and a piano player gave Foy his intro. Honey was to come in four bars later. Upon her entrance, she started singing immediately and doing the dance steps as well as Eddie Foy. The act flowed right away.

"Wait a minute," said Carroll, still shouting. "That's my Red Dust girl. Who said you could take her?" Honey and Foy stopped dancing.

"Mr. Carroll," Foy said calmly. "Take a look at her. Don't you think the public should see her sing and dance instead?" There was a moment of silence while Honey held her breath.

"Okay," said Carroll. "And by the way, Honey, congratulations."

Foy's head jerked instantly to look at Honey. She was smiling out at the audience and was not at all surprised by Mr. Carroll's recognition.

"Hello, Daddy," said Honey on the telephone from her apartment. "I want you and Mother to come down here and see me. I'm one of the principals in Earl Carroll's show, working with Eddie Foy." She could tell that Everett was thrilled. Even her mother recognized Eddie Foy's name.

Honey made arrangements for them to come down on Saturday and stay at the Monteceito. Mr. and Mrs. Perry arrived in Hollywood on December 6, 1941. They saw their daughter's name on the marquee at the theater and were stunned by it. Everett was ecstatic to see his baby on stage. Emmaline was forced to go along with it, although the time that Honey had been away from home had been Emmaline's happiest time in years. She just wanted to see Honey's act and then get home as fast as possible. Honey persuaded Eddie and his adorable wife, Mac, to have dinner with her parents after the show. The Foys didn't mind doing it because they were family-oriented, coming from a vaudeville heritage. They liked showing people around Hollywood. Just as they all were standing in front of Honey's dressing room getting ready to go to the restaurant, a delivery boy came up to the girl and asked, "Where is Honey Perry's room?"

"I'm Honey Perry," she said. The boy handed her a dozen long-stemmed red roses. Honey was flabbergasted. "Who would send me these?" she asked.

"Open the card and let's see," said Mac.

Aloud Honey read, "From your very secret admirer."

"Uh-oh," said Eddie. "Do you think someone's after you?"

"I don't have the slightest idea who could have sent them, really," said Honey.

Everett looked uncomfortable during this exchange, and Honey just put the flowers in her dressing room, stared at the card again, and then went back into the hall. They all left the theater and got into Eddie's car.

"I'm going to show you the Sunset Strip from beginning to end," said Eddie. "It starts just about here, but really picks up speed at Schwab's Pharmacy. That's where that cute little blonde Lana Turner was discovered."

Honey didn't tell her parents that she hung out there as well.

"On your left," continued Eddie, "is the Garden of Allah Hotel. All the New York writers stay there. Errol Flynn and Humphrey Bogart have been known to take their girls there. It's quite a place. Don't let Honey near there. There's the Trocadero, a big nightclub, and right near it is the Colony." The car pulled over near Doheny and Sunset in front of Dave's Blue Room. "Okay, everybody out," said Eddie.

Honey loved the blue decor. It was her favorite color. As they walked through the bar to their table, she spotted Sheila sitting with a good-looking man in his late twenties wearing glasses.

"Sheila, what are you doing here? I had no idea you knew about this place," said Honey. "You know Eddie and Mac, and these are my parents. Dad and Mother, this is one of my roommates, Sheila, who is also in the show with me." Honey was a little puzzled that Sheila hadn't mentioned anything about Dave's but she dismissed it. She was so happy to be in the famous Dave's Blue Room with Eddie Foy, Jr. She was happy to be in his act and very happy about the flowers in her dressing room. Things were very good indeed.

At seven-fifteen the next morning the phone rang in the girls' apartment, and when Honey answered it her father was screaming on the other end of the phone.

"The Japanese have bombed Pearl Harbor! We're at war! All you girls get dressed right now. Pack for an emergency. Your mother and I are coming right over."

Honey rushed into Sheila and Penny's room and told them what was happening. Penny stared to cry. Sheila put her arms around her and comforted her.

"Quick, turn on the radio," said Sheila.

They all got dressed and were sitting paralyzed on the couch in the living room. When Honey's parents arrived everyone was frightened and upset. They didn't know what was going to happen to the world. They didn't know whether they were going to live or die.

"Don't worry," said Mr. Perry. "I lived through World War One. You just must learn to ration things and be prepared at all times. The chances of anything happening on our shore are remote."

Throughout the day they listened to the radio.

"You'd better stock up on food," said Emmaline. Honey and Penny went to the market and found themselves faced with crazed people. They were pulling all the canned goods off the shelves and buying anything that wasn't nailed down. They too hurled themselves right into the fray and bought as much as they could. When they got home Sheila told them that Earl Carroll's was shutting down for forty-eight hours to assess the situation.

Emmaline was badgering Everett to go home, and he could understand why she wanted to be near their own things. It was her way of coping. Honey went to the station with them.

"I'm so afraid to leave you," said Everett, gently touching Honey's hair.

"Don't worry, Daddy, I'll be fine," said Honey. "It's still scary, but Sheila and Penny and I will stick close together."

"We'd better get going," Emmaline said impatiently. "You two probably haven't noticed, but people are running around here like it's the last train out. I don't like it, and I want to go home."

For the first time Honey noticed the chaos and the sudden appearance of many young men in uniform. It unnerved her a bit. "Good-bye, Mother," she said as she brushed her mother's cheek with her lips. "Dad, we'll talk to each other every Sunday morning, okay?" She saw her father nod and then turn away before the tears started.

After about a week the fear was down to a dull ache, and Hollywood began to open its business doors again. People were going to be cautious, but they were going to carry on. All the gang in the show decided to volunteer at the USO in Hollywood. The women had two choices. Either they could work in factories, which was not appealing to Honey, or they could assist in putting on shows and cheering up the boys by entertaining them and dancing with them. World War II aside, it did not escape Honey's consciousness that the environment of the USO would be good for her career.

About a month into the war, Honey was spending her days at the USO and her nights at the theater. She was exhausted, but she was loving every minute of it. "Miss Perry, please," said the voice at her door.

She opened it, and a deliveryman was there with a dozen roses. Honey had completely forgotten about the secret admirer. Who was he, anyway? she thought, and during the next two shows she made a point of looking out into the audience to see if anyone was staring at her. When she looked at a front table and saw Robert Taylor, she almost fainted. He was smiling at her and at one point tipped his glass toward her.

The next day she found herself making sodas with Bette Davis and Hedy Lamarr. She could barely get the ice cream in the glass. "So," said Bette, making that one word sound like a command. "Are you going to volunteer for the transcriptions? You should, you know. You've got a good voice."

Honey couldn't believe Bette Davis even knew who she was. "In the Mood" was blaring from the speakers as she tried to carry on a conversation. "Thank you very much, Miss Davis. I'm sorry, but I don't know what a transcription is," said Honey.

"Put some more seltzer in here, will you?" barked Davis. "Armed Forces Radio is going to start recording some of the shows that go on in here. Those recordings will be shipped overseas to the boys all over the world."

"Oh, I'd love to help," said Honey, realizing that if Bette Davis liked her singing, maybe there were more people out there who would hear her and maybe she'd get another movie.

Honey soon found out that volunteering for transcriptions meant much more than just performing. The USO needed volunteers to go to the packaging factory and pack up the "platters" to get them ready for mailing. There were thousand of packages that needed making up and addressing. Honey enlisted Sheila and Penny to help her. Even though Sheila was interested in the war effort, she had begun seeing Hal Murphy, the fellow Honey had seen her with at Dave's. Hal was a very talented composer who was being used more and more by studios to create movie scores.

Honey heard a knock on her door, and the delivery boy

was there again with more roses. Honey laughed and said, "Are you sure these aren't from you?" Just as the boy was about to answer the question, a gorgeous man in a tuxedo stepped into Honey's view.

"He's sure," said Robert Taylor.

Honey was speechless.

"Aren't you going to thank me for the flowers?" he asked. "It's taken a lot of roses to get your attention." He extended his hand and reached for Honey's limp one. She was really doing the very best she could to pull herself together. "Are you busy tonight?" he continued.

Honey heard herself say, "No." The USO would have to live without her for once.

"Gather your things and come with me, Miss Perry."

"Please call me Honey," she said, reaching for her coat and purse.

"My name is Robert."

She just smiled at him. She was trying to get a grip on herself, but she was very nervous. He walked her down the backstage corridor, and heads were popping through doors to see what was happening. Some of the line girls started to whistle. By the time they reached the exit Honey was mortified. "I apologize for their behavior, Robert. They're so unsophisticated."

Taylor looked at this beautiful girl in her early twenties and laughed his head off.

As they walked toward a gorgeous black Packard touring car, she was trying to remember whether or not he was married. She had a funny feeling that he was, but at this point she was fairly sure that it didn't matter to her. They drove along Sunset past the Colony and the Troc. Her heart sank a little when she realized he wasn't going to take her to any of the clubs. She would have loved to walk into one on Robert Taylor's arm. Along the way he asked her where she was from and how she got to Los Angeles. It was not scintillating stuff, and he seemed to be killing time until his destination. When Sunset met the ocean he turned and drove for about ten minutes until he was in front of something that was so big it looked like a beach club. There was an awning out front and a circular driveway. There were no parking attendants, and Honey thought that was strange. He stopped the car in front of the door and went to the other side to let her out. Once at the front door he took out a key and let them in. It was very dark and clearly not a private club. He turned on the lights in the foyer, and Honey felt as if she were in a public library because the space was so big.

"Where are we?" she asked.

"This is Marian Davies's beach house that William Randolph Hearst bought for her," explained Taylor.

"You're kidding," exclaimed Honey, looking around excitedly.

"Of course I'm not. She's hardly ever here, and they let me use it from time to time," explained Taylor.

Honey's head was spinning. He took her into a room off to the right. It was totally paneled in mahogany, and it had the faint aroma of furniture polish. There was a huge crystal chandelier in the center of the room, and two walls were covered with books. They even had one of those ladders where you could climb up and go from shelf to shelf. Taylor walked over to one of the bookshelves.

"*Moby Dick*," he said as he pushed a book into the wall a few inches. Honey saw the wall rise up into the ceiling and a full bar come out from inside. She was trying to remain calm, and it wasn't easy. Taylor was divine, with his slicked-back black hair and long eyelashes. She could easily fall for him. She was also aware that her career hadn't yet found that extra push, and maybe this was it. She would watch and wait to see his next move. She sat down on one of the matching pink brocade sofas on the Persian rug. He was mixing some drinks.

"Here," he said as he walked over to her. "This is a stinger. I'm sure you'll enjoy it." He sat down next to her. "I'd like to show you something," he continued.

"I'm sure you would," retorted Honey.

Taylor laughed again. "You are some character. I never know whether you're just off the boat or whether you wrote the book. Here, take this in your hand."

"What!" said Honey.

Again he laughed. He gave her his pocket handkerchief and took off his jacket. "And what am I supposed to do with this?" asked Honey.

"I'm going to teach you how to fold this for a man."

He made her fold it three times, getting the corners just right, and then he okayed her work.

"Very good," he said. "Now I'm going to show you what else you can do for a man." She smiled as he looked deeply into her eyes.

He told her to stand up, and she did. Honey could feel herself start to shake a little bit, and she didn't want him to see it. She watched him take all the down pillows from the couch and place them on the floor to make one gigantic fluffy playground. He never took his eyes off her while he was doing it. Honey didn't know what to do with her hands. They felt like two anvils hanging at her sides. She started to cross them on her chest and then thought better of it.

"Now do exactly as I tell you. Take off your shoes and stockings."

Honey was shocked, but she did as she was asked.

"Good. Now take off all of your jewelry and then your dress."

She was standing there frozen with nerves, delight, and curiosity. He wasn't being bossy, really. It seemed like a game. She was now wearing a pink bra, beige panties, and a garter belt. She wished she had worn the matching panties, but it was too late for that.

"Very, very good. Now take everything else off."

As she did that, he went to the record player and put on Bach's Brandenburg Concerto No. 5. Honey noticed that the music was very precise and ordered. He circled her now very slowly, taking in her completely nude body from all sides.

"Magnificent," he said.

She turned around to look at him. His gaze was intense and serious. She could sense his demeanor changing.

"Lie down on your stomach on the pillows."

She noticed that he remained fully clothed. He had, in fact, put his jacket back on. She saw him go to the bar and get a bottle of something.

"Just shut your eyes, my beauty. I want to surprise you." His tone was not menacing, just direct.

Honey felt him bend down and get closer to her. She then felt a trickly substance at the nape of her neck, heading down her back. The heady smell of the plum brandy got to her. He moved even closer, and she could feel his breath on her neck. His tongue darted out like a snake all over her neck wherever the brandy was. It then very slowly began tracing the liquid path down her spine. She couldn't stop the gasp that escaped from her throat.

"Whatever you do," he said, "don't touch me and don't move unless I tell you to." His voice was now hoarse and deeper. He traced her entire body with his brandy-coated tongue.

She discovered crevices she didn't know she had. When the brandy moved into the crack in her buttocks, and the tongue followed, she didn't know if she could take it. His asking her not to move heightened her desire. She couldn't help but jump as his tongue found its way deeper inside. Suddenly his teeth were biting her. She moaned.

"I told you not to move," he growled, and then he softly slid his tongue back inside. It seemed like he stayed there for ages.

Honey hoped he would never leave. She loved it when his tongue began to make its way between her legs to the precious front of her body, deliberately never quite hitting the right spot. He was making her crazy. Then he suddenly stood up.

"Don't open your eyes. Just turn over."

She did as she was told. Listening very carefully, she could hear the sounds of him getting undressed. It was almost as if he were unzipping to the time of the music. He was standing astride her when he commanded her to open her eyes. He looked like a Greek god. From her point of view, of course, the sight was amazing. "Actors do know a lot about angles," she said aloud.

Ignoring her, he knelt down over her, handed her the brandy, and said, "Here, put some all over 'Bobby.' "

Again she did as she was told. She was mesmerized by him and was willing to do anything. His slow technique was masterful.

"Now shut your eyes and don't move." He moved up on his knees so he was hanging over her face, his brandy-coated foreskin touching her lips. She opened her mouth gladly. She had never been so excited. Just as quickly as he was there, he was gone. "Bobby" was the teaser, and she couldn't get enough. What Robert's tongue did to her while she was on her back was nothing compared to what "Bobby" did. But not once did he go inside. He went all around, even down to her feet and back, until she was moving and begging for him. Just when she thought she was going to scream, he was between her legs.

"Now, my beauty," said Taylor.

Everything exploded around Honey, and she couldn't think. She felt as if her whole body had just elevated into another stratosphere. She had never felt such feelings before. She knew now how special she was, and she never wanted the feeling to stop.

When Penny woke up the next morning she found the apartment empty. She was still getting used to the fact that Sheila was spending a lot of time at Hal's, and it was difficult for her without her. But now to walk in the living room and find that Honey's bed had not been slept in as well really made her feel lonely. She was sitting at the kitchen table having some coffee when she heard the key in the door. It was Honey.

"Where have you been?" asked Penny. "It's not like you not to come home. I was worried."

"You'll never believe me if I told you," said Honey, sitting down at the kitchen table.

"Just tell me and we'll see," Penny begged. "Please?"

"I was with Robert Taylor," said Honey.

"Right," said Penny, "and when I left Clark Gable this morning he told me he was meeting Robert for lunch today."

"Okay, I knew that's how you'd take it, so if you don't want to hear about the most incredible night of my life, I'm not going to tell you."

Penny sat for a minute and then spoke, eyes wide. "You're not kidding, are you."

"No, and he's picking me up to play tennis this afternoon with Lana Turner and some lawyer."

"What!" Penny shrieked. "Wait till Sheila finds out about this. Boy, have you hit the jackpot! But isn't Robert Taylor married?"

Honey's eyes darkened. "I don't want to know about it," she said.

And so Honey's life changed, but not in public. She soon realized that Robert wasn't going to really take her anywhere important, but she was so wild about him she didn't care. She would fit him in whenever and wherever she could. She was learning tricks from him that she never imagined. She tried hard to keep from falling for him because of his wife, but she couldn't control herself. She thought about him every waking hour. Even her auditions didn't seem to distract her. He was too glamorous, too powerful, and it fed her identity too well. She had hoped that it might help her career, but the secrecy was necessary. Everyone told him how talented she was, but it didn't seem to interest him. About seven months later he began to have problems seeing her, saying his wife was putting demands on him.

"Well, would you look at that," Penny said as she and Honey were dancing with some sailors at the Friday night dance at the USO. "Guess who's here?"

Honey turned around, expecting to see someone interesting, but she was not prepared for Mr. and Mrs. Robert Taylor. People started to applaud as they walked through the room toward the guest area. Robert spotted her as he walked through and smiled. Honey could barely contain her rage. All logic went out the window. She wanted to be on his arm. The pain of being the "other woman" was suddenly unbearable. After a few minutes, when his wife went to go help in another area, Honey joined the crowd trying to get his autograph. She managed to get to the front of the line.

"May I have your autograph, Mr. Taylor?" said Honey with venom dripping from her lips.

"Certainly," he said as he scribbled something on a piece of paper and handed it to her. Honey took the paper away and opened it up. It said, "Sorry, didn't know—accident."

Some accident, thought Honey. It didn't matter that Robert was substituting for another star who couldn't make it, and that he was just trying to do his best for the war effort. Honey immediately ran out the door. She didn't know how much longer she could take it.

She didn't return his calls for three weeks. Finally she talked to him and agreed to go out to the beachhouse.

"I'm very glad you came here today, I was worried about you," he said when he opened the door. He was wearing a white tennis sweater with maroon-and-blue trim, white slacks, and white shoes.

The sight of him made Honey forget all the thoughts she was having. He was truly the most gorgeous man she had ever seen. Robert saw her melt.

"I'm so sorry," he said. "I never want to hurt you." He shut the door behind her and grabbed her. He covered her face with kisses, and before she knew it they were on the floor in the foyer right under the sixteenth-century tapestry.

Honey didn't know how she was ever going to get out from under his spell. She was almost powerless. The ease with which their bodies now flowed together was matchless. They anticipated each other's every need, rolling over and over until they had ended up in the dining room, wringing wet and totally spent.

As she opened her eyes slowly, she saw him looking at her in a peculiar manner. "What's wrong?" she asked.

"This is very difficult for me to say," Robert said tentatively.

Honey instinctively reached for her clothes to cover up.

"Something is going to happen tomorrow," continued Robert, "and I don't want you to hear it on the radio."

"My God, what is it?"

"I've been under a great deal of pressure about the war. The studio can pull very long strings to keep me out of the army, but after a while I look like a traitor to my fans." He paused for a second. "Tomorrow I'm enlisting in the army. The press will be notified early in the morning, and I'm being sworn in at noon."

Honey reached out to hold him, and she started to cry. "I'm frightened. I don't want anything to happen to you," she said. Robert accepted her embrace, and then he got up.

"Don't worry about me. I'll be fine, I'm sure of it," he said as he got dressed.

Honey got up, dressing herself along the way, and said, "I love you. I'll wait for you. You'll come back safely. I'm just positive of that." She threw her arms around his neck and started to nuzzle him. Robert stiffened just a bit and removed her arms, keeping her hands in his.

"When I come home, Honey, we can't see each other anymore. I can't keep doing this to my wife," said Robert.

"How dare you?" Honey pulled away sharply. "I'm not just some kid who's new in town. It may look like that to you, but—"

"But you are wonderful," said Robert. "I care about you. We had a grand time together. I want to thank you for it."

"You mean thanks for the job well done, don't you?" said Honey. "Are you going to tip me on your way out?"

Robert was shocked by Honey's anger.

Honey grabbed her purse and opened the front door. This is the last time I'll be used, she thought, remembering Alii, then Sam. Next time it's my turn. Robert ran after her just in time to see her take her keys and scratch her initials on the side of the Packard touring car.

Sheila and Hal were married six months later on February 13, 1944, and both Honey and Penny had been happily involved in the preparations. They loved being bridesmaids. Hal got a contract at MGM in the music department, and Sheila celebrated by quitting her job at Earl Carroll's. As time wore on, Penny and Honey saw less of Sheila together. Honey was tired during the day because she worked at night, but Sheila and Penny still met for lunch frequently. Penny really missed Sheila. On the one-year anniversary of Sheila and Hal's marriage, Honey and Penny were invited to a dinner at Dave's. Honey loved to go there, but she rarely was invited. She never would have gone alone or with another woman, but she had begun to feel that she was in a rut. She did her seven shows a week, but even that was becoming monotonous.

When they arrived at Dave's, Honey was immediately caught up in the excitement of the room. She loved it. Even the smoke didn't bother her. They spotted Sheila and Hal and went over to the table. Once there, Honey couldn't believe her good fortune. Sitting right in the middle of everyone was Sam Lewis. She hadn't talked to him since she'd first arrived in town. She knew he was embarrassed, and she never pursued him, thinking there were other ways in store for her. His father had made him VP of Metropolitan Studios. No longer was he handling just the theaters. He was really in the movie business. And he definitely had not married. He looked at her and tried to cover up his awkwardness.

"Sam, I'd like you to meet two of my best friends, Honey Perry and Penny Collins," said Sheila.

"Nice to meet you both," said Sam as he looked at Honey on the word *both*.

Okay, thought Honey. I'll play it your way. Penny, knowing nothing of Sam's past, looked at him as if he were buried treasure and immediately engaged him in conversation. Honey's eyes moved around the table until they landed on a man with a friendly, open face and a great smile.

"Oh, Honey. I'm so sorry," said Sheila. "I forgot to introduce you. I'd like you to meet Philip King."

They shook hands, and it was as though an electric jolt went through them. Honey saw him feel the same thing. It was so strong that it shocked them. She felt heat rising on her neck and she reached for a glass of water.

* CHAPTER 6 *

"Good morning," said the deep voice as Honey answered her phone the next morning. "This is Philip King. I hope you don't mind, but I managed to get hold of your number."

"Should I ask you how you did it, or remain impressed with the mystery?" teased Honey.

"Oh please," said Philip, "let me stay a genius for as long as possible." They both laughed and started feeling incredibly comfortable with each other. "I would very much like it if you would join me for lunch sometime this week," Philip continued. "Is today good for you?"

"Yes," answered Honey. "That would be fine. Where would you like to meet?"

"Well, do you know where Metropolitan Studios is?"

"Yes, I do. Where should I go once I'm inside the gate?" asked Honey.

"Go to the commissary, but use the side entrance into the executive dining room. I'll see you at twelve thirty."

Honey hung up and was ecstatic. She had graduated to the executive dining room. She smiled, remembering that it was only a few years ago that she was thrilled just to walk into the commissary. She had heard that Sam Lewis, Sr., was famous for his love of food and had hired the nighttime chef at Chasen's, a little restaurant on the Strip famous for its chili, to be his chef in the executive room during the day. It was quite a coup for the studio. Dave Chasen and his wife, Maude, were former vaudeville performers who catered to the tastes of people in the entertainment business. They had recently moved from the original chili restaurant into more elegant surroundings, and now all the executives were taking their wives there for dinner. It was quite the place. On more than one occasion, it was known, if a star was trying to decide between contract offers from Metropolitan and another studio, it was the chef who swayed them. A hobo steak went a long way toward sealing a deal.

Philip could spot the beautiful blonde in the emerald-green suit very easily from his table by the window. The big corner table was Sam Sr.'s and Sam Jr. had a smaller table in another corner without a window. In the executive game, the corners were better and the windows were premium. The way Philip saw it, the studio was divided into two types of executives, "creative" and "noncreative." If you worked with writers, actors, and directors, and had the power to push a script along, you were in the creative area. Executives who did deals, worried about money, and planned production schedules were "noncreative," and it took skill in both areas to run a studio smoothly. Sam Sr. had them. Jr. was creative, but he had no understanding of money since he gambled all of his away. As for Philip, he was so happy that he was inside a studio, he didn't care that for the moment he was a noncreative executive. He knew he was there as "Mr. Fix-it," and the time would come for him. His love of the creative side of show business was hard to stifle, but he contained himself. It was difficult for him, though, when the biggest female star on the lot, Paulette Wilde, was unhappy about scripts being sent her and he knew what would be better for her. He could sense Sr.'s growing disenchantment with Jr., but it was difficult for Philip to capitalize on it because of the family connection, and he was grateful to Sam for getting him into this world in the first place.

The door opened to the executive dining room and in walked the most beautiful girl Philip had ever seen. Honey indeed was wearing a green suit, with a black silk blouse and black pumps with matching handbag and her white-blonde hair long and perfectly waved. She smiled right at him and sat down. All eyes were on the two of them because they made such a striking couple. Out of the corner of her eye Honey spotted Sam Jr., and she nodded. She quickly turned her attention to Philip.

"How are you?" she asked.

"How long do you have?" he countered.

"Well, I have an early rehearsal at the theater," said Honey.

"I really must come and see you. I love live performing more than anything. I get inside a theater and it gives me chills," said Philip.

"Me too," said Honey. "It doesn't matter what kind of theater, either—whether it's live or a movie screen. I really think it's all magic."

Philip just stared at her. "I hope I don't sound too silly, but I can't get over your hair. It's the most beautiful color I've ever seen. It looks like honey."

Honey laughed.

"I know," said Philip. "You've probably heard that a million times. I'm sorry."

"Don't be," Honey said sweetly.

He just knew this was the girl for him. They seemed to have the same rhythm. He thought she understood how he felt, and that was hard to find. After they finished their butterfly steak with mustard sauce and creamed spinach, they couldn't stop talking. The dining room slowly emptied, but it was obvious that they didn't want to leave. "Won't you stay with me a little while longer?" asked Philip. "I'd like to show you around the lot."

"I'd really like that," said Honey. "I can stay for a little while, but then I have to go home to get ready for the rehearsal. I'm never late for Mr. Carroll."

Philip stood up, helped her with her chair, and then they wandered out into the sunlight. "To me, just being here on the lot is fantastic. And I even found a magical place where I go when I need a break to think. May I show you?"

Honey nodded, smiling. They walked about three blocks before Philip stopped in front of a big sound stage building in the back of the lot away from all the others. He took out a key and let her in.

"Welcome to my secret world," he said.

Honey gasped as her eyes feasted on a wonderland of fantasy. He had taken her to the storage area for all the sets. She ran to the living room of a southern mansion from the Civil War period and said with the appropriate accent, "Oh, look, kind sir, I'm Scarlett O' Hara!" Then her eyes went to the western saloon. Before he could say anything she strode onto that set, her hands resting on the "pistols" on her hips. "You have until noon today to get out of town or you'll have to answer to me," she growled.

Philip laughed, reveling in her delight, then walked over to a shipboard set and leaned on the railing. "Oh, Miss Rogers, won't you come dance with me in the moonlight?"

"Why, Mr. Astaire," replied Honey, "I thought you'd never ask." She gracefully stepped on board, holding the "skirt" of her gown. Her feet were poised for dancing, and she extended her hand. Philip took her in his arms and started to sway her; softly she started to sing, "Heaven, I'm in heaven . . ." For a few moments they really were Fred and Ginger. Philip was a surprisingly good dancer in spite of his slight limp, and he knew all the words to "Cheek to Cheek." The magic of the moment was a revelation for both of them. They stopped singing and just looked into each other's eyes. She loved how his hands felt touching hers. She felt safe for the first time in her life, felt real love for the first time. He leaned in to kiss her, and she was lost in the softness of his mouth. It honored her. It didn't ravage her. She was stunned.

When she went home before the show, Penny wasn't there, and Honey thought she was going to explode with the news. She did the show in a daze, and finally, after the show, she raced to her dressing room to change, wanting to get out as fast as possible. As she went flying out the stage door she almost collided with him. "Honey"—Philip smiled, draping an orchid lei around her neck—"this is for you."

"I can't believe you did this for me," said Honey, her eyes beginning to mist over.

"I just wanted to do something different for you," he said. "Would you like to go to the Trocadero tonight?"

Honey's mouth dropped open. "Why, I'd love to, but I'll have to go back to my house to change first."

When they walked in, Penny was in the kitchen. It was the first time Honey had ever brought anyone home. "I'll leave you two to get acquainted while I change," said Honey after the introductions. Within ten minutes she was dressed to kill, wearing a black strapless taffeta sheath with her hair pulled up to one side.

"I like this guy, Honey. You'd better watch out."

Philip laughed and helped Honey with her wrap. It was midnight and the perfect time to go. "Have you ever been to the Trocadero before?" asked Philip.

"No, I haven't," answered Honey.

They pulled up in front of a one-story building with a circular driveway filled with fancy cars. The maître d' greeted Philip by name and showed them to a table near the dance floor. Honey couldn't stop looking around. The whole back side of the building was glass, and it overlooked the city. Everything was white, including the pillars. There was glitter in the white paint, and everywhere you looked it seemed as though stars were shining. Over at the next table sat Lana Turner and the attorney Greg Bautzer. Honey had heard of him. She was nervous about Lana seeing her. There was no question that she would remember her from their tennis games with Robert Taylor, and Honey was curious to see what her reaction would be. Within seconds she was waving.

"I didn't know you knew Lana. I haven't met her yet and I'm a studio executive. How do you know her?" he asked.

"Oh, we used to play tennis together," said Honey, hoping he wouldn't ask more questions. The music from Xavier Cugat's orchestra was reaching a frenzied pitch and drowning out conversation. "Fred and Ginger" headed for the dance floor and "killed 'em."

"What are you doing tomorrow night after the show?" Philip asked as they walked back to their table.

"I'm not sure," answered Honey.

"I have to be at a dinner with our distribution branch, but afterward I'd like to meet you at the theater again. Is that okay?"

Honey found his eagerness endearing. "Of course it is," she said. "I'll be there for you."

This was the beginning of Philip picking Honey up every night after her shows for about three weeks. Things were proceeding exactly as Honey had hoped. She was so thrilled to be at the Troc with a movie executive. She felt as if she belonged now. Hollywood was her town. But she was a resident, not a star, and that did not make her happy. As much as she was falling for Philip, her goal was to be a great movie star. In this case, she thought Philip was very compatible with that goal.

"I'll be back later," Penny said as she headed toward the front door.

"Oh, no, you don't,"said Honey.

"What do you mean?" said Penny. "What's the big deal?"

Honey stood up and walked over to her. "The big deal is that you've been avoiding discussing with me the fact that ever since Sheila got married you disappear like clockwork every Wednesday afternoon for four or five hours. Normally

I wouldn't think anything about it, but you've been so evasive whenever I asked you that I can't take it anymore. Where are you going? This time I want to go, too!'' Honey was defiant in her strength.

Penny took a long moment and said, ''All right. Yes. Perhaps it's time.''

Now Honey's curiosity was really aroused. ''Oh, good. Where are we going? What should I wear? What's happening?''

Penny was a little more relaxed now. This was beginning to amuse her. ''Just dress as if you were having lunch at a nice restaurant. Hurry. I'll wait for you.''

Honey was ready in a flash, wearing a simple brown-and-beige print dress. Penny had on black pants and a sweater. ''Let's go,''said she.

''Go where?'' Honey pushed in an exasperated tone.

''You'll see,'' replied Penny. They drove to the Musso and Frank Grill, one of the oldest restaurants in Hollywood on Hollywood Boulevard, open since 1919. Once inside, Honey saw that the walls were wood-paneled with English riding scene wallpaper on the top half of each wall. The booths were green leather.

''This is what restaurants are like in New York, Honey,'' whispered Penny. The maître d' approached them and recognized Penny immediately.

''Hello again, madame. Your friends are already here.'' He showed them to a booth along the wall.

Honey noticed as she went by that coat racks were built into each booth. When she got to the table she saw Sheila and two women sitting there. Sheila was not surprised to see her, but Honey was confused. Why wouldn't they have invited me to have lunch with them before? she thought.

''Welcome, Honey,'' said Sheila. ''I'd like you to meet Kate Gallery and Ellen Elliot.''

The two women each offered her a hand as she sat down. Honey knew Kate was married to the well-known comic

Freddie Gallery, and she recognized her from her pictures. Kate was a pretty ash blonde in her mid-twenties wearing horn-rimmed glasses. Ellen Elliot had jet black hair done in a simple bob. She was dressed in black to go with her hair, and she seemed nice. Ellen, it turned out, was married to Freddie's agent, Jack Elliot. Honey had heard of him, too. Was this some sort of gathering to further careers? she wondered. If that was the case, then she was highly offended that she hadn't been asked earlier. Obviously the restaurant was familiar with this group, so this gathering must have been happening for some time.

"Well, it's very nice to see all of you," said Honey. "How do you all know each other? I never heard Sheila or Penny mention you."

Sheila responded. "Dear, dear, Honey. There is a time and place for everything. Why don't we just enjoy our lunch. I've ordered the flannel cakes for you. They're the specialty here, and you'll love them. They're wafer-thin pancakes with the circumference of a dinner plate, almost drowning in melted butter and syrup. It's the best. I also ordered some cream of tomato soup to start with. We always have this unless for some reason somebody is craving the sauerbraten and potato pancakes with creamed spinach. You've got to try the sourdough bread, too. It's amazing."

Honey couldn't imagine why Sheila was babbling on so about the food. She was acting a little crazy. Honey still didn't have a clue as to what was happening. She noticed that Kate was very delicate, with a slight southern accent. She was very intelligent but was comfortable with it. There was nothing overbearing about her. She was soft-spoken, with beautiful manners. Ellen, by contrast, was brittle, with a biting wit. Extremely bright and very funny. Rather than talk a lot, Honey decided to listen to them so she might figure out what was going on.

"You know, Freddie's not so sure he wants to renew with Metropolitan," said Kate.

"Oh, come on," said Ellen. "You know Jack's right. He'll push the deal up and then he'll sign. Big Sam's a smart guy. He won't want to lose Freddie and you know it."

That was interesting, thought Honey. Maybe I'll tell Philip about this. "Do you know Philip King?" she asked.

"Jack says he's a real star waiting in the wings," answered Ellen. "Apparently he's this legal whiz with some very well-placed friends, but he'd better get out of contracts and into picture making. That's really where the action is."

Honey was impressed with Ellen's candor.

After they all paid the check Sheila said, "Everybody ready?" Everyone nodded except Honey. "Okay Penny. You take Honey. I'll go in my car, and Kate and Ellen can meet us there."

"Right," answered Penny. Honey just followed. She realized at this point that she was not going to get any information. Whatever was going to happen was just going to unfold in front of her eyes.

The group went in a caravan and stopped in front of a California bungalow house on Seward Street south of Sunset Boulevard near Earl Carroll's. It was a white wooden house with a cement veranda and porch, with a neatly trimmed lawn and rose bushes along the walk.

"Who lives here?" asked Honey, following them to the front door.

"Never mind," said Sheila, inserting a key in the lock.

"But this isn't where you and Hal live," said Honey, who was getting very confused.

"I know," said Sheila. "Just follow us."

Honey found herself in a charming house furnished in rattan with matching print floral slipcovers. The floors were hardwood, and there was a white throw rug in front of the fireplace. The kitchen was yellow, with a little breakfast nook. Next to the kitchen off the living room there was a dining room with countrylike table and chairs. Through the window one could see a backyard that was fenced in with trees, and there was furniture on the lawn.

"This is a very comfortable house," said Sheila. "There are two bedrooms and a large bath."

"Are you suddenly in the real estate business? I don't get it," said Honey.

"You will," said Penny. With that, Kate and Ellen held hands and walked toward a bedroom. Penny put her arms around Sheila and said, "Which one of us would you like to join?"

Honey was mute and wide-eyed. How could she have not known about this? she asked herself. She had lived with Sheila and Penny!

Penny, seeing her discomfort, said, "Well, you wanted to know where I go every Wednesday, and now you do. Say good-bye to Kate and Ellen—you'll be seeing them again—and come with us."

Ellen and Kate waved and went into their bedroom. Honey followed Penny and Sheila into theirs. "I'm coming in here with you, but I just want some questions answered and then I'm leaving."

Sheila and Penny's love nest was all in lavender, the bed covered in lavender satin. Honey sat down on a chair and said, "I'm a big girl. You two can do what you want. I'm just upset that I didn't know about this, and I can't figure out why you married Hal."

"I do love Hal," said Sheila. "We have a great life. Sometimes women just need a little extra something from another woman who really understands. We don't want to hurt anyone. We just really need this kind of intimacy. It keeps us going."

"We decided we could trust you," Penny chimed in. "We wanted to tell you right from the beginning, but we didn't know you well enough, then we felt terrible lying to you once we got to know you and you became a friend. It's not right to lie to a friend, and we're sorry. All four of us chip in for the rent here. I get to pay less because I'm not married. It's like our private club. We know that telling this to you is not an invitation to participate. We just thought you'd like the conversation and the communication. Kate and Ellen are fantastic and they're well-connected in the business. Any time you'd like to join us for lunch we'd love to have you. We really care about you.''

''Well, at least I don't feel left out anymore,'' said Honey, feeling better. ''And besides, those flannel cakes are the best thing I've ever tasted. See you at Musso's.'' Penny handed Honey the keys to her car, saying that Sheila would drop her off. Honey heard Mabel Mercer's ''In Love Now'' coming from Kate and Ellen's room as she walked through the living room. As she sat in the car she felt a little strange. She didn't really want to belong to their club, yet she did feel left out, and she didn't really understand what Sheila was talking about in terms of a ''need.'' Honey wasn't ever going to ''need'' anybody. That would cripple her plans. She started to imagine what was going on in there, and then it was too much for her. She was going to go home and give herself a facial. That was her need at the moment.

''I hope she's okay,'' Penny said after Honey left. ''Do you think we did the right thing?''

''Don't worry,'' said Sheila. ''She's very bright and she'll be fine. It will be good for us to have another ally in town. I certainly know we don't want her for an enemy.''

Penny placed her hands on Sheila's shoulders and said softly, ''You're right, but forget her for now. I really love you, and a feeling this good can't be wrong.''

Sheila kissed her, and without taking her lips away she whispered. ''Be ready for me when I come back.'' While Sheila was in the bathroom, Penny turned down the bed. She had put a comforter under the bottom sheet, so the bed was really soft. She undressed and went to the closet to put on a matching lavender satin nightgown. She knew how much Sheila loved everything to match. She turned on the radio to the station that played Billie Holiday, Helen Morgan, and mostly sexy torch songs. She lit a candle on either side of the bed and got in. ''Stardust'' was playing as she saw Sheila enter the room. She was wearing a long satin purple robe with nothing underneath. Penny loved how she could see the outline of her body against the satin.

Sheila loved Penny's body even more. It was picture perfect, the way a movie star's body should be. She had broad shoulders, and her breasts were divinely ample and beautifully formed. Even more important, they were extraordinarily sensitive. Penny's skin felt like satin, too. It was hard to tell where the nightgown ended and the skin began. Sheila just loved to gaze into her eyes and melt into the sensation. Penny loved Sheila's touch. She sometimes joked and called her "Magic Fingers." Sheila felt as though her fingers and mouth were blessed with extrasensory devices. There was almost a current that ran through them. She knew she could stroke just Penny's face repeatedly and it would lead them to complete satisfaction.

After fifteen or twenty minutes of Sheila caressing Penny's face, Penny began to make soft little moans. Sheila knew it was time to move her hands to Penny's breasts. Sometimes she would use just one finger for stroking, and sometimes she'd use ten. It was just how the mood struck her. As her hand strayed down to Penny's breasts, the nipples were already like rocks. Sheila deliberately kept her touch feather light, and Penny's moans grew a little louder. Sheila started to squeeze the nipples with her fingertips . . . just hard enough to straddle that fine line between pleasure and pain, then she scooted down and put her mouth on the left nipple while still squeezing the right one. She used a random pattern of soft strokes and very fast licks, then switched to little bites here and there, sometimes doing everything so fast that she would almost do both nipples at once in her mouth.

The love that Sheila felt for Penny was not just excitement. She truly loved to make her happy. Her lips traveled even lower now. She raised her head and took both of her arms and pushed up Penny's knees. She then wrapped her arms under the knees and began kissing the unbelievably soft skin of the underside of Penny's thighs. Penny's writhing made Sheila even more inspired. She felt as if her head were between two satin pillows. It was a feeling she loved. She opened her mouth and ran the edges of her teeth up and down the whole length of the inner thigh, making sure that enough saliva made it slippery and exciting. She was getting closer and closer to that magic triangle, and Penny knew it. Her breathing was changing. When Sheila was almost ready to land she took care that the touch of her tongue was very light. It was deliberately too light. This was Sheila's favorite part. It was like joyously pressing one's face into the most delicious birthday cake in the world. By the time Sheila got to the "frosting," Penny cried out in ecstasy. Sheila was aching for Penny now, and she quickly raised herself up on Penny so their triangles were touching. They moved together very rhythmically, and held each other closer while Sheila joined Penny in that heavenly moment.

"I love you so much I want to cry," said Sheila. "We must always protect this." They could love each other in private and be best friends to the public. They had the best of everything.

When Philip met Honey after the show that night, she was never so happy to see anyone. She didn't want to share the secrets of the afternoon with him because she was determined to be loyal to her friends, but she did want to feel safe in his arms.

"I just loved you and Eddie Foy," said Philip. "God, Honey, you're so talented. You really should be bigger than Rita Hayworth. I'll have to do something about it."

This was what Honey had been waiting for, and it was an added bonus that she fell in love with him along the way. They went back to Dave's that night and continued to tell each other all about their lives. When Philip started talking about his Jewish heritage, a little alarm sounded in Honey. She remembered cracks her mother made behind Alii's back because of his ancestry. Emmaline loved to make a big deal out of Everett's WASP lines and his senator father. A kid who used to be called Pinky Cohen was not what her mother would like. When the conversation got around to the meeting of parents, they decided that Honey would meet Philip's mother, Dora. Philip would send a studio car to San Diego for his mother, and they all would have lunch in the commissary. Then the next weekend, Philip and Honey would take the train to San Francisco and meet the Perrys. This all sounded very serious to Honey, but as yet Philip had not asked her to marry him. She was presuming that he would, of course. She also found it very interesting that he wasn't pushing to go to bed. He was very respectful, and she liked that. It actually took about a month for all the plans to be coordinated, and Honey was going to ask for time off from the show to go to San Francisco.

The day before they were going to leave, Dora was going to come up for lunch. But Philip had another plan on his mind. He asked Honey out for the Thursday night before all of this was going to happen. He told her he was going to take her to a night game of the Hollywood Stars baseball team. Honey was aware of how much the Stars meant to Philip. They were his "team." She had heard all about the gang from box 303, but she had never been asked to go. It was male territory. She couldn't believe that Philip was going to include her. She loved the idea that she was going to get even closer to his friends. She had little interest in baseball but a great deal of interest in meshing with Philip's life. He picked her up and drove her to the stadium. Only Philip would wear a blue suit and tie to a baseball game. Honey had noticed that he was always very properly dressed. She had on navy blue pants and a beautiful beaded sweater with red, white, and blue beads. When they got to box 303 it was empty.

"Where's the gang?" asked Honey, looking around. "I thought I was going to meet them."

"Oh, they'll be late tonight," answered Philip, beaming from ear to ear. "Here, sit down. Would you like some popcorn and a Coke?"

Honey said that she would, and Philip went to get the food. While he was gone, Honey looked around her. She saw an array of characters and felt an energy that was exciting. She just loved being in Hollywood. It never ceased to excite her. Philip was back quickly, in time for the first pitch. Honey started to enjoy the game because she loved the atmosphere. Two innings went by, and she could sense that Philip was starting to get nervous.

"Are you all right?" she asked. "You seem jumpy. The Stars are playing well. What's the matter?"

"Nothing," replied Philip. "I'm absolutely fine." He sounded more as though he were trying to convince himself of that.

As the third inning ended, an announcer came on and said, "Ladies and gentlemen, would you please turn your attention to the sky above." Suddenly a stunt plane swooped very low across the field, carrying a banner that read "Honey will you marry me? Love, Philip."

A cheer surged skyward from the stadium crowd, and Honey's jaw dropped open. She looked at Philip, who had tears in his eyes, and threw her arms around him.

From the people directly around them in the stands, a cheer came up that soon grew into a standing ovation. Philip pulled a ring case from his pocket and placed a beautiful sapphire-and-diamond ring on Honey's engagement finger. "This ring has been handed down in my family for generations, my darling," said Philip. "It may not be very large, but it couldn't be more precious to me."

Honey was crying by now. She had never dreamed that anything this wonderful could happen to her. She was in Hollywood, California, with a gorgeous man who had one of the brightest futures in the business. A plane with her name was flying overhead, and thousands of people were clapping while she was in a spotlight. "I love you so, Philip," said Honey, holding him close. "Our dreams will all come true. I promise, this is only the beginning."

They were so excited, it was impossible to stay and watch the game. They ran through the parking lot, holding hands and just screaming. It was a feeling that neither one of them wanted ever to lose.

"Let's go to the Trocadero for champagne," Philip suggested. Even without a reservation he managed to get a table, difficult because of the stunning popularity of the new singer who had opened there last week, Lena Horne. Honey and Philip were kissing and toasting, totally oblivious of the Hollywood debut of Miss Horne. They soon realized that they didn't want to be in public anymore, and Philip called for the check. The valet brought their car around quickly, and without saying anything Philip drove Honey to his apartment on Hayworth, just south of the Sunset Strip, and two blocks east of Schwab's Pharmacy. He parked in the garage in the back and went up the back stairs. It was a nicer apartment house than the one Honey lived in, but by no means was Philip living "high." The apartment was decorated in black and red and looked very "Chinese." He had black carved Oriental furniture and red walls and grey-and-red carpet. It wasn't opulent, but it was in good taste, a simple one-bedroom apartment, with a kitchen, living room, and a bathroom.

"My darling," said Philip, "don't even bother getting used to this place. I have my eye on a small house on Swall Drive, just at the beginning of Beverly Hills. It's perfect for us." He took her in his arms to kiss her again, and she succumbed readily. They had been behaving themselves for so long during the courtship that they were ready to explode. "I love you, Honey," said Philip, lifting her in his arms and carrying her to the bedroom.

Honey had never felt this kind of love before. With Robert it was a fantasy gone wrong. With Alii she was just a child. But this was very real. Very real. This was going to be her life. She looked into his blue eyes and saw a love that was pure, and it made her want to envelop him and keep him safe, to protect him from harm. She didn't know what it was in her that sensed he needed this, but she knew that he did.

He placed soft kisses all over her face. She had never felt

such sweetness. As his hands moved gently across her body, she felt the newness of the touch, the insecure pressure of his fingers. He was undressing her now, very slowly. He gently placed the beaded sweater on the side of the bed. Her pants he folded on top of the sweater. He went to get a cashmere robe out of the closet to cover her with while he undressed. His body was very strong across the shoulders, and as he walked toward her she wanted him to ravage her on the spot. The combination of pure love and excitement was almost driving her mad.

He began kissing her on the neck and then went down to her breasts. And then he did something she had never felt before. He took his eyelashes, by placing his eye very close to her nipple, and by opening and closing his eye, he made his lashes tickle her nipple. She started to giggle, and then it made her start to ache. He was so persistent with it. He wouldn't stop. When his head started aiming lower she wondered if he was going to do that between her legs. If he did, she didn't know if she could stand it. But he did do it. The feeling on her inner thighs was joyous beyond belief. It was like feathers teasing her. Her thighs started to tingle as his lashes moved about with abandon. She began to writhe uncontrollably. Just when she could stand it no longer, he raised up and slid himself into her. She was so wet that she could barely hold on to him as he moved. The pulsing of her muscles trying to keep him inside proved only more exciting for both of them. She thought that she would never be able to catch her breath again. Her whole body started to feel hot, as if it were going to explode. She could feel him melting into her. When they came together Honey started to cry with joy. She wanted to grab him and never let him go. She ached with love for him.

When Honey walked into the commissary to meet Philip and his mother, she was supremely confident. She had been nervous in the morning, but by the time she arrived at the studio she was in great shape. Once she saw Dora, she realized there had never been a reason to be nervous. She was a short woman in her early sixties with a face like a little doll. Everything about her was petite, right down to the little gray curls. You could see how much she loved her son, and although she would be concerned about his choice for a marriage partner, all she really wanted to see was that he was happy.

"You look like a nice girl," Dora said as she and Honey shook hands. "Do you love my son?" she asked before Honey even had a chance to straighten out her skirt.

"Very much, Mrs. Cohen. I plan to make my life his life."

She reached her hand across the table and put it on top of Honey's, giving it a pat. "Good boy, Philip. You have my blessing."

"Did you hear that, everyone?" said Philip to the twenty or so other diners in the executive room. "My mother says it's okay!" Applause rang out, and when a waiter arrived with champagne, Honey realized she was going to like being Mrs. Philip King very much.

As Honey and Philip sat on the train to San Francisco, she was filled with apprehension. Her mother wasn't a sweet little lady, and Philip didn't know that. He booked two rooms at the Clift, a beautiful hotel off Union Square, explaining that he didn't think it was right for them to be in one room with her parents coming. Honey had called them to ask that they drive to San Francisco and meet them in the Redwood Room at the Clift. It was a very grand room, all paneled in redwood with a very high ceiling. Honey thought it would be a good setting for everyone to meet because it would be more difficult for her mother to make a scene there. She had Philip order martinis, and they were waiting for Emmaline and Everett when they arrived. She hadn't seen her parents in a long while, and she realized she wasn't looking forward to it at all. She was, however, looking forward to her mother's reaction to Philip.

"It's nice to meet you, son," said Everett as they shook

hands. Honey hugged her father and perfunctorily hugged her mother.

"Tell us all about Hollywood," said Everett. He ordered a straight bourbon for himself and some hot tea for Emmaline.

"We are having a wonderful time, sir," said Philip. "I'm working very hard at the studio, and I hope that I can do something significant there."

"I'd love to act in another movie," said Honey, hoping that Philip would hear it. "I've been at Earl Carroll's long enough."

Philip cleared his throat and then said, "Mr. and Mrs. Perry, I have something important to discuss with you." Honey thought it was a wonderful coincidence that the piano player started playing "Cheek to Cheek," and she took Philip's hand. "I'm very much in love with your daughter, and I have asked her to marry me."

"What was her answer?" asked Everett.

"She said 'yes.' "

"Where are you from?" asked Emmaline, not reacting to the previous conversation.

Philip then told her his history, schooling, and about his family life.

"You do what every Friday?" asked Emmaline.

Philip started to repeat his answers, and Honey actually saw the hair on his neck start to stand up. "We light a candle to begin the Sabbath. It's very important to our people."

"And exactly what kind of people is that?" said Emmaline.

"The Jewish people," Philip shot back, barely able to contain himself.

"I did not raise my daughter to marry one of you," Emmaline said haughtily.

Before Philip could respond, Everett stepped in and said, "Emmaline, dear, I think we should see how happy our daughter is and wish her well, don't you?" Emmaline sat in silence.

While Honey was mortified by her mother's behavior, she had provoked her reactions. She never wanted her mother bothering her and Philip anyway, and this was the perfect solution. Now Philip would support her when she insisted that her parents not be at the wedding or be included in holidays. She looked at Philip and was very sorry that he had to go through this, but Honey knew it was for the best.

* CHAPTER 7 *

Honey would have loved to have a dream wedding, complete with movie stars, a grand hotel reception, a towering cake, and a giant limousine to take her away on her honeymoon, but that did not happen. Since the family situation was complicated, they were married by a justice of the peace, with Jerry Geisler as best man, Sheila as Honey's matron of honor, and Penny as her maid of honor.

The ceremony was over very quickly, with both Honey and Philip surprisingly nervous and thankful they weren't saying their vows in front of a lot of people. Honey hadn't told her parents she was getting married. They phoned Philip's family right after the ceremony, and Dora was delighted for them and understood about the quickness of the proceedings. Philip and Honey took the wedding party to lunch at a charming French Restaurant, Les Frères Taix, in downtown Los Angeles. They looked rather conspicuous when they entered. Honey was wearing a white wool suit and hat and carrying a bouquet of white gardenias, and Philip was in his usual blue suit, this time with a gray satin tie and a boutonniere. They were a noisy group, calling for champagne at noon, and soon the whole restaurant was in on the act. Taix specialized in a wonderful *suédoise* soup of pureed peas and vegetables, with hot sourdough bread. This was followed by a roast chicken and French fry dinner. Hardly anybody tasted the food. Honey was so in love with Philip that she didn't care that at the moment she wasn't in the Beverly Hills Hotel. She had never seen a more handsome man in her life. She was Mrs. Philip King, wife of the VP for business affairs at Metropolitan Pictures. How do you like that? she thought.

They drove down to La Jolla, a little seaside town just north of San Diego. They checked into the honeymoon suite of La Valencia Hotel, a beautiful Spanish hotel on a cliff overlooking the ocean. When they got to the room, Philip said, "Oh, no, Mrs. King, let me," and swooped Honey up in his arms, carrying her across the threshold. He carried her right over to the bottle of champagne with the card marked "Mr. and Mrs. Philip King."

"Oh, Philip," exclaimed Honey, "Mr. and Mrs. Philip King. That's the first time we've ever seen that. I'm going to save it. I'm going to save everything for the rest of our lives, darling, because I want to remember every moment."

Philip kissed her and walked her over to the bed, where he laid her down as gently as if she were a newborn. "Just stay like that. I'm going to pour us some champagne."

Honey watched as her dream man took a few steps away from her. She loved his strength. The fact that he was short didn't bother her at all. She saw him as a powerhouse.

"For you, Mrs. King," said Philip as he returned with two flutes of champagne, and touched his glass to hers. "May our lives revolve around the happiness of this moment, my darling. I honor you with my life and my love forever."

"I'll be right back," said Honey, smiling at her groom on her way to the bathroom where the bellman put her things. Philip has the most gorgeous smile, she thought. She entered the dressing room area and suddenly got very nervous. It was as if she were a virgin again. It was different with Alii, and certainly with Robert, she suddenly thought. She realized now that she hadn't loved them. She never cared what Robert thought. She just had a good time. This time she really wanted to make Philip feel special. She took off her suit and put on a white satin bias-cut gown that sensuously hugged her body. Over the nightgown she put a white marabou feather jacket, and then she slipped on white satin high-heeled mules. She noticed when she looked in the mirror that her hair was almost the same color as the feathers.

She's a honeymoon night vision, thought Philip as she came toward him smiling. He was already in bed, and when he lifted the covers off himself, all of Philip King was showing, and she could see he was very happy to greet his bride.

She sat on the bed and leaned toward him, and he brushed his face through the feathers for several minutes before he took off her jacket. His hands explored the satin-covered body very slowly. She felt him take the bottom of her nightgown and lift it toward her head. Together they took it off. He then took the feather jacket and began to let the feathers trace her body. She could feel them tickling her breasts until you could see the nipples through the feathers. His mouth quickly covered her right nipple, feathers and all, and the effect was dazzling. With his teeth, he dragged the feathers lower and lower, and soon she was swirling in them. He was on top of her and took her with such force that she forgot who she was. She couldn't think at all. It was as if they were silently announcing to each other that they would never part. The rhythm of their bodies took on a separate existence.

After they were calm again and lying in each other's arms, Honey reached for more champagne for both of them. After a while, she picked up the feather jacket, turned to Philip, and said, "Now, it's your turn."

He did as he was told, and she stood over him just perfectly to keep her "best parts" in view. The feathers were driving him crazy, and they started laughing. In all the giggling she lost her footing and fell on his chest, legs astride, feeling him hard, throbbing behind her. She raised and lowered herself just a little bit at a time so they each would crave one another more. Their breathing and concentration became paramount. Interesting, thought Honey. He was totally hers at this moment in time. Until she made the move no one would be satisfied. She knew that he was craving her, wanting her. This was a new feeling for her and one that she liked. He was groaning for her now, and she loved it. She could feel him pushing himself toward her as his hips went up and down hungrily.

"I need you," he urged from below.

"How much, darling?" purred Honey, letting him agonize a few more delicious seconds before lowering herself onto him. The ride was exquisite. They both could sense that something different was happening.

"I love it," said Philip.

Honey had never heard a man react to her this way. She had always felt like the pupil before, but with Philip she sensed something had changed. She could tell that he wanted and needed her, and that gave her the upper hand. It was something that excited her, and she was going to cultivate it and never give it up. Philip, too, felt excited. He trusted Honey. He knew he could be totally free with her, and he felt she knew what he was thinking.

After the weekend was over, she and Philip returned to Los Angeles to their new home on Swall Drive. The house was a one-story stucco Spanish bungalow with a small lawn in front, a larger one in back, and a covered patio area. Nothing about the house was that large, but Honey and Philip were ecstatic. To Philip it was a dream come true. To Honey it was a perfect starter house. Philip had his secretary furnish it in traditional browns and greens, with new kitchen appliances and linens, but he thoughtfully left lots of room for Honey to pick things out.

Honey liked to plan things, and the first thing she wanted was a dinner party. Right from the beginning of the marriage she was more ambitious than Philip, and she knew that together they could be very successful in Hollywood. Philip was bright, quick, likable, and lucky. Several times early in his career he'd been in the right place at the right time, and he'd delivered. But she didn't want to rely on luck. She'd take advantage of her lunch group's intimate perspective on Hollywood and ask their advice.

"I'd like to have a dinner party as a surprise for Philip," she explained the very next Wednesday when she joined her friends for lunch at Musso's. "Of course all of you and your husbands, such as they are, are invited." Honey started laughing, and the girls took the crack the way it was intended.

"I think you should invite Flora and Sam Lewis," said Ellen Elliot.

"And of course Sam Jr. He's so boring, hopefully he'll decline," added Kate. "Freddie met a new comic when he was passing through Chicago named Danny Thomas. He's this really funny Lebanese guy married to a very sweet girl named Rosemarie. The studios are hot on him."

"That's right," said Ellen. "I heard Jack talking about him. They're meeting this week because Jack would like to represent him. If you have Flora and Sam, I'll tell Jack and he can use that to get Danny to come to the party. I'm sure Sam wants him for Metropolitan, and that way everybody is a hero."

Honey knew she'd done the right thing. These women had been around and could tell her firsthand how the game was played. She really wanted to be a good wife for her husband. "Ellen, what did you do before you met Jack?" asked Honey.

"I was his secretary. I really wanted to be a writer, and in fact I'm writing a screenplay at home right now to surprise him with."

"That's great. I hope you can get an agent," Honey said jokingly. "And what about you, Kate?"

"Well, I used to be an actress. I met Freddie in summer stock and just followed him to Hollywood. Fortunately he married me, since I'm the one with the brains. You see, I don't care how many other girls he sleeps with—'cause I've already got mine," she said, squeezing Ellen's hand.

They all know how to make it work for themselves, thought Honey. She was going to watch them all at her party for sure.

She decided not to keep the party a surprise from Philip. She wanted him to be rested and ready. Her guest list was looking very good. Flora and Sam, Ellen and Jack, Sheila and Hal, Kate and Freddie, Danny and Rosemarie, and she asked Jerry Geisler to bring Penny. Sam Jr. declined the invitation, saying he'd be out of town. That made everything perfect. The night of the party she would not let her nerves get the best of her. She was going to handle it, and everything would be great.

Honey decided to have Chasen's send over a vat of their chili. She was going to make a big salad and as a unique touch serve a Hawaiian sweet bread she'd learned to bake in the islands as a child. She wanted to be different. She wanted people to talk about her gatherings. She knew that Chasen's was newly popular, and she doubted if anyone had served their food at a private party. She hired a bartender and a maid and ordered all red and yellow carnations as flower arrangements. Aside from the fact that they were the colors of Philip's alma mater, USC, the chili was red and the bread was yellow. Honey thought it was nice to have some sort of theme for the evening, even though it was probably noticeable only to her.

At seven P.M. the first guests arrived. She and Philip raced to the door together, excited to have guests in their house for the first time. She took one last look in the mirror, pleased with what she saw.

The Gallerys, Elliots, and Thomases arrived together, the women in cocktail dresses, the men in suits. When the bartender came and asked for their order, Ellen shot Honey a "good move" look. There were crudités and nuts on the table. Within a few minutes Flora and Sam Lewis arrived. Honey had never met Flora, a plain, stout woman with a kind face, who looked like the wife of a deli owner. But Honey would never underestimate her. Last to arrive were Jerry

Geisler and Penny. Geisler looked uncomfortable in an intimate social situation, but Penny would bring him out.

"I've never heard of anyone serving Chasen's food in their home yet," exclaimed Sam Sr. "What a find you have here, Philip." And he put his arm around Honey's waist.

Honey could see Danny Thomas over in the corner looking a little nervous, so she walked over to him. "Hi," she said, taking his arm and winking at Rosemarie. "I've heard that you are fantastic. Now I know you haven't been here very long. I haven't really been here all that long, either, but let me tell you something. The ones with the talent always win in the end, but they had better surround themselves with good people. Some of these studio guys in Hollywood are real rats. They wouldn't know what a family meant if they ran over it. Choose carefully. You're a good guy, and I only let good people in my house."

From across the room, Philip watched wondering what Honey was up to.

After dinner, Hal Murphy walked over to the piano and started playing, and soon Sheila, Penny, and Honey were harmonizing. "You could give the Andrews Sisters a run for their money," shouted Sam over the applause.

Kate and Ellen looked at each other and smiled. The evening was going well and might turn into one of those great nights. Kate could see Freddie and Danny itching in their seats to have a turn in the spotlight. Honey also saw what was going on and whispered something to Hal, who then hit an attention-getting chord.

"And now, my friends, I'd like to ask Danny if he'd sing a song for us," said Honey.

Danny told a few jokes and then did "Danny Boy." He was great, and Honey could tell he really appreciated having the chance to perform in such a setting for the head of Metropolitan. Freddie was up next and was hilarious.

Then Hal said, "Ladies and gentlemen, if you would all take your seats, Honey Perry King will now sing for us."

Applause broke out and quickly subsided as Honey walked

to the piano and began a flawless "Embraceable You." In midsong she went over to Philip and sang directly to him, and by the time she was through, there were more than a few tears. She followed with "How Deep Is the Ocean" and closed with "I Can't Give You Anything but Love." She practically got a standing ovation.

"Son," said Sam Sr., coming over to him as the guests were about to leave, "you have a remarkable woman on your hands. Congratulations, my boy." Philip beamed, so proud of his wife he could barely speak.

"Honey, you must join me for tea soon to meet members of my Angels of Hollywood group," said Flora.

"I would be honored, Mrs. Lewis," said Honey. "The Angels are really special."

"Please call me Flora, dear, and thank you so much for a lovely evening."

With that, everyone left. Evenings like this, Honey thought, are almost as fun as having my own opening night. Almost.

Honey almost fainted when her party showed up in Louella Parsons's column two days later. She called Philip at the office to share the news with him.

"That's wonderful, dear," he said with all the enthusiasm of a man studying a contract at the same time. "I'm very glad you're happy."

Honey was a little disappointed with his reaction, but she dismissed it because he probably was busy. She wanted to dedicate herself to making Honey and Philip King successful. It was her job. Philip had other things to do. She sent a thank-you note to Louella and hoped that one day she might invite her to her home if the party was important enough.

When Philip came home from the studio that night, the house was completely dark except for a candle on the coffee table in the living room. He put down his briefcase and called for Honey. "I'm in here," he heard from the back of the house. As he walked down the hall he saw that there were more candles along the walkway. They were votive candles in clear jars. Philip was wondering if he was being sacrificed at the altar, but he was very interested in going to the bedroom. Inside he saw Honey wearing all white satin, reclining on a satin sheet, the latest Frank Sinatra melody playing softly.

"I'll help you, darling," said Honey as she slowly got off the bed and started to take off Philip's clothes. Once that task was completed she walked him back to the bed. As she sat at the head of the bed, she stretched her legs out, saying, "Lie down on top of my lap, facedown."

Philip obeyed immediately, intrigued by Honey's demands. She started to scratch his back, and he loved it. It relaxed him. She lulled him into it and began to run her hands down to his buttocks. She took her fingertips and ever so slightly ran them over each cheek. The effect was very soothing. She used them like little soft squiggles, and Philip began to giggle a little bit.

"Oh, so you think this is funny, do you?" said Honey. "Maybe I should stop tickling you. You're having too much fun. This might be better for you." Slap! went her hand on one cheek.

"Ow!" said Philip. "What are you doing?"

"You'll see," said Honey, and slap! the hand went again.

"Wait a minute," said Philip.

"Just relax, darling. I'm doing this because I love you. Just start to feel the rhythm of it," said Honey. And she proceeded to make him sound like an Indian war chant drum. But the regularity of the hit began to make him want it more. Once the initial stinging turned from pain to pleasure, he couldn't get enough. She could feel him grow hard underneath her. He kept wanting to turn to get to her, and each time he did she slapped him harder. Finally he was so excited he lunged at her, ripped off her nightgown, and took her ferociously. Honey's excitement at figuring the perfect balance to their sexual relationship threw her into shrieks of delight.

Philip, who always prided himself on being a gentleman, was shocked by what had happened and by how much he loved it. He was really hooked on her, and that's the way she wanted it.

"You're a smart cookie," said Jerry Geisler to Honey while he smeared some chopped liver on a bagel slice at Hillcrest Country Club. "Hillcrest understands chopped liver," Geisler said. "You have to have the right balance between the eggs, onions, and chicken fat to make it all work."

"I'll remember that, Jerry," said Honey. "I want to remember everything you tell me," said the bride sweetly. "I love my husband so much. I want to get to know his friends better so I can better understand him and make his life easier."

Geisler was impressed with her sincerity. "Pinky's a nice guy. There aren't many real ones around. He cares about people and tries to help them, sometimes even when he's in danger. Now that's either a saint or someone who needs a little savvy by his side."

Honey's curiosity was piqued. "What do you mean, Jerry?"

Geisler proceeded to tell her how Philip saved Sam from the gamblers in the vacant lot. Honey couldn't believe it. Philip had never told her anything. No wonder Sam and Flora Lewis were so nice to him. "Lemme tell you something else, too. Most executives are scared of actors because actors have the real power. It may look to you like the studio head is powerful, but just let Gary Cooper be upset about something and the executives get very nervous. Philip is really well liked by actors. He doesn't seem to be afraid of them, and they trust him. Keep concentrating on those associations. He'll be more protected that way."

Honey wasn't quite sure what he meant, but she knew it was important for their future.

* * *

A short while after her lunch with Jerry, Honey hit upon the idea of having a woman's night dinner on the first Monday of every month at her house. It started out with her usual gang of girlfriends, but after the first monthly dinner they decided to ask two new people each month. It was only natural that Kate and Ellen would be the first to ask new people and that they would gravitate to actors' wives. It was their fourth dinner, and the girls were very happy at the turnout. When Kate asked her friend Rocky, who was married to Gary Cooper, after the second one, Rocky had such a good time that she asked Afdera Fonda for the third one.

"Mrs. Fonda," said Honey. "It's such a pleasure to meet you. Please come in." Afdera Fonda was wearing a spectacular hat with a small plume coming out of it, and Honey made a mental note to start wearing more hats.

"Rocky, how are you?" said Afdera, rushing to her friend's side. "How's Coop? Did you get that contract situation worked out?"

Honey's ears were at attention.

"Not really," said Rocky. "I know they'll come around, but Gary just hates the negotiating game. He feels he's worth a certain price and he's made a fortune for the studio and they should pay him."

That night when Philip got home, Honey was ready for him. As she handed him a drink she nuzzled close to his neck and said, "I have something that you want. . . ."

"You always do, darling," said Philip. "Are we going to start it here or wait until after dinner?" He loved how she teased him. It always got him excited because he never knew what she would think of next to do.

"In time," said Honey. "But first let me tell you about Gary Cooper."

As Philip listened, he realized how valuable her information was. Philip was proud of Honey, wanting her to be happy and busy since her career was not developing the way she wanted it. He encouraged her to enjoy socializing.

After a few months, Honey was very chummy with Mrs. Gary Cooper, Mrs. Robert Lafontaine, Mrs. Henry Fonda, Mrs. Eric James, Mrs. Joel McCrea, Mrs. Fred MacMurray, Mrs. Humphrey Bogart, and Mrs. Richard Callaway, women who were married to some of the biggest stars in the business, some of them under contract to Metropolitan. It was decided that the girls would have a Sunday brunch so their husbands could meet, too.

Honey realized that she hadn't heard from Flora Lewis in a long time. She was sure that Flora had meant it when she'd invited her to tea; she'd probably just forgotten. Honey wanted to invite Louella Parsons to the Sunday brunch, but she was worried that if Louella wrote it up, Flora would be hurt if she was not invited. She thought it might be good for Flora and Sam to see how well Philip mixed with her new group of friends, and she hoped that they might then promote him out of business affairs. He was invaluable to them in that area, but he, and she, would be so much happier in the creative area. The problem was Sam Jr. Philip would never do anything to hurt him, and his parents were so loyal to him that they wouldn't move him, even at the prospect of jeopardizing their studio because he couldn't do the job as well as someone else. Honey decided it was time to start making things happen, and she invited all of the Lewises.

The morning of the brunch arrived, and Philip and Honey awoke feeling on top of the world. Neither of them wanted to leave the bed. Sunday morning was one of their favorite times to make love . . . lazy, sensual, lasting for hours. When Philip reached for Honey and began to kiss her neck, she stopped him gently.

"I want you so much that I won't settle for anything less

than our extravaganza, darling. I'd rather have nothing than a substitute.'' She put her hands on his face and kissed him deeply, leaving him wanting much more. ''C'mon,'' she said, getting up. ''This is our day to shine.''

Honey had worked with the caterer the night before to set up the house and the yard. Her budget was not unlimited, so she made up for it by being clever. She was going to have a western barbecue with sausages and ribs on the grill, grits and scrambled eggs done in the kitchen, and homemade biscuits from the oven. She wore a red-and-white gingham dress with a full skirt, her blond hair pulled back into a ponytail. She had Philip go into wardrobe and get a full-fledged cowboy outfit with spurs. She had the usual gang there, consisting of Kate and Freddie and Ellen and Jack.

''Here, taste this,'' she said as she forced Sam Lewis, Sr., to eat grits for the first time.

''What is it? It looks like baby cereal,'' he said with a horrified look on his face.

''Just do it for me, please,'' said Honey, smiling at him. Just as he put it in his mouth there were screams of delight at the front door. She and Sam rushed to see what was going on. Coming up the block was Gary Cooper and his wife, Rocky, on horseback. They were met by applause as they arrived on the lawn, and Coop said, ''Where can I tie up my horse?'' Honey thought he was enchanting. He had real presence.

As soon as everybody was finished eating, out from the kitchen came a lone country violinist playing square-dancing tunes. Honey encouraged Philip to get up and dance with her, and soon the others joined in enthusiastically. At one point Honey noticed that Richard Callaway and Eric James, two of Metropolitan's biggest stars, were gathering a crowd around them.

''Let's go see what's happening,'' she said to Philip.

''Mine's bigger than yours,'' said Callaway.

''Not true,'' said James. ''I'll show you mine anytime you want.''

"Boys, really," said Honey, affecting a southern accent. "Is this proper for a Sunday?"

"Well, my dressing room IS bigger than his," said Callaway.

"Tell you what," challenged James. "I'll arm wrestle you for it. If I win, I get it."

"Deal," said Callaway.

Sam Lewis was laughing, but Philip was not, recognizing a potential problem.

"Hold it," said Philip. "Tomorrow morning I'm measuring both dressing rooms. If they aren't the same size, I'll make sure they're equal within forty-eight hours. I'm sure Sam agrees with me." Honey was watching Philip's command of the situation with admiration, and she hoped Sam was doing the same.

When Louella's column appeared it was almost anticlimactic. The whole town had heard about Honey's Down Home brunch. The stories about wives bringing their special breakfast dishes, Gary Cooper riding in on a horse, and Richard Callaway and Eric James arm wrestling made the gossip rounds by nightfall. Honey had done it. She was now a talked-about hostess. She wasn't Mrs. Jack Warner, but she was still young. It was really very simple. If you want to be Mrs. Jack Warner, you have to have a Mr. Jack Warner, and VP of business affairs just won't do. Well, she had time, and she was just beginning.

With Philip's first substantial raise they put the Swall house on the market. Honey had her eye on a Colonial house on Bedford Drive in the best section of Beverly Hills. The Swall house sold very quickly at a handsome profit, which enabled Honey to step into the probate timing on the other property. The house, designed by Paul Williams, was a beautiful white brick with white columns across the front. The shutters were dark green, and the red-brick walkway to the front door was lined with perfectly groomed rosebushes. The house was sold with the existing furniture. It was early American, and Honey detested it. She very much wanted to go out and decorate it her way, but they didn't have enough money. It was a big step supporting a house of this size, and they needed to take their time customizing it for themselves.

Flora Lewis also had begun to respect and acknowledge Honey, and she invited her to her first tea with the Angels. It was more of the Hollywood old guard than her new set, but it was important for her to belong, and she went gladly. It was her goal to blend the old and the new and let time take care of the changeover. But key to all of this was helping Philip get the position he wanted. He was hanging out with the boys at Dave's Blue Room a lot, and she realized he was just hungry for a real show business environment, something he was not getting at the office. Honey was trying not to feel as if she were being taken for granted a little bit. What she did not realize, though, was that Philip was beginning to feel second place to Honey, beginning to notice how much her "information gathering" on his behalf took away from her wifely attention to him. He'd begun to resent it just a little bit. Her raw ambition disturbed him, yet he knew she was doing it for him. He just wasn't completely sure what she was up to.

"Mrs. King is here, sir," said his secretary.

Sam Sr. had been surprised when his secretary told him that Honey King had asked for an appointment to see him.

"Please show her in," said Sam.

"Sam, thank you for giving me some of your time," said Honey as she swept in the room wearing a yellow silk suit and a wide-brimmed matching yellow hat, with shoes, gloves, and purse to match. Combined with her towhead blonde hair she looked like a butterscotch sundae. Sam was dazzled, and Honey knew it. He showed her to a couch in the corner. It would be too formal to have her sit opposite him at the desk.

"Flora tells me you're being a big help to the Angels. You got a whole shipment of dolls donated to the hospital. She really appreciated that," said Sam.

"I think the work Flora does is very important, and I'm honored that she asked me to participate," said Honey.

"Well, what can I do for you?" said Sam.

"Actually, I think you and I are about to do a lot for a lot of people," said Honey as she rested her hand on his knee just for a second. "I want to tell you how grateful I am that Philip is at Metropolitan. I think this studio is the most artistic of them all, and you really seem to have your finger on the pulse of the public. I feel as though Philip and I are part of the family. I'm very protective of Metropolitan, and I always want it to come out on top. I look upon you as Philip's father since his own father died a number of years ago. That's how he feels about you, too."

"You know how much I appreciate that, my dear. You and Philip are like my children," said Sam.

"I've heard something, Sam," continued Honey. "I come to you today because you must have this information. I wouldn't want you to be caught in second position on this."

"What is it? What's going on?" he asked urgently.

"You know that I'm around a lot of women who are married to studio executives," continued Honey. "I recently overheard a conversation that Mrs. Darryl Zanuck was having with someone. A man as smart as you is aware that there is a lot of money in Europe in the film business. I'm also sure you know that people over there are very eager to get involved with Hollywood."

Sam was listening intently. He'd had no idea that Honey was this smart. He knew she was a loyal, loving woman, but he had no idea about this side of her. Philip was even luckier than he'd thought.

"I understand that Darryl Zanuck is going to open a European branch of Twentieth-Century Fox in Europe within the next six months," continued Honey.

Sam was surprised, but he didn't let it show.

"He is going to either appoint someone from his staff to be the production head in Europe or he is going to look for an executive outside the company. My Philip loves Metropolitan. It was always his dream to work at a studio, but you know as well as I do that he's worth more than just running your legal department. I realize he's a great lawyer and you need him, but he's an even better showman. More than anything he wants to move into the production area."

Sam was now getting very nervous. Honey looked at him, and her mood changed. She started to speak, and her voice was hesitant.

"It would break my heart if Philip had to leave you." Her eyes started to tear up. "But it is breaking his heart sitting with contracts all day. I see it at home. He's just not happy."

He took her hands in his. "My dear, please don't cry. We are a family. We will work this out," said Sam.

Honey paused before speaking. "Don't you think that Sam Jr. would enjoy living in Europe?" she asked sweetly.

A click went off in Sam's head. Honey was handing him the perfect scenario to put Sam where he might be better and save the father-son relationship at the same time.

Honey continued, "He seems so lonely here. I think he would really like Europe. He could have a whole new life. Maybe he'd even meet someone and fall in love. Of course, that would leave the position of head of production open . . ." Honey let her voice trail off as she looked at Sam. A slow smile started on her lips as she could see Sam Sr. focus in on the whole package. "You see?" she said. "It's perfect. You beat Zanuck and you give Sam and Philip a better life. Just one big happy family. There's only one thing I'd like you to do. I would like you to not tell Philip that I had anything to do with this. I love him so much. I'd rather stay in the background and let him have all the joy. You don't mind, do you?" She kissed Sam on the cheek as she stood up to leave. "I hope you agree that this is a good plan. It's important to keep our family together. I look forward to hearing from you."

Sam just stood there stunned after she left. He would really have to give a lot of thought to her proposal. That would have to wait, however, until after his three o'clock meeting was over. He had to pay attention to that. He was meeting Freddie Gallery and his agent, Jack Elliot. Freddie was their biggest star, and his last three pictures at the box office had brought in most of Metropolitan's profits last year. His contract was up in three months, and he had offers from every studio. Sam couldn't afford to lose him, but he didn't want to be bled to death, either.

After everybody said their hellos they got right down to business.

"Look, Sam," said Jack. "It's very simple. Freddie's number one and it's time to pay him what he's worth. This is a two-way street. He has abided by the terms of his first contract, which were not that lucrative. Of course they shouldn't have been that rich since it was his tenure here that made him a star. Now that you make so much money from his movies, it's only fair that he get more money. I'm not telling you anything you don't know."

"So what do you want?" asked Sam.

"I want a two-year deal. Ten thousand dollars a week the first year, twenty thousand the second. Plus ten percent of the studio stock."

"What!" screamed Sam. "I have never heard of such a thing!"

"Well, it's time you did because it's Freddie's name that's boosting your stock. He should get some of it."

"Now here's what I want," said Sam. "I want a five-year deal. No stock. Five thousand dollars in year one, seventy-five hundred year two, ten thousand year three, fifteen thousand year four, and twenty thousand in year five."

Jack laughed. "In your dreams, Sam. Should I just pick up the phone now and tell Jack Warner we accept his deal? He's sitting by the phone."

"You may be bluffing or you may not," continued Sam. "Freddie is sitting here not speaking. But I know him, too. I knew him before you. He's a loyal guy. He's not going to screw me over."

Freddie smiled.

"Okay, Sam," said Jack. "How about three years. Seventy-five hundred in year one, twelve thousand five hundred in year two, and twenty thousand in year three. Plus five percent of the stock."

Sam glowered and paced. "Okay," he said after a few minutes. "You've got a deal." He extended his hand to Jack, but Jack didn't take it.

"Oh, by the way, I forgot to mention one more thing that is very important to Freddie. He only wants to deal with Philip King. He feels that Philip understands actors and material. Your kid's a nice guy. I don't want to hurt your feelings, but Philip's the only one any of my clients want to deal with from now on."

Jack extended his hand now to Sam's. Sam slowly brought up his hand for Jack to take. "This has been a very interesting day, gentlemen," said Sam, not quite knowing what hit him. "You will have Philip King."

"I'm glad our family is still together," said Jack.

Sam smiled. Hadn't he heard those words once today already?

Two days later Philip came home from the office holding a bottle of champagne and a dozen white roses. "Honey, Honey!" he shouted from the front door. "Where are you?"

Honey came running from the upstairs. "What is it? What's happening? Are you all right?" she cried.

"I have the most wonderful news, darling," said Philip. "I've just been made head of production for the studio!"

"I'm so happy for you! You've wanted this for so long," said Honey, throwing her arms around him. "Let's open the champagne right now!" They toasted each other and then danced to their favorite Frank Sinatra record, slowly making their way to the bedroom.

"Lie down and wait for me, darling," said Honey as she went into her bathroom. After a few minutes she came out wearing a black satin teddy, black stockings, and high heels.

In her right hand she was holding a doctor bag. She could see Philip's eyes light up at the sight of her. She saw him watch her every move as she took out four black leather thongs. "Turn over," she said, her voice getting a little tense. Philip did as he was told, and she carefully tied each one of his limbs to the bedposts, then climbed on top of him and started licking the back of his neck with her tongue.

He was tingling with excitement. She went into all the crevices, particularly those where she knew he was ticklish. It drove him crazy. Seconds before he could take no more, she pulled a sandpaper-covered Ping-Pong paddle out of the doctor bag and struck his beckoning rear end. Philip gasped. It was much harder than anything he had felt before. As she hit him time and again his cries of pain turned to the moans of utmost joy. And then she just stopped and waited. His body stopped moving and then started in again quickly. It was aching to be touched again.

"What's the matter, darling? Is there something you want?" taunted Honey. "Let me hear you."

Philip begged for more. They both were going over the edge, and they loved it. Honey was consumed with power as she magnanimously untied him, turned him over, and mounted him. Perfection, thought Honey, sheer perfection, as she gave in to her own ecstasy.

The next morning Honey met Ellen and Kate for breakfast at the Beverly Hills Hotel coffee shop. They took one look at each other when they all got there and started laughing. How neat it all was. Freddie and Kate make much more money. Jack and Ellen make more as a result of the percentage, and with Philip as the head, Honey gets what she wants and Freddie and Jack and all of Jack's clients have a friend at the top.

"Honey, you're the best," said Ellen, toasting her with orange juice. "I have a surprise for you that you weren't expecting. Half of what Jack gets is always put under my name in the bank. Since the stock idea was yours, I am going to give you one-quarter of Jack's stock in Metropolitan. You'll have better use for it than I, I'm sure."

Honey pretended to be shocked and delighted. In fact, she was well aware that it was a payoff, and it was one she expected and deserved. "Oh, my God, thank you so much! I'll always remember how thoughtful you were," and then she hugged her. It did not go unnoticed in Honey's mind that she was the only "outsider" who knew about the "love nest" and that as she and Philip grew more powerful it would behoove people to make them happy, but she was going to take Ellen's gesture at face value for now. Ellen had been very helpful to her right from the beginning. Ellen was impressed by Honey's eagerness to learn the business side of the business and helped her by taking contracts out of Jack's files and letting Honey study them. Honey was now as familiar with deals as Philip. She wanted to be. A part of her felt that she needed to take care of him in every area. She even checked with him to make sure that he put into his new contract a clause that guaranteed him five percent of the gross receipts of every movie made under his regime, and if the picture grossed more than five million dollars, anything over that would be converted to shares of stock in the studio. This was big stuff for a new production head to get first time out, but Honey knew Sam Sr. sensed the power, and Philip got everything he wanted.

As for Sam Jr., he was not heartbroken to leave town. There was a little jealousy at Philip's rise, but he really wanted to get away. He felt inadequate in Hollywood and planned to make a name for himself in Europe. The timing really was right for everyone.

Now that Honey had Philip in his new position, she could turn her attention back to the house. It was time to give away the old furnishings and turn it into her dream house. She was going to make each room of the house a different fantasy, in memory of the scenery warehouse where she and Philip had first met. First, she remodeled the backyard so the pool looked like the outdoor one at William Randolph Hearst's San Simeon. Inside, she went room by room and dream by dream. The dining room was Georgian from the South, with navy blue walls, blue-and-white Wedgwood china, and a Chippendale dining set. The oil paintings were originals depicting the Civil War. The den was painted dark hunter green. The furniture was brown leather and mahogany, and all the walls were paneled wood. There was a beige, green, and brown plaid carpet, but the most striking feature of the room were the two walls of bookcases and the brass ladder that could be pushed anywhere. Honey did add one more touch, a bar hidden in the bookshelves that revealed itself when a book was pressed. Upstairs, their bedroom was peach and blue and very Louis XIV, with a veranda that overlooked the pool. The guest room was American Colonial, with a four-poster bed covered with a chenille bedspread. The poolhouse was a Grecian fantasy . . . all white with blue accents. Honey's favorite room_was her bath and dressing area, which she decorated with smoke-colored mirrors and black tile floors and sinks. The lighting could range from high for makeup to dim for a very special bath. Music was piped into all the rooms, but the pièce de résistance was the "Arabian Nights" living room in red and gold, with huge sweeping canopies, tents, and gigantic brocade pillows. When it was all done, she walked through the house room by room, feeling the beginnings of contentment.

* CHAPTER 8 *

Honey had been waiting in the den nursing the same martini for about an hour. Philip was late again. It had begun happening more and more since he had gotten his new job. She knew he was probably legitimately working late, but she had just about had it. He was a good man, but his lack of attention to her, his failure to help her career, and his lack of appreciation for her work was making her angry. She was beginning to find more joy in life from the recognition of her intelligence by Kate and Ellen.

When Philip pulled into the driveway he wasn't happy. He loved his job at the studio, but he wasn't happy about the changes he felt in Honey. She was so sweet when they met, he thought he was marrying an angel. He loved how she helped him. But now it was different. There was an edge to her that he never knew was there.

He found her in the den, and they kissed on the cheek.

"I have the most wonderful idea, Philip," Honey said after she gave him a drink. "I want to give the most incredible party that Hollywood has ever seen. It will be the perfect send-off for our new home." He wasn't elated, and she could see it. "What's the matter? Don't you like the idea?" she asked.

"Oh, Honey," Philip said, sighing, "I'm sick of hearing about parties and gossip. I wish we'd just spend some time on us instead of everyone else in town."

Honey exploded. "How dare you say that? What do you think I do it for?"

"I'm beginning to think you do it for yourself," answered Philip. "It certainly doesn't do anything for me."

"Oh, no?" said Honey in a tone he had never heard before. "Who suggested most of the amendments in your contract with Sam? Who do you think got you to be friendly with the stars at the studio? Do you think I was giving barbecues because I like baked beans? You don't have the slightest idea about anything."

Philip was stunned. Part of him realized there was a grain of truth to what she was saying, but the depth of the ambition she revealed unnerved him. "Why don't we just go in to dinner now, shall we?" he said.

Honey didn't say a word, but her mind was going a mile a minute as they went to the dining room.

Honey decided that she was just going to get on with it. If Philip didn't understand, it was his problem. She knew she was right. She knew what she was doing. The invitations went out the next day for the "Arabian Nights Costume Ball" to be held in Philip and Honey's home in four weeks. Nothing pleased her more than to plan a party. She felt that each time she did it she was advancing Philip and herself. It was almost like conquering a country. She met with various caterers and judged them on their ability to come up with creative ideas and food. She was always better than any of them and usually went with the company that would take her orders the best. It was just easier that way. She had florists "audition" arrangements in her living room. She made them leave their samples and then used them around the house. She met with the band leader to go over every single song he was going to play; no song could be played without her approval. She had the top set decorator at Metropolitan do sketches for the backyard to see if his ideas would work. A party was something she worked on for at least five hours a day before the event, and now she had the money to do it right. Because each room in the house had a different style, she was going to give a theme party once a year in honor of each room. It was only fitting that the first one be Arabian for the living room. Next year she'd give a "Rhett and Scarlett Ball."

Within days all of Hollywood was talking about the party, and people who were not invited were prevailing upon friends who were to get an invitation. Honey held firm to her original guest list. She might expand next year, but she knew that if she gave in this year, her party would seem less exclusive.

Philip just went along with it, realizing he really enjoyed Honey's parties. Underneath it all, though, he was disappointed that Honey did seem to derive more pleasure from her "position" than from their personal life.

A few days before the party Honey began to notice that she didn't quite have her usual boundless energy. When Philip came home from the studio at nine P.M. he found her lying down in the bedroom.

"Are you all right? This isn't like you," said Philip.

"I'm not sure, Philip," replied Honey. "I feel so tired. I just don't understand it."

"Well, tomorrow morning I'm calling the doctor and you're going right in. We're going to fix this immediately." Philip squeezed her hand and went to his dressing room.

Honey was pleased that he cared. When she woke up the next morning she was nauseated and felt terrible. "I must have the flu," she said.

"Tired and morning sickness? You don't have the flu, darling," said Philip. "You're pregnant!" Grinning, he rushed to hug her.

Honey started to cry. She wasn't so sure she wanted a child yet. She had things to do. "Do you really think so?" she said. "I'm not so sure. It's probably that I've been working so hard on this party."

"Darling! Why the tears?" Philip was a little taken aback. He would love to have a child. "Why don't I just drive you to the doctor and we'll find out?" he asked.

"Oh, not yet. Let's wait a few more days and see what happens." Honey threw herself into the party even more. But the tiredness persisted, and at the end of the week she allowed Philip to take her to get a pregnancy test. The doctor confirmed it almost immediately. Philip floated to work. He would love being a father. Honey, always resourceful, looked to the future. All right, she thought to herself, it's time for the dynasty to begin. Our son will inherit the studio. We'll wipe the Zanucks right off the map.

Louella Parsons was the first to arrive. She always liked to get there early with her husband, "Docky," so she didn't miss anything. That way she could also get a better table than Hedda, although Honey had placed them at equal tables on either side of the room. Sheila and Hal Murphy arrived next with Penny and her beau of the moment, actor Donald Hudson. Esther Williams and Ricardo Montalban arrived together because they were shooting their movie nearby.

To carry out her Arabian Nights theme, Honey had tented the whole backyard. She'd hired dancing girls and had all the waiters dressed like Valentino in *The Sheik*. There were special tables inside and out draped in brocade satin and set on short legs so guests could sit on large puffy pillows on Oriental carpets. The Lester Lanin Band was there from San Francisco, too.

"I can't believe you actually have live camels on your lawn, Honey," said Clark Gable.

"I did it for you," said Honey. "I think things should just be outrageous and we should let ourselves go." Clark had come with Hedy Lamarr and Paulette Goddard, who were trying to take his mind off the death of Carole Lombard. It was not an easy task. "I want you to go to the very first waiter you see and ask him to show you the couscous. Go on," urged Honey.

Then Sheila came up behind her, dressed like a harem girl. "He really is gorgeous, isn't he?" said Sheila.

"Yes, but Penny's probably better than he is!" cracked Honey.

"Watch out, friend," Sheila cautioned. "You never know who's behind what veil at this party."

With the passing of time Honey felt better about Robert Taylor and invited him with his wife, Barbara Stanwyck. It did not escape Honey that it would be a coup to get him to leave MGM and come to Metropolitan. She would have to work on that. Robert and Barbara were standing by an open fire pit, watching two chefs roast the lamb kebabs. Robert kissed her on the cheek when she approached them.

"Make sure you spend some time with Clark this evening. He needs special attention," said Honey.

"Don't worry, well take care of it," said Barbara. "You're so thoughtful. We'll be glad to help."

"Now I want you both to be sure to taste the b'stilla. It's like a Middle Eastern chicken pie with eggs and powdered sugar. Be adventurous," Honey called back as she breezed over to greet someone else. She glanced out in the crowd and saw Flora and Sam with a man in a sheik's outfit wearing a mask. His eyes were burning through her, and her gut told her it was Sam Jr. When had he gotten back from Europe? Why was he back? It had to be for the quarterly meetings. She would get answers. As she was fuming, she saw Philip go up to the bandstand and stop the music.

"Ladies and gentlemen, I'd like to call my wife, Honey, up here," said Philip.

Honey walked to the bandstand to applause. It made her want to sing. Philip put his arm around her and said, "Honey and I have something to share with you tonight. May I have a drumroll please? We are going to have a baby." The orchestra started playing "Rockabye Baby," and there were hugs and cheers all around.

In all the activity Honey's eyes met Robert's, and he tipped his glass to her.

Honey whispered to Philip, "What's Sam doing here? I don't like him around."

"It's only three days. He's just here to give me a report," answered Philip. "He's actually doing a fairly decent job."

"Three minutes is too long," Honey said testily. "Get him out of here, he wasn't invited."

"Could we just focus on this happy occasion and not talk about business for once?" snapped Philip.

Honey smiled at the crowd.

The invitation read:

> *The Angels Give a Shower for Honey King*
> *Place: The E. L. Doheny Estate*
> *Time: 3 P.M. High Tea*

Honey had placed it next to her makeup mirror so she could see it while she dressed. To be invited to the Doheny Estate and be the honoree was more than a dream come true for her. The Dohenys owned most of the land in Beverly Hills and the oil that came out of it. They were so rich that they looked down on movie stars, and only the most prestigious occasion would get them to open their home. Since Mrs. Doheny had her own charitable foundation and saw no need to do anything else, it had taken the Angels eight years to recruit her into the organization. Finally the pressure of Mrs. Doris Stein, wife of Jules Stein, founder of MCA, did the trick. To have Mrs. Doheny on your roster put you over the top.

Honey finished brushing her hair and looked at herself in the mirror, hating the way she looked. She felt like a blimp. She had only eight weeks to go before her due date, and she was exhausted from decorating the nursery. Both she and Philip had decided they would have it done like a train station. It would be all in blue, of course, and the crib was specially built to look like a locomotive. Around the top of the walls they had a shelf built with actual track on it and an HO-gauge-size train ran around it, complete with lights and whistles.

They had a carpet painted to look like railroad tracks, and an engineer's hat awaited the baby's arrival. They wanted him to feel like a leader already, so of course he should be the one to run the train. It was important to Honey that her son learn leadership abilities at an early age. She was going to constantly reinforce that with everything he did.

"Look at that," cried Sheila. "It's a little sailor suit. Isn't that adorable?"

Sheila was seated next to Honey in the solarium of the Doheny Estate, all glass with a white marble floor. The furniture was sea green wicker, and there were colorful flowers and plants everywhere. The house looked like a national monument. Honey was taken aback when she went into the dining room to see more silver than she had ever seen in her life. The tea service looked as if it had been set up for the British royal family, with scones and clotted cream, homemade jams, finger sandwiches of watercress and egg, smoked salmon, and individual pastries flown in from Paris. Standing behind the table were five butlers in white tie. It was an awesome sight. Honey was surrounded by the most powerful women in Hollywood and Beverly Hills, and she loved it. She was in her element. She was learning from them, and in her mind she would soon be the most powerful of all. If she couldn't have her acting career, she would simply take over the town another way.

"Your house is so beautiful, Mrs. Doheny," Honey said appreciatively. "How long have you lived here?"

Mrs. Doheny laughed gently at the "newcomer." "This has been in my husband's family since the twenties, dear," she said. "I'm very glad you like it. Would you like to see the grounds?"

"Yes, thank you," said Honey, realizing she wasn't quite in the big leagues yet.

Six weeks later Philip stood looking through the glass of the nursery of Cedars of Lebanon Hospital at his baby girl, realizing that in his life no moment would be greater than this one. She was the most beautiful creature he had ever seen. Her resemblance to him was unbelievable. She had wavy dark hair and blue eyes. He knew that all babies were born with blue eyes, but he hoped hers would stay that way. He was so happy with a girl. He would see to it that she had everything she wanted. He would take her to musicals and plays and let her watch movies being made. He had such plans. He wanted her never to have a bad moment. He practically flew back to Honey's hospital room.

"I love her! She's beautiful. Oh, thank you, my darling," he said as he held Honey in a tight hug. "Our little girl is the best."

Honey hugged him back politely. She felt his joy, but she only wished she could share it with him. A girl did not fit into her plans. It scared her. Girls were trouble. You couldn't control them. She was unconsciously going back to her own childhood, and the memories weren't good. She knew she could raise a son. She didn't want the competition of a daughter. The look on Philip's face when he talked about her was a knife through her heart.

"I have the perfect name for her," Honey said quickly.

"What is it?" asked Philip.

"I'd like to call her Powar, spelled with an 'a,' not an 'e.' She's gorgeous just like Tyrone Power."

"Powar . . . I have never thought of the word as a name for a girl or anyone, actually," Philip said slowly.

"Darling, our daughter should have a strong name, one that will motivate her all her life. You'll see. She'll love it later on." Just then the nurse brought in the baby and placed her in Honey's arms. Powar started to cry.

"May I hold her?" asked Philip. When Powar was placed in Philip's arms, her crying stopped and she looked up at him. "Look! She's smiling. That's my little girl," Philip cooed.

"She's just hungry. I should feed her now," said Honey, almost feeling jealous. Philip handed Powar back to her, and

Honey offered her breast to the baby. Powar rejected it. Honey tried again and was rejected. The nurse could sense Honey's frustration and hurt.

"Don't worry, Mrs. King. This happens in many cases. She's just going to be a bottle baby, that's all. I'll bring you a bottle for her."

Honey looked at her husband and her child, who bore no resemblance to her, and she felt like a total outsider.

Powar's room was redecorated with pink accents, but the basic color was still blue. They changed the carpet and painted out the bed, although the shape was still a train. They also kept the real train. Every evening as soon as he got home, Philip would come and play with her. He had Honey bring her to the studio at least once a month, and he would go from set to set, showing her off. Powar made her movie debut at the age of one in the arms of Lana Turner, who was on loan from MGM. Philip built a special playroom for Powar by combining three offices on a lower floor of his building. He only took Powar when Honey needed to go out, but he loved it so much he began to look for excuses to take her. "I want to start a nursery school on the lot. That way Powar can be there every day, and the stars and directors and producers can bring their kids and we'll be one happy family."

"Philip, for God's sake, don't you think you're carrying this to extremes? There are perfectly lovely nursery schools right near our house."

"Of course there are, darling, but who could beat growing up on a movie lot? Wouldn't you have loved growing up on a movie lot? It's a beautiful fantasy for a child. And for our child it can come true."

"Yes, but I don't think it's necessarily a healthy place for a child to be every day. She needs a regular school environment. I realize that Beverly Hills is hardly normal, but it does put her into the real world a little bit more." Honey realized that she wasn't going to win this one, but she did get Philip to promise that it would only be for nursery school and that

Powar would go to El Rodeo, the private school in Beverly Hills, for grades one through eight.

From the very beginning, the child preferred her father. Babies don't hide their emotions. It was as simple as that. Honey and Powar tolerated each other, but Honey was determined that her values be instilled in Powar, too. She encouraged her to be the best at whatever she tried and told her repeatedly she could get whatever she wanted if she was "good" and "worked hard."

"Powar, show your father the picture you painted in nursery school," said Honey when Philip came home from the office, and the four-year-old ran to get the picture.

"Honey, can't you just let her be free to express herself without always having to show something for it?"

"Here it is, Daddy," said Powar, showing him a red blob on a piece of paper.

"That's really beautiful, dear. I think red is a wonderful color," said Philip. "Did you have fun painting it?"

"Oh, yes," said Powar, jumping up and down.

"What is it, Powar?" asked Honey.

"It can be whatever she wants it to be, isn't that right, my baby?" said Philip.

It annoyed Honey when Philip did this. Whatever the child wanted was okay with him. He had no sense of training and planning. Powar's response to him also made her crazy. They were just devoted to one another. It was as if they were the same person. They could talk for hours and go places without Honey and be as happy as could be. Honey thought that Philip was constantly making her out to be the bad guy. Well, somebody has to assume responsibility here, thought Honey, and I'll do it.

"Isn't that a fire engine?" Honey asked. "That's what your assignment was. You were told to paint something red. What else is red that you could have painted?"

Philip looked at Honey to say, "Give the kid a break," but before he did Powar answered, "Santa!"

"Good girl," said Honey. "Now you can go to bed and look at the pictures in the Santa book. I'll get it for you." With that she picked Powar up and whisked her away.

Philip saw the longing in Powar's eyes when she looked at him, and he wanted to rescue her and take her away.

Philip's tenure as production chief had been highly successful right from the beginning. Sam Sr. was pulling back a bit with age and letting Philip run things. What he didn't know was that frequently Honey would read the script and suggest actors to cast or rewrites with ideas to make them better. She was invaluable to Philip and one of the main reasons that Metropolitan was such a giant. Honey was doing this for her family, she told herself. Now that Powar was in El Rodeo, it was time to start thinking of the Kings owning the whole studio. This would have to be orchestrated carefully, and she didn't know how Philip would feel about it. But one thing she did know, he wanted to build that studio for Powar. He never once mentioned doing it for his wife. When it came to Powar, no one else entered his thoughts. Most of the time this hurt Honey deeply, but just this once she might use that tunnel vision to help her win the studio.

It had been over six years since Sam Jr. had left for Europe. He had only been back to Hollywood once, and Philip thought it was time to go see for himself how the European operations were going. He hated being separated from Powar for two weeks, but he was looking forward to a break. He was on a nonstop merry-go-round of meetings and parties. He and Honey had no time to relate to just each other. It was true that she was responsible for getting him his new deal with John Wayne's company. He was grateful for that. But their time at home was spent talking about caterers and seating charts.

"I told you," said Philip, dressing in his customary navy blue suit, "that I had to be at the office early today. *Desert*

Sands is in trouble, and Sam and I have called a meeting with Fitzgerald. He's usually a fast director, but this time something has gone wrong. Paulette Wilde is screaming her head off and wants him replaced. I don't want her unhappy, but it will cost too much money to replace him and reshoot. We'll go so far overbudget that we'll never recover.''

"I know," said Honey, giving him a playful slap as he tried to tie his tie, "but I need you to check out the table for Saturday night. It will only take you five minutes. I don't know whether or not Humphrey Bogart and Eric James get along, and if you're trying to get Bogart for a picture, is it better to sit him near you, or flatter him and put him in between Paulette Wilde and Ann Sheridan?''

"Honey, I told you that I don't have time to get involved in your little parties. I have to pay attention to business,'' said Philip.

"Oh, really?" said Honey, eyes flashing. "When will you realize it's my little parties that bring you most of your business? If I were you, I wouldn't alienate me. This is a tough town, and you need help to stay alive.''

Philip walked briskly to the door. "I can't believe you'd say that. Right now I'm going to keep a picture alive. You worry about the vichyssoise!''

He hoped that Honey would want to go to Europe with him, and he asked her the next evening.

"Are you going to work or will we have time to ourselves?" Honey asked.

"I have to spend a lot of time with Sam. I've never seen our company over there, and it's important that I know firsthand what's going on,'' Philip explained. "We might have to have dinners with our business contacts over there as well. I wish it were different, but hopefully we can sneak away for a day or so.''

"Let me get this straight," said Honey. "You want to go to Europe to do business for the company that I helped you build, and you want me to just figure out a way to amuse myself while you work. Then at dinner you'll trot me out to enchant someone for business and then maybe we can go sneak away somewhere for a few days or maybe not?'' Honey was screaming by the time she got to the end of the sentence.

Philip was stunned. "I am getting sick and tired of you making me feel inadequate, as though I can't handle anything at the studio by myself. I was doing very well before I ever knew you."

"Right, Mr. Big Boy. Mr. Strong." Honey was pushing him in the chest now as she talked. "Wanna see how strong you are? I'll show you." She reached in the bathroom drawer for her hairbrush, the one with the wire bristles, and smacked him as hard as she could on the seat of his pants.

Philip whirled around in the heat of anger, barely controlling his urge to hit her. She was humiliating him, and he was furious. Then she shocked him by hurling herself into him and kissing him hard, biting his tongue. She felt him change his body posture. He was getting turned on, and they both knew it. They fell to the floor, and she ripped off his pants and grabbed the hairbrush again. She was striking him unmercifully, breaking the skin, and he loved it. She could feel him go over the edge. She knew she had him. It didn't matter how much power he thought he had anywhere. She knew where the real power was now, and so did he. When he managed to get her on top of him, he could feel the rug burning into his buttocks. He was genuinely hurt this time, but he wanted her as he never had before. Why did his desire for her supersede common sense? As they both rode each other into oblivion, part of him was sickened, but not enough to ever want to stop.

Philip was meeting Sam in Paris because they wanted to expand their operations to France. They had done very well in London originally, and then they'd added Rome. He flew first class on TWA, and when he stepped off the plane in Paris as production head for a major studio, he started to laugh. Not bad for a gimpy Jewish kid, he thought.

He was met by a limo driver and taken to the Ritz, the most glamorous hotel in all of Paris. When he walked through the lobby he couldn't keep his eyes off the crystal chandeliers. There was a message from Sam at the front desk to meet him in the Solarium for tea, so Philip checked in and had his bags sent up to his room. He spotted Sam in a corner of the Solarium. The table was covered with the finest linens. Limoges china and the silver place settings looked as if they were about to be shot for a magazine. A harpist was playing when Philip sat down.

"No wonder you don't want to go home," said Philip.

"This is the best thing that could have happened to me," said Sam. "I love it here. We have reservations tonight at Tour D'Argent. Not only will you see the most beautiful restaurant in Paris, but we will be dining with Laurent LeJeune."

LeJeune! "Good work, Sam. I'm impressed. That would really set us up here if he joined Metropolitan." They were served finger sandwiches and tea, and Philip devoured them. "The food on the plane was awful," he explained. Sam politely asked after Honey and Powar, and Philip showed him pictures. "Isn't my daughter incredible, Sam? Can you believe it? Look what has happened to us."

The view from Tour D'Argent was spectacular that evening. The bridge from Île de la Cité to Île St.-Louis was lit up like a diamond necklace. Philip and Sam, in black tie, were led to a rear table by a window. LeJeune was already there and rose to greet them. He was a big bear of a man in his early fifties, with a slightly grumpy disposition. Sam greeted him and the young woman with him.

He turned to Philip and said, "I'd like you to meet Laurent LeJeune and his daughter, Genevieve." There sat an innocent-looking woman with light auburn hair and green eyes. Her skin had a slightly pink color and looked like porcelain. She couldn't have been more than twenty-two years of age.

Philip shook LeJeune's hand and then focused on Genevieve. How could Sam have failed to warn me? he thought.

"*Bon soir, monsieur,*" said she.

"*Enchanté de faire votre connaissance,*" replied Philip.

She laughed at his accent. "I am sorry. I don't mean to be rude. I am flattered that you tried to learn our language."

"I'm just glad I remembered something right from the phrase book. I could have asked you where to find the men's room instead," said Philip with a smile.

Philip and Sam sat down, and Philip let Sam do the talking for a while, which gave Philip time to think. Was Genevieve Sam's girl? Was she really LeJeune's daughter and not a mistress? He was dying to know. It took all his concentration to keep his mind on business, and he felt conflicted about it. He was so busy concentrating that he barely noticed the foie gras with Calvados followed by *saumon en papillote.* Too bad. The food tasted as good as Genevieve looked.

They all made arrangements to meet the next afternoon for a tour of a French studio. Philip hoped Genevieve would join them, but he didn't say anything. He was trying to keep his emotions in check, and above all he didn't want Sam to know how he was feeling.

In the car on the way back to the hotel Sam said, "Okay, her mother died five years ago. From that point on she has been at her father's side. He raised her to be his director of photography, and she has done his last two pictures. She's very good, and no, I'm not seeing her. No one knows anything about her except that she works all the time."

Philip was uncomfortable that he was so transparent. "Really, Sam. I'm a married man." Those were the only words he could get out without sounding unconvincing . . . or unconvinced.

Genevieve was indeed there the next day, the day after, and the day after that. It was becoming obvious to all of them what was going on. Sam just looked the other way for a while, but then he set up a breakfast with Philip at the hotel.

"Philip, I know your personal life is none of my business, but we need to talk. LeJeune is stalling. He thinks you're using Genevieve to get him to sign."

"That's ridiculous," said Philip.

"I know it is, but you have to convince him of that," continued Sam. "He knows you're married, and he doesn't like it. We need him on our side."

"Don't worry, I'll take care of it," said Philip. He met Genevieve at Café Flore on the Left Bank. It was becoming their favorite place in all of Paris.

"What is the matter, Philip?" asked Genevieve. "You look upset." He told her of his conversation with Sam, and she said, "Oh, don't worry. I'll take care of my father. Everything will be all right."

"I appreciate your wanting to help," said Philip, "but I don't need a woman to do my business for me." He could see right away that he had hurt Genevieve, realizing she had no idea about his situation at home and couldn't possibly know how sensitive he was. "I'm sorry," he said. "I didn't mean to insult you, nor do I mean to be ungrateful or disrespectful. I believe I can pull this off myself, but I certainly would appreciate a good word," he said as he took her hand.

By the next morning LeJeune's signature was on the contract and delivered to Philip's room.

Philip was tortured. It didn't matter that things weren't perfect at home, he did not want to be thought of as a liar. On Friday morning he cabled Honey that he would have to stay a few more days. He told Sam that he was going back to Los Angeles. And he and Genevieve disappeared. They checked out of the Ritz very early in the morning and took the train to Nice. From there they rented a car and drove to Cap d'Antibes on the French Riviera. Sitting on a cliff overlooking the Mediterranean was one of the most romantic places in the world, a castle called Hôtel du Cap that had been turned into a hotel. They checked into chambre douze, a room that overlooked the water and had a private pathway to the Mediterranean.

The sun was barely coming through the curtain when Philip awoke and looked over at Genevieve, who was still sleeping. The sunlight gently covered her skin. He had never seen or felt anything that luminescent. It was like a baby's. Her eyelids started to flutter, and she slowly opened them and smiled up at him.

"*Bonjour, gentilhomme.*" She kissed him and then said, "Today I will show you a very special spot. My father took me there during the festival as a little girl."

After a breakfast of tea and croissants, they ordered a picnic lunch made up by the hotel and took off in their rented Citroën, driving to Cap Ferrat, a little town about thirty minutes away. The corniche roads on the French Riviera were beautiful, and the drive sent them into ecstasy. Genevieve stopped at a remote point on a cliff and motioned for Philip to get out. After they walked through the trees for about five minutes, there was a little path that led all the way down to the beach. "This is China Cove," she explained. "I don't know why it is named that, but I think it is magical."

Philip looked around and saw that they were standing in a cove that was big enough for one small boat. The ocean was deep blue and flowed onto a little beach that led to a cave.

"Come in and listen," said Genevieve as she raced inside. Philip followed her in and heard the ocean sounds magnified by the shape of the cave. He was surrounded by the rush of the water.

Looking at Genevieve, he thought he had never seen anything so beautiful. Underneath a flowing white diaphanous shirt she was wearing a red bikini that looked as if it were made from scarves. And her skin. Next to the shirt it was glowing. She started eating a peach, and a little juice trickled down her chin. Philip leaned over, and with his tongue he smoothed it away. She put the peach in his mouth, and he bit down generously. She placed her mouth on his, and together they shared the fruit. The feel of her skin on his mouth was unbearably exciting. He wanted to swallow her whole face. He covered her face with his mouth, letting the lips relax and feel every pore. She pushed off his shirt and started kissing his nipples. That had never been done to him before. The flick of her tongue became more urgent as it slid down toward his pants. She freed him from his zipper and engulfed him with her mouth. Philip raised his hands behind him, lost in ecstasy as he felt the ocean lapping at his toes. In a flash he turned her over, wanting to be inside her at the height of his pleasure, wanting to leave a part of him with her because he didn't know if he would ever see her again. He had not experienced such gentleness and love for a long time.

After a few days passed, Philip showed up in Sam's office in Paris.

"Well, well," said Sam, "the escapee has returned."

"Why don't we just skip that and go right to the business we have to discuss before we go home," said Philip. "It's great that we have LeJeune, but I'd like an update on your meetings in Italy and England."

"As I told you before, MGM has a stranglehold on England. As for Italy, I have had one meeting with Del Vecchio Films where they seemed to be interested, but I haven't been able to get them back to the table."

Philip sighed just a little bit before he spoke. "Sam, you're not giving it your all. I thought things would be better than this. I want you to go back to England and find out the top three small independent filmmakers. Get to know them. Make them your friends and talk at least two of them into getting into business with Metropolitan. Let MGM go for the big stuff now. Find the newcomers and make them stars. You should know that's how it's done. Get on a plane. Go to Italy. Don't use the phone. Just sit in his office until Del Vecchio sees you again." Sam was fuming, and Philip could see it. "Turn your anger into ambition for the company. Don't waste your time getting mad at me. Get mad at Louis B."

"Don't worry, Philip. I'll put my anger to good use," said Sam as Philip was getting up to leave.

* * *

When Honey's mail was delivered her heart jumped when she saw the envelope with the French stamp on it. She had heard very little from Philip except for the cable. How sweet it was for him to write to me, she thought, ripping it open. But inside were pictures of Philip and Genevieve. Nauseated, she ran to the bathroom, uttering a cry that came from deep inside her. The betrayal that she felt was one of the most painful things she had ever experienced. She tried to keep quiet because she didn't want anyone to hear her. She could hardly breathe, and she thought if she splashed water on her face, she might calm down. It worked a little bit. She felt faint, but she had the presence of mind to reach under the sink and get a paper bag to breathe into. It calmed her down in about ten seconds. She took deep breaths, then opened the door and walked back into their bedroom. Her emotions kept switching now from devastation to rage. Who would send the pictures? And why? The handwriting on the envelope was American. Sam! she thought. He was just waiting for something like this.

Philip called from Paris the following day and told the housekeeper that he would be home the next night around seven, not knowing that Honey was deliberately not answering the phone. All the way home in the plane he thought about Genevieve. He felt terribly guilty yet exhilarated by her. He loved her sweetness. She was a young lady of simple tastes who would be happy running in a field or picking berries somewhere. She loved the art of cinematography, and as her eyes gazed at the pictures of life around her, her mind was like a camera. She was so different from the women he knew in Hollywood who worried about their nails. She could care less about Hollywood. He wanted Powar to see more of life than the back seat of limousines and wished he could take her and spend time in the French countryside with Genevieve. But that was fantasy. Reality was awaiting him at Bedford Drive. Maybe he hadn't been as attentive as a husband should be, he thought. Maybe everything was his fault. And maybe

Honey was just being a good wife. By the time he pulled up to the house he'd convinced himself this was the beginning of a new start on his marriage. He wasn't going to think of Genevieve. He was just going to be as good a husband as he could be.

Honey heard his key in the lock. She was seated in the living room wearing peach wool slacks and a matching sweater, her blonde hair brushed and glowing. She was calm. She was concentrating. She was ready.

Philip walked in carrying his bags and put them down immediately when he saw her. "Honey," he said delightedly, and went to kiss her.

She offered her cheek quickly, which took Philip aback slightly. "Sit down, Philip. We have something to discuss." She motioned toward the couch. Her tone was determined. There was no anger in it, but it was very powerful. Philip couldn't imagine what was going on. She placed the pictures in his hands and watched him turn white. He opened his mouth to speak, but nothing came out.

"Now listen to me very carefully," said Honey. "By noon tomorrow you are going to sign over five thousand of your shares in Metropolitan to me. That will give me exactly fifty more shares than you. Your remaining stock, plus what I have obtained through various means through the years, will give us enough shares to remove the Lewises. I will allow you to be president and CEO to save your reputation, and only the two of us will know that you have to answer to me. I want you to call an emergency board meeting for three P.M. tomorrow. As soon as the meeting is over you will fire Sam Jr."

Philip was dazed. He started to speak, but Honey interrupted him.

"Don't bother. Either you do this, or I show the pictures to Powar. She certainly is old enough at twelve to understand about her precious daddy."

Philip found his voice. "I can certainly understand how

you feel about me. What I did was terrible. But don't you ever threaten to upset my daughter or use her as a tool for something.''

"Just follow my instructions and everything will be fine. I've moved your things to the room adjoining ours. That way Powar will never know we are not in the same bed. I'll see you at three P.M. sharp.''

Three P.M. came very quickly, and Philip was waiting when Sam and Flora Lewis arrived with the other five board members.

"Philip, I don't understand what this is all about," Sam bellowed. "What do you mean calling for a board meeting without my knowing about it?''

Philip asked ~veryone to sit down. He wanted to control all of Metropolitan, but this was not the way he wanted to get it. This was not the way he did business, but he knew now this was the way Honey operated. It disgusted him, but he wasn't going to say no to her. He was in no position to do so. He noticed that nowhere in her speech did she ever mention Genevieve or his giving her up. There must have been a reason for that. Honey had a reason for everything.

"Sam, I am nominating myself for president and CEO of Metropolitan, and I'm buying you out.''

"My dear boy—" Sam laughed. "Do you really think I would ever give you enough stock, even though your contract is generous and up till now well deserved, to put you in that kind of position? This meeting is adjourned." He started to push back his chair when he `.eard a side door open behind him.

"Oh, no, it's not," said the woman's voice. He turned and saw Honey, dressed magnificently in a hunter green suit. She strode to the table and opened up a briefcase full of stock and documentation of value with proof from a bank that she and Philip were the majority shareholders. Sam stopped cold.

"It's nothing personal," said Honey. "It's just good business. With Philip owning the studio it will be much more profitable than with Sam Jr. running it. Your remaining stock will be worth even more money in the future, Sam. If you want, we can buy you out right now, or you can keep the stock, announce your semiretirement, and we'll put you in charge of the film library. You have lots of choices.''

The headline in *Variety* read KING PICTURES FORMED, LEWIS RETIRES. Honey wanted to have it framed. But she knew it was time for a change. Television was becoming more and more popular and needed to be dealt with, even though she felt that it was beneath Metropolitan. Honey was very happy. She and Philip were at the top of the mountain. She looked around her British den as she was reading *Variety* and thought, Hmm. I think this summer's ball will be ''Ride to the Hounds.''

''Thank you all for coming so early this morning,'' said Philip, greeting his department heads for the first time as owner of the studio. He studied the ten men looking at him from around the table in the boardroom. He liked what he saw. They were awaiting his every word. ''We all want the same thing in our work . . . quality that is profitable. We work in one of the few industries that is a fishbowl. Our product is judged every day by how many people buy tickets to see it. Do you ever wonder why it is called 'show business'? I think about that sometimes. I love the 'show' part because I love entertainment and people. Now that I own this studio I have a duty to be concerned about the profit margin as well. For the next six months I would like a weekly detailed report from each of you on your projects. For the two people in charge of developing scripts and working with writers, I would like you to meet with me every Monday morning. No idea should be passed on or put into development without my approval.''

Philip looked around at some of them shifting on their seats.

''This is called King Pictures now. If something goes

wrong, it's my problem. Your problem will be if that happens. I really believe that we have a special opportunity here. I will see you all here every Friday at this time."

Powar awoke to the sound of her mother screaming, "Listen, Father. My little girl wants to go to your school. I already gave you twenty thousand dollars. How many pews does it take to get into the ninth grade?" Powar pulled the covers over her head. Her mother's behavior constantly embarrassed her. There had to be another way to get through life. She was sorry now that she'd mentioned to her mother that some of her friends were going to Catholic school once they left El Rodeo. She did want to join them, but not at the expense of massacring a priest, which was obviously what was happening in the next room. If your father is Jewish, you don't get in. It's that simple. It doesn't matter if he owns one of the most successful movie studios in the world. Powar thought it was disgusting that some people in the world thought her blood was "tainted." It was very confusing for her. She could tell that everybody liked her, but each time she wanted to join something with her friends there was a "problem," whether it was that so-called pious organization Job's Daughters, which segregated all Jewish girls into one group and didn't even let in Catholics, or the Coronet Debutantes, the group for only the Christian daughters in Beverly Hills and the west side of Los Angeles. None of this made any sense to her when Clark Gable would greet her by name and kiss her on the cheek. If she was that special, why was she constantly made to feel inferior? It was difficult for her because she received such mixed messages. Powar believed her mother when she said that she was the smartest and the prettiest, but she kept being rejected by things that her mother thought were important. It was very confusing. Why would her mother want her to go for certain things if she knew up front it might be a problem? But Powar did feel loved by both parents. She admired her mother's tenaciousness and organization. And her father was the most wonderful person in the world. Most of the time the love and attention lavished on her by her father made up for any problems. She wanted to be a leader in life to please him. He was the most important person to her. If he said she was the best, then she was. Powar tried to love her mother, but it was difficult. Her mother seemed to always be doing things "for" her, but they were things that Honey thought Powar should do. She rarely asked Powar what *she* wanted to do. Whenever her parents fought it seemed to be about her. She knew her mother hated it when she went to the studio, but that was the place Powar loved more than anything in the world. She loved watching any kind of entertainment, and from the youngest age she had the gift of analyzing what was good and bad about it. Her advice to her father about films for the teenagers was unerring, and he had come to rely on her a lot. Powar could feel her mother's resentment over this.

"Powar, would you open the door, please?" said Honey.

Honey hated it that Powar always had the door to her room shut. She was always threatening to have it taken off by the hinges. Powar opened it. "I just had a wonderful idea," Honey continued. "You didn't want to go to Our Lady of Faith that much, did you?" She kept on talking without giving Powar a chance to answer. "I've arranged for you to go to Westborough. You'll be much happier there."

"I guess twenty thousand dollars wasn't enough to impress God, Mother," said Powar.

"One day, young lady, that mouth is going to get you in trouble," Honey said.

"Gee, I wonder where I got it from?" said Powar. She thought her mother was clever but about as subtle as a truck. She preferred her father's good manners, a much better way to get things done.

Westborough School was actually fine with Powar. She already knew some kids who were going there. Being the "daughter of" was the norm for that school. Learning arithmetic with her friend Liza Minnelli was no big deal. Liza was just a kid like everybody else, only she had more obvious home problems. Liza and Powar got to know one another when her mother, Judy Garland, did a turkey of a movie for King Pictures a few years back. Garland needed the money, and Philip was talked into making a picture he knew was bad because Honey wanted Garland to have a job. Liza and Powar met in the studio "playroom," which by now was decorated for the teenagers they'd become, with a jukebox and a bowling alley. By the time they both went to Westborough, they had become friends. They also traveled the celebrity child birthday circuit together.

The first year that Powar was at Westborough Judy Garland gave a birthday party for Liza. When the invitation read "party dress," everyone thought that it was the signal for their first "adult" party. No longer would clothes from Pixie Town do. No longer would the presents come from Uncle Bernie's Toy Menagerie, although one was never too old to stop in there for a drink from the lemonade tree. Powar was taken to Saks by Honey, their first "adult" outing together. She was excited as they entered the store. They didn't quite know what floor to go to. On the fourth floor was the children's department and the teenage area. The third floor had clothes for all ages. There was no need yet to go to the designer floor on two, so they decided to go to the fourth floor and look in the teenage department.

"Go and pick out anything you like, Powar," said Honey. "I'll meet you in the dressing room."

Powar was thrilled. She spent a great deal of time going through the party clothes, trying to find something that didn't look childish. She wanted to look like a lady, not a little girl. She picked a number of dresses, trying to stay with white, beige, or gray. She would rather be on the third floor finding something in black, but she knew her mother would never go for it. She gathered her dresses and took them to the room. She saw her mother sitting there with a saleslady pointing out different dresses to show Powar.

Powar sensed trouble. "I'm just going to try on this beige one, Mother." She held it up.

"You really don't want to try that one, do you?" said Honey. "The color is so boring. Here, try on this pink one. You'll love it. See how the organza goes over the taffeta. It's really pretty."

"I'd rather try on the beige one," said Powar.

"Oh, just do this for me, Powar. It's not that difficult."

"I don't like the pink dress, and I don't want to wear it," said Powar. "I'm going to try on the white one." She just wanted to get it over with, to get home and go to her room, where she felt at peace. White it was.

The day of the party Powar wore a cream-colored silk sheath, pearls, and little dyed-to-match silk pumps. The heels were one and a half inches high, and the look was perfect. Liza's house was within walking distance, and she didn't want her mother to drive her. She wanted to set out on her own, which is exactly what she did. Her dark hair was long, and there was a gentle breeze that made it sway as she walked. Powar was a beauty and seemed to be escaping that "awkward" stage. She had her father's full mouth and her mother's good bones. As Powar walked up Bedford Drive and turned right on Elevado, she felt really cool, just like Annette Funicello or Sandra Dee. When she started walking down Rodeo toward Liza's house, she was shocked to see a live elephant on the front lawn. Why am I wearing a dress to a circus party? she asked herself. And why weren't we told about this? She had a funny feeling that something was about to go terribly wrong.

In the backyard Powar saw little tables and chairs and clowns and small rides for young children. Judy Garland hadn't noticed that Liza had grown up into a young woman! It was a mortifying situation for Liza. Her friends were ignoring the clowns and the rides and were just sitting around talking. Liza had been forced to dress in one of those organdy pinafore dresses with Mary Jane shoes and silk socks that turned down to make the perfect cuff. Just at the moment when the strain was so thick you wanted to die, a creature in blue jeans, penny loafers, and a flannel shirt appeared on the top of the wall that separated Liza's house from her neighbor's.

"Hey, Liza, I escaped. Turn on some music and let's get on with this!" She then jumped and made a perfect landing. Powar could see Liza's whole mood change.

"Everybody," Liza yelled. "I want you to meet Cheryl Crane." Powar had met Lana Turner's daughter when they were much younger. She had some vague recollection that they used to ride the horses together at Beverly Park on Saturdays when their fathers would take them there. Cheryl confirmed it and was happy to see Powar.

"Cheryl, you know Candy Bergen, don't you?" said Powar. The girls said hello to each other, and then everybody started dancing and it really turned into a party. All that was missing were the boys, thought Powar.

Philip was now on a schedule where he would go to Europe four times a year to oversee "production." Honey didn't care. As long as he showed up for important events it was fine with her. She could find ways to amuse herself, and besides, nothing was more important than remaining "Mrs. Philip King." As far as she was concerned King Pictures was her creation. She attended every board meeting, read every script, and went in the office every week to read the interoffice memos. Philip did nothing to stop her.

"I just read *Golden Gate,*" said Honey as Philip was getting ready for bed. "I don't think it will make any money, and you really shouldn't go ahead with it."

Philip did not hide his annoyance. "We already have Gary Cooper for the lead, and there's no way it will miss with him."

"Yes, it will. He's great, but not if there isn't a story that people care about. This script is slow, and you don't care about the people. And if you don't care about the people, the movie won't work. I want it canceled."

"Are you going to pay off Cooper his two hundred and fifty thousand dollars?" Philip yelled.

"No, I'm going to find a script that's better and talk him into that one. I'm having lunch with Rocky tomorrow, and all will be fine. Nobody wants her husband in a bomb."

Philip sighed and walked into his room. "Good night, Honey."

Honey smiled. "Good night."

Philip never strayed too far anyway because he wanted to be near Powar. That was a string that was comforting as well as disconcerting to Honey. Well, soon it would be time to discuss where Powar was going to college. She felt it was important for her to be on her own and not hanging around "Daddy" all the time. At least that was what she told herself. The truth was she was jealous that Powar took whatever was left of Philip's attention and Powar clearly preferred him. She thought a wonderful school like Vassar or Sarah Lawrence would be good.

"What!" Philip exclaimed when she brought the subject to his attention. "Powar is going to USC. Aside from the fact that it's my school, it's the very best school for Powar. They have the best cinema school. It would be ridiculous to send her away from everything she wants. She was born to be in this business. The studio is her home."

"Is there anything wrong with her having a well-rounded education?" asked Honey. "Shouldn't she be given a chance to explore other things as an independent person?"

"Don't be ridiculous! She can do all of that at USC. I paved the way for her there just as she will pave the way for her children," said Philip.

Just then Powar walked briskly into the room. "I could hardly help overhearing the two of you argue about my future. How about asking me what I think? I'm the one who has to go to the school."

Honey then broke the silence. "All right, Powar, what do you want?"

"Of course I want to go to USC. It's our family's school. I've been going to their football games for years with Daddy. I love it there. Does that really surprise you, Mother?" Powar turned and walked out of the room triumphant.

"Fine," said Honey. "Powar can go to USC, but I want to go to work alongside you at Metropolitan. I'm tired of working in the background. I want an office next to yours and an announcement in the press."

"You've got to be kidding. I would look like a fool," said Philip. "You're already recognized by everyone as having tremendous influence."

"I want the real thing," Honey shouted, "and I want it now! I'm responsible for getting you King Pictures. I'm responsible for attracting the stars. I'm responsible for giving you the information that puts you one jump ahead of everybody else."

"Over my dead body will you run the studio publicly. Things are staying exactly as they are." Philip walked out of the room, turning his back on Honey.

Powar wouldn't let the animosity between her mother and father ruin her graduation luncheon. Her parents were letting her have a grown-up luncheon in one of the private rooms at the Luau, the chic Beverly Hills restaurant owned by Steve Crane, Cheryl's father. Powar loved to go there with Cheryl and the other kids from Westborough. It looked like a tropical island with bridges and waterfalls and big canoes that hung overhead next to the colored lanterns. During the week there was one long canoe that served as a salad bar. Honey had started taking her there as a child during their shopping expeditions, and then her father carried it on Saturdays when they were at the studio. When she was old enough, the girls would go on Saturday afternoon and order red fruit punch drinks that came in coconut shells. They would pretend that they were young starlets just like the ones they read about in the magazines. Natalie Wood was always going there with Nick Adams. Sometimes Elvis Presley would sneak in with Yvonne Lime. It really was the place to be. Powar couldn't wait until she was old enough to go there on a date. When Steve saw the kids there on Saturday he would send over plates of spare ribs, fried shrimp, rumaki, and egg roll. They would try to stay as late as possible to see who would come by for cocktails. Even though Powar was accustomed to seeing the biggest stars in her own living room, she longed to catch a glimpse of Troy Donahue or Frankie Avalon. She knew that her idol Annette wouldn't be there. Someone's virtue had to remain intact in Powar's eyes.

Powar could barely contain her excitement when the day finally arrived. Liza and Candice were going to be there, along with Barbara Hutton's son Lance Reventlow, Natalie Wood's kid sister, Lana, Jack Wrather, Jr., the son of the man who created the "Lassie" show on TV, and Tim Pantages Considine from the Mickey Mouse Club. He was the son of Rodney Pantages, a friend of her father's, and when Philip found out Powar would have done anything to meet Tim, he invited him as a special guest to the graduation luncheon. Powar had on a mustard-colored spring cotton tweed linen suit with a silk blouse. Her parents gave her pearl-and-diamond earrings to match the pearl necklace she had gotten for her sixteenth birthday, and she wore it that day. There was a graduation cake with a Trojan horse on top, the USC mascot, which Powar had asked for. She had begged her mother not to turn this party into one of her extravaganzas and so far everything was okay. She was a little shocked to see the USC Marching Band in the parking lot playing for everyone's arrival, but she really enjoyed it. At least her mother refrained from having the horse, Traveler, the Trojan mascot, there, too.

Her parents arrived just in time for the cake, as planned. Right after the singing, Honey saw Philip motion to Powar. He then left the room, and in about thirty seconds Powar followed him. A few seconds later Honey went after them to see what was going on. She stopped a few feet behind them. In the Luau there was an alcove on the way to the restrooms. The alcove was above a bridge, and Honey could hear every word by staying underneath. Philip was talking.

"Powar, you have such talent. You have been by my side in the business from the day you were born. Your instincts of story and casting are extraordinary."

Honey was beginning to burn.

"This envelope is for you on this very special graduation. You'll know exactly what to do with it. I'll always trust you. I love you very much."

Honey heard Powar take the envelope and then start to cry.

"Oh, Daddy. I'll never let you down. I don't know how to thank you. This is incredible."

Honey then quickly marched up the bridge to find Powar holding a document that made her sole trustee to $18 million worth of King Pictures stock—one million for every year she had lived.

Powar hugged Honey and thanked her in her excitement. She hadn't had time to compute the fact that Honey had had nothing to do with it. "Can I show this to my friends, Daddy?" Powar asked.

"Of course you can," replied Philip. He kissed her again and said "Happy graduation."

Honey waited three seconds until Powar was out of view, and then she slapped Philip across the mouth as hard as she could. People in the restaurant turned in their direction, and he grabbed Honey and pushed her into the men's room. Fortunately no one else was in there.

"What are you trying to do? Get this in the papers?" said Philip, trying to keep his voice down.

Honey took a swing at him again, only this time he caught her arm. "What's the matter, was I aiming in the wrong place, sweetie?" said Honey.

Philip was mortified that she knew his deepest secrets and desires and would use them against him.

"As long as I live I will never forgive you for giving Powar what I so rightly deserve and have worked for. You and I built that studio, and you and I should have a say in where the stock goes. Your foolish gesture now makes me an untouchable majority stockholder. Every night when you go to sleep and every morning when you wake up, you are going to wonder what I'm about to do. Let's see how you can live under those conditions."

POWAR

* CHAPTER 9 *

When Powar was going through sorority rush at USC, she took one look at the Kappa Alpha Gamma house and knew it was for her. It looked just like her house on Bedford. All the sororities wanted her, and she felt accepted. There was no mention of her ancestry or religion, but she was the exception. The daughter of King Pictures would be welcome anywhere. Very few pledges were allowed to live in the house. Most were forced to live in dormitories. Supposedly Powar was allowed to live there because she was from Los Angeles and it would be "more convenient." Even she didn't buy that one. If they wanted an occasional star at a party, she would provide it. She was having a great time, and it didn't matter to her.

All the upstairs bedrooms were pretty institutional-looking, filled with single beds or bunk beds all covered with brown bedspreads. The furniture was early thrift shop, but Powar didn't mind. She loved the idea of fitting in somewhere. She was assigned "the Annex," an add-on wing of the house over the garage. There were three single beds lined up in a row all right, but this was very different. Each bed had a brand-new flower-printed quilt. There were matching curtains on the windows and Impressionist prints on the walls. A brand-new television, radio, and record player setup was on the large chest of drawers. Powar was confused because she thought pledges were supposed to have the worst rooms in the house, but she didn't say anything. She'd just wait. There was a tiny closet for each person and a shared bathroom that looked like a bus station. There was a giant living room, two dens, and a very large dining room and kitchen. It was the first time Powar had been away from home, and she loved the freedom. She was the first one in the Annex, and she chose the bed on the end nearest the window and farthest away from the door. She was lying on her bed figuring out how many cinema and TV classes she could fit into her schedule when she heard someone enter. She raised her eyes and saw a five-foot-eight Barefoot Contessa type with jet black hair, white skin, and a smile that could melt Cleveland. Her eyes were slightly Oriental-looking. She had to be that incredible blend of Eurasian where the formula of Oriental and Caucasian was mixed just right.

"Hi, I'm Maria Jong."

Powar sat up and smiled. "Hello, Miss Universe. My name is Powar King. Wanna be a star?"

Maria giggled and looked away shyly. She obviously did not get the joke.

"Is this your first time away from home?" asked Powar.

"Oh, no," answered Maria. "I came right here from boarding school. I haven't lived at home since I was twelve." Oddly enough, even with Powar's bravado, it was she who was a little nervous about being away from home. Maria's strength underneath her shyness caught Powar's attention.

"I think we'll be very good for each other," said Powar, extending her hand. "Welcome aboard."

"Have you noticed that this room looks very different from all the others in the house?" asked Maria.

"Yes," Powar said resignedly. "Don't pay any attention. I think my mother has been donating again."

Maria didn't get the joke but didn't pursue it.

* * *

Powar and Maria took USC by storm. It was a miracle any studying got done. Maria ended up as the assistant society editor for the *Daily Trojan,* and her first assignment was to write a weekly column called "Parties and Pinnings." Whenever she went to cover the parties, Powar went along with her, and as a result boys were constantly coming over to the house to see them.

"Put on that new one by the Contours," shouted Maria. The Annex was getting famous for having impromptu dance parties in the afternoon.

Powar tossed her cinema book and began dancing. Soon some of the other girls came in, and then the housemother showed up.

"You know this is study time, young ladies. Music can be from five to seven."

Powar turned off the record player. "I'm sorry, really."

"Phi Sigs on one, Phi Sigs on one," the cry rang out suddenly. That was the phrase that was used in the sorority if men had come in. Their fraternity was announced, and "one" meant the floor they were on.

"Phi Sigs for Annex!" was the next message. They went downstairs and saw Steve Ball, the president of the frat with his buddy Donald Siller.

"See, I told you they'd be here," said Steve to Donald. "We have a great idea for you two."

"I can just imagine," said Powar.

"No, seriously," said Steve. "We are going to start the Phi Sig Little Sisters, and we want you two to be the first ones we name. We're going to have ten of them and invite them to all our events. You will wear a special pin and everything. We're tired of Sigma Chi getting all the Sweethearts. It's time our house did something. What do you think?"

Powar and Maria looked at each other. "That's really cool," said Maria. "Let's do it!"

"Absolutely," said Powar.

"Great!" said Donald. "Can you come over after dinner and we'll serenade you on our porch?"

"We wouldn't miss it, would we, Maria?" said Powar.

The day after being serenaded, Powar was having lunch with her father at the studio. Ever since she was a child she'd been having "business" lunches with him and always preferred to eat in the executive dining room rather than his private dining room. She liked to be near the action. Sometimes she even asked him if they could eat in the main dining room with everybody and anybody who worked at Metropolitan. Today was one of those days.

"Okay," said Powar, "You give me the title, and I'll tell you what they do."

"Fine," said Philip. "There's a first AD."

"That's an assistant director whose job it is to run the set and make sure the actors are on time," answered Powar.

"Good," said Philip. "Now you see the woman over there? She's an executive story consultant."

"This is too easy," said Powar. "She supervises and makes suggestions on a script and works with the writer and the producer, or in some cases she's the writer of the script. You know, I think I'm ready to do all these jobs, not just know what they are."

"Spoken like a true King," said Philip. "Maybe you did get some good things from your mother after all."

"God, she's tough to live with," said Powar, "but she's an amazing woman."

"Yes, she is," Philip said without wanting to go into more.

"I can't wait until I graduate," continued Powar. "I learned so much just by growing up here, and now I'm learning the technical things in school. I have to tell you now, though, that my favorite part of the business is television. I think you're making a big mistake by not going into it, Dad. Most of the other studios are doing it, and you're missing a lot of money that can be made. The business is changing under your feet."

"I know it, honey, but I'm not the only one who owns part of this studio. I'm doing it as fast as I can," explained Philip.

"I understand the problem, Dad, but I'd get a move on if I were you."

Philip laughed. "You really are some kid. I love you."

Powar immediately started writing movies for the cinema class to shoot. Her father would occasionally loan them equipment or sets, and the second film she produced and wrote won first place in the student film awards for freshmen.

The girls from the Annex really did try to "belong" and be accepted by their sisters. They rode their bikes back to the house every day to have lunch, volunteered for committees, and tried to get in the spirit. As with all groups, there inevitably was a split. KAG was run by seniors, who were its officers. They were very conservative, plastic-looking girls who wore little skirts and sweaters and heels. They were properly dressed at all times and had no sense of humor or style. There were really two heads of the house, both from the conservative suburb of Pasadena. One was the moon-faced June Roberts, who dressed and walked as though she had a broom up one of her orifices, and the other was the slightly overweight Maureen Worthington, who acted like Scarlett O'Hara most of the time. It became apparent that they were very jealous of the girls in the Annex, whom they dubbed "the Rebels." They pretended to be virginal angels and tried to paint the Rebels as trash. Powar couldn't understand this kind of treatment since she and her friends made the house more popular than it had been before they arrived, and it was her impression that June and Maureen were spending an awful lot of nights out of the house. Powar was curious about sex, considering it was something one did not do casually. She still believed you should be married first.

Things really came to a head when Powar suggested that she write and direct a short musical play for the sorority to enter in the annual Trolios Talent Show, a competition between the sororities and the fraternities, with each participating house doing a skit. KAG had never won before, and it was something Powar really wanted to do. She wrote *A Day in the Life of KAG*, taking current rock hits and changing the lyrics. June and Maureen were furious that the other members of the house voted it in.

The rehearsals took three weeks, and Powar had never worked so hard. Not only did she write the lyrics and the book, but she had to mimeograph the scripts, direct and costume the girls, and produce all of it. It was the fall of 1963, and USC was a little Eisenhower world encased in a glass bubble. The rumblings of racism and unrest in the country were not heard at all. Nothing interfered with their luncheons, dances, or football games. Going to USC was a time away from reality, and the tension-free environment was glorious. Honey and Philip were coming to the talent show. It was going to be held in Bovard Auditorium in front of the whole student body. Powar was nervous, but it was from excitement rather than apprehension. She thought her miniature musical was terrific. She knew her parents were in the audience, but she didn't have time to see them before the show. She had to get everyone ready.

When the time came for KAG, Powar's heart was racing. She loved live entertainment. Even though she directed the show, she was going to dance in it to make sure that people remembered their moves. It made them feel more comfortable to have the director on stage with them.

"Okay, everybody," said Powar. "Take your places, please. Dancers, in the front. Good. Everybody looks great. June, make sure your sleeves are rolled down." And she continued, enraptured with leading a group of people in a show. "Remember your spacing and don't forget your split on the second chorus to make way for Treesh."

Maria had been too shy to participate, but a sister named Treesh was singing lead, and she was wonderful. When the entire show was over, KAG won first place and Powar went on stage to accept the trophy.

"I'd like to thank all my sisters for working together with me on this. We've had a great time. Fight on!" she said as she raised her fingers in the V for victory sign that belonged to USC. It would only be a short while before that V sign would stand for peace across the land, but at USC it would never mean anything except "victory." Philip and Honey were waiting backstage to congratulate her.

"Powar, you were wonderful," said Philip, practically picking her up. "You're so talented! This is just the beginning, sweetheart." Powar looked to Honey.

"Congratulations, dear," she said, giving her a kiss on the cheek.

Powar, even in her excitement, noticed that her parents weren't relating to each other at all. It made her sad, but that lasted only a second because her sisters surrounded Philip to thank him for arranging special screenings for them and giving them tours of the studio. This was the first Honey had heard of these activities, of course. When all the girls turned to congratulate Powar, Honey said to Philip, "What tours? What screenings? What more aren't you telling me? Next you're going to put them all in a movie. I can see it now, *Sorority Rock.*"

Philip, instead of playing into it, decided to be smart and said, "Good idea, Honey. Why don't you come up with a treatment?"

The next morning it was school as usual. At around eleven-thirty Powar and Maria were standing outside their history class when a shout rang out. "President Kennedy's been shot!"

It was very hard to hear among the noise of the students. "It sounded like she said something about President Kennedy," shouted Maria. "We'd better find out."

Powar and Maria went with what was now a growing group to find a radio, and within a couple of minutes they found someone standing in shock on the lawn in front of Founders Hall. Within a few seconds the entire campus had fallen silent. Cars stopped, nobody moved. Just then June and Maureen walked by, oblivious of what had just happened. Powar stopped them and told them that Kennedy had been killed.

June said, "Oh, good. Now Goldwater will have a better chance to win," and she and Maureen started walking away.

Powar was stunned. She and Maria just stood there, not knowing what to do. Pretty soon people were wandering back to their dorms or houses. Lunch was being served at the house when they got back, but people were hardly eating. They were in the den downstairs, watching the TV set. Powar was horrified and couldn't watch. It was just too painful. Instead she decided to drive to the studio to be with her father.

As she drove along the streets of Los Angeles she noticed cars pulled over to the side of the road, the drivers sobbing with their heads on the steering wheel. All the cars had their lights on even though it was the middle of the day. All the radio stations switched to very somber classical music or news. On the sidewalks people were walking slowly in a daze. Powar had a terrible headache from crying, and she parked at Fairfax and Wilshire to go into the Rexall Drug Store to buy aspirin. Inside the store it was absolutely silent. No one was talking to anyone. The few people who were in the store were walking up and down the aisles by rote. Tearstained faces nodded to each other. There was a heaviness in the air that you could almost touch. Breathing was difficult. All Powar wanted to do was get to her father. When she got there, a gate guard had tied a black band around the pole of the main gate. As Powar drove onto the lot she could see that production had stopped on all the sets. Actors and crews were just standing around in a state of shock. When she got to her father's office she rushed right in. Philip was sitting turned around in his chair facing away from the desk toward the window. He was just staring. When he saw Powar they embraced wordlessly and cried in each other's arms.

It took several weeks before the campus got back to normal. People went through the motions of their lives, but it was meaningless. John Kennedy had been the bright light for this generation that believed in government and supporting your country. It didn't matter that most of the USC students were Republicans, as were their parents. This was an issue of pride. When Lyndon Johnson became president, it all died. Powar and Maria were studying in their room when the phone in the hall rang. Powar went to answer it.

"Maria, your mother is on the phone," she called. The voice on the other end of the line had a soft Asian accent. Maria had always been very private about her background, and Powar had been unable to get her to reveal anything. Maria never went home for the weekend. Powar rarely did, but she did frequently spend Saturdays with her father at the studio. It was interesting to Powar that Maria's mother was calling.

Maria did not make eye contact with her as she want to the phone. After about fifteen minutes she came back to the Annex. She was a little shaky. "Powar, I need you to go somewhere with me tomorrow. I know I haven't been very cooperative when you tried to talk about my childhood. I'd feel better if you would just come with me tomorrow, and you'll be able to understand everything. I couldn't ask anyone to do this but you." Maria was near tears.

Powar hugged her. "Of course I'll go with you. Where are we going?"

Maria explained that she hadn't been home since she was about twelve years old and that her mother wanted to see her. "I have seen my mother," she said. "I wasn't abandoned or anything like that. I just never liked going home. You'll see."

Tomorrow couldn't come too soon for Powar. She'd wondered for so long where this beautiful creature had come from, and today she might get an answer. They both awoke bright and early. It was early in June, just before the end of the semester, and it was warm. They dressed in cotton skirts and tank tops. Maria had a blouse on over hers. Maria asked Powar to drive, and they got into Powar's 1957 powder blue

Thunderbird. Maria told her to drive to Sunset past the Beverly Hills Hotel. It was an area that Powar knew very well, and they continued past the huge estates of Holmby Hills. Maria was not speaking, so Powar kept driving and waiting for instructions.

"Just past the east gate of Bel Air you're going to turn into a driveway," Maria finally said.

"Okay," said Powar. Bel Air? This was not the kind of neighborhood she had expected, yet the tuition for boarding school and USC was very high, and Maria was not on a scholarship.

"Turn right here," said Maria. Powar couldn't believe where she was going. She'd been at the house many times as a little girl. It was a mansion easily as big as her parents', if not bigger, with a front lawn the size of a football field and a tennis court complex so big that it took up a second lot west of the house. There was the Tara-like veranda across the front of the house that overlooked the lawn and a circular driveway in back of the house that was actually the front entrance. The whole thing looked like Jefferson's Monticello.

It was the home of Nathan Blumenthal, owner and publisher of *Hollywood Newsday*, the entertainment industry trade paper. Philip and Honey King had carefully cultivated his friendship through the years for obvious reasons. Honey loved the coverage, and Philip made sure that a large portion of King Pictures' advertising budget went to the paper each year. Blumenthal was a real character. He was a very large man with few manners. It didn't matter how much money he had, he still dressed and acted like a bum. He had come to Hollywood because he was thrown out of Belmont Park racetrack for trying to fix horses. Hollywood Park was in its infancy and fresh territory for him. He hung around the stables and made friends with the trainers and exercise boys. He knew that the big shots hung out at the Turf Club, and he'd butt into their conversations, giving them "tips" and classified knowledge he had about upcoming races. A lot of the studio boys listened, and as he proved himself more and more picking winners, they began to tip him heavily for his advice. One day after the third race, Nathan was out at the stables, and a young guy he recognized as a "gofer" for Irving Mendelbaum told him the boys wanted to see him in the private room of the Turf Club. This is very unusual, thought Nathan as he went upstairs. He walked into the room to see seven of the most powerful men in Hollywood seated at a table. There was one empty chair, and Mendelbaum motioned for him to sit.

"Nathan, we have an idea that we've been discussing for some time," said Mendelbaum. "There is a venture that we would like to start. It's highly confidential, and we know you won't breathe a word of it. I'm sure you know of the paper *Variety*. Well, we don't like it because we don't own it. It's too powerful only because it's the only paper for our industry. If there were another paper with equal circulation and backing from the studios, we'd be very happy. We need a guy to front the operation, and that's you."

Nathan was mute.

"Don't worry that you don't know anything about journalism. We'll staff you with the best reporters and columnists around. You just talk to us every day and keep your nose clean, and we'll all be very happy."

"Whatever you say, guys. I'm yours," said Nathan.

Nathan was set up in a building on Wilshire Boulevard, offices in front, the printing operation in the back. The Rexford Corporation was the name used on the masthead, and Rexford Press was also the printing corporation.

Mendelbaum lived on Rexford Drive in Beverly Hills. So much for the cover. The first issue of *Hollywood Newsday* was on the stands within six weeks, and it was successful right off the bat. Nathan immediately let the power go to his head and started acting like William Randolph Hearst. He talked "Rexford" into buying him the mansion on Sunset, saying it would be good for business . . . and he was right. His Sunday afternoon parties and Friday dinners soon became legendary. The three guest houses on the property were kept filled with women, which the studio boys loved. It was more tasteful than going to a whorehouse. Nathan had thought of all the angles.

"I know this place," said Powar as they drew closer. "I spent a lot of my childhood here. This is Nathan Blumenthal's house. What a character. My parents know him well, but they never really liked him."

Those comments did not help Maria. She turned to Powar and said very sadly, "Please, this is very hard for me. Just stick by me."

Powar was sorry she had spoken too soon. They got out of the car and rang the bell.

"I am Maria Jong, and I'm here to see my mother," Maria spoke as a butler opened the door.

"She's in her quarters. I'll go get her."

Powar's mind was working overtime. Again she couldn't contain herself. "What's your mother doing here?"

Maria answered her slightly impatiently. "She's the house-keeper. I was born on these grounds."

This was startling news for Powar. As she had gotten older she had heard from her father about the guest houses at Nathan's, but the connection to Maria was hard to imagine.

Mei-Ling entered from the dining room, an elegant-looking woman in her late forties. Mother and daughter just stared at one another. They really knew each other through letters and had had very little face-to-face contact through the years. They reached out and hugged each other tentatively.

"Mother, I'd like you to meet my roommate, Powar King."

Mei-Ling looked at Powar. "Of course. I knew you when you were little. You're Mr. and Mrs. King's child, who liked avocado sandwiches, right?"

Powar laughed and said, "Yes. It's very nice to see you again."

The sound of boot heels on marble made everyone turn around. Mei-Ling tensed at the noise. The presence of Nathan was upon them. The years had made him dress a little better, and he wore his power as if he were more accustomed to it.

"Did I hear Philip King mentioned?" he bellowed.

"Yes, you did. I'm his daughter, Powar. It's been years since I played here, but I remember it well." She shook his hand as firmly as he shook hers.

Nathan's eyes naturally went from Powar to Maria as he took her hand in his. The last time he had seen her she was a troublesome twelve-year-old. "Maria," said Nathan as he held on to her hand too long.

Mei-Ling turned to ice.

"You two must come to the backyard right now. We're having a wonderful Sunday gathering," said Nathan.

Powar was apprehensive. Being here as a child with parents to protect you was one thing, coming as a guest was another matter; but they had no choice.

Maria stayed back to visit with Mei-Ling in her house, and Nathan walked Powar into the backyard. A glance around the yard indicated a major party, with buffets, tables with umbrellas, two bars, and about fifty people. From one glance it looked like actresses trying to make it and East Coast ad agency men trying to get into the studio business. It turned Powar's stomach because it all was so obvious. She had spent her life at business parties, and this was not her idea of a good time. She decided to go to the far bar at the end of the pool. It was quieter over there.

As she was walking along the pool she saw two young men looking at her, and as she passed by them they deliberately raised their voices.

"What do you think, Falk?" said the one with the reddish hair. "Is she SC or UCLA Film School?"

"Oh, definitely USC," answered the one with brown hair. "Very old money, I'm sure." They started to laugh as Powar stopped and looked at them.

"Deep is more important than old, gentlemen. My name is Powar King." She thought they were sort of cute and smiled her biggest smile. They didn't seem as creepy as the rest of the crowd. She extended her hand to the redhead, who reminded her of Ned in the Nancy Drew books.

"Hi. I'm Andy Stromberg, and this is my friend Falkner Cantwell. You can call him Falk, and he's as snobby as his name sounds."

Her eyes shifted to Falk. He was handsome and well aware of it, very slick with longer hair that looked shiny, as if it had pomade on it.

"You're Philip King's daughter?"

"Yes, I am, and I do go to USC."

Falk laughed.

"What's so funny?" asked Powar.

"Oh, nothing. It's just that Hollywood sons and daughters are so obvious," answered Falk.

"Obviously talented, is what I think," countered Powar. "And what do you hope to do, Falk?" she asked, anticipating a story of hopes and dreams.

"I'm VP of nighttime programming for Premier Broadcasting Company."

Powar could tell he loved saying that to her. Now she remembered who he was. She'd read about the Golden Boy who'd said he was going to turn an upstart network into a major player. She looked at him again, and he reminded her of Alain Delon or that gorgeous gas station attendant in *Umbrellas of Cherbourg*.

Falk saw her sizing him up, and he was delighted. Having Philip King's daughter intrigued by him might be an interesting move.

Andy knew what Falk was thinking, and he knew Powar was in over her head. Why was it every time he met someone nice, Falk got her? Just once he wished he could meet somebody without him being around. He just couldn't understand why Falk's "rude" technique almost always worked.

"These gatherings happen every Sunday afternoon," explained Falk. "Why don't you come back next week?"

"I'll think about it," answered Powar. "Right now I'm going to find my friend."

Andy smiled and said, "It's really nice to meet you."

Falk wasn't even paying attention by then. He was swirling his lemon wedge around the top of his chilled glass containing a straight shot of Stoli and seeing who was a more important person to talk to.

Nathan was gazing at Maria and Powar getting into their car when he allowed his mind to wander back to the day Mei-Ling had come into his life. He'd gotten a call from Mendelbaum.

"Clear out one of the houses, Nathan, I have someone coming over who will be a permanent resident."

Nathan never messed with Mendelbaum, he just did as he was told. About six o'clock that evening a beautiful Chinese girl arrived by cab. She was standing in the foyer when he first saw her, very petite, about five one, looking like a little doll. She had a beautiful, chiseled face and an elegant way about her. She bowed.

"My name is Mei-Ling Jong. Mr. Mendelbaum said you would know what to do with me."

Nathan could barely contain himself. "I will show you to your quarters," he replied.

When Mendelbaum arrived the next day he told Nathan that Mei-Ling's mother had worked for him for many years and that Mei-Ling had been raised in China by her grandparents. Mendelbaum had been sending money over there to keep her mother happy, and it had been used to give her English lessons. "This one doesn't get passed around. You got that, Nathan?" growled Mendelbaum.

On the days Mendelbaum was not around, Nathan watched her endlessly. He could see Mei-Ling starting a garden around her house. She usually wore a red cotton Chinese robe and little white slippers. She seemed so removed from what life had assigned her to do. He couldn't stand it when he saw Mendelbaum go into her house.

After about a year of this torture for Nathan, Mendelbaum lost interest in her. It was so abrupt that it took Nathan by surprise.

"I have a short attention span, Nathan. Put her into regular service now," said Mendelbaum. By regular service he meant that it was open season on her for the rest of the boys, but Nathan had other ideas. The next day he went to visit her while she was gardening.

"Mei-Ling, I think it's time for you to have a new job. I'd like you to tend to the big house. You can cook and clean, can't you?" asked Nathan.

"Of course I can. I thank you for the opportunity, sir." And then she bowed.

Nathan soon saw to it that it was necessary to "work on a story" at home during the day. He was up in his study when he heard the door open. Mei-Ling did not expect to find him there. She was wearing the uniform he bought for her, a white cotton stiffly starched maid's uniform with white stockings and white ballet shoes. Her apron was white satin trimmed in lace.

"I'm working at home today. It's fine if you clean around me. There's no need for you to leave," said Nathan. He pretended to go back to his work, but he was watching her move. She had a feather duster that he insisted she use for the furniture.

"Would you clean under the bed, Mei-Ling?" asked Nathan. His breathing changed the minute she bent over to reach under the bed. He loved the chase of the first time. He knew exactly what he wanted, and he always got it.

It did not escape Mei-Ling that he was watching her. This kind of situation was simply her lot in life. Men had been using her since she was thirteen.

"My desk needs dusting," said Nathan.

She came over to where he was sitting. The feather duster was right near his fingertips.

"Let me show you how to use this properly." He took the duster from her and let it graze very slowly across her hand.

A shock went through her, and Nathan felt it, too. "This way is even better," he said as he told her to close her eyes while he raised the duster to her face.

She felt the feathers sliding back and forth. "Do you like that?" asked Nathan.

"Oh, yes, sir," replied Mei-Ling.

"Exactly how much?" continued Nathan as the duster kept working.

"Very much, sir," Mei-Ling replied.

"I am your master, Mei-Ling," said Nathan.

"Yes, sir, I know that," she said.

"You must do everything that I tell you to, you must do everything to please me," he continued.

"Yes, sir."

"You are very young and need to be taught certain things. I want you to take off your uniform, leaving the stockings and garter belt. Do it quickly and then lie across my lap."

Mei-Ling did exactly as she was told.

Nathan took the feather duster, pulled down her panties, and started stroking her pearly white buttocks. "You are very beautiful, little one." He started rocking back and forth with each stroke.

She could feel him swelling under her. He was taking the feathers and deliberately letting them slide down between her legs. The repeated touches in just the right place made her throb.

Nathan could feel it too as he lifted her from the chair and placed her on the floor. He unzipped himself and heard Mei-Ling gasp at his enormous size. Nathan loved it when that happened. He waited for it each time. He tossed the duster away and started using his fingers.

Mei-Ling was moaning.

"Not so fast, little one. You are just learning this, and you must do what the professor says," said Nathan.

At that moment, Mei-Ling finally caught on that Nathan was acting out some sort of fantasy. "Yes, master," she said.

That really excited Nathan. "Open up for me, little one, open wide and you will learn it all."

He knew she couldn't resist him. They both knew, and they grabbed on to each other and were locked in rose haze. They rolled over and over, their passion knowing no bounds.

Mei-Ling was screaming now. She couldn't get enough.

Nathan loved to do that to young girls. The faster they went, the more he liked himself. He got dizzy with the speed as he felt his brain go numb. He was no longer thinking. There was only body.

On the ride back to school Maria and Powar were talking a mile a minute. Maria told her how Nathan had paid for her schooling and taken care of her mother all these years. She did not talk about her father. Powar couldn't believe how they might have even met as children if Maria had been around. The coincidence was amazing. Powar then told her about Andy and Falk. Maybe Maria might like Andy, Powar thought. But all Maria could talk about was Nathan. She was mesmerized by him.

* CHAPTER 10 *

Honey walked into her bedroom and put her briefcase on the bed, kicking off her Jourdan pumps. Right . . . my bedroom, not ours anymore, she thought. She thought for a second and realized she didn't know whether she wanted it to change. She never said anything about Philip's repeated overseas trips, feeling it was beneath her. She had other things to do. Her charity work, the studio, the family name. And when she was standing on that podium feeling the lights and hearing the applause of all Hollywood as she was honored as "Angel of the Decade," it made up for the empty bedroom . . . almost.

She walked into her dressing room, unbuttoning the jacket of her St. Laurent suit, and furiously threw it across a chair. She could not stop thinking about Philip's graduation gift to Powar. Her fury would not go away. His obsession with their daughter was bad enough, but the family and business crossover wasn't right. Even though she was still the major shareholder in King Pictures, some of the control of the company was now in other hands, and it didn't matter that it was her own daughter's hands. She hadn't made King Pictures a global success to be a party to handing out gifts. There would be plenty of time for Powar to inherit at the right time, years from now.

She changed into a mauve crepe lounging suit with matching velvet flats trimmed in gold and was walking down the stairs when she heard him at the front door.

"How's the Rock Hudson project coming?" she asked, following Philip into the living room. "Did he report for work today?"

Honey had warned him not to hire Hudson. His late-night exploits and drinking were becoming known in Hollywood, and *Dawn* was an important picture.

"You're stalling, Philip," Honey said.

"Okay. You were right. He showed up, but he was too puffy to shoot. We could only do long shots."

Honey countered, "You should have taken a chance on that Eastwood kid I told you about, but it's probably too late for you to use him. At least you hired Irena Wayborn. I told you she was going to be the next Brigitte Bardot."

Honey's voice faded as he walked to his upstairs dressing area and undressed for a steam after a difficult day. He hated it that Honey was always right on business decisions, yet a part of him never lost the original respect he had for her. He sighed, undressing. There were times when he wanted to move to France permanently. He made sure that every year he went to the Deauville Film Festival and took Genevieve with him. He'd even bought her a beautiful home on the Normandy coast. A few times when Powar was younger she went to the festival, too, and met "Daddy's friend" Genevieve. As the steam enveloped him he took pleasure in remembering the first time Powar met Genevieve. She was ten and loved Europe immediately. She was fascinated by the people with different accents, and she loved it when her father took her for a walk to all the little shops in Deauville.

"Do you have TV here?" she asked the woman trying on a hat in the millinery shop.

"Yes, we do," she answered.

"How many channels?" asked Powar.

"Two," replied the woman.

"Only two?" said a horrified Powar.

"We are lucky to have that. We only got TV a few years ago," the woman continued.

"Hmm. Do you have any kids?" asked Powar, trying on a beret.

"No, I don't," said she.

"Are you lonely?" asked Powar.

The woman looked at Philip for a second and said, "Sometimes I am, but most of the time I'm very busy with my work. I also love my country house. It's a beautiful place to be."

"Ooh, I'd like to see it. I've only been to cities. Can we go, Dad?" asked Powar.

"Well, honey, this nice lady has to ask us first," he said.

Powar looked at her and said, "My name is Powar King, and this is my dad. We won't hurt you or anything. Please let us go with you. We won't stay very long."

The woman bent down and put her hands on Powar's shoulders. "I think that I would love to show you and your father the countryside. My name is Genevieve LeJeune. It's nice to meet you." She took Powar's hand and smiled at Philip, who was beaming. He'd thought it would be better this way, and he was right.

The last time they saw one another was one of the most glorious times they ever had together. Instead of staying at Genevieve's home in Honfleur, they went back to the Riviera to a little town called St.-Paul-de-Vence. There was a charming inn called La Colombe d'Or, which was also a four-star restaurant. It catered to the very artistic crowd. The inn had been started years earlier, and the original owner had accepted paintings from customers who couldn't pay. They were the early works of Van Gogh, Cézanne, Pissarro, and Monet. The food there was as good as the art. Philip was excited to be there because he heard that the American writer James Baldwin lived there, and sure enough he met him at the bar the first night. It was a thrill for him. He was so excited he could barely taste the quenelles nantua, swimming in the delectable sauce, as they were placed before him.

Genevieve had no trouble at all. Food to her was more important than Baldwin. She insisted on ordering the complete meal to please Philip. Veau Normande with petites haricots verts and pureed carrots was next. Philip smiled as it was brought to the table. "You really love to watch the apple brandy swirl through the cream, don't you?" he said.

"I did this for you as a prelude to dessert," Genevieve said seductively.

Philip couldn't wait to see what she had in her ever-adventurous mind. When they finished, the waiter came over to the table.

"Would you please have our dessert brought to our room?" asked Genevieve.

Philip followed her eagerly back to their room. The ceiling had exposed wooden beams painted sky blue. The same blue was on the shutters. The furniture was simple, hand-carved wooden fare. The bed was plain with a painted blue headboard, but what was on the bed was special. France was famous for its sheets. They were an extra soft cotton placed on top of a feather mattress. On top of this was a huge down comforter. Slipping in between these sheets was like getting into a baby's bed. A clear vase of freshly picked flowers was on the nightstand, and only candles lit the room.

"You can't take a shower," Genevieve said cheerfully. "Your body must be absolutely dry. Just take off your clothes and meet me in bed."

Philip did as he was told. He saw her disrobe and then take out a brush that looked like an old-fashioned men's shaving brush. She then brought out a can of glistening white powder.

This was the sixties, Philip thought, but Genevieve wouldn't use drugs.

She got in next to him and dipped the brush into the powder and smiled. "Now just lie back," she said.

She started with his face and brushed it slowly. He felt the tickle of the bristles, but he liked it. She dipped the brush again in the powder and began brushing him all over. The sensation on his bulging manhood was awesome. When she went lower and finished his feet she looked at him and said, "Now brush me."

Philip loved it immediately. There was something very sensual about feeling every part of her body through this silky brush. When he was finished covering her with the powder, she threw her arms around him and pressed him to her chest.

"Eat me, Philip. Lick your dessert."

As soon as Philip tasted the powder he knew why she'd used it. It tasted like dust from honey, and the sweetness of that coupled with her own natural taste drove him wild. There was no pain here, only pleasure. So different from Honey. He felt good about himself. Being inside Genevieve was like being surrounded by comfort and love. The beauty of it made him feel truly loved. His entire body was pulsating now, and he was holding back, not wanting it to end. Just at the exact moment he was about to come, she surprised him by pulling him out of her and onto her stomach. He exploded, and his juice was turning the honey dust back into liquid. She took that mixture in her hands and rubbed it on his chest and rolled in it. He had never known such wild passion. Genevieve was teaching him about pure love, the thing he'd thought he wanted in the first place, so many years ago. Tears covered his face. It broke his heart that he did not have this happiness at home, and he didn't know how to make everything all right. Genevieve held him and didn't ask any questions.

It was difficult for Philip to sit at the dinner table with Honey that night. He wanted to be on the next plane to France. But Honey had plans for him.

"I have been giving your idea of a television division a lot of thought, Philip. King Pictures should not get mixed up with this upstart medium. We hardly know anything about it. I don't think you should expand. Let the others do it. They'll spread themselves too thin, and you'll be one of the few pure movie studios left. There will always be room for that kind of operation." Honey was actually just vamping for time. TV might be a good idea, she just needed to study it more so she could control it.

"I'm sorry," said Philip. "I've already hired Ron Frankel from Warner Brothers to head up the division. I think there's a big profit to be made."

"How dare you do that without consulting me?" Honey shrieked. "I could pull the plug on it right now if I wanted to. You're only doing it because Powar loves television and you're creating a TV division so she can work there after graduation."

"Listen to me," shouted Philip. "Movie business grosses are dropping. People are staying home watching television because they can get something for free. If we don't start competing in it, I don't know how long we can expect to stay in business at our current level. If we have a TV division, we can produce and own our own programs. There are three ready-made sources to sell to, and if a show is a hit, it can run forever and generate millions of dollars in income. We have young kids under contract who we're paying practically nothing to. We can stick them in the shows, make back our money, and turn them into drawing cards."

"Everyone in Hollywood looks down on television, Philip. People admire our family and who we are because we stand for quality and greatness in Hollywood. We have a tradition to uphold. Hollywood is movies, not television!" Honey countered. "What kind of premiere are we going to have for some unknown kid starring in a western that costs $1.98? You're selling out and turning us into commoners!"

"Who are you kidding?" shouted Philip. "Have you forgotten that my last name is Cohen, not King? And since when have you become a descendant of the Royal Family? This isn't about television, it's about Powar and your insane jealousy over our relationship."

"No, it's about how you've never given me the respect I deserve for really running King Pictures all these years. And you'll pay for it!" Honey stormed out of the room.

* * *

Powar was surprised that TV production turned out to be her favorite class. She'd been surrounded with movies every day of her life, but the time she spent after school, locked in her room watching "American Bandstand" and "Soupy Sales," had taken hold of her creative imagination.

Today she was sitting in the director's booth in her class, doing a run-through for her final test. She'd learned how to light, operate the camera, be a technical director by operating the cut and dissolve switches, and, as a director, call the shots. Naturally she liked that best.

For her final she could produce and direct any show she wished, and she picked her own college version of "Bandstand," which enabled her to work with all the things she loved. She picked the music, rehearsed the couples, and she would have emceed if she could have. As a joke she had her blond "Justine and Bob" couple, her brunette "Kenny and Arlene," and her bouncy "Pat Molitierri." They were going to dance to Bobby Darin's "Splish Splash."

"Okay, camera one," said Powar into the headset she wore in the booth that allowed her voice to be heard by all the cameramen. "Give me a longshot of couple number one and hold it. Camera two, I want a close-up of couple three and then I want you to widen to a medium shot when I cue you. Camera three open on a close-up of our MC, and then when I cut I want a master of the whole stage."

Powar loved being in the booth. She hit the mike so her voice was heard by everyone in the studio. "I'll cue the music, wait for Dick's intro, and then just dance your little hearts out. Ignore the cameras and have fun. Applaud when the music stops. Wait for your cue, and thank you, everybody."

Powar turned to her assistant, Nathalie, and said, "Follow me." They went onto the studio floor to camera three. Powar had a brown paper bag with her, and she took a small paper cup out of it with a hole the size of a quarter in the bottom.

"Nathalie, when you see the red light go on this camera during the dance section, I want you to hold the cup up to it, touching it, and move it around in a random manner."

Nathalie didn't have a clue why she had to do this, but when the teacher saw the tape of Powar's final he understood. The TV department was very new at USC, and it hadn't yet received enough donations to get special effects on the electronic board, so Powar had invented one herself. The professor, a dinosaur named Mitchell Channing, should never have headed up the department. He was impressed with Powar's abilities, but he himself was over the hill. The new technology was too much for him. He knew enough to give her an A in the course, though.

"Come in, Powar dear," said Honey, opening the front door. She was wearing a turquoise taffeta hostess gown, Chinese lantern earrings, and diamonds flashing from every visible appendage.

As Powar followed her mother into the study, she realized how much she hated going home, hated that she'd agreed to bring her grades to her parents at the end of each semester so they'd have an excuse to have dinner together. It was unbearably difficult when they all were together. Powar could sense their unhappiness with each other, and the tension always gave her indigestion.

Honey was carrying a glass of wine and didn't offer Powar any.

"Thank you, Mother, I'd love a glass of wine." Powar smiled and sat down on her favorite easy chair.

"Your father will be here momentarily. How's school?"

Just as Powar was about to answer, Honey interrupted her. "Next Saturday we'd like you to go with us to Kirk and Anne Douglas's party. Their son Michael has graduated and he's coming home to be an actor. His stepmother is just sick about it. She wanted him to be a lawyer. It's a much safer profession," Honey continued, asking questions nonstop but never wanting to hear the answers. "They're giving him a party to celebrate his graduation, but Anne's just putting on a good front for everyone. It would be good for you to go. You've been hiding out at USC too long, and you should see the boys again. Peter Douglas is exactly the right age for you, and I don't think he's going to be an actor. You should spend some time with him.'' She paused for a second.

"I don't like to be pushed into doing things like that, Mother, and you know it. I can lead my own social life,'' said Powar.

"She's talking about the Douglases again,'' said Philip as he rushed to hold Powar. "I'd like you there, Powar. I want to show you off. You're the most beautiful daughter in the world.''

"Of course I'll go, Daddy, but I'm going to bring my roommate with me.''

Honey didn't comment.

"How did your TV final turn out?'' Philip asked.

"It was great. I got an A,'' answered Powar, her spirits rising. "It's so incredible to be in that booth and see all the shots in front of you. You can pick what you want when you want it. The immediacy and intimacy of it are fantastic. It's absolutely the wave of the future.''

Honey almost choked on her chardonnay. "Powar, dear,'' she began, "I'm sorry, but you're wrong. TV will have its place and appeal to a certain audience, but movies will always be the premiere business.''

Powar couldn't stand it. "Wake up, Mother. You're so out of touch. Nothing will replace the big screen, but if Daddy doesn't start producing his own TV shows, he's going to be in trouble. Don't you know that Warner Brothers supplies at least half the programming to ABC already?''

This was a familiar scene to Philip. Whenever the discussion turned to business it was always the same. Powar was as smart as they came. She was a "baby'' Honey, and Honey resented it terribly. How sad it is, thought Philip, that Honey doesn't just nurture her and keep the dynasty going.

"TV is déclassé, Powar dear. I've raised you to be proud of what we represent. You're so like Philip. I can't get either of you to understand the tradition that we must uphold."

"I don't know what's wrong with either one of you," said Powar. "I'm shocked that Dad hasn't gone into TV before this. It's so obvious that it's the right thing to do. And regardless of what else I might think of you, Mother, I do know you're extremely perceptive in business, and I can't even believe we are having this discussion."

"Dinner is served," said Honey, nodding to Lupe, their housekeeper, who had quietly appeared in the doorway. She swept out of the room.

Powar no longer wanted to stay for dinner. Her stomach was already starting to go, but she couldn't figure out a way without hurting her father. As she walked into the dining room she knew it was Chinese night, one of her mother's "themes." Now she knew the reason for the earrings. Fortunately Powar liked Chinese food, so it wouldn't be too awful. "Remember Ah Fong's, Dad?" asked Powar. Philip nodded, smiling. "I loved it when you took me there in the late afternoon to shell peas with the waiters. I couldn't believe it when I saw them in all the Charlie Chan movies."

No matter what Honey did she was left out. The connection between Philip and Powar was simply unbreakable. All she wanted was for Powar to notice that she had tried to do something Chinese for her. Honey yearned to ask them why they never took her with them on their explorations, but she thought better of it. She didn't want to seem weak. It was going to be another one of those dinners when there were lots of words but nobody communicated. It was the story of their lives.

"It's your turn, Maria," said Powar as they were walking from the house to the Coliseum for the football game against University of California at Berkeley, better known as "Cal." USC students really disliked that university. It was a public school that catered to a radical population that was protesting and did not believe in the same values the USC students did. The game had taken on the proportions of a class war.

Maria was not listening. Powar tapped her on the shoulder. "Didn't you hear me?" she asked. Maria seemed to be day-dreaming all the time. "I said it's your turn."

"My turn for what?" asked Maria.

"I need you to go to a party with me tonight. My parents are going to be there, and they insist that I go. It's at Kirk Douglas's house."

"All right, I'll go, but how long do I have to stay?" asked Maria.

"What is wrong with you? You're moody. You're distant. I don't get it."

Maria insisted she was fine and then started talking about the game. Now it was Powar who let her mind wander. Was Maria nervous about graduation, just a few months away? She hadn't talked much about what she was going to do when she got out, except to write. Maybe that was it. Powar was also getting restless. She'd been in school long enough. It was time to go out and do something in the real world. She knew she could go to work at King Pictures any time she wanted, but that was such an obvious move. She'd have to inquire about other opportunities, and quickly.

"Hurry up. I don't want to miss 'Conquest,' " said Maria, running to their seats in the student section. "Conquest" was the theme of the USC Marching Band and a highlight of every event. For football, the white Trojan horse, Traveler, would come out and dash around the whole field just before the game, ridden by "Tommy Trojan" in a warrior suit, while the band played this incredible song. All the students loved that moment and didn't want to miss it. Since this was one of their last football games as seniors, they didn't want to miss a second of anything. True to form, USC clobbered Cal.

As usual, the sorority house was crawling with alumni after the game. It was a tradition that a late afternoon tea be held with the actives and the alums after each game. Powar wondered just what kinds of lives these women led if they needed to keep returning to the house week after week. She could understand wanting to go to the football games, but then they should get on with their lives. The majority of them were very plastic. It was the pom-pom set without a sense of humor. Most of the time she could tolerate them, but when they interfered with her life or started offering her pompous advice, she had had it. "Let's cut out of here," said Powar.

"This is how you show up to go to a party?" shrieked Honey when she saw Powar and Maria at the front door, both scruffy from the football game.

"Don't pay any attention, Mother," said Powar. "We'll be just fine in an hour. Give us a break."

Philip had to sit through a good thirty-five minutes of Honey's bitching about Powar's appearance. "Don't worry, Honey. She's going to be fine. Just calm down."

Maria entered the room first, her long black hair flowing over her shoulders and just touching the top of her red sheath. She looked stunning. Powar had chosen a black cocktail suit with a turquoise silk blouse that looked wonderful with her eyes.

"You both look beautiful. You're so grown up you take my breath away," said Philip as he gave each girl a kiss on the cheek. "What young ladies. Shall we go?"

"Maria and I want to take our own car," said Powar.

The Douglases' French Regency house was just a few blocks away, and this evening there was valet parking in front for the guests. It was a very formal house done completely in Louis XIV. When Philip and Honey arrived they were immediately cornered by Frank Sinatra and his date, Juliet Prowse, so Maria and Powar were left to fend for themselves. Most of the people were out in the backyard, which was so large that the pool didn't need to be covered over for a dance floor. There was enough lawn for everything. Powar spotted Rona Barrett, the columnist, who wrote for all the movie magazines and had just started a regular broadcast on local KABC News. Powar was enthralled by her.

"Hi, I'm Powar King, Philip and Honey's daughter. I have really wanted to meet you. This is my friend Maria."

"It's very nice to meet you both," said Rona. "Your parents have mentioned you to me several times. I think you're just finishing school now, isn't that right?"

"Yes," answered Powar, "and I can't wait to get into the business. Do you mind if I ask you a question?"

"Not at all," said Rona.

"Why did you decide to go on TV?"

"I realized that TV is the future, my dear. I just know that there will be magazines on the air and much more entertainment news on programs coming up, and I plan to be in on all of it," answered Rona.

"Please let me know if there is anything I or my family can do for you. I think you're terrific." Powar was just thrilled to meet her. She was as nice as Powar hoped she would be.

Powar turned to talk to Maria and ran right into Falk Cantwell.

"Now she's mine, Rona," said Falk.

"You better go for it, Powar," said Rona. "It's not every day a girl gets a one-on-one with the legend." She winked at them and left.

"How come you never came back to Nathan's?" asked Falk. "I saw your friend, but you never came with her."

Powar was stunned about this revelation but didn't show it. "I just wasn't comfortable in that atmosphere," she answered.

"Would you like a drink? I need a refill," said Falk.

"All right," Powar answered.

"What would you like?"

"I'm not sure. I really don't drink," said Powar.

"I'll get you one of mine," he said.

Powar looked around for Maria and couldn't find her. It was not like her to disappear. She glanced over to where Falk had gone and saw him talking animatedly to her mother. I didn't know Mother knew him, Powar thought. I wonder why she never mentioned it? Then Falk was back with two Stolis with lemon. From Powar's first taste of it, she loved the velvet glide of vodka down her throat.

"I can see you are enjoying that," said Falk.

"Definitely," said Powar, wondering why she was so drawn to him. He was obviously a shark, but a very smooth one. It was more than his job. Powar's father owned a studio, so a network VP didn't scare her at all. There had been something about him from the very beginning. He had an element of danger about him that was exciting. He was wearing a dark gray glen plaid suit with a white shirt and burgundy-and-gray tie. He was immaculate.

"When do you graduate?" asked Falk.

"This June, and yes, I think I want a job in television," Powar said.

He smiled. "There are some people I have to see here, but why don't you meet me at Chasen's at nine P.M. for dinner. I'd like that very much." Powar agreed to meet him as the last bit of vodka dripped down her throat.

She went to look for Maria in earnest and came upon a crowd of people surrounding someone. Powar recognized the actress Jessica Walter, who had just made a name for herself starring in the movie *The Group* with Powar's friend Candice Bergen. Powar thought Jessica was a terrific actress and would have loved to meet her, but she wanted to find Maria.

"Powar, we've been looking for you," said Anne Douglas. "We want you to see Peter and Michael."

Just then they were joined by Army Archerd, the extremely popular columnist for *Daily Variety*. Powar had not seen him since she'd graduated from high school. Her parents had the utmost respect for him.

"Army, have you seen Michael anywhere?" asked Kirk.

"He's in the dining room with a sensational brunette," Army replied.

Now Powar knew where Maria was. After a few minutes she excused herself. She spotted the giant ice towers of shrimp, lobster, and crab and immediately recognized a Chasen's-catered table. Next to the seafood display was steak tartare and all the condiments, followed by a whole fresh smoked salmon with capers and pumpernickel bread. At the other end of the table was the beluga caviar and Michael and Maria. Powar just stood and watched them. They made a striking couple. She could tell that Michael was certainly interested. They hadn't stopped laughing. Maria was shifting her weight from foot to foot, something she did when she was excited. Michael was busy making different versions of caviar for her to taste . . . just lemon (the proper way), with sour cream, with onions and egg . . . a lovely taste test. The onions and egg was the winning combination, judging by Maria's expression. Suddenly all animation went out of her face. She stared straight over Michael's shoulders into the face of Nathan Blumenthal. Michael turned, too.

"Nathan, thank you very much for coming," said Michael.

"The pleasure is mine, believe me," said Nathan, not taking his eyes off Maria. "May I borrow this lovely lady for a moment?"

"Of course," said Michael.

Powar quickly went over to Michael. "Mistake. Big mistake," she said.

"What are you talking about?" he asked.

"You should never have let her go," said Powar.

"You know, you haven't changed since we were kids. Shy you are not," Michael said as he kissed her on the cheek. "So, are you going to enter this rat race?"

"C'mon, Michael! It's the family business, and I love it," replied Powar.

"Let me take you to see Peter," Michael suggested. "My mother made me promise to do that if I saw you." Powar went along reluctantly.

For a while Powar looked for Maria and couldn't understand where she'd gone. She thought about asking some people at the party for their impressions of Nathan, but she didn't know whom she could trust. Even at her age she knew that one had very few true friends in Hollywood. She felt a tap on her shoulder and turned around to face Andy Stromberg.

"Hi," he said. "Falk told me I might run into you." He had a really sweet face. He really was like Ned from the Nancy Drew books.

Powar felt comfortable with him right away. "Do you mind if I ask you a question?" she said.

"Of course not," he replied. "I will always try to do anything I can to make your life easier."

An unusual comment, thought Powar, but she let it pass. However, she couldn't help but notice the way he looked at her. He was like a golden retriever puppy. "Who is Nathan Blumenthal, really? I know he's a publisher and he has his parties, but I've heard some pretty bad stories. What do you know about him?"

Andy nodded in a resigned way. "Your parents probably never told you anything. You were too young."

"Too young for what?" asked Powar.

"Nathan is sort of a pimp who was put in business by the studio heads many years ago. He's a very secretive man, but, well, I feel uncomfortable going into the rest of it," said Andy.

"Please tell me. I need to know for sure," explained Powar. She looked so concerned that Andy went against his better judgment.

"He likes young girls, and he always keeps changing them. There is one, however, who he has had on the property for years. He never lets her go."

"Who is that?" inquired Powar.

"Mei-Ling, the housekeeper. She was top of the line in her day. Word has it she's the trainer for the newcomers."

Powar was going to be sick.

"Are you all right?" asked Andy. "I knew I shouldn't have told you this. You need to get away from here. Let's go to the Luau and have drinks and hors d'oeuvres and pretend these people don't exist."

Powar's mood brightened. "How did you know I love the Luau? I had my high school graduation party there."

"I didn't know that," explained Andy. "I just named a

place that makes me very comfortable and hoped it would rub off on you."

Powar was amazed at his sensitivity, and she was a little torn. "I'm really sorry, but I made plans to meet Falk at Chasen's. I'm majoring in TV, and there's so much he can tell me."

Andy's heart sank. He was going to lose again. "Well, maybe some other time," he said, and walked away. Coming to Hollywood had been difficult for him because he was not duplicitous and conniving. He had graduated from the University of Pennsylvania seven years earlier and come out to Hollywood to write original screenplays. He'd secured a job as a reader for an independent movie production company, reading other people's scripts and either recommending them or not to his bosses. He had hoped that this would give him an entree into selling his own scripts. He'd had an offer from another company after being in town for two years, to write some scripts for them. They were low-budget horror movies, but it got him into the Writers Guild and paid his rent. He had been working on his own movie script for a year now, and soon he was going to send it out to see if someone would buy it. He wasn't going to give up.

Powar went into the kitchen, looking for a phone. She wanted to call the sorority to see if Maria had returned. She had not. Powar was more worried than ever and wasn't sure she could sit through a whole dinner. It was ironic that she had to be so concerned about someone else during this important dinner. Falk Cantwell was the first real man to ask her out. She was glad he'd picked Chasen's. Her parents had taken her there for her birthday each year for as long as she could remember. Her mother even had done their den to look like Chasen's, with dark wood and green leather.

"Not again," Philip said tersely as he and Honey pulled into their garage after the Douglas party. "Powar would love to work in the TV division, and it's time for us to start discussing it. Graduation is coming up."

Honey continued in her icy tone. "Philip, I told you I believe it would hurt her rather than help her. People will just say she got the job because of us, and she'll have to keep proving herself for the rest of her life. Call one of your friends and let her work there and learn. You're not thinking about her welfare."

Honey's argument was so good, Philip almost fell for it. But not quite. He had to always remember that Honey's goal was what was good for Honey and no one else. "Powar is a King, and Kings work at King Pictures. We take care of our family. That is what I built it for." He was adamant.

"That's what *you* built it for?" screamed Honey. "Just because you sit in that office, don't think for a second that you did it by yourself. You've hurt me terribly, Philip. I've never told you that and I'll never admit it again, but you had better remember who owns the cement that your chair is sitting on."

Philip was caught. She was right. She did hold the controlling interest. His voice softened. "I hate what we have become, Honey. We had dreams together, and it's all turned so ugly." He touched Honey's hand and she pulled it away.

In tears she said, "It's too late," and left him sitting in the car alone.

"Good evening, Miss King," said Julius, the maître d'. "Are your parents joining you this evening?"

"No, I'm meeting Mr. Cantwell." Julius smiled and showed her to booth number one. There actually were two booths called number one, depending on whether or not you wanted to be in the small section of booths to the right of the door or the first booth to the maître d's left. The right was more intimate, and the left was an announcement of your presence. Falk Cantwell was in number one on the left. Just his choice of booths alone gave Powar some insight into him. He stood up when he saw her.

"My dear, what would you like to drink?"

Powar answered that she would have what he was having.

She loved ritual with her food, and it amused her how Falk was so fastidious with his drink and went through a very specific procedure of squeezing the lemon and circling it around the top. Philip had taught her the joys of sitting down and relaxing with a drink and an appetizer and then reading the menu in absolute silence. As a consequence Powar hated it if someone talked to her during the menu-reading time. Each morsel of food mentioned on the menu took her on a fantasy trip. Falk started talking to her as she was reading, and she put the menu down.

"To the future," he said, raising his glass to her. They clinked glasses.

"Falkner, how are you?" said the voices going by the table. Powar looked up and saw Angie Dickinson and Burt Bacharach. She thought that nowhere in the world could there exist a more beautiful couple.

"Powar, I'd like you to meet Angie and Burt. And this is Powar King," said Falk.

Angie took her hand and smiled the warmest smile. "Are you Philip's daughter?" Powar nodded. "I've heard you are a very bright young lady."

Powar liked her instantly. She could tell that Angie was totally genuine.

Tommy and John, the captains, came over to the table to take the order. Powar and John remembered each other from the days when he was a busboy at Musso's and Philip would take her in there.

"Have you decided, Powar? Is it the steak Diane, the butterfly steak with mustard sauce, or the filet of sole Veronique?" John knew her so well.

"Steak Diane, please, with one of your Caesar salads to start," said Powar.

"No creamed spinach?" asked John.

Powar laughed. "Of course I want creamed spinach."

"And for you, Mr. Cantwell?"

"I'd like the hobo steak and sliced tomatoes," he said.

Now all they had to do was wait for the cheese toast to

accompany this. When two more Stolis arrived the waiter pointed to the end booth, where Marlo Thomas was smiling at them. She and Marlo used to run into each other at Uncle Bernie's, and then Marlo had preceded her at USC. She loved what Marlo was doing with "That Girl," the first show on TV that featured a single woman in the lead role. Powar was feeling fantastic. She was out without "Daddy" in a grown-up restaurant. These were not her peers, but they were close enough in age not to treat her as a child. It was a world she wanted desperately to join, and she wanted to do it on her own. Falk was certainly the first key to it that had presented itself. She was prepared to interview at all four networks starting in May, but she doubted that a better opportunity than the one sitting next to her would materialize.

"All right, your graduation is coming," said Falk. "Why does television interest you so much?"

"Well, I know you might think that movies would be my first love, and I do love them. But sitting at home in my room growing up, the television set became my private world. Those people on the small screen were my friends. That's the difference in the media. A movie star is not your friend. It's an untouchable idol that is twenty feet high. When it comes to television you welcome people into your home, and you don't do that with strangers."

Falk was impressed with her. "You're absolutely right about the difference. Most people don't understand that."

Powar continued. "What is the same about the two media is the story. You can't have anything without a good story. Understanding that everything comes from the material is crucial. If the story doesn't involve you, nothing else matters. I don't care who stars in it. I think that's the problem with some people working in the development areas. They don't have good story sense. I think that's what I have, and I know I can put it to good use. I see things and concepts as a whole and can translate them into scripts and see that they are cast correctly."

"If I may ask," Falk began, "why don't you go to work in your father's TV division?"

"I'm the one who encouraged him to start it because I knew what TV was going to become. I love him very much, and I know that he wants me there. I just want to prove something on my own first. How did you come to PBC?" Powar asked.

"I came to them from the advertising business. I knew what sponsors would buy, and I worked closely with all three networks. They saw that I could 'marry' sponsors with show ideas, and when Arthur David wanted to start PBC he called me. He needed someone who could bring in the sponsors and come up with programming ideas. Working at a young network presents all kinds of opportunities. We can be more experimental, and we have more freedom. We're the smallest one now, but it won't be that way forever."

"So you don't have an exclusive arrangement with a studio to supply a lot of your programming?"

Falk smiled broadly. "No, Powar. Gee, do you think we might know someone who could set that up?" They both laughed.

While they were waiting for their cars he took her hand and kissed her on the cheek. "Please call me on Monday and we'll set a date for you to come to the network and I'll show you around."

* CHAPTER 11 *

Maria was apprehensive as they waited for the Aston Martin. Nathan had insisted that she have a drink with him and now had a hold of her arm. She didn't know what it was about him that mesmerized her, but the power of Nathan's presence just kept overwhelming her. His gruffness should not have been appealing. His weight and size should have frightened her. It was not that he was grossly overweight, but he was just a very large man. Maria thought he must be six feet four. She knew he was in his fifties. She tried to put out of her mind the thought of her mother. She could fixate on why and how her mother came to be involved, but she would rather not. She was angry with herself when she started the pretense of visiting her mother more, realizing it was just an excuse to get to the house. She also hated lying to Powar. She and her mother would be together in the guest house and within ten minutes Nathan would be there, wanting to show Maria how to play tennis or running a movie for her in his screening room. Maria felt the outrage from her mother, but the two of them never discussed what was happening. It was as if her mother accepted Nathan's hold on people. When Nathan was alone with her he was always a gentleman. She felt his energy, but he never did anything about it physically. They both needed this cat-and-mouse game, and Maria wondered how long it was going to go on.

Nathan opened the door of the car for her. Maria had loved Aston Martins ever since she'd seen the one in the James Bond movie. This one was British racing green, her favorite. She loved the smell of the leather in the car and all the gadgets in the dash.

"Where are we going?" she asked.

"Why, are you nervous?" said Nathan.

"No, you're my mother's friend, so you would never hurt me," Maria said cleverly. She could see that annoyed him.

"We're going to a place that very few people know about in Hollywood, but I think you'll like it. I don't show it to just anyone."

Nathan turned the car toward Hollywood and away from Beverly Hills. Just before reaching Highland Avenue he turned onto a winding road going up into the hills under a sign that read "Yamashiro Sky Room." It was a very beautiful drive up to the top, slinking through the trees as fast as the car could go. Nathan handled it like a master.

The car pulled into a private driveway in front of a two-story Japanese house. But it couldn't be private, thought Maria, since there was valet parking. Huge teak-carved doors opened up to reveal a beautiful Japanese courtyard with a garden and waterfalls. Maria heard koto music and soft voices and felt transported to another world. When she looked to the left she saw a dark bar with a window overlooking the whole city. To the right was a dining room with hand-painted screens and low tables with pillows to sit on. All the help was dressed Japanese style, waitresses in kimonos and obis and men in hapi coats. Maria saw that Nathan was immediately recognized by the staff. They nodded at him and bowed as he entered.

"What kind of place is this?" she asked.

"Sometimes one finds out more by observing and not asking," replied Nathan. They were led by a gentleman to the bar on the left and were seated in a corner by the window. A large bottle of sake arrived with two cups.

"You never pour your own sake," explained Nathan, reaching for the bottle. "Now you pour mine."

Maria did.

"It's the custom of the country," continued Nathan. "I'm going to teach you a lot about Japanese customs."

As the hot sake filled her throat, her body jumped a bit, feeling it go down inch by inch. She looked around and saw that most of the people were Oriental. "Do you know that I'm majoring in journalism?" she asked nervously.

"Of course I do," he replied. "Who do you think told your mother to suggest that to you if you ever showed any interest in writing? She showed me some of your letters when you were younger, and I could tell you had talent. They were very entertaining. You have a good imagination. That kind of imagination will serve you well in life both professionally . . . and personally."

Maria was continually puzzled by him. Just when you tried to have a logical conversation there was an undertone. However, her anger at her mother showing him personal letters superseded any other feelings, and that was exactly the emotion Nathan wanted to get out of her. She didn't know that, of course, but things were going precisely as he planned. When they finished the bottle of sake a gentleman garbed in traditional Japanese clothing came to the table.

"Are you ready now, Mr. Blumenthal?"

"Yes, Fukuda," answered Nathan.

Nathan stood up and gestured for Maria to follow.

When she stood up her mind was bursting with confusion. She felt she was in over her head, yet she was paralyzed and couldn't turn back. They returned to the foyer and walked to the back area of the courtyard. Fukuda bowed as the shoji screens opened to a fully furnished Japanese living room with tatami mats, teak tables, and futon bedrolls. Everything in the room was sea green, and painted on the main wall was a gold leaf mural of a tree with a bird in it. Suddenly a Japanese woman dressed in a geisha costume approached Maria.

"I will see you in an hour," said Nathan. "Just follow Sachiko and do everything she tells you to do." It was an order, not a suggestion.

For one second Maria's independent streak took over and she almost told him she didn't take orders from anyone; but that was quickly silenced by her intense curiosity. She didn't know whether it was his mystery or his power, and at that moment she didn't care if she had an answer.

Nathan left the room through a side door to the left of the mural. There was an identical door to the right, and Sachiko walked through, and so did Maria. She found herself in a dark alcove. Sachiko opened a section of the floor by lifting up a trap door. As she did that, huge amounts of steam filled Maria's lungs. Maria followed Sachiko down the ladder through the trap door and found herself in a stone grotto with a natural underground spring running through it. The spring formed a freshwater pool, and Maria saw women bathing in it. Everywhere she looked she saw naked women, some jumping from the fresh steam pool into the icier pool, some lying on special mats surrounded by nude handmaidens who seemed to be doing incredible things to their bodies with oils and special scented materials. Maria was the only non-Oriental there. A young girl came over to her and told her to take off all her clothes. Maria was self-conscious, but she did it, getting into the freshwater pool as fast as she could. As soon as her skin touched the water she felt a sensation of calm come over her. The spring water had bubbles in it that played with the skin like a massage. She was surrounded by the warmth and the steam, and her breathing eased. It was as if there were magical powers in there. As she began to walk, her feet felt large underground rocks and she sat on one and closed her eyes. The only sounds she could hear were rushing water and the trickling of steam down the walls of the cave. The effect was hypnotic. She was finally relaxed.

Suddenly she felt four hands on her body. She opened her eyes and gasped as they physically thrust her from the steam pool to the icy one. Her whole body zinged in response. Her original emotion of hate turned to pleasure at the shock of it. She stayed there for two minutes and then was led by the handmaidens to the massage area. She lay down on a raised platform and was surrounded by four women holding rough-looking sponges. They dipped them in flower-scented water and went to work. Every area of Maria's body was being scrubbed. It was abrasive, but it felt good in a bizarre way. They rolled her over and scrubbed her backside. That was a more sensitive area, but she withstood it. They turned her face up again, and she felt a mixture of something being applied to her face. It smelled like cucumbers and milk, and that's exactly what it was. From her neck down she felt hands covering her with a warm satiny substance that was different from the cucumbers. It smelled very sweet.

"What is this?" she asked timidly.

A voice said, "It is honey, milk, and bananas. Please do not ask questions. Just experience."

Maria felt like a fruit salad that was being kneaded. She heard the scurrying of feet, and then she felt the waves of water. She was being rinsed off with water from barrels being poured over her. When she was suitably rinsed, they washed her hair. She was then wrapped in a towel, and someone blew her hair dry with an electric dryer. That was the only modern convenience in the grotto. When her hair was dry they took off her towel and she felt her skin. It was so soft that she felt like a newborn. They held out a gold brocade silk geisha robe for her to wear and put tabi slippers on her feet. Sachiko reappeared.

"Please follow me," she said. Maria was led back to the ladder in the alcove and told to climb to the top.

Nathan was dressed as a Japanese warrior, with a sword strapped to his kimono. She could tell by the glow of his skin that he, too, had experienced the wonders of the cave.

"Don't speak," said Nathan in an imposing voice. His

kimono was red and black, and it suited him. He rolled down the futon and looked at Maria without a smile. He walked over to her and put his hands on her shoulders and guided her down to the floor. Her robe was still on and tied at the waist. He bent down and reached into a drawer in the table and pulled out white silk cords. Maria's eyes were wide. He took one limb at a time and tied it in a special knot that was a reverse of a slip knot—if you pulled on it, it got tighter. Each wrist was tied to a heavy table leg. Each foot met the same fate.

Rising to his full height, Nathan stared her in the eyes and slowly drew his sword, placing its tip on her forehead. The look in his eyes was mesmerizing. She felt as if she were part of a ritual. The tip of the sword was very frightening. She had to shut her eyes because the sight of the tip from her angle looked as though it were going to slice her in two.

He started moving the sword ever so slowly over her face, down her neck, and resting it between her breasts. It stayed there for a long moment and then started moving again. The straight path changed, and she felt the sword cover her left nipple and caress it. She jumped and the ropes got tighter. The cold steel through the silk was devastating. She felt ashamed of feeling excited, but the sensations were too overwhelming. The sword was moving again. Her right breast was aching for it, but it tricked her. Instead it went down to her waist. She heard material rip and realized her sash had been cut. Nathan used the sword to pull away her robe and leave her exposed. She opened her eyes in time to see him take the gold handle end of the sword and place it right between her knees on the floor. She heard it traveling closer to her. She was tingling all over. When the gold hit its mark, probing her, teasing her, she couldn't contain her cries, she was being driven crazy. As she squirmed it didn't matter to her that the cords were biting her flesh. Nathan lay down on top of her and devoured her mouth. The sword never stopped its pulsating motion. Nathan began to move his body in time with the sword. Just when she thought she would go off the edge, it was inside her, only it was warm and hard and very big. Nathan knew right when to make the switch and make her feel as she had never felt before. Maria almost flew up to the ceiling with ecstasy. She knew that for the first time she was experiencing what it was to live. Her body was floating. She wanted him again right away, and he knew it. He always knew it.

Powar drove to the sorority house as fast as she could without getting a ticket. When she pulled into her spot in the alley and noticed that Maria's car was not there, she didn't have a good feeling. Powar went up to the room and started watching the "Tonight" show, but she could not concentrate. She turned it off and picked up one of her cinema textbooks. That wasn't any good, either. She got ready for bed and turned out the lights.

Maria crept in around two A.M. Powar heard her, but she didn't want to let her know. She thought it was better to let her get some sleep and see how she behaved in the morning.

When Powar woke up for real the next day, Maria was still asleep. Powar went for a walk to the corner restaurant, Woody's, where she met some friends for breakfast. She hurried back and found Maria awake.

"Hi, I missed you last night. Where'd you go?" Powar asked a little too quickly.

"Oh, I just went for a long drive. I needed to have a break. I've been under a lot of pressure lately," said Maria.

"Anything I can do to help?"

"No thanks, Powar."

"You know, Michael Douglas really liked you," said Powar.

"Mm-hmm," replied Maria as she started to get that glazed look again. "I can't think about him right now," she said.

Powar didn't want to be a nudge, but she didn't want her friend to get hurt, either. She was going to have to keep an eye on all of this, but for right now her first priority was

Premiere Broadcasting Company. She would give Falk one week to call.

Powar was due in Falk's office at PBC in ten minutes. His private line rang.

"Yes, Honey," he said. "Everything has been taken care of. I'll call you back later, and by the way, she's really just what we've been looking for."

Honey hung up the phone with mixed emotions. She wanted Powar away from the studio, but she didn't want to do her any favors, either.

Falk liked sitting in his steel-and-glass skyscraper overlooking the Sunset Strip. Other networks had offices and studios together on big lots, but because PBC was the "new kid" in the network business, they had to rent studio space for their productions. But Falk knew that soon they'd be able to compete. He'd make sure of it.

"I can go in looking like I already work there or I can look more like the college student who needs to be molded," said Powar to Maria as they were trying to figure out what Powar should wear.

"From what I've observed of Falk, his ego would like to mold you, but it would be far more effective to look the part. You want to knock him out and let him know you can do the job. I think that's more important. Wear the navy-blue-and-white suit with the white silk blouse and the navy-and-white spectators," advised Maria.

Powar agreed and got dressed, then had Maria do the finishing touches on her makeup.

PBC's decor reflected its upstart reputation. Unlike the more traditional networks that were decorated like hospital institutions or eastern boardrooms, PBC was wildly modern, its lobby three stories high. When the elevator opened on the right floor, you would walk out into a geometric design of chrome and glass and practically look to the sky from inside.

Huge plants towered a full story, and the black leather couches were so big you sank into them. Everything about the lobby was big; probably the designers and the owners of the network thought it was a masterpiece of manipulation because anyone walking in would feel small and intimidated. It never occurred to them that their motives were so transparent that people in the industry laughed every time they had to come there for a meeting. It didn't work on Powar, either, who, when she was engulfed by the couch, actually laughed out loud. The moment of levity was interrupted by a secretary coming to get her.

"Miss King? I'm Mr. Cantwell's secretary, Nancy Hobson. He's ready for you now. Please follow me."

Powar walked along a corridor with offices on either side. She noticed that the ones to her right, the outside offices, had a picture window and an inner glass wall, so if the executive chose to keep a curtain open, he or she could watch everything. The offices on the left were windowless and much smaller. Falk's office was on the corner, and when Powar was shown in it was hard for her to focus on him when all around her was the city displayed through floor-to-ceiling glass walls. The effect was dazzling.

"Welcome to PBC," said Falk, extending his hand as he came around from the desk that was carved opaque glass on black wood. He was dressed in black, with a white shirt with very faint pinstriping and a dark green tie.

Powar looked around and saw that a mirrored bar took up one wall. On the other wall was a giant screen. There was a door next to the bar that obviously led to a private fully equipped bathroom. Placed perfectly around the room so they could see the screen from any angle were three black leather couches.

"Don't even sit down," said Falk. "I want to show you around. You will notice as we walk down the hall that there are different kinds of offices. The ones with windows are for vice-presidents and directors, and the cubicles with no windows are for managers. This whole floor is offices, and here is our main conference room."

Powar peeked in the door and saw a twenty-foot-long table with black chairs lined in a row in front of a big screen.

"On the second floor we have two screening rooms. One looks like a large public theater, and the other is smaller with a stage and lights for run-throughs of different projects."

Powar noticed that in front of every office sat a secretary in a station done out of black-lacquered wood. Powar and Falk had just about come full circle. They were standing in front of an outside office two doors down from Falk's.

"Hi, Mara," said Falk to the fiftyish efficient-looking woman who was sitting there. "I'd like you to meet Powar King. Powar, this is Mara Burson." The two women smiled at each other politely.

Falk walked past Mara into the uninhabited but decorated office and asked Powar to join him inside. As he sat on the couch he asked Powar to sit behind the desk. "Just do it," he said laughingly. "I want you to see what it feels like."

When she sat down on the chair and put her hands on the desk, she felt the magic. Falk sensed it immediately. "Feels good doesn't it?"

Powar just smiled.

"Powar, this is your new office," said Falk.

Her heart flew into her mouth. "What do you mean?" she said.

"You heard me. You were right for this network from the day you were born. Normally you would start out as a program executive supervising current programming, meaning what's on the air already. But in your case I'm going to take a risk. As you pointed out to me so well, some studios have agreements with networks to supply series, and we don't have that, but I have had an idea for the past year, and I didn't quite know how to implement it until we talked. I think that networks should go to the studios and have them make special two-hour movies just for television. No one has thought of it yet, and I think it will put PBC on the map as a major player. Who better than you will have a better frame of reference for working with me? Naturally I think we should approach King Pictures first and set up, say, a two-year exclusive deal, where you can act as the liaison and supervise everything. Because this will be a new division, I'll have to approve all programming, but I need you to wade through the ideas and come up with recommendations. It would be the perfect marriage.''

Powar was so excited she could barely hear what he was saying.

"Of course you'll have all the perks that go with the job . . . a secretary, an expense account, all travel expenses, a parking pass, insurance . . . all the necessary things. Powar, I really need someone with your brain and background! I need you! The third member of our group will be Timothy Foster, who'll run business affairs, so we'll always have a grip on the finances. Listen. You graduate in six weeks, so you can start full-time then. Your salary will be thirty-five thousand dollars a year. I hope you'll start spending time here regularly though school isn't over yet. We have a lot to do and great things ahead of us. Well?''

Powar just sat there and stared at him. She'd been dreaming of this for years. She didn't care what kind of connections had gotten her this opportunity, she was going to go over the goal post with it. "Falk, I am very grateful for this offer, and I'm incredibly excited about the creative challenge. You did pick the right person for this.'' Powar stood up and shook hands with him. "Are you free for lunch?'' she asked.

"Of course I am,'' answered Falk. "I'll meet you in the lobby in a few minutes. I just have to make a call.''

As soon as lunch was over, Powar drove directly to King Pictures, which was south of Beverly Hills in an industrial area. As she pulled into the parking place at the studio, saying, "Powar King,'' she remembered the thousands of hours she'd spent here as a child. Sometimes her father would pick her up after school with a surprise hamburger made just for her from the commissary waiting in the car. They would then go and watch whatever was being shot. On Saturdays he would take her onto a sound stage and have her operate the lights or show her how the booms worked. He would let her sit behind his desk and pretend to run the studio. She loved it when he played an agent trying to sell her something. She knew more about the picture business by the time she was ten than most adults ever did. After her college graduation her technical skills combined with her upbringing made her an invaluable commodity. She raced to her father's office.

"Madge, is my father in?" she asked. "I have to see him right away."

"He's in with Freddie Gallery. Let me buzz him."

"That's not necessary, not if he's with Uncle Freddie." He was her favorite comic as well as one of her favorite people. She loved the fact that her parents were so close to Freddie and Kate. Many were the nights she used to crash their card games with Ellen and Jack. Those were some of the nicest nights she could remember as a child. Her parents didn't seem to fight as much with that group around. She went flying through the door.

"Daddy, I have the best news. Hi, Uncle Freddie. You have to hear this, too."

"Well, what is it? I've never seen you this excited," said Philip.

"I've just been offered a job at Premiere Broadcasting starting something called movies-made-for-television," said Powar. "Can you imagine that opportunity?"

Philip tried to look happy. "Did you take it?" he asked.

"Of course I did. You know how I love TV." Powar softened a bit and added, "I know how much you want me to work here, Dad. I didn't forget that, but there will be time for that, plenty of time. I just wanted to start on my own first. You understand, don't you?"

"Of course I do. I love you," said Philip.

"And I have a great idea on how we can work together on this anyway. I'll tell you about it later. I'd like you to have lunch with Falkner Cantwell and myself. Do we have a proposition for *you!*'' Powar ran off, looked back, and said, "Tell Mother for me. I've got to get back to school and tell everybody.''

"You can tell her yourself. She's due here in about fifteen minutes," answered Philip.

"She's on the lot," Philip's secretary whispered through the intercom.

Philip nodded encouragingly to Powar.

"Well, I guess I'll be going," said Freddie.

"Good move," said Powar.

Honey waved to Freddie as they passed in the doorway. "Well, well, two at once," she said, looking at Philip and Powar.

"Yes, we're celebrating, Mother."

"Oh, really? Why?" she asked nonchalantly.

"I'm going to work at Premiere Broadcasting in charge of a new division to make movies just for television."

Honey smiled broadly. "What a wonderful idea! I'm very happy for you." She said it so naturally that part of her actually believed it.

Powar and Philip looked at each other.

"That's great," said Powar. "I didn't think you approved of television. I'm surprised by your reaction."

"But I always want the best for you, Powar, and I do know what's best." Curiously, Honey actually did feel she'd done a good thing.

Maria had been dreading telling Powar what her plans were going to be. Maria had enjoyed her years in college more than anything. When she was in boarding schools she hadn't had a friend like Powar, who could draw her out. She'd just "read" her way through her childhood, never able to figure out why she couldn't go home. Had it been something she'd done? She kept trying to get good grades so maybe then her mother might see her. The letters from her mother had been beautiful, but they never went so far as to welcome her into her life. She knew her mother lived in a grand house where she worked, but that was about it, and she knew she had no brothers or sisters. She never had a pet to grow up with, so she'd started a bear collection. Her favorite was a very soft beige furry bear with sensitive eyes named Edgar, who went everywhere with her and sat on her bed in the sorority every day she was in college. He was the best friend she ever had, until Powar King had come along. Maria had loved her energy from the moment she'd met her. To Powar, life was fun, and she lived it to the fullest. It was something that Maria needed to learn, and she was happy to go on the "ride" with her. Maria was somewhat aware of her looks. She knew a five-foot-eight-inch Eurasian girl with long black hair and hazel eyes was not your average-looking girl. She just never focused on it. It must have been fate to run into Powar, because her world crossed Maria's and they might never have known about each other. She respected how Powar kept her distance when it came to discussing Maria's family. Maria trusted Powar and wanted to confide in her. She had always missed having a sister in her life. She sensed that that was the way Powar felt as well.

Maria could hear Powar's T-bird as it flew into her parking space. Powar came into the room, and they almost shouted each other's names at the same time.

"Maria! The greatest thing has happened. I have a job! I'm going into television."

"What happened? That's great," said Maria. Powar went on to tell her about her meeting with Falk, and Maria was thrilled for her.

"We're growing up, aren't we, Powar?" said Maria.

"Isn't it wonderful?" said Powar. "There's so much I want to do." Then in a more subdued mood, "But it's going to be strange leaving here, Maria. I had the best time with you." A few seconds passed, and they just looked at each other. There were tears in Powar's eyes. "We have to keep seeing each other. But where are you going to be?"

Maria swallowed and then started in. "I have a job, too,

Powar. I'm going to be right here in Los Angeles writing for *Hollywood Newsday*." Maria could see Powar fighting the mixed emotions.

Powar put her arms around her and said, "Maria, I'm worried. I know it's a good writing job for you, but I don't trust Nathan. We haven't discussed him because I just felt you didn't want to hear me. You still don't, but I wouldn't feel like a friend if I didn't tell you my concerns."

Maria pulled away. "Can't you just be happy for me? It's one of the most powerful papers in town."

"Maria, that's not what we're talking about and you know it," continued Powar. "What exactly did he offer you? I want to know."

Maria replied indignantly, "A bungalow at his house to live in, two hundred and fifty dollars a week salary, and he promised me my own column within six months. I'd be crazy not to take it."

"You're going to live at his house?" said Powar, her voice rising. "You can't do that. Don't you know what he does? He makes women slaves. We can't agree to those kinds of arrangements anymore. We have to fight for our rights."

"I don't blame you for not getting it," said Maria. "But as my friend you have to trust me. We each fight for what we want in our own ways. You'll see. I'll be okay." She put her hands on Powar's shoulders and said, "Please, just trust me."

Powar could say no more. "When are you leaving?" she asked.

"Friday," said Maria.

Maria was surprised how quickly she could pack four years of her life into a car. When the car pulled up, the butler took it and brought her things to her bungalow. She'd dreaded a scene with her mother upon her arrival and was surprised no one was there to greet her. The bungalow had been redone all in tones of gray. There was a carpet of subtle squares of light and dark gray with light gray walls. In the corner there was a French day bed made out of iron, which was painted gray and covered with a gray satin spread. Across from the granite fireplace was a couch that consisted of overstuffed gray flannel pillows. The bungalow was only one large room and a bathroom, and it looked beautiful. Maria was very touched. Within seconds of her stepping inside, Nathan was upon her. She could feel his presence even before seeing him.

"Do you like it?" he asked.

"It's gorgeous. Thank you very much," replied Maria.

"How gorgeous?" asked Nathan as he came closer.

"Very," answered Maria as she pressed her body to his and threw her arms around him. Nathan kissed her so hard that she nearly choked on his tongue.

"Meet me at seven in the dining room," he said. And then he left.

Mei-Ling was still nowhere to be found, and Maria thought she should not bring it up. When it was seven, she walked to the dining room. Nathan preferred to have drinks sitting at the head of the table rather than in a cocktail area of the house. Maria remained standing.

"Sit," he said, indicating the head of the table opposite him.

Maria obeyed. Just then the door to the kitchen opened and Mei-Ling appeared with the salads. Maria was startled to see her mother serving. She knew Nathan used her for dinner parties, but this particular situation was appalling. Maria felt her mother's anger and embarrassment and Nathan's enjoyment of the scene. She knew there was nothing that could be done about it right away, but there would be a different plan in the future. Maria knew that she was not strong enough to deal with her Nathan obsession yet, but she was strong enough to know that the obsession went both ways in this case.

After working a few weeks at the paper, Maria knew that she was really hooked. There was no comparison to the *Daily Trojan*. This paper made a difference to thousand and thousands of people, and whatever she wrote had a real impact.

The offices were in a building that had been a barbershop in the thirties. In fact, you could still see where the barber poles were painted over along the walls. When you walked in the door there was one huge front room completely paneled in dark wood with a fireplace that was at least five feet high. It looked like the living room in San Simeon. This room served as the reception room, and grand it was. Nathan's power was felt right from the front door. The room behind was the city room, filled with desks for reporters. The editor sat at the head of the circle of desks. Nathan, as the owner-publisher, sat upstairs in an office that looked like a living room with another fireplace and a bathroom suite. Nothing in the paper was printed without his approval, so the editor, a young man in his thirties named Wilson, ran up and down the stairs all day.

Maria loved sitting at her desk and typing along with everyone else. When they were all typing together the cacophony was music to her ears. The never-ending pulse that beat every second through that room and each body in it was addicting. She knew that good contacts were the key to success, and she was surprised to find how many people she had met at Nathan's during college came in handy now. The first weeks at the paper she put her plan into action. First, studio by studio she'd ask the head of public relations to lunch. She'd then ask to do a production story interview with the head of the studio or the VP of production, then follow that interview with a visit to at least three sets to films that were shooting. She figured that would take her at least six months, and by then she would know most of the important people at each studio plus a large number of stars and directors. The perfect place to start out would be King Pictures, of course. If Philip King would give her an interview personally, it would be page one. She decided not to consult Nathan, wanting to wait to knock his socks off with her professional prowess. What she didn't realize was that most of the powerful people in Hollywood knew that she was Nathan's and would talk to her anyway. Either way it didn't matter because she worked so hard and was so good that Nathan couldn't deny her talent.

"I just got Coppola, Puzo, and Evans to sit down for an interview," said Maria as she walked into Nathan's office four months later.

"Impossible," said Nathan. "They hate each other since *The Godfather*. No one can get them to talk to one another."

"Well, I did," said Maria.

"When was this?" asked Nathan.

"I've been working on it for weeks. The best neutral place was a bungalow at the Beverly Hills Hotel. I used your card and rented one for the day. The interview was over about forty-five minutes ago."

Nathan started to laugh.

"What's so funny, Nathan? I told you I was good. I've given you everyone from Lew Wasserman to Robert Redford. And now I've accomplished the impossible. I want my column. I delivered, now it's your turn."

"You're doing great," said Nathan. "I'll keep my word, and I told you that it would be appropriate after a certain amount of time here. Just keep up the good work. You know I take care of you very well."

True to his word, two months later the daily column "My Turn" by Maria Jong appeared on the inside front cover.

* CHAPTER 12 *

Maybe it was something about fastidious, short men. They felt they had to compensate all the time. Whatever it was, Powar did not like Timothy Foster. When she went into his office to discuss the budget, the feelings started coming as she looked around and saw green-and-camel-plaid sofas and wooden duck decoys everywhere. Here was a guy from the East Coast who tried to pretend that he wasn't in show business. King Pictures' business affairs department was crawling with men like Foster, but Philip King wisely never gave them any creative control. The fact that she was sitting in Foster's office having to fight for budgets was appalling to her, and she was convinced that this kind of management would ruin broadcasting.

"The made-for-television movie is a brilliant idea, Tim. Yes, we will deal with companies that are fiscally responsible, and yes, if they go over budget, the deficit will come out of their own pockets. But don't make them have to beg for every budget item. Everything is in the experimental stage, so you can't just arbitrarily start making up rules. Just give them the set fee and let them go. PBC is doing something innovative here, and I don't want to be stifled by you," said Powar.

"Well, young lady," said Timothy, "I'm the head of the financial area, and I have no intention of disappointing this company with inappropriate spending. You're running the creative side, under Falkner, of course, but you should deal more with the production companies I tell you. They will deliver on time."

Powar looked at the list in her hand. Spelling-Goldberg, Daniel Gerber, Levinson-Link at Universal, Fred Von Zelnick, Chuck Fries, Isenberg-Abrams, Christiansen and Rosenberg, Bill Beller, and Jameson Warren. There was not one woman producer on the list.

"This list is fine as a starter, Tim, but you know we're going to sign an exclusive deal with King Pictures, and we'll give them first crack at ideas."

Foster was squirming in his navy blue blazer with a burgundy-and-navy-striped tie. "As you wish."

Powar and Falk approached Philip King's office optimistically. Everybody knew they were going to make a deal, which was unusual for Hollywood. Yet Falk had a responsibility to his company, and so did Philip, so they had the formal meeting.

"Hello, everyone," said Philip. "Welcome. I'd like you to meet Michael Josephs, our business affairs head. It's just a formality. I thought the conference room was not necessary. Why don't we just sit around the coffee table."

"What number do you think would be fair as a commitment?" asked Falk, jumping right in.

Philip was thrown by Falk's eagerness. It was impolite to just start right in negotiating without a little pleasant conversation. "Ten would work nicely," he said, not so sure he liked Falk. "That number at one and a half million per movie would be excellent."

"As you know, Mr. King, we want you to be exclusive to PBC. But we can't anger our other suppliers. So we have to give them a few commitments," said Falk.

"That's true," Philip said. "On the other hand, by our

being exclusive to you, you are limiting where we can sell.''

"Well," said Falk. "Why don't we come up with a number that we both can agree on. What do you think, Powar?''

"I think a fair compromise would be seven movies at one and a quarter million," she said, looking at her father.

Philip smiled and said, "Agreed.''

"We'd need approval over your stories," said Falk.

"I know you have a responsibility to the broadcasting public," said Philip, "but you must agree not to be unreasonable. And if you don't like a story, we're free to sell it elsewhere.''

"Done," said Falk. "Mr. King, it has been a pleasure.''

"The pleasure is mine," said Philip as he hugged his daughter.

"Here's the rest of my plan," Powar said to Falk in his office after being at PBC a few weeks. "Mystery/horror stories, crime stories, and love stories are surefire categories in the movies, and should also work on TV. We also can do best-selling books if we can fit them into two hours. My idea is to do an announcement story in *Hollywood Newsday*. A friend of mine works there and will give us the front page. We say that we want to meet with writers, agents, and producers who might have the material we're looking for. Then, let's take well-known television stars and cast them in these movies. That way we'll have a built-in audience from the beginning. Not all of our series stars are that successful yet, so let's mix them with more successful ones from other networks to bring new viewers to our channel.''

"Powar, you're so bright it's unbelievable. I want you to go full speed on this and set up the interview for me as soon as possible," said Falk.

Powar was taken aback when Falk assumed he was going to do the interview. This was her whole campaign. She was about to learn the first lesson in network politics—how to take credit for the good things and duck the bad.

"We'll do a separate press release about the King Pictures association," said Falk. "There's no need for an interview with that yet. Trust me, Powar. I know exactly how to use the press."

The reaction to movies for television was extraordinary. Powar's office was swamped with people pitching ideas. Within three months she had a full development slate of twenty scripts being written. She and Falk would then choose which ones they would shoot. Powar also set up meetings with certain actors to see what ideas interested them. There was still a tremendous gap between movie actors and TV actors. The movie people scoffed at TV movies in the beginning, but Powar knew it would only be a matter of time before a certain subject would attract one of them to cross over to TV.

Philip introduced Powar to Joan Wimberley, a writer-producer of a hit romantic comedy for King Pictures called *Together Again*. Powar admired her work and was looking forward to meeting her. Joan was a very pretty blonde in her early thirties with a great sense of humor. She and Powar felt they shared a lot of the same values, and hit it off immediately. Joan wanted to do a movie about two women, one black and one white, working as secretaries in the same company competing for the same promotion. It would show the different problems each faced and how they could form a friendship under difficult circumstances. Powar felt it could be sold as an "event" rather than just a "woman's picture." Falk okayed it reluctantly after Powar pointed out that it would be surrounded by a movie about seven sexy women deserted in a haunted house and another that would be a ripoff of *The Poseidon Adventure*. The budget for each movie would not exceed $800,000. With the network selling advertising for $50,000 a minute, there should be a profit of $200,000 per picture. If the ratings were really successful, they would charge even more money for the advertising time.

It took almost nine months of work before PBC would air

its first movie. Naturally Falk picked *Seven Desperate Women* as the opener, complete with promos showing women in torn clothes screaming. Powar understood, though. It was crucial to get the ratings the first time out. Everybody from the other networks would be watching, and if PBC was successful, the others would soon follow. Falk had been very careful not to mix business with pleasure and hadn't asked Powar out since she'd joined the network, but he asked her to dinner at his apartment to watch the debut.

Falk lived at the Empire West, a New York–style condominium building just below the Sunset Strip. As Powar entered the building she wondered if Falk was going to be businesslike tonight. Part of her hoped he wouldn't. She had been saving herself a long time for the right man. No one in college ever deserved her, so no one ever had her. She was proud of being a virgin. She had high standards and was going to stick to them. Powar walked toward the front desk, dressed perfectly for the occasion in a black pants suit with a gray silk shirt and just the right amount of jewelry. "Powar King for Mr. Cantwell, please."

A Chinese butler opened the door to Falk's apartment, and Powar walked into a sea of beige—beige carpets, curtains, couches, chairs, tables, and lamps. The only touches of color were occasional peach pillows and fresh flowers in warm tones. Falk appeared wearing a slate-blue-and-camel-tweed blazer, slate slacks, and an open-necked powder blue shirt.

"Welcome, my dear," he said, kissing her cheek.

Powar noticed that his hand was very smooth. He led her to a den that was all leather. Not only were the couches and walls brown leather, but he even had little leather pigs to sit on. The bar was all mirrored and, of course, had leather bar stools. There were crystal dishes on the counter filled with nuts, and in the center there was a large bowl filled to the brim with caviar and two wooden spoons with two lemon wedges next to them. Hmm . . . impressive, Powar thought. The butler returned and poured two Stolis and then ran the lemon wedge around the glass. He presented them on a silver tray and left. Powar could not help but notice the extensive collection of pre-Columbian pottery. The pieces were everywhere.

"Come sit by me," said Falk as he took his place at the end of the sofa and put his feet on a pig. Powar joined him on the couch but put her feet on the floor. "How's *Friends and Foe* coming along?" asked Falk.

"I think we really have something. The script is dynamite. I'd love to get Marlo Thomas and Cicely Tyson to star in it. We both know Marlo and we could approach her personally. She's the toast of Broadway with her play right now, but when that's over I'll bet she'd like to do something prestigious in another medium. Our project is it. Cicely Tyson is hot off *Miss Jane Pittman*, and hopefully she'll be interested, too. Unfortunately her agent, Jim Bethcel, is an idiot who can barely read, but he can be taken care of."

Falk took a bite of caviar. "And what else have you observed now that you're becoming a network veteran?"

"Well, there is something else that is peculiar," said Powar.

"What?" asked Falk.

"It's about tonight's movie. It's well done and should be a ratings hit. That's not my problem. But you look at the movie and you realize that it was shot entirely in one set. There were no other locations, no exteriors, and it took place in a twenty-four-hour period so the actresses never had to change clothes. There were a few special effects and of course salaries, but I've been studying the budget compared to what's on the screen, and there's no way Bill Beller could have spent eight hundred thousand on that production."

Falk took a sip of his drink before answering. "You haven't checked overtime and meal penalties, and union overages, have you?"

"No," answered Powar.

"Well, there you go," said Falk. "Let's have dinner."

He walked her to a red-and-black-lacquered Chinese dining room where the female half of the Chinese couple started serving a lavish Chinese meal. Powar told Falk stories about Ah Fong's restaurant and her childhood, and they were having a wonderful time. He served plum wine, which Powar loved, won ton soup, hot and spicy shrimp with Yang Chow fried rice, and cashew chicken surrounded by fresh broccoli. Fresh lichee nuts were served for dessert. Powar could tell they weren't canned, and again she was impressed with Falk. My mother may be a character, thought Powar, but at least she taught me about the finer things in life.

After dinner they went into the screening room next to the den. It was filled with plush couches of burgundy velvet. The velvet theme included the walls. The room was totally soundproof. Falk had a wall-size screen that could show movies or TV shows. The butler arrived with yet another silver tray. This time two crystal champagne glasses were upon it, filled with what looked like a chocolate milkshake.

"It's a mixture of vodka, Kahlúa, cream, and ice whipped up in a blender. Try it," said Falk.

Powar thought it was really delicious. Falk turned on the set, and the newly designed PBC TV Movie graphic appeared.

"It's real! What a thrill it is to watch something you did go out to millions of people. I only wish we were leading with a quality product. I know we have to get the viewers hooked on a viewing pattern before taking chances, but isn't it sad that quality is a chance in the entertainment business?"

"Don't be so serious," chided Falk. "There's room for everything. Enjoy it all."

When the movie was over Falk's phone started ringing off the hook. Powar listened as he said, "Thank you," over and over again. She wondered if her phone was ringing, too, since she'd done most of the work.

"Well, we're a hit in this town," said Falk. "Now all we have to do is get the overnight ratings in the morning. Congratulations, Powar." He leaned over and kissed her softly at first, then, feeling her respond, he increased the pressure and moved his whole body closer to her.

Powar felt the strength of his hands on her back, and

lightning rods went through her. This is what it's supposed to be like, she thought.

Falk drew back, gazed into her blue eyes, and pushed back a strand of black hair. "Well, Ms. King."

Powar smiled back at him. "Yes?"

"Come with me." He walked her to the bedroom. It was a room fit for a prince. All the furniture was carved antiques with marble-covered tables. There was a raised fireplace and a bedroom set that looked as if it were from a medieval castle in France. There were faces carved in the headboard and footboard. The linens were exquisite, either Pratesi or Frette. He handed her a turquoise silk Fernando Sanchez robe and showed her to the bathroom.

"I'll see you in a few minutes," he said as he shut the door.

Powar found herself in a blue-and-white bathroom where the fixtures were all gold swans. There was a gigantic tub set in blue tile with a white plaster border that was so wide you could lie down across it. It looked like bathrooms in Greece. She noticed a complete set of women's toiletries on the sink. They were unused. She wondered how many times a week he replaced them. She used some mouthwash and then rubbed Dior cream all over her skin. She put her robe back on and very tentatively entered the bedroom, suddenly losing her nerve. Her fear was overcoming her excitement. She sat on the bed and felt very awkward. She noticed that the lights had been lowered and classical music was coming from somewhere.

Falk returned, wearing a black cashmere robe with satin lapels and silk tassels at the end of the sash. He had on matching black suede slippers. He was holding two more glasses of his special "milkshake" and toasted her as they took a generous sip. They put down their drinks, and he sat on the bed, just staring at her. She didn't know what to do. He gently pushed her shoulders back on the pillow and started kissing her. As soon as she felt his lips she knew it was right. Her body was melting into his, and she wasn't afraid anymore. His mouth was soft and gentle, and he used his lips a long time before she felt his tongue. He wasn't rushing her at all. His manner was flowing and almost lazy. The whole time he kept moving his hands on her back like a massage. The effect was magical. His tongue started darting in and out, more rapidly than before. Powar thought it felt like a teasing snake, and she was mesmerized by it.

He took off his robe and pushed hers away. They were skin to skin now, and she had never felt skin like his. It was softer than hers. He moved slowly all over her as if to touch every pore with his own. He started kissing her all over, continuing to use his tongue like a snake. Powar loved being treated like a baby in this way. She felt his lips float all over her and then remain sensuously between her legs. He felt like moving velvet. She really wanted him. She could feel her body getting very warm. It was almost burning. Powar could no longer feel the top of her head because she couldn't think anymore. She had lost control, something she had never done in her whole life. She felt him push gently inside her, felt him sense that she wasn't that experienced. It hurt a little bit at first, which triggered her mind back to reality. But in the next second the hurt went away and she was seized with the most delirious feeling she had ever felt. She let loose with a fury and started to writhe.

"Grab me. Tighten your thighs and move more," said Falk.

Her senses heightened even more. Her legs were numb and her arms were floating. Her heart was in her throat, and she started to cry.

She didn't want to act like a little girl in front of him, but she couldn't help it.

When Powar walked into her apartment the next morning and called her answering service, there were messages galore for her. It made her soar. She decided to return Maria's call first.

"So you really liked it?" asked Powar.

"Didn't you see your review?" Maria asked. "I fixed it so 'commercial' didn't sound like a dirty word. I concentrated more on the genius idea of movies made for television. Why don't we have lunch at Musso's next week to celebrate? I have my own table there now."

"Musso's?" said Powar. "I don't know. My mother still goes there a lot. On the other hand, I think I like it. Let's go on Wednesday. I want her to see this. She didn't even call to congratulate me, but then why do I keep hoping for the impossible? My father sent flowers. I'll see you Wednesday."

Powar was a little nervous about seeing Falk at the office. She had never been in this kind of situation before and wasn't sure how people behaved. She made up her mind to be thoroughly professional and just see how he played it. When they ran into each other in the hall, his smile told her he remembered everything. She wished she were having lunch with him today instead of a boring business meeting with the man in charge of the nuts-and-bolts production at Bill Beller's company. She knew she had to do it since their first collaboration was very successful, but Fred Grossblatt just rubbed her the wrong way. He was probably just going to ask her for a multiple deal because they'd turned out a winner for PBC and had successful track records at the other networks. He just did not have a creative mind. It was simply one of those necessary lunches.

She'd set the meeting at La Scala in Beverly Hills. At least she knew the food would make her happy. You could always trust a chopped salad and a mozzarella marinara to get you through the day. She was the first to arrive and delighted to run immediately into Andy Stromberg. He jumped up so fast when he saw her that he nearly knocked over the table.

"Powar, I'm so happy to see you! I was going to call you this afternoon to tell you my good news. I rewrote one of my scripts into a play and it's been optioned for Broadway. Can you believe it!"

"Oh, Andy, I'm so happy for you. It's what you've always

wanted," said Powar. They hugged soundly, almost jumping up and down together like two kids. Powar then looked down to see the young woman sitting in the booth with Andy. She was not happy at being ignored.

"Powar, I'd like you to meet Franny Melton." Gazing up at Powar was a woman somewhere in her early thirties, a little older than Andy, with a slightly pinched face. She wasn't unattractive, she just didn't make a particular visual statement. She had curly brown hair and weak, darting eyes that she kept trying to focus on Andy. Smiling her most sincere smile, Powar shook hands with Franny and commented on what a lovely occasion this was.

"I'll call you this afternoon," said Andy.

Fred Grossblatt soon joined her at her booth. He was a little overweight and dressed in clothes that were too loud for a person of his size. As he talked, Powar noted that a little trail of sweat was forming on his upper lip. She just wanted the lunch to be over, but she knew she should strike some sort of deal with him. She was having a hard time paying attention to what he was saying. First of all it was boring, but second, her eyes kept going back to Andy and Franny. She was really happy for him, but she couldn't shake the ominous feeling about that woman. It was unnerving.

"Powar, are you listening?" asked Fred. "I just proposed a four-picture deal to you and you didn't respond."

"I'm sorry, Fred. I don't mean to be rude. I'm concerned about a friend of mine. You have my full attention now, I assure you."

"Look," said Fred. "You've been at the network almost a year now. You've had wonderful success and you're making some good deals. If you say yes to us or any production company, you put a lot of money in our pockets."

"Frankly, Fred, I've never thought of it that way. I just want to get the best product on the screen, and the network gives you the budget to do that. If you go over, you have to pay out of your own pocket," said Powar.

"That's true," said Fred, "but how many companies go

over? Some do, but some don't, yet each time we make a movie we ask you to give us a larger budget.''

"What's your point?'' asked Powar, who was getting a bit annoyed.

"My point is that you're a salaried employee on a fixed income who has the power to make other people very wealthy. Don't you know how PBC is run?'' he asked.

"Obviously I don't know whatever you're about to tell me, and I wish you'd get on with it.''

"Relax,'' answered Fred. "It's time you really learned about the business. Several of your cohorts over there are being rewarded for their efforts.''

Powar just looked at him.

"Take Marvin Lewis in daytime programming. His fee is ten thousand dollars for a series commitment, five thousand for a pilot, and five hundred a week for every week the show airs.''

Powar was so stunned that she just kept her mouth shut.

"We have a couple of people in nighttime series as well who get even more money. And don't think your area is so clean. When we get a licensing fee we take one hundred thousand right off the top for a TV movie. I'd like to offer you fifteen thousand out of our cut each time you give us a movie to make. We'll set up an account for you at a bank we use. Just let us know what dummy corporation names you want to use and we'll put it in motion.''

Powar had to use every muscle in her body not to show her anger. She was appalled and shocked. "Fred, this has been a fascinating conversation. I'll consider everything you've told me and I'll let you have an answer as soon as possible,'' she said.

"Good,'' replied Fred. "Why shouldn't everybody be happy?''

Powar drove back to the network as fast as she could. She wanted Beller and Grossblatt prosecuted, along with the PBC employees Fred named. She would not be associated with anything illegal.

"Nancy, I need to see Falkner immediately. It's urgent."

Miss Hobson buzzed Falk and passed along Powar's message.

"Have her come in," he said.

Powar burst into the office and told him everything that had happened. Her adrenaline was running on overdrive, and Falk could sense it. "Here's my plan," Powar said angrily. "I want to call Fred Grossblatt tomorrow and tell him I'll take him up on his deal. I want him to set up an account, and when I get the very first check we can turn it over to the police and clean this place out."

Falk got up and put his hands on her shoulders. "Calm down. This is dangerous information. We are a vulnerable network and don't want a scandal. Under no circumstances are you to tell Fred Grossblatt anything other than to decline his offer. Do that tomorrow. What I want you to do right now is go back to your office and write a memo to me describing everything that you've learned today. Don't make any copies of it. Bring it back to me and I'll lock it up in my safe. Once you see me do that you are never to mention this incident again. Is that clear?"

Powar had never seen Falk so quietly focused. She hadn't thought about the damage that could be done to the company if this got out. "Yes, of course. I completely understand," said Powar. "I should be back with the memo in about an hour."

"Don't worry," said Falk. "In time I'll see that certain executives are removed quietly."

When Powar left the room Falk picked up the phone. "Timothy, it's me. Dissolve the Bainbridge Corporation immediately and transfer the money to Williamson in the Caymans under the Trilogy account."

Powar thought going to Musso's would relieve some of the tension of the week. King Pictures was such a clean company, it was unnerving for her to discover the PBC situation.

Maria was waiting for her at the front door. It was no accident that Maria's table was right next to Honey's. They were the two best tables in the place—the booths against the left wall in the middle of the restaurant. Honey was very surprised to see Powar and got up to kiss her cheek. Too many years had gone by for Ellen and Kate and Sheila and Penny not to have noticed the lack of relationship between mother and daughter. Powar said hello to all of them and noted to herself that they were aging well.

"Congratulations on your movies, Powar," said Ellen. "You're quite a hit."

"Thank you very much. I appreciate hearing it," said Powar to Ellen as she looked at her mother.

"Well, Powar, you know your father and I have always been proud of you. This is what we expected to happen," said Honey. "And how are you, Maria? I enjoy your column very much. Nathan has always been one of my favorite people."

Maria smiled and nodded as she and Powar sat down in the next booth. "You inherited a lot of your mother's brains and instinct," she said to Powar.

"I don't want to hear that," said Powar.

"That's ridiculous," said Maria. "There are so many morons in this town you should be grateful for brains wherever they come from."

Powar noticed there was more of an edge to Maria since she'd gone to work at the paper.

"There are so many people who are out for themselves, you just can't stand by and play it the regular way. Do you know that the editor before the one we have now repeatedly took one hundred dollars from press agents under the table to give a story the page one banner headline? Do you know why he did it? Because it's supposed to be such an honor to be a reporter or have a column that the papers can get away with paying you almost nothing. And we all do that because we want the exposure and the power. The poor editor couldn't feed his children. That's why he took the money. Luckily I'm not in that position.''

"We're all in some sort of position, Maria," said Powar.

Maria decided not to pursue that avenue of conversation anymore. She had her own plan for Nathan within the next two years, and Powar would see it in due time.

When Powar came back from lunch Andy Stromberg was waiting for her in the lobby. "You never called me after we ran into each other," said Powar. "I'm glad you're here. Come in. Please hold my calls, Mara," said Powar as she led Andy inside her office. "What's happening? You look a little funny."

"The backers pulled out of my play," he said.

"Oh, I'm so sorry. That's a terrible break. Do you think you can find some new ones?"

"I'm going to try. I quit my job because I thought I was going to New York. Would you like to go out and have some ice cream or something?" Powar thought he looked so upset that she couldn't resist him.

"Sure, let's go," she said.

They went to Wil Wright's on the Sunset Strip. "Don't you just love how the ice cream sticks to the roof of your mouth?" asked Powar as she licked a double vanilla cone.

"Of course I do. It's the butterfat. Wil Wright's uses more of it than Baskin Robbins, or any other place, for that matter," explained Andy.

"I have an idea," said Powar, changing the subject completely. "You have a great mind for story. My father is always looking for help in the story department at the studio." Andy interrupted her. "I didn't come to you today for a job. All I wanted was ice cream."

"I believe you, but why not do it? It's perfect. You help my father and get paid while you're looking for backers. I know it's only temporary. We both get something out of it. I'll set up the appointment. That's what friends do for each other.

"So tell me about Franny," she said.

"She's very attentive and organized. She cares for me a great deal," said Andy.

Powar thought she would not ask the next obvious question but leave well enough alone.

* CHAPTER 13 *

Maria loved going on Vegas junkets, and in the three years she'd been going, the drill was always the same. Whichever press agent was handling the star of the night would simply arrange for a limousine to pick her up at the office and take her to the airport, where she'd board a plane, usually chartered, reserved for the press, celebrities, and VIPs flying up.

At the hotel she would check into one of the best rooms of the house, everything courtesy of the hotel, of course . . . everything but the gambling. That was fine with Maria. She hated gambling, never understanding the concept of risking money you already had to probably lose it in search of more. She remembered the last time she'd been up in Vegas for Connie Stevens's opening at the Flamingo-Hilton; she and Connie had gone to play together after the show.

"This table looks good," said Connie, the focus of every guy in the place with her cascading blonde hair and her rhinestone-studded one-piece body suit. It was about two A.M., and she had just finished two smash shows in the main room. "C'mon, Maria, I'm in the mood to celebrate. I want you to play," said Connie as she handed her a fistful of $500 chips.

"I can't do it, Connie. For one thing it's your money, but for another it's too hard for me to take."

"Then let's get some champagne and you can watch," Connie replied. "Maybe you'll feel like it later."

As soon as they sat down at the blackjack table a crowd came around. Connie put $1,000 worth of chips in her square. She got two cards facedown. Maria looked over her shoulder and saw that she had sixteen, a difficult hand. The dealer showed a queen. Connie doubled her money and said, "Hit me." Maria thought she was going to throw up right there. Connie got lucky with a four. The dealer hit with a ten and went over. Connie got almost $5,000 back.

"Isn't this fun? I knew you'd like it," said Connie.

"Right," said Maria, almost choking on her champagne.

Connie told the dealer to let it ride. On the next hand she lost it all and didn't care. She and Maria went to the coffee shop, where Connie rounded up some of her band members.

"Okay, guys, let's go!" she said.

"Now what are you doing?" asked Maria.

"We're going on our desert run."

"What's that?" continued Maria.

"You'll see," Connie said.

With that they all went out into the parking lot and got into a rented van with a huge moon roof. They drove for an hour directly out into the desert. The van parked in the middle of nowhere, and somebody took out a portable tape machine and started playing jazz tapes. They all lay back in the van and watched the stars until the sun came up. Maria loved it.

Tonight's opening at the Las Vegas Hilton was for Ann-Margret, who was represented by one of Maria's favorite press agents, Dick Grant of Rogers and Cowan. She loved to go to Vegas and hang out with him because he had such a biting sense of humor and he loved to have fun. This was Ann-Margret's first live appearance since the terrible accident she'd had in Lake Tahoe when she'd fallen from a ladder and crushed one side of her face. Maria had met her originally when one of her TV specials was airing and she'd gone to her house for an interview. Ann-Margret and her husband, Roger Smith, lived in the old Humphrey Bogart–Lauren Bacall home off Benedict Canyon. It was up a private road and looked like a Connecticut farmhouse.

Ann-Margret and Roger explained that they loved to live in a place that let them escape from Hollywood. Ann-Margret had been very shy and nervous during the interview, but Maria could tell she was a sweet person with a strong core of inner strength.

When Maria checked into her room she started to laugh. Dick Grant had promised her a surprise, and he'd stuck to it. Her room was a junior suite decorated all in red velvet. Even the walls were flocked in it. The four-poster bed was on a platform and enclosed by sheer red organdy drapes, and the ceiling over the bed was all mirror. If the occupant chose to roll out of bed on the right side, he or she had better be careful. Just two feet from the bed was a raised round bathtub, six feet in diameter, with cherubs on the wall that would spit water into it if you pressed the right button. There was also champagne and fruit from the hotel and flowers from Ann-Margret and Roger. These amenities were very thoughtful, but Maria was so used to getting this treatment by now that she almost didn't notice them.

Maria was the queen of *Hollywood Newsday*. The paper had done a reader survey and found out that 85 percent of their readers turned to her column first in the morning. Her haul last Christmas was so gigantic that she'd had to hire a moving van to get the presents home. Whenever she went to a play or nightclub she was in the front. Movies and TV shows were screened privately for her. It got to be that she wouldn't even grant an interview to someone who was pushing a movie or TV show if she hadn't seen it or at least read the script so she knew it was good. She was tough, but she was bright and she'd earned the respect of the town. Her only blind spot was in thinking that no one knew about her personal life. Everyone knew, but because she was so good at what she did, they never thought of her as somebody's bimbo.

After she unpacked she went to the health club and had a massage. The show was a dinner show, but the food was so bad nobody ate there except the public. Maria was going to have dinner with Roger and Ann-Margret's co-manager, Allan Carr, a real character. He was very grand and entertaining and very smart, and he had a great eye for talent and knowing what to do with it. They went to the Bacchanal Room at Caesar's Palace, the most luxurious room on the Strip, where the waitresses were dressed in togas and every man at the table was massaged by these women in between courses. Maria found all of this very sexist and wasn't in the greatest mood.

"Isn't Powar King a friend of yours?" asked Allan Carr.

"Sure. We went to college together," Maria replied.

"Falk Cantwell is trying to use Powar to get close to Ann-Margret. He wants to take her specials away from NBC. I think it might be interesting to work a tie-in with King Pictures so Roger and I can produce. Do you think Powar might talk to her father about that?" asked Allan.

"She won't do it unless you come produce for her at PBC. She's as smart as you, Allan. Maybe even smarter," said Maria, laughing at the expression on Allan's face.

After dinner they went into the showroom and sat at the best table in the room, the center booth in the first row of booths behind the long tables. Ann-Margret got a standing ovation as she came out on stage. The act was great, with home movies, motorcycles, and fourteen dancers doing a special number, "I Love Being a Dancer in Ann-Margret's Act." It was a triumph. The hotel gave her a party in a private penthouse, and people were pushing and shoving to get in.

"You were awful, just awful," said Don Rickles as he entered the room. "But not bad for an immigrant."

"Gee, Don," said Maria, "may I quote you for my column?"

"Of course, inscrutable one." He bowed. "Gotta go," he said as he spotted Debbie Reynolds and George Burns coming in the front door.

Maria grabbed a martini and walked around, listening to bits of conversation. "Do you think Ann-Margret's going to be charged back for this food?" said one guy.

"Her face looks great," said Joan Rivers, a comedienne from New York who was becoming the hottest opening act in town. "I want the name of her surgeon for later."

Maria stayed for about an hour before she decided she'd had her fill of people giving her stories. She walked back to her room, thinking it was a great life and she wanted as much as there was to get, but there was one thing she still didn't have, and it was time.

It was time she took her rightful place alongside Nathan. She was tired of being just a guest at his parties. She was well known and powerful enough in her own right to stand up to whatever anyone might say. So without clearing it with Nathan, she orchestrated a dinner party for Burt Silverberg, the president of CBS. She put together a power list that included Falk and Powar, Leonard and Wendy Goldberg, Valerie Harper and Dick Schaal, Mary Tyler Moore and Grant Tinker, and Carol Burnett and Joe Hamilton. Burt would enjoy seeing his stars, and Powar and Falk would love the chance to get to know them even better. The group would make for interesting conversation and clever moves.

Maria and her mother had long given up the pretense of trying not to pretend there was a changing of the guard. Mei-Ling had just accepted it and hoped she'd have a better life in her next incarnation.

"I need to confirm the menu with you for tonight, Mother," said Maria. Mei-Ling looked up at her with disdain, and Maria tried not to notice. Her mother was receiving good care, and that was that.

"Do you remember that recipe Hope Smith gave to Powar and me? It was done with New York steak where you dip it in olive oil and seasoned bread crumbs and garlic and cook it in a skillet?" Maria asked.

"Yes," answered Mei-Ling.

"Good," said Maria. "I need it for fourteen people. Burt

and Nathan love steak. Let's have scalloped potatoes, steamed asparagus, and butter lettuce and tomato salad. Put a creamy French dressing on the salad and make lemon pie for dessert. This is a real American group. Serve the burgundy with dinner. And I'll be upstairs if you need me."

Maria had simply told Nathan he needed to be home that evening by six P.M., and he'd been too busy to ask her why. But when he came home and saw the dinner table being set and all the preparations for a party, he got upstairs as fast as he could. "What's going on here?" he demanded.

"Why don't you come in and find out?" said Maria in a low tone.

The sight of her stopped him cold. She was now a far cry from the inexperienced girl in the Japanese bathhouse, and he was constantly amazed at her ability to get to him. She was wearing a Catholic girls' school uniform, a navy blue jumper with a white cotton long-sleeved blouse, navy-and-white saddle shoes, and white bobby socks. The initials *OMGC* were on the breast pocket. Her black hair was in a ponytail.

"Mr. Headmaster, Sister sent me to you. She said I was misbehaving in class," Maria said with a straight face.

"What did you do, young lady?" asked Nathan in a stern tone.

"I talked back to Sister," Maria confessed, highly amused by Nathan's fantasy games.

"That requires serious punishment. No student here is ever allowed to talk back to the teacher. Come here." Nathan sat down on the couch in her dressing room and patted his knees.

Maria walked to him slowly. She dropped to her knees. "Oh, sir," she "sobbed." "Please don't punish me. I'm not a bad girl. I didn't mean to do what I did. I'm so sorry that I gave away my rosary beads. I know that they were blessed by Father Johnson and given to our late Reverend Mother before I was lucky enough to earn them."

"You are bad, Maria, very bad," replied Nathan. "You are in this office repeatedly for these kinds of lapses. I think that we have to put an end to this behavior once and for all. Get up on my lap. You know what to do.'' Maria stepped back and took off the outer garments of her ''uniform.''

"Continue, young lady," said Nathan.

Maria hesitated. "No, sir. This isn't right. You must be reported to the bishop."

"How dare you be insolent to me?" screamed Nathan. He jumped off his chair and charged toward her. He pushed her to the ground and roughly shoved her slip up around her neck.

Maria felt his teeth between her legs. "You're hurting me," she yelled. She slapped him on top of his head to stop her pain. The game was getting out of hand.

"Hurting you? *This* is hurting you!" he said as he virtually skewered her with his now too ample "equipment." His hands grabbed her face to keep her from screaming. He was ramming her repeatedly, but then he felt something happen. He saw her start to crave it.

Maria arched her body and begged for more. She wrapped her legs around him like a vise to keep him deep inside. They rode each other until she screamed rapturously.

She felt herself get hot and start to tingle, and that feeling spread like thousands of shooting needles throughout her body. As she went over the top her arms went numb.

Nathan was fully spent and remained inside her as the two lay exhausted on the floor.

"Nathan?" whispered Maria. There was no response. He was still off somewhere. "Nathan," she said again.

He grunted.

She leaned in closer. "I'm pregnant. You will marry me in two weeks. We'll make the announcement at dinner tonight." And then she got up and left him sitting there with his pants askew.

She walked into her dressing room, pleased with herself. Everything was working according to plan. Deep down in her soul she knew that Nathan wanted children. That was really the key to him. He never admitted it to her, but she had overheard him talking to Schenck at one point, worrying about who would run his empire long after he was gone. Schenck had two children whom Nathan cared about a great deal. While marrying was never one of the goals, Maria knew he wanted a son to carry his name. Anyone who had his name on a masthead and lived in a house as big as the White House wanted to leave something behind. Maria wanted a part of that, and getting pregnant was the answer.

The guests were in the library, sampling the Petrossian pâtés on the hors d'oeuvres table when Nathan and Maria entered the room. They looked perfect. She had on a black strapless taffeta hostess jumpsuit, and he had on a gray cashmere smoking jacket and black pants. Maria had bought it for him a while back, and he rarely wore it. She thought it was interesting that he'd chosen to put it on tonight. Maria was delighted to see Powar first. "Where's Falk?" she said, embracing her.

"He had to go to a last minute meeting. He was really upset that he couldn't make it, but he told me to hold down the fort. He'll be sorry he wasn't here. I see what you were trying to do," added Powar, looking over at Carol Burnett and Mary Tyler Moore talking to each other.

"Let me introduce you," said Maria. She took Powar over to Carol and Mary. Much to Powar's surprise, they both complimented her on her movies at PBC.

"I think what you're doing is excellent," said Mary. "It will upgrade television."

"Needless to say," added Powar, "if either one of you has a favorite novel or original idea that you would like to do, I wish you'd call me. We would be honored to work with you."

Just then Burt Silverberg joined them. He put one arm around Carol and the other over Mary's shoulders and smiled at Powar. "Are you enjoying getting to know my 'girls,' Powar?" he said territorially.

"Absolutely," said Powar, "They're terrific women. Don't worry. I know they're your series stars, but it's okay if they do a movie for me. I know you won't mind." Powar smiled genuinely as she walked away. She didn't dislike Burt at all. She thought he was a brilliant programmer and showman, but this was business, and she would simply love PBC to do a movie with Carol and Mary.

Dinner was served, and Powar was seated between Burt and Grant Tinker. That made her very happy. Maria and Nathan were at the two heads. Powar could never bring herself to do something that stupid.

Maria noticed that Nathan was being unusually quiet, but it didn't matter because the guests were engaged in a debate over whether or not hour-long dramas were on the wane in favor of half-hour situation comedies.

"The point is that the half-hour vehicle is cheaper to produce and has a better syndication life," said Burt. "It's all economics."

"What about quality and the network's responsibility to provide good programming for people?" asked Powar.

The group stopped talking to wait for Burt's answer. Nathan tapped on his wine glass with his knife instead. All eyes went to him, including Maria's. "I have an announcement to make. My darling Maria and I are getting married in two weeks. To Maria," said he, raising his glass while the others did the same.

Maria heard a crash in the kitchen and hoped her mother hadn't dropped the lemon pie.

Powar suddenly felt abandoned, upset that her friend hadn't confided in her. She knew that Maria knew she wasn't thrilled with Nathan, but Powar could now see the advantages. It wasn't a choice she would make for herself, Powar thought, but she came from a different background from Maria, and their years together as friends had made her understand that growing up without a family made Maria's needs different from hers. She looked around the table and realized she missed Falk. She had tried not to let the idea of marriage get into her head. Her opinion on marriage was soured by seeing her parents' unhappiness, but she couldn't help wondering what a good one would be like. She and Falk were perfect for each other. She had never felt things before the way she felt them when she was with him. Now all she wanted to do was leave the party and be with him. Hearing about Maria's plans made her long for some permanency in her life, and she was taken aback by the strength of these desires. They never were in her head before . . . or so she thought. As soon as people went into the living room for after-dinner drinks, Powar told Maria that she needed to leave.

"Please don't think I'm rude. I just need to do something for myself right now. I'm very happy for you if this marriage is what you want. You know I love you."

"I understand . . . and thank you, thank you," Maria whispered as she hugged Powar.

Powar drove to the Empire West as fast as she could without getting a ticket. The doorman took her car and waved to her. It was eleven P.M., and her arrival was a little later than usual, but the man at the desk just pressed the button to release the elevator to her without calling ahead. He knew her so well that it wasn't necessary. Powar felt good that these people accepted her as Falk's other half, and she started fantasizing on what it would be like to live here full-time as Mrs. Falkner Cantwell. Powar King Cantwell, she thought. She rang the bell, and the houseman let her in.

"They're in the dining room," he said, and disappeared.

Powar thought, *"They're?"* not *"He's"*? She decided to approach the room cautiously. She didn't know where the strong feelings of trouble came over her, but she could barely breathe. She was very careful not to let her heels tap the marble. She tiptoed to the area of huge ficus trees at the entrance of the dining room. It was possible to see in the room if you went behind the trees and looked through. Powar heard women's voices as she slipped in behind the trees. She looked around the room and saw five women sitting on chairs in a circle; a sixth chair was not occupied. They were having drinks and were very well-dressed. They seemed to be of varying ages, having a wonderful time. Falk was nowhere to be found. Powar recognized her mother's friend Ellen, which surprised her. She didn't know Ellen knew Falk.

Suddenly a woman in a flower print dress stood up and said, "Who's next?"

"I am, honey," said Ellen as she got up off the chair and lay right down on the floor.

Powar could not believe what she was watching. She had no idea what was going to happen or what kind of game they were playing. The woman in the print dress with a very low-slung wide belt didn't seem to be as refined as the other guests. She walked toward the area where Ellen was on the floor and lowered herself on top of her, flinging Ellen's legs almost over her head! The woman on top began thrusting wildly and screaming in a high-pitched tone. This is the sickest thing I have ever seen, thought Powar.

She wanted to leave, but she just couldn't understand what this had to do with Falk. She was totally dumbfounded. Her feet became unglued, carrying her into the dining room as fast as she could go.

"What's going on here?" she screamed.

The woman in the print dress jumped off Ellen and looked in Powar's direction in shock. As she did that, Powar's eyes couldn't help but go to the red rubber dildo strapped onto the belt. She was speechless as her eyes made the one-second jump to the face of bewigged, bejeweled Falkner Cantwell. Powar felt the blood drain out of her as she stumbled out of the room.

The ladies were stunned into silence and tried to get out of the room as fast as possible themselves without running into Powar downstairs. Falk was left alone, shaking. He pushed a button, and a panel in the mirror over the buffet slid back, revealing a video camera. He switched it off, then walked over and dialed a phone number.

"You stupid idiot!" said Honey, exploding completely. "You've ruined everything."

"Don't give me that attitude," Falk snarled. "I'm the one

who's been taking all the risk with these little blackmail evidence sessions for you. I'm the one who's out front!''

''Right,'' Honey snapped. ''And you're the one who loves this little 'pleasure game,' Falk, so don't tell me you've been put upon. We've been having these get-togethers for ages without a hitch, and the first stranger who walks in has to be Powar?''

''Listen, lady, I did everything you wanted. I gave your daughter a job. I slept with her so you could even control that part of her life,'' Falk screamed. ''I told you everything that was going on between King Pictures and PBC. Believe me, I earned everything you think you gave me.''

She was calm again and ice cold. ''Remember who has the tapes, honey.''

As she hung up Falkner knew he was no match for this one.

The next morning Honey was still angry. She looked over at the empty pillow next to hers. Just for a second she wondered what had happened to them. They had been young and so much in love. Ready to have happy, fulfilled lives. Yet they had delivered publicly and financially. She didn't dare allow herself to wonder if the trade-off was worth it. Owning King Pictures and Hollywood itself would do nicely. As long as he showed up at her parties and kept King Pictures on track, she would be happy. She got up and went to her dressing room to call Falk.

''How are you this morning?'' she asked.

''Coping,'' said Falk. ''I'm not looking forward to the office this morning for obvious reasons.''

''Nonsense, dear,'' said Honey. ''Just remember all the contingencies we discussed at the beginning, and you'll know what to do.''

At ten A.M. Falk arrived at the office wearing a navy blue suit and vest, white shirt, and navy foulard tie. ''Call Timothy Foster and Powar King and ask them to be in my office in one hour.''

A shiver went through Powar when she got the message. What was he going to pull? she thought. He certainly wouldn't want to rub her the wrong way. If he were smart, he'd give her a new title plus a raise to keep her mouth shut. She had a contract, so that wasn't a problem. She wondered if he could break it. He probably could, but she'd break him first. She sat back on her chair and tried to think of things she'd learned about corporate policy just by listening to her parents at the dinner table for years. She was deep in thought when her intercom buzzed.

"Powar, this is Timothy. I just received an unusual message from Falkner. Are you aware that there's a meeting called for eleven?"

Relief came over Powar. If Timothy were there, how bad could it be? she thought. "Yes, I'm aware of it," she answered. "I'll meet you in your office at five to and we'll go in together."

Powar had been up all night "on the tiles." She was so sick, it was worse than food poisoning. Every fluid in her body had erupted with disgust. She swore to herself she would never be this hurt again. She had dressed well that morning. It was time for the Chanel suit with matching Chanel shoes and handbag with a silk blouse. She looked like one of her mother's friends about to have lunch at the Bistro, and she thought that would make Falk crazy, since he certainly seemed to be involved with that type. It was Powar's perverse pleasure trip. She was glad she was going to see him today. She just had to keep from killing him, that's all.

She was right on time to meet Timothy, and off they went. Falk's seven-foot door was closed tight. Miss Hobson opened it immediately when she saw them coming. Falk was seated behind the desk in his best chairman of the board pose. He rose when they entered.

"Good morning, all. Please be seated. We are here today to talk about a special project. Every once in a while something comes along that requires attention from executives in the company who wouldn't ordinarily deal with that area. For some time now I have been looking for a show to go five days a week that will revolutionize daytime television."

Powar couldn't believe that he'd just launched into his speech without even looking at her. She thought he must be made of ice.

"I needed something different from just game shows and soaps," he continued. "I believe the housewife at home needs to have an entertaining fantasy every day that takes her away from her chores. If you were ironing in Omaha in a snowstorm, wouldn't you just love it if you could go to Hawaii every day for thirty minutes? Of course you would." He wasn't waiting for answers. He just kept talking while Powar stared right through him.

Powar had no idea where this conversation was going, but whatever "vision" he had, she felt certain the timing of it was not accidental.

"I've contacted Bill Beller. Before he did TV movies he was a great variety show producer. Six weeks from now we are going to be on the air live every day from Hawaii with a thirty-minute variety show starring Eddie Wing! I'm sure you know him from your trips to Hawaii. He is like the Hawaiian Tom Jones. The women love him."

"What women?" asked Powar. Falk ignored her.

Powar knew who Eddie Wing was. When she was a teenager and her parents took her to Hawaii a few times, she saw his show. She thought he was repulsive.

"Falk, I have a real problem with this," Powar interrupted. "I think your idea of a variety show from Hawaii is interesting, but you have to get another host who is more contemporary . . . like Helen Reddy! Her song 'I Am Woman' is number one, and she's right in tune with the times."

"This is a done deal," Falk replied "The contracts have been signed, the budget has been approved, and everything's a 'go.' Sets are being built as we speak. Powar, you're the best person at this network to oversee the initial production with your theater and show background. You leave in forty-eight hours to go to Hawaii for the next two months. Get this thing on the air and on its feet, and you can come home after two weeks of air shows. Timothy and I will run the movie division during this temporary period. I know how vested you are in the overall success of PBC, and we need your help now. You've worked with Beller's company before, and he and Fred Grossblatt are there waiting for you. Aloha." He stood up and waited for them to leave the room.

Powar didn't talk to Timothy. She just turned and went straight to her office. So Falk was going to play it this way? Okay. He's going to get it from both barrels as soon as I'm ready, she thought.

"Andy Stromberg on line one, Miss King," said Mara.

"Oh, Andy, I can't believe you called just now. We have to talk," said Powar.

"I did it this time, Powar," said Andy. "Through some producers I met at the studio I met some new backers for New York. This time it's the Nederlanders, and it's all set. I've been reworking the play, and I made one of the two families black. It makes everything so much more moving and funny. I think I really have something now. It was worth a few years' wait. I'm going to be leaving the studio and going to New York with it in the next two weeks."

"Do you want me to send you a pineapple?" asked Powar.

"What kind of a response is that to the news I just told you?" asked Andy.

"It's a response of someone who's very happy for you, but someone who has been forced off her job into exile in Hawaii for two months to baby-sit a lounge singer. Meet me at the Farmer's Market at the Mexican place in an hour. Please?"

The Farmer's Market was an old complex of wooden buildings at Fairfax and Third in the middle of Los Angeles. Built in the twenties, it had been turned into a tourist attraction, but it also was a fun place for natives to go. There were food stalls selling every kind of food—Mexican, Chinese, Italian, American, and Barbecue. Powar bought a tostada for herself and Chinese rice and vegetables for Andy. They were on the table at his place when he arrived. Powar didn't really know why, but whenever she was in a crisis she looked to him.

HONEY DUST / 239

"Well, it looks like we're about to become world travelers," she said. She didn't want to dampen his enthusiasm for the great playwriting opportunity ahead of him. "I am really happy for you," she said. "I just know you'll be able to pull it off."

"Thank you," said Andy. "I really am excited, but what is this about Hawaii? It doesn't make any sense."

Powar thought carefully about what she was going to tell him. If she told him the truth about Falk, it would be horrifying to both of them, and then he might confront Falk. It was better to say something else. "For some reason Falk is interested in putting Eddie Wing, a Hawaiian sex symbol, on the air during the day. He thinks the housewives will go crazy for him. I don't think so, and daytime isn't my area, but he thinks I should go supervise the show because of my background. Believe me, I am not looking forward to it."

"I can see why," said Andy, "but turn it around to a positive thing. You're being given a vacation in Hawaii. Why don't you just play on the network's time. It couldn't take that much of your day to supervise the show. Just relax."

"I can try," said Powar, "but God only knows what will be going on at the network while I'm away. I'm really going to have to be careful."

"What's the problem, Powar? I've never heard you talk like this before."

"I think that I'm learning that I grew up in a sheltered environment in a family-owned business. I learned a lot about clever business tactics at the dinner table, but I was never in a position of being unprotected. It's very difficult."

"If you're having a problem in that area, then you feel that someone is out to hurt you," said Andy. "Who is it? I want to help you."

Powar was afraid she had said too much. "You can't help me this time, Andy. I have to take care of it myself."

"Can't Falk help you? He obviously cares about you a great deal. He has from the day you two met," said Andy, trying to hide the disappointment he kept deep inside.

"I'm on my own this time," Powar said, looking very much like a little girl.

Andy put his hand over hers. "I want you to call me in New York whenever you need me. I'll always be there for you."

"I'm really going to miss our lunches," said Powar. "Pink's hot dogs and the museum cafeteria just won't be the same without you."

Before Powar knew it she was on a United Airlines flight to Hawaii, and she was miserable. She knew she had to do it because of Falk's position within the network. She simply was not as powerful as he was. She even liked Hawaii, but these were just not the circumstances she wanted.

When she landed, there was a limousine waiting to take her to the Royal Hawaiian Hotel on Waikiki. Known as the "Pink Palace," it was the most luxurious hotel on the beach, almost like being at the Beverly Hills Hotel on the sand.

Powar was shown to a corner suite overlooking Diamond Head and all of the beach down to the Halekulani. She was told that all her expenses would be picked up by the network, of course, and she was being given an "extra" allowance of $500 a week. Falk is sure trying to keep me happy while I'm away from things, she thought, having every intention of spending the $500 plus charging enormous amounts at the hotel. She was going to make Falk pay through the nose. If she had to be here, they were going to know about it, and she was going to have a gigantic vacation that gave her time to plot. She knew she had to do some work because she didn't want the show to be bad. Falk could use that against her with Howard Pohlmann, the chairman of the board of PBC, and she wouldn't have that happen at any cost.

As far as Powar could tell, PBC had spent hundreds of thousands on the show. They had to have been paying triple time for two crews to work around the clock in order to meet their air date. They had to convert a hotel dining room into a studio by knocking out a wall so it was open to the beach.

The idea was to make this a sort of Hawaiian "House Party," with a family of regulars, tourists doing stunts, guest stars singing, and a roving camera shooting travelogues of Hawaii. This was all fine except that Eddie Wing was not showing up to rehearsals. His nightclub shows went very late at night and then he had to "tend to" his fans, and that took until five or six in the morning, so he could never make an eleven o'clock rehearsal. The plan was to rehearse at eleven and then do makeup and tape between two and three P.M., when the light was just right on the beach. Since the show was live, Eddie either had to read from cue cards or study his script. But he would do neither, thinking he could "wing" everything. The few times he showed up for rehearsal he was barely awake. Beller finally designed a special piece that fit in Wing's ear that served as a minispeaker. Someone offstage would read his lines to him, and then he would say them. The only problem was that it caused a time delay, and if Wing was having a conversation with a guest star, it was impossible for that person to understand what was going on because Wing threw off his or her rhythm. Once Powar realized everything was going to be a disaster, she sent a memo to Falk through proper network channels, copying Pohlmann on it, saying she had done everything she could and that Beller had promised her he could pull it off. She stressed Beller's personal relationship with Wing, so if it was a failure, it would be Beller's and not hers.

Powar eventually worked out a very nice schedule for herself. She would wake up every morning and order room service to be brought to her terrace. She would have half a papaya with a fresh lime, a waffle with coconut syrup, and passion fruit juice to drink. She would occasionally switch to guava juice and macadamia nut pancakes for variety. She would then read the papers and the trades and make calls to the Mainland.

Around ten-thirty A.M. she would put on a bikini and go to the beach. The beach in front of the Royal was roped off from tourists and riffraff, and beach boys attended to guests' every need. The beach was the best for swimming in all of Waikiki, you could walk out in the water for almost a mile. Outrigger canoe rides left every half hour in case you wanted to go for a boat ride. At eleven-thirty Powar would saunter back to the pool snack bar, run by a nice Hawaiian lady named Barbara, where she would have either a tuna or an egg sandwich with an iced tea. Sometimes she might have a patty melt or tuna melt with a coke. A little after noon she would walk down the beach to where the show was being done. After the first few days of rehearsal when she saw crew members in shorts and bathing suits, she decided to wear her bikini to work. Unfortunately it was the first time Wing decided to show up at a rehearsal.

"My, my, is this what TV executives look like?" Wing asked lasciviously. "Had I known, I would have agreed to do this show sooner."

Powar reached out to shake his hand. He grabbed it and pulled her to him, trying to kiss her on the mouth. Powar pushed him as politely as she could before he could connect.

"That may be the way they do things in the islands, but I'm from Beverly Hills," she said, trying to make light of it because he was on her network.

"That's okay," said Wing. "The longer you're here, the more Hawaiian you become. I'll wait." He laughed and slapped one of his bodyguards on the back as he headed to his dressing room.

Now I have yet another thing to add to my misery list, Powar thought. From that point on, when he did show up, Wing wouldn't leave her alone. He had his bodyguards follow her if she went for a drive around the island or out to dinner at night. It was horrible, and she was desperate to get out. During breaks in rehearsal when the craziness got to be too much, she would rent a paddle boat and paddle as far out as she thought would be safe. She would then turn the boat around and sit there, looking back at the "studio." It was her only escape.

She was also watching everything very carefully, since Fred Grossblatt was around and she knew there had to be something funny going on. After his first attempt to bribe her, she'd called him and refused politely, and he'd never brought it up again. Every time he looked at her in Hawaii she felt he was thinking she was an idiot for turning down the money.

In going over the budget for Eddie Wing's show, she saw that the cost of production was $80,000 to deliver five thirty-minute shows. That was a fair price. But when she checked quietly with the PBC accounting department, she found that Bill Beller Productions was being given $200,000 per week for the five shows. She wasn't shocked this time; she simply wondered what the deal between Beller and Falk was. Something had to have occurred for this show to be put into production so fast. She also remembered that Beller and Falk were represented by the same attorney, who was also the business manager and accountant for the show . . . who, by the way, was buying up real estate in Hawaii. Forget this for the moment, Powar kept telling herself. Concentrate on coconut syrup and sun as long as you're stuck here. That calm attitude would last about an hour, of course.

"Now don't you worry," said Franny, putting on her coat. "Everything is going to be perfect tonight."

"How can you say that?" asked Andy. "My whole life could fall apart four hours from now." It was opening night for Andy's play, *Neighbors*.

Franny got very close to him and cupped his face in her hands. "I believe in you completely. You are very, very talented, and your time has come. You are the best writer in the world. Now put on your coat and let's go to the theater. Broadway is going to get a present from you tonight. They're very lucky to have you."

"You really know what to say to me, Franny. I really appreciate it," said Andy, hugging her. They were living at the Wyndham, a reasonably priced hotel that rented suites with kitchens over a long period of time. It had been three months since Andy's lunch with Powar at the Farmer's Market.

Andy was sitting at the bar at Sardi's, after spending a good hour on the phone with Powar hoping that she might calm his nerves. They spoke at least three times a week, their calls helping each other get through difficult times. He couldn't believe that he was at Sardi's. Just like the movies, he thought. I'll wait for the reviews and then I'll know what to do with my life, or without it, as the case may be. Broadway was in need of a good comedy. Not since *A Chorus Line* had anything opened to such anticipation. His head was getting full of people saying, "Neil Simon, move over," but he didn't allow himself to believe that for a second. He was just praying he'd get through the night.

He had brought Franny with him. She made him feel important. He could tell that she loved him very much, and he allowed himself to get carried along in this because he didn't want to tread on Falk's territory, but he wished that Powar were with him tonight. He was going to have to learn to accept just friendship from Powar. They had a strong one. He should be happy with that.

"Honey," said Franny, hurrying up to him, "look who's here. It's Arlene Francis and Virginia Graham. I just loved them when I was growing up. I want to go talk to them. Introduce me."

"Franny, I don't know them. How can I introduce you?" asked Andy.

"They'll know you," she said. "Everybody knows you tonight. Never mind. I'll go introduce myself."

Andy shook his head and berated himself for always thinking of Powar. Franny really would be good for him. She loved him, plus she could take care of herself, and she saw to it that he was taken care of.

He checked his watch and realized that the papers should be out within five minutes. The producers were in a private room upstairs, while he preferred the distraction of the crowd in the main part of the restaurant. He checked his watch again as the producers came down to the bar.

"They should be here soon," said one of them.

"You wait outside and get them. I think I'll stay at the bar," Andy said. He saw Franny in animated conversation with Arlene and Virginia. Franny was managing actually to get a word in, and Andy laughed out loud at the sight of the three of them. Then he began to notice that people were starting to stare at him, waiting to see his reaction to his fate firsthand. He felt as if he were in a display window on Fifth Avenue with vultures looking inside for a bite. Suddenly Vincent Sardi came rushing toward him, gesturing grandly.

"Mr. Stromberg, we have a special table for you."

The producers were right behind him, carrying copies of the papers and screaming, "We're a hit!" Franny was jumping up and down and trying to get through the crowd to congratulate him. She was getting a little hysterical. Within what seemed like seconds, the whole restaurant started applauding. Then there was that moment of silence when someone was about to make a speech.

Producer Jimmy Nederlander said, "We'd like to call upon our author, Andy Stromberg. Without him there would be no *Neighbors*."

Andy looked at the floor. Then he heard Franny say for everyone to hear, "Isn't this the perfect time to announce our engagement, darling?"

A cheer rang up in time to cover Andy's gasp. She went to kiss him, and he looked around at the crowd of smiling faces waiting for him to speak. He looked at her and then at the crowd and realized that this was indeed a special moment in time. "Absolutely," he said as cheers rang out from everyone.

Powar was awakened by Andy's call the next morning. As soon as she heard his voice she knew the play was a success. "Kerr said what in the *Times*? Read it to me. . . . Oh, I'm so happy for you."

Andy read a number of the reviews to her, and she savored each and every word. "I wish I could have been there," she moaned.

"I do, too," said Andy. "Listen, I have something else exciting to tell you."

"What else could there be?" Powar said flippantly.

"Franny and I are getting married in the spring."

Powar's mood hit the floor so suddenly that she was taken by surprise at the intensity of it. She tried to recover quickly. "Oh, Andy, congratulations. That's very good."

"Then you're happy for me?" Andy said a little too cheerfully.

"Of course," said Powar. "I wish you all the best. Listen, I have to get ready for the taping now, but we'll speak really soon."

He said good-bye, and then she hung up. She had never felt so lonely. She was stuck on the island with no real friends. She missed her father and Maria enormously, but she felt now that she'd lost her best friend. She was ecstatic about the success of his play. She was less ecstatic about Franny, but she couldn't think of a reason that he shouldn't marry her. Neither she nor Andy had mentioned the word *love*. Powar had made him promise not to sell the TV or motion pictures rights of *Neighbors* until he talked with her. She couldn't tell him why she'd made him promise, but it was very important to her. Of course he'd said yes.

About a month into the show, she began going to other islands for the weekend. She went to Kauai and stayed at Coco Palms, the resort where the cast stayed when *South Pacific* was being shot. There were individual "huts," and it was very beautiful and much more tranquil than Waikiki. She liked Kauai better than Maui or the big island of Hawaii. She needed to think, and Kauai was a perfect place for that. She knew she couldn't just sit in Hawaii and let Falk toy with her career. She knew he wanted to exile her to save himself in case she talked to anyone, but it wasn't going to work. She had to come up with something before her time was up on the island, otherwise Falk was certain to extend her commitment to the show. He never called her anymore, and any orders from the network came by memo to her and Bill Beller at the same time. The longer she was in Hawaii, the more her movie division slipped away from her and the more her reputation was hurt.

Powar remembered hearing her mother say constantly when she was growing up, "Go in armed when you want something and don't look back." So she pulled her ace and called PBC chairman of the board Howard Pohlmann, asking to meet him confidentially at the Bel Air Hotel on Friday. He accepted. She had known him through her parents and knew him better than she ever let on. Something told her from the very beginning just to keep her mouth shut and do good work. There was no need for anyone to know who she knew and how well. She was planning on using that strategy throughout her whole life. Pohlmann was a very quiet man who just showed up for board meetings. He never took a hands-on approach anymore, but his word was the final one at the corporation. He looked like a kindly grandfather, but that and his quiet nature covered up his corporate killer mind.

She never told anyone at the show that she was leaving. She left the Royal through one of the kitchen entrances at four A.M. so she wouldn't be followed by Wing's guards, took a bus, and then switched to a cab to go to the airport. She waited for the eight A.M. flight to leave, very calm and purposeful. She arrived at the Bel Air Hotel on Thursday night and checked into one of the special suites overlooking the pond with the swans. It was a beautiful setting and perfect for her mission.

She saw to it that the English muffins, jam, and tea were ready when Howard arrived Friday morning. She knew it was his favorite. It also took less time to eat than eggs or cereal, and she needed "short food." Their meeting could not last long; it was going to be hit and run. Powar opened the door wearing a beautiful Hawaiian print dress in shades of blue, a reminder to Howard that she was being forced off to an island. It was never spoken of by her. The dress should do it.

"What a pretty outfit, Powar," said Howard.

"Thank you very much, sir. I'm so glad you could see me. I would never have bothered you if it hadn't been important. Please sit down and join me in an English muffin, won't you?"

They were seated on the facing love seats placed right at the window by the pond. Classical music was playing in the background. "As I'm sure you are aware, the movies that I'm doing have managed to knock off ABC and put us in third place for the first time. The area we should tackle next, and the one that will knock off NBC so we have a shot at taking over CBS, is comedy. We have more and more affiliates who want to see our movies, and the buzz is on that we're on our way to really having a voice in broadcasting. I know this is something you want very much. I'm also aware that King Pictures has been very helpful in securing stars to star in our movies. But the public wants to see comedy more than anything. You just aired a show called 'Fabulous Fifties' that looks like it could be very strong. There's a character on the show called Boxer who's been getting a lot of mail. I think we should make him more the focus of the stories. He's what will make the show successful."

Powar could see that she certainly had his attention, so she continued after spreading black raspberry jam on her muffin. "I love to watch it settle in the cracks, don't you?" she asked Howard, showing him the muffin. "I'm sure you know that Andy Stromberg's play, *Neighbors*, about two families, one black, one white, is the biggest Broadway smash in years. It is a play that just cries out to be a TV series, not a movie. Andy has received inquiries from all the other networks as well as Warner Brothers and, of course, King Pictures. If we had the rights, we could put it on after 'Fabulous Fifties' and use the Boxer character to do some promos for it so we wouldn't lose the audience. Both shows have a family audience. We could then start building a comedy powerhouse on

Tuesdays and make a real dent in the ratings, which of course would translate into more advertising dollars for the company, and we would really be taken as a contender." She saw Howard put down his muffin.

"Here's a telegram from Andy Stromberg giving King Pictures the rights to *Neighbors* for one dollar and specifying that he will only okay a deal with a network if I'm personally involved." She placed it next to Howard's plate. "I think that it's time for me to supervise all programming." She paused. "I know what you're thinking. What would you do about Falkner Cantwell? Well, I think he would make a terrific independent producer. Let's face it, a producer makes more money than a network executive ever can. He's been working in the top job for five years. I'm sure he'd appreciate an exclusive production deal with guaranteed series commitments. As for me, I know I would have no trouble getting out of my contract by just asking Falk for a release, but then I would go to CBS and produce *Neighbors* for them, and that won't help PBC at all. Why don't you think about our conversation, and I'd love to hear from you in Hawaii by Monday."

Howard looked at her a moment, and then a smile broke out on his face. "You have some genes, Powar. Your mother couldn't have handled this better herself." He stood up and kissed her on the cheek and left.

Falk finished reading the latest development reports and smiled. He was very pleased with how smoothly things were running at the network. The one hitch was Powar, exiled in Hawaii. He thought about her all the time. He was still painfully embarrassed by what happened, but he had to take care of himself. Compassion was not part of the "success" program. All he needed was to keep her away for two more months and he'd be able to put his plan into action. Howard Pohlmann had agreed to see him Monday morning, and he doubted if Howard had any idea about the shake-up in personnel he was going to propose to him, but he was certain he'd go along with his plan. There had never been a problem between the two of them. Howard had respected the job he had done through the years, particularly when they'd started with so little, so he couldn't refuse him now that things were going so well.

"Come in, Falk," said Howard, motioning for him to join him on the couch. There was a tray of coffee and bran muffins on the table. "Would you care for some coffee?"

"No, thank you," said Falk. Both men then began to speak at once, but Falk had to defer to his superior.

"Falk, I've been thinking a great deal about the good things you have done at PBC, and I want to reward you," said Howard.

Falk was taken aback by this. First, he had called the meeting, not Howard, and second, "rewards" could be a dangerous thing. He listened in rapt attention. Maybe he's going to make me vice-chairman, he thought.

"You are one of the brightest minds around when it comes to picking and producing quality commercial shows. What PBC really needs is a production company exclusive to us who can deliver these fine shows. I want to insure that that kind of product can go nowhere else. In return for that, I will guarantee that production company one on-air series per season, thirteen episodes, and three pilots each season. This is an extraordinary opportunity both financially and creatively. I can think of no person other than yourself who should have this opportunity."

Falk's mind was racing. Was this the Velvet Sledgehammer? Howard was speaking again.

"I knew you'd be very eager to get started, so I've taken the liberty of arranging for your entire office to be packed for you and delivered to Columbia, where we have leased space. The company, of course, will be called Falkner Cantwell Productions."

Falk opened his mouth to speak.

"No, don't thank me, my boy," Howard said quickly. "I

knew you'd be grateful. Miss Hobson will be joining you there, too. It's a great studio. I love their commissary. Order the Chinese chicken salad. Your lawyer is meeting right now with ours to iron out a new deal. Congratulations!'' He stood up and extended his hand. ''You're going to do a wonderful job for us. Oh, by the way, I am promoting Powar King to your position. You two work so well together, it will be just like old times.''

Falk found himself out in the hall. He turned on his heel in a way that would make Hitler proud and walked down the hall to the men's room as fast as he could go without causing comment. He dropped to his knees when he got in the stall, and the cold porcelain on his forehead was the first good thing that had happened to him all morning.

Falkner Cantwell hadn't gotten where he was without being brilliant, and within fifteen minutes he knew what to do. There wasn't even time for ''flop sweat.'' He had to pull this off, and quickly. He marched confidently back to his office and called Army Archerd at *Daily Variety*. ''Army, I have a big announcement, and I want to give it to you exclusively. I'm leaving PBC to form the first independent television production company that is exclusive to one network. It's a history-making concept that Howard Pohlmann and I have been planning for months. The official announcement will be next week, but I wanted to tell you first. Joining my company will be Timothy Foster for business affairs, and we'll announce more employees shortly.'' He could feel the adrenaline flowing. He was on a roll now. ''Our offices will be at Columbia. Let's do an in-depth story later on in the week, Army, but you can run with this right now. Thank you very much. I'm very excited about this.''

Falk hung up from Army and buzzed Miss Hobson. ''I want the following calls placed in this order: *The New York Times, Advertising Age, The Wall Street Journal*, and the *Los Angeles Times*. Ask for the business editor. But just before you start placing the calls, send a memo to every executive in this building and have them in the main screening room at noon. Tell them I will have a short announcement, and then they can go to lunch."

He turned and looked out the window, teeth clenched. It could be worse. After all, he could become a richer man because he would own a percentage of the shows up front. But the damage to his ego was of such proportion that someone was going to pay dearly.

The halls had been wild with rumors for about forty-five minutes, and the seated executives were squirming in their nervousness. A meeting like this was never called unless something terrible or something wonderful happened. At noon on the dot Falk strode to the front of the screening room, cleared his throat, and made the announcement sound like the Second Coming, exactly as he had to Army Archerd. To hear him tell it, it was the greatest achievement in all of broadcasting, and he almost believed it himself as he felt the excitement building from his audience. Just as the applause was ringing in his ears, the door to the screening room opened and Howard Pohlmann appeared.

"Falk," he said so everyone could hear, "why don't you let me make the rest of the announcement?"

Falk had no choice but to turn the stage over to him. He clenched his teeth together so hard that he felt the pain all the way into his head.

"Ladies and gentlemen, I give you our new leader, someone who will make us the number one network, I'm sure, Powar King!" The door opened and Powar walked in the room and joined Howard on stage.

"Thank you very much for that applause. I will take it as a vote of confidence. I know that I have taken on an awesome responsibility, but I hope that my love of our industry and my hard work, along with yours, will give us an even brighter future." Powar then reached for Falk and, standing in between Falk and Howard, took their hands in hers and raised them over her head as she smiled triumphantly.

* CHAPTER 14 *

Maria and Nathan's wedding was big news in Hollywood, but they angered a lot of people by getting
married in secret to avoid prying eyes. Maria had
insisted that they just go away to Santa Barbara and have a
judge marry them at the Biltmore. She didn't want a million
people commenting on something so personal. She asked
Powar to fly in Friday night from Hawaii in order to make
the wedding on Saturday; then she could be back in Hawaii
on Sunday so the shooting schedule wouldn't be interrupted.
The only witnesses were Powar and Nathan's lawyer, Oscar
Portugais. Immediately after the ceremony, which took place
on the putting green, there was a wedding lunch in the front
dining room overlooking the sea.

Maria leaned over and whispered to Powar, "Maybe he
just wants to get to the bedroom? He's in an awful hurry."

"Then let's give him what he wants and get out of here,"
said Powar, who started shoveling food in.

Maria knew Powar was there only to support her as a friend
and that she had no love for Nathan. She decided to just make
small talk and get through it.

Once she and Nathan were alone, she started to kiss him.

He pulled her off of him, saying, "No, not while you're with child. It wouldn't be right."

Maria was shocked at his double standard, but she let it go.

Mei-Ling had stopped talking to Maria altogether. The thought of Nathan being the father of her grandchild was too much for her. About three months into the pregnancy, when Maria was just starting to show, Mei-Ling did not show up to serve breakfast one morning. After a few minutes of being annoyed, Maria began to wonder if everything was all right. When she buzzed Mei-Ling's bungalow there was no answer. Maria walked quickly from the dining room to the garden and knocked on the door of the bungalow. Again there was silence. She pushed, and the door was open. Inside, Maria saw that there was nothing left except the furniture. Every personal possession was gone, and so was Mei-Ling. Maria looked around for a note or something, but nothing was left. All she could see was empty tabletops, an unfilled closet, bare cupboards, and blank walls, but her mother's faint perfume was still in the air.

She sat down on the couch and felt as empty as one could feel with a baby growing inside. She started to cry for all the lost years. She grabbed her stomach and doubled over. "Mother," she sobbed, the tears falling on the brown-and-yellow print sofa. She hugged the pillows closer to her, trying to turn them into her mother, a woman she'd never shown her love for. Now it was too late, and she couldn't stop the crying. As much as she wanted to stop, she couldn't. Her crying slowly gave way to an anger about her lack of control. She didn't want to be soft. She wouldn't get anywhere being that way. She had to get her strength back. It was the only way she could maneuver her future. This baby was the key to everything. It was the cement to her empire.

Honey was seething. Powar had landed on the cover of *Time* with the headline THE DYNASTY CONTINUES. Tracing her family history, *Time* made the analogy of father-daughter moguls and talked a great deal about King Pictures and how well trained Powar must have been to have turned out so well. Honey was astonished. *Time* referred to her great parties and hostessing legend, but not once did they make the connection between these efforts and the success of King Pictures. The article made it sound as if Philip and Powar had done it all themselves. To the world, Honey reveled in having her child on the cover of *Time*, but privately she was having a difficult time. To maximize what had happened and turn it into a plus, she gave a *Time* party for her daughter, with *Time* covers throughout the ages covering the walls of the private room at Chasen's. Philip and Powar didn't really want to go because by now they saw through Honey's antics, but she'd sent the invitations out without checking with them, and by the time they found out about it they had to go, of course.

The network's publicity department worked with Honey, so all of the press were there. Army Archerd, Rona Barrett, Marilyn Beck, Joyce Haber from the *L.A. Times*, Vernon Scott of UPI, Polly Mellen of *Vogue*, and even Helen Gurley Brown showed up.

Powar decided to be very conservative and wear a black Chanel suit with gold chains. When she walked in everyone applauded, and she looked over to see that her mother was applauding, too. Honey was dressed all in white as if she were a bride. By now Powar had given up guessing what her mother was going to look like. It was easier that way. After an appropriate time for people to devour the fresh seafood buffet, Philip King stepped up to the microphone.

"Ladies and gentlemen, I'd like to toast my daughter, Powar King, for proudly carrying on our family tradition of quality work for the public. Her mother and I are very proud of her."

Powar smiled and lifted her glass to her father and then walked to the mike. "This is quite an honor, and I'm really overwhelmed. I'd like to toast all of you for honoring me, and I'd like all of us to toast my parents. Thank you." And then she did everything she could to get out of there as fast as she could.

Powar and Andy got "Neighbors" on within six weeks, and it was a hit. Things were beginning to turn around for PBC just the way Powar had hoped. By the second year of the show, Powar and Andy had a great working pattern. She would be in her office every day until four, and then she would meet him at the production office he had set up at one of the bungalows in the Beverly Hills Hotel.

One day in June, Powar went over to discuss adding a character to the show for the fall season. "Do you remember that actress I pointed out to you named Caroline Spencer? She's the one who was on that daytime show 'The Daring and the Dangerous' at CBS?" said Powar.

"Yes," Andy said.

"I think she's the next Grace Kelly," said Powar. "She's beautiful, and she can do comedy. I think we should add her to the show and have both families trying to get her attention. It would be really interesting if there was triangle for her involving both the white and black young men."

"Powar, you really are a genius," said Andy. "Only through comedy could we get that kind of story across at this time."

Powar smiled. She loved working with him. He was so bright and kind. So different from Falk. She saw Falk now only at business meetings.

"Mr. Cantwell and Mr. Foster are here," Miss Burson said over the intercom.

Powar braced herself. She had to see them, it was part of her duties, and she was sure they hated it more than she did. Unfortunately for Falk, anytime he wanted to shoot a show, he had to get approval from Powar, as did all the independent producers.

"Powar," Falk said almost superciliously as he entered

her palatial office and shook her hand. Timothy just nodded to her.

Falk was wearing a charcoal-gray glen plaid suit, slate blue shirt, and a charcoal tie. As usual, his clothes were perfect, but ever since Powar had surprised him at his "party," that's all she saw when she looked at him.

"Good morning," she said to both of them. "Let's sit over on the couch." It would have been too much of an insult to Falk to ask him to sit across from her at her desk. The right protocol, even though she despised him, was to take him to the more casual area of the office because of his previous position at the network.

"We'd be happy to do so," said Falk.

"Let's get right to it, shall we?" said Powar, now dispensing with any more pretense.

"Fine," said Falk. "We want to do a one-hour show that takes place in a Las Vegas hotel. Everything will be shot on location—"

"Another location show?" said Powar alluding to the Hawaiian fiasco and wondering what kind of side deal he'd cut with the hotel.

"I think you should hear the premise first," Falk countered. "The story will revolve around the hotel owner, who is a young, good-looking Howard Hughes type. We have a gorgeous assistant manager he's interested in, a wisecracking older woman dealer, a young kid who's a bellman, plus different real entertainers each week and all the guests we want."

"It's perfect formatting, Powar," said Timothy, jumping in. "We will do more than one story each week, and we can mix drama and comedy."

As Powar was listening she realized that it was a hit show, and it galled her. Falk was talented, and she couldn't deny it. "It sounds good. Why don't we do a two-hour movie to kick it off, and then I'll give you an order for thirteen episodes and we'll see how it's doing. I think Elaine Rich will be the perfect network supervisor for the show. Report to her on all casting, producing, directing, and writing suggestions for the pilot. Then we'll decide how we'll proceed on the episodes.''

Falk was furious that Powar wasn't going to supervise it herself, but he couldn't say anything. He had to play by the rules in this office, but once he left the building he knew how to handle things.

When the labor pains came, Maria couldn't find Nathan. She had him paged at the racetrack where he usually was, and there was no response. The next call was to Powar, who came over immediately to take her to Cedars-Sinai Hospital.

"You still have to be driving the T-bird from college, don't you?" joked Maria as she tried to fit in the front seat.

"I'll never be separated from this car, and you know it," said Powar, "but in this case I think I had better drive yours." They struggled out of the T-bird and slipped right into the comfort of Maria's Cadillac.

Maria was frightened by the pains. "Can't they just give me some medication the minute I hit the door?" she asked. She doubled over again. Powar drove faster. "This is not my idea of a good time," said Maria.

"Don't worry. We're almost there," said Powar.

Once they were in the hospital Maria was quickly taken to her room, while Powar began leaving messages for Nathan at strategic spots.

A doctor was asking Maria to count backward. She was only too happy to comply. "What took you so long?" she asked drowsily as she went under. When she woke up she was in her room and Nathan was pacing.

He asked gruffly, "How do you feel?"

"Fine," answered Maria. "What did I have? A boy or a girl?"

"A girl, and she's very beautiful," he answered. "She has your coloring and features and my size. She's a really long baby."

"I know you wanted a son, Nathan. Don't worry. The next

one will be a boy, I promise," said Maria. The thought of having another baby was abhorrent to her. She didn't enjoy one thing about the first one, but she knew she had to keep trying until she had a male heir. "I want to see her," she said.

"The doctor is with her," Nathan explained. "He would only let me see her through the window. He said something about some tests and we could see her tomorrow. He's coming to talk to us at ten A.M. tomorrow."

"And that's it? You didn't ask any more questions?" Maria said excitedly.

"Try and relax. I told you I saw her and she looks good to me. That's all I know," said Nathan.

Their "discussion" was broken by a nurse coming into the room pushing a cart full of flower arrangements. It was only then that Maria looked around the room and saw so many flowers that she thought she was in a funeral home. "I guess the *Hollywood Newsday* baby is big news today in town," she said dryly. "Nathan, I want you to call the doctor right now." Before he could answer, the nurse returned with a shot for Maria.

"The doctor ordered this for you, Mrs. Blumenthal." And she gave it to Maria before she could say anything.

"I want to see the doctor now, Nathan," Maria said again, but quietly fell asleep.

Nathan got to the hospital at 9:55 A.M. and walked into Maria's room as he saw the doctor coming toward him. Dr. Eugene Melinkoff was head of OB-Gyn for Cedars-Sinai and the gynecologist Hollywood preferred. He had a very calm look about him. He looked a lot like Ozzie Nelson, and he used that to his advantage, particularly in cases like the one he was about to face.

"Good morning, folks. Nathan, please sit down. I know you are concerned because my actions with your baby have been a little unusual. Let me assure you that your child is very healthy."

"Thank God," said Maria.

"Yes, you must relax, Maria," Dr. Melinkoff continued. "There is a situation that we have to discuss. It is a rare one, but again, let me assure you that everything is going to be fine."

"What is it, doctor?" said Nathan.

The doctor paused before answering. "She has a condition that has an unusual name. It's called ambiguous genitalia."

"What!" Nathan shouted.

"Please, just give me a chance to explain all this. Every once in a while, a child is born with a penis and a vagina. We don't really know why it happens. It just does. What we do in this case is see which organ is developing faster over the first six weeks of life. If they are developing equally, we make the baby a female because that is a less risky operation."

Nathan interrupted. "So what you're telling me is that we don't know whether to name it John or Joan?" he bellowed.

Maria started to cry.

"I know this is a shock," the doctor continued. "It is my best guess right now after examining the baby that she will be a she. Unfortunately, she will never be able to have children of her own, but she will have a normal, healthy life. Occasionally she may have to take hormones, but that is a simple thing."

Nathan stood up. "Great, doctor. We'll call her Jonna." And with that he walked out of the room.

Dr. Melinkoff went over and took Maria's hand. "Don't worry. I promise you everything will be fine."

"I'd like to see her now if I could," Maria said cautiously.

The doctor buzzed the nursery and had the baby brought in. Maria extended her arms and cradled her child. Holding life for the first time was magical. She never knew she was capable of feeling such love. Maria looked at her and prayed that she wouldn't make the same mistakes her mother had. She was determined that Jonna's life be a healthy, successful one, and she would stop at nothing to see that it would happen just that way.

"Franny and I have finally set a wedding date," said Andy.

That caught Powar by surprise. He had hardly mentioned her during the past year.

"We're going to get married the first week the shows can go on hiatus. I've been so busy over the past year I never gave it a thought, but Franny really wants to get married, and we have been engaged for two years."

"Congratulations, Andy. I hope you will be very happy." Powar heard the hollowness of her tone and hoped he wouldn't pick up on it. He didn't seem to be very happy, either.

"Let's take a break," said Andy. "Follow me."

Powar was happy to. They needed to change the atmosphere around them. They walked to his car, which he kept in the garage of the hotel. "Where are we going?" asked Powar.

"It's a surprise," Andy said. He drove up Coldwater Canyon, the street next to the hotel. At the top of the canyon was Mulholland Drive. There was also a side street called Franklin Canyon, which not many people noticed. Andy turned on it and drove to the gate, which had a sign that read "Private Property to Los Angeles County." He was taking her to the Franklin Canyon Reservoir, a place her father used to take her to when they wanted to hike in the city and feel like they were miles away. She couldn't believe that Andy knew the same place.

"I can't believe this," said Powar. "This is one of my favorite places in the city. I have to show you something." She got out of the car and climbed over the fence. Andy followed her, smiling at her enthusiasm. She ran toward the lake and stopped in front of a tree. On the tree Andy saw a heart carved in it with "P.K. loves P.K." inscribed inside.

"My father did this for me. I'm so glad it's still here."

Powar's eyes started to fill with tears. "I miss seeing him. My mother spent my whole childhood trying to keep us apart, and it's still hard to see one another. We have our business meetings, of course, but I miss the times like this. Imagine, my own mother, Andy. I hate her for the way she uses people and tried to separate my father and me. You know, she's jealous of what I've accomplished . . . but I've learned so much from her, too. Oh, I don't know what to do. Between dealing with my parents and running a network I don't have time to pay any attention to anything personal. Sometimes I think the treadmill is unbearable, and then I realize the excitement of it is what gets me through life." Powar stopped her rambling suddenly and looked at Andy, saying quietly, "Sometimes I don't even know what I'm talking about."

"Powar, just try to breathe calmly for a second. Realize that you are a highly visible woman trying to work within the Hollywood system. Even with your name you still have to work harder than any man. You know you have to give it your all. Give yourself a break. Look what you've accomplished. Go visit your father." Andy put his hands on her shoulders. "Why don't you call him tomorrow and go to the studio for lunch or just kidnap him and take him here on a picnic. Don't let her win. Don't allow her to separate you."

He was so understanding and gentle. Powar wanted him to hold her, but that wouldn't be right in view of the wedding announcement. They just looked into each other's eyes and didn't say a word. Almost with a sigh, Andy took his hands away from her and reached down to pick up a sharp rock. He turned to the tree and carved "A.S. & P.K." They walked to the car holding hands, not saying a word.

"How could you do this?" screamed Powar, waving an invitation under Honey's nose. "I don't even know why I'm asking you the question. Since when have you ever cooperated with someone else in this family? Why should I be surprised now?"

Powar found herself standing toe to toe with her mother in the kitchen on Bedford. Honey was not fazed. "What seems to be the problem?" she asked stonily, running a hand through her blonde hair.

"Well, Mother, I told you I wanted to give a wedding reception for Andy as my present to him."

"You mean Andy and Franny, don't you? She's such a nice girl."

"Look, Mother, I hardly thought you would put only your name and Dad's on the top of the invitation and invite all of your friends. Now it looks like just another one of your extravaganzas. I wanted this to be something special from me. I wanted a classic wedding reception in perfect taste. I don't want a carnival theme or a Greek reception or any other creative thing you can think of. Now listen to me. You and I are going to do this together. If I find that you have ordered one thing without my approval, I'll move the party to the Bel Air and make you stay home."

Honey just looked at her and then said, "Fine, Miss *Time* magazine. We'll see who throws the best parties. You go right ahead and plan everything."

"I will, Mother, and here's what's going to happen. The party will have an all-white theme. We'll even have swans floating in the pool. There is a new chef that Patrick has just hired at Ma Maison named Wolfgang Puck. He says he's great. Let's have him cater everything. Michel Richard will do the cake, and we'll have the Lester Lanin Orchestra flown in from San Francisco. Flower Fashions can decorate. Now that's what's going to happen."

"Tell me, Powar," said Honey. "You seem to be awfully involved in this. I know Andy is important to PBC, but is he really *this* important?"

Powar started to leave the room and turned to face her mother. As she opened her mouth to speak Honey said, "Is Falk going to be Andy's best man? They used to be so close. In fact, all of you were close. What kind of trouble are you asking for here, dear?"

* * *

Growing up Franny Melton in the apartments south of Olympic Boulevard below Beverly Hills hadn't been easy. It would have been easier to be in Cleveland and read about how the other half lived than to be a few blocks away, so close to the right side of the tracks, looking in. Her parents were schoolteachers, and although that was a noble profession, it brought in little money. Franny had always been told to do her homework and then get a college education, but academics simply didn't interest her. She was a "meet the right guy and move in better circles" person. She had been reading magazines and the society pages of the *L.A. Times* since she was a little girl, and she knew she belonged in that world and didn't care how she was going to get it.

After she graduated from high school she went to work in the men's department at Bullock's department store in Century City. What better place to meet successful men? she thought. Century City was a high-rise office building development on the land that was formerly owned by 20th Century-Fox. There was the Century Plaza Hotel and a shopping center soon after the office buildings were built. Most of the buildings were filled with lawyers, agents, bankers, and other businessmen. They all went shopping at some time or other, and Bullock's was known for being a hipper store than the Broadway, which was next door. Every day when she went to work, Franny would do herself up and be the most charming girl in the world to her customers. Even when she saw a wedding band she was charming, thinking the man might have a single friend. Occasionally customers would ask her to parties and she would go, always driving herself and never staying late. She was on a canvassing mission. If the right guy wasn't there, she would leave after a little while.

One day a good-looking young man named Nicholas Parks came in to buy a tie. He was going to a surprise birthday party for a friend, and he needed something very specific to give to him. He said the friend was kind of a shy guy, who didn't even have a date on his own birthday. When Nicholas joked and said he'd like to give Franny as a present along with the tie to his friend, she agreed. And that was the night that she met Andy Stromberg.

"I don't know what to say," said Andy, looking down, mortified. "I don't really think this is right. You shouldn't allow yourself to be treated this way."

"Well, I appreciate your concern, Andy. And if I were normally the kind of woman who gave herself away to strangers, I would agree with you," said Franny, smiling her best smile. "But this is a joke. I work at Bullock's. I'm a good girl. Really I am."

"Now I feel even worse. Now I'm an idiot," said he. "Some birthday this is."

Franny reassured him again, "Don't be ridiculous. You're not an idiot. Let's go eat some cake and forget about this. Let's just pretend that we met at the party like normal people, okay?" She liked him a lot, and she especially liked that he wrote scripts and was trying to do some good work in the business. She respected those ideals. She liked him better than the shark who had invited her to the party. She'd recognized early on by checking out the successful crowd that Andy was going to make it and was someone she should hang on to.

It had not been an easy road. Andy's friends did not take to her right away, especially Powar King. Franny sensed she should stay as far away from her as she could. It was a tribute to her resourcefulness that she managed to hang on and land Andy. Tonight's wedding reception would be just the first jewel in the Hollywood crown she was planning to place on her head, and the fact that it was at Honey and Philip King's house was beyond her dreams. More than anything she wanted to do what Honey had done. She was going to use her wifely status to become the queen of Hollywood. Of course, Honey was already on the throne, but there would soon be room for a younger one starting out. Franny was patient, she would wait. She hadn't sold socks in the men's department for two years for the fun of it. She had earned tonight, and she was going to savor all of it. Every last star who was there was going to be her friend before the night was over.

Andy and Franny had eloped to Arizona the weekend before the reception. She'd wanted Andy all to herself without any interference from his friends. If she was finally going to get him to marry her, it was just going to be the two of them. Andy was rather shy about parties, anyway, and getting married privately suited him just fine.

Franny was getting dressed upstairs at Honey's. Andy was in a separate room. Franny thought it would be cute for them to wear wedding attire even though they'd married in nice streetwear. Andy was going to wear white tie and tails, and she was in a gown designed by Estevez with a pearl bodice and long train and starched lace veil.

As she dressed in a guest room that overlooked the backyard, Franny was taking everything in because she wanted this house to be hers. She loved how the yard was terraced on different levels. The first level was off the family and living rooms, and it had a long head table set up for the occasion. On the second level were tables for guests. The third level contained the orchestra and the dance floor, and the fourth level had more guests. Honey put the orchestra in the middle so it would be easier to get to from all levels. Franny marveled at Honey's ability to give such fantastic parties, and she hoped that someday she could do the same. She was going to give at least two dinner parties a week at home for Andy, to see to it that his career kept moving in the right circles. Franny was upset that Andy had let *Neighbors* go to TV. She felt he belonged in the movies and that TV was too average a medium.

She could see guests wandering about, looking so beautiful. There were hors d'oeuvres stations all over the yard on all levels, as well as hot things being passed. There was also a bar on each side of each level. All the help was dressed in white, and all the tables for guests as well as the hors d'oeuvres tables were solid white. The waiters were even using silver trays with white lace doilies on top. She knocked on Andy's door.

"Honey, honey, open up! You have to see this!" she said.

Andy opened it, and when he saw how beautiful she looked, it warmed his heart. He felt terrible for not wanting her sexually. Oh, he was capable of performing, and he assumed it was pleasant all around, but there was no magic. But he knew she was good for him. He just wanted to write and not be bothered with the social side of life. He didn't care where he had dinner or what he was eating. He'd just go along with her. It was fine with him. He kissed her as passionately as he could. "You look beautiful, Franny. This is a wonderful moment," he said.

"We will always have these, honey," said Franny as she took his hand and dragged him to the window. Andy looked out and was dazzled by it . . . so dazzled that he'd rather just stay upstairs and not face it.

"Let's go," said Franny, taking his hand again and walking to the stairs. He followed along and took a breath.

Honey was at the foot of the stairs as they came down to applause. Franny had never felt more in her element.

"Congratulations, my dears," said Honey. "Now you stay with me, and when I go outside you stay just behind the wall. When you hear the orchestra play the 'Anniversary Waltz,' you come out."

They did as they were told and heard Honey announce over a loudspeaker, "Ladies and gentlemen, please welcome Mr. and Mrs. Andy Stromberg!"

Franny and Andy walked out and right into a spotlight. Andy thought he was going to die. Franny waved to the crowd.

Powar was standing on the fourth level, looking up. She was wearing an elegant deep purple silk suit. "Who does she think she is—Princess Margaret?" she said to Maria. The two of them were busy eating duck quesadillas with Barbara Walters. The food was extraordinary. Powar spotted Natalie Wood and Robert Wagner and motioned to them to join her group. There were kisses all around. Powar loved Natalie. She thought she was absolutely luminescent on the screen. She had seen *Rebel Without a Cause* and *Splendor in the Grass* so many times, she could do all the dialogue. She made a mental note to tell Andy to write a movie for them.

"Who is this Franny person?" asked Natalie. "She called me up last week and asked me to lunch. She implied that you told her to call."

Powar shook her head. "Uh-oh, we've got another live one. I didn't tell her to call you. She probably wants to get into SHARE. Be careful. I think she has some long-range goals in mind."

"She seems so eager to please that it's hard to refuse her," Natalie said.

"Just keep your eyes open at all times," cautioned Powar, taking a moment to reflect on what was happening around her. It was a perfect party, from Roger Moore and Michael Caine to Faye Dunaway and Marlo Thomas.

"I really think you should do another Broadway play," Andy was saying to Marlo a few minutes later. "Powar has asked me a few times to think about something for you, and I do have some sort of idea starting. Would you be interested?"

"I certainly would. I'll be happy to read anything," said Marlo. Andy was pleased, knowing that Powar would love the whole idea and then want to turn it into a TV series.

Honey announced that dinner would be served and to please take your seats. Powar had arranged the head table so she would sit on one side of Andy with Franny on the other. Falk was placed on the end of the table. She was sorry he had to come at all, but it was polite to Andy to have him. She was surprised when her mother did not place herself at the head table during the seating chart planning, but when Honey placed herself between Sidney Poitier and Cary Grant at table number two, it all made sense. "Do you see where my mother is sitting, Andy?" she asked.

"Yes," he said, starting to laugh. "It takes so little to

make her happy." They both laughed together. "Do I really have to stay here?" Andy said. "I'd rather be at the Carnegie Deli."

"Yes, me too, for a while," said Powar, cutting into foie gras sautéed with pears and black-currant brandy.

"Save me a dance, please," he said.

Philip was seated at his own table with industry executives, lawyers, and Barbara Stanwyck, who was a real kick to talk to. As charming as she was, though, he had a hard time keeping his mind on the festivities. He kept looking at Powar. He was so proud of her. He missed seeing her on a regular basis and felt that he would love to lure her back to the studio. She had become so successful, so fast, that she was beyond being president of the TV division of King Pictures. She was running an entire network. The only way he could get her would be as production president of both movies and TV. He would have to relinquish that title and just keep "chairman." That wouldn't go over well with Honey, and she had the stock to block it. He was very uncomfortable with the situation, and it was eating away at him. In fact, he was getting indigestion more and more lately and was not enjoying the food tonight, even though he knew it was very good.

He looked over at Honey, sitting next to Cary Grant. Honey had been pressing him to make Grant an incredible offer to return to acting. But Philip knew it would never work. Cary was a man of his word, and if he was retired, that's the way it was going to stay. Still, Honey never took "no" for an answer, and she had been staring at him for twenty minutes to come over to her table and ask Cary. He didn't want to do it, but he went over anyway.

"Hello, dear. I was just telling Cary what a wonderful idea it would be for him to do some movies for us. Sidney could direct him in just the perfect script. Wouldn't that be terrific?"

All eyes went to Cary. "Thank you. I am flattered. I am also permanently retired from acting," said Cary. "Honey, would you like to dance?"

"I'd love to," she answered, and gave Philip a look that

said "I have just begun to work on him." She then turned to Clint Eastwood and said quietly, "You don't mind, do you?" And she waltzed off.

"You need a break," Powar whispered into Andy's ear. "Meet me on the tennis court in five minutes." Powar got up as if to circulate and moved through the crowd to the staircase below level four, which led to the court. In a few minutes Andy joined her.

"Thanks, I couldn't take it any more. Franny's talking to Farrah Fawcett and someone named Blair Lawson, so she'll be happy. Who's Blair Lawson?" asked Andy.

"Oh, she's from a very wealthy land development family. I think her grandfather started Westwood."

The tennis court was not lit for the evening, and it was a little dark. "I'm going to show you something very special. Just follow me," said Powar.

She took him through the back gate of the court into a really wooded area. "I could tell you needed rescuing. Just watch this." She stopped in front of a thick hedge and pulled on a pine cone that was hanging. The hedge swung open to reveal a small cabin and a child's garden that had not been tended to for years. From the outside, the cabin looked like a gingerbread house. It had windows with little lace curtains and a glass oval front door. "Come on in," said Powar, and she opened the door.

They both bent down slightly to go in. It was fairy-tale enchanting inside, with furniture that looked as if it had been built for elves. It was carved out of wood, and the seats were covered in paisley fabric. There was a fully furnished living room and kitchen. There was also an actual working stove and a record player and TV in a cabinet. Off to the side was a working bathroom painted pink with flowered wallpaper. The sink came up to Andy's midthigh level. He heard Powar put on the sound track to the movie *A Summer Place* and smiled.

"C'mon," said Powar.

Andy followed her to a small staircase in the back of the room that he hadn't noticed. She bounded upward, with him at her heels. She loved the look on his face as he was discovering her secret space. His eyes roamed around a room that was completely padded with chintz wall covering, red cabbage roses everywhere. On the floor was a huge mattress that took up the entire room. Powar flopped down on it and said, "Here's where I used to have my slumber parties. Oh, look! Here's a Nancy Drew book that we never finished reading aloud to each other. I divided my time between this place and my room in the house until I was about sixteen. All the kids from the neighborhood used to hang out here. They liked it better than their own homes. I can't tell you how many of their parents drank and argued, and this was a safe haven. We'd make cookies, read, laugh, and just save ourselves."

And then the feeling engulfed her. Powar realized she was where she felt the safest of all, with the person who made her feel safe. Andy was the soul mate she had been waiting for her whole life, and she had never allowed that thought to materialize. She couldn't help it now, and she was appalled that it came to her in the middle of his wedding reception.

Andy looked at the woman he loved, knowing what she was thinking. He had waited so long for this moment, and he'd been so sure that it would never come. He knelt down on the bed. Powar could see that he had tears in his eyes.

"I love you, Powar. I've always loved you. I loved you from the second I saw you, and my own insecurities let you get away. I tried to tell myself that Franny is good for me, and she may be, but what have I done? This night is supposed to be a highlight of my life and I've never felt worse."

Powar was crying now as she took his face in her hands. "It's not your fault alone. My stupidity with Falk didn't help matters. There just has to be a way to save this." For a second, she started to laugh. "You know, if you wrote this in a script, no one would ever believe something like this could happen. Talk about bad timing."

"In certain moments, Powar, you sometimes can't choose. You just act."

They held each other hungrily. Powar then began to loosen his tie and unbutton his shirt. "I love you. I love you now and forever." She looked at him very directly and then slowly began to speak. "I Powar, take you, Andy, to be my husband . . . in sickness and in health, for richer for poorer, for better or worse. I promise to love you, honor you, and cherish you, till death us do part. This is your real wedding, Andy." He kissed her, and she felt a magic she had never experienced. It was a lightness, almost a giddiness of one floating among the clouds.

They gently took their clothes off, stealing as many kisses as they could, touching everywhere, feeling each other for the first time. Whatever had gone before this moment was being erased from their history. To find out what real love feels like is very rare, and they both knew what was happening. She felt his lips all over her body. They were like warm butter seeping into her skin. He was slowly licking and kissing her entire body like lazy syrup. When he turned her he raised himself over her. He took his hand and guided his precious gift to Powar and just touched her silken V gently, stroking her over and over. They both knew they wanted to delay the moment they had been waiting for until the last possible second. They knew it would change their lives forever.

When she took him inside her, waves of love washed over her. With every breath she took it was like a wave of gold enveloping her being. Tears came to her eyes as she tried to meld her body into his. They were joined together, and at that exact second they each knew the meaning of destiny. Powar could barely hear the sound of the music as the passion between them cut out all reality. She felt him come inside her and knew that she would never be without him again. She climaxed after him, holding him, floating into him. When it was over they were barely breathing, holding each other for strength, knowing a line had been crossed.

"Oh, Andy, what are we going to do?" cried Powar. "I've never been so happy and so miserable in my life."

"We'll handle it. We'll just have to handle it," said Andy, stroking her hair to calm them both down.

"I know, I know. We're good at handling things," Powar replied, wiping the tears from her eyes.

"I'll go back first," said Andy, "and then you come in about ten minutes later, okay?"

Powar agreed, grateful that he knew she needed some time to compose herself both physically and emotionally. She took one last lingering look at him as he took his clothes and left the room.

After about twenty minutes, she was at the gate, ready to return, hoping no one could look at her and tell what had just happened.

"Powar, how are you?" shouted Kate Gallery from the shrimp table. "You look divine. I've never seen you look so happy."

"Thanks, Kate," said Powar. "I've got to go in the house for a second. Please excuse me." She didn't want anyone to see her emotional pain, and she knew she couldn't bear to see Andy come back to be with Franny. She made it all the way to the back door when Franny suddenly came out of it. "Oh, Franny! I haven't had a chance to congratulate you yet. Are you having a good time?"

"I certainly am," said Franny. "This is so exciting. I just met Steve McQueen, and I'm still shaking. Do you know where Andy is? I can't find him."

"No, I haven't seen him," said Powar. "Listen, I need to go in the house for a few minutes. I'll see you shortly." She ran to her childhood room and shut the door, just in time to burst into tears.

Maria circulated among the guests, mentally taking notes for her column. The beauty and taste of the reception was breathtaking, she thought. Everything reflected Powar's taste.

Nathan had refused to come, but it was now typical behavior for him. Ever since Jonna was born, he had turned his back on her, blaming her for Jonna's problem. He acted as if it were her fault that Jonna had a "problem." Maria never forgave him for treating Jonna so coldly. She lavished attention on the child and constantly told her how pretty she was, but it was not enough to counteract Nathan's damage. Maria knew that Jonna couldn't understand what she had done to make her father disapprove of her so, and she was a very unhappy child. She hated him for that and was glad he was gone. Except for one area, Jonna was developing like a beautiful girl, very tall for her young age and large-boned. Unlike Maria and Mei-Ling, Jonna did not have the shape of the Oriental eye. Hers were jet black and set wide apart, and her hair was also jet black and very straight and thick. Maria had taken Jonna to two other specialists during the first three years of her life, and both agreed with the original opinion. It was correct for her to have an operation to make her a girl, but no operation existed that could make her have a period and be fertile. It was impossible without a uterus. Maria finally accepted it and knew one day she would have to explain everything to her daughter.

Philip swung around from his desk and gazed out the window, thinking about Genevieve. It seemed she was more in his thoughts than ever; in fact, a day never went by that he didn't think of her. He had begun to regret that he'd never married Genevieve and brought her to Hollywood. Honey would have thrown a fit, but he could have dealt with that. What he couldn't do was disappoint Powar and upset her life. Powar had gotten to know Genevieve fairly well, though, having been to the Deauville Festival with him several times. But Powar was a grown woman now, with her own life. Perhaps . . . He rubbed his chest.

Two months had gone by since he'd felt that strong indigestion at the wedding reception. Ever since his botched back operation when he was at USC, he'd avoided doctors as much as possible, but the indigestion was now happening almost daily and Rolaids didn't touch it. So he'd reluctantly made an appointment with his internist, Dr. Jesse Leibman, who also was the finest heart specialist at Cedars.

"Philip, we need to do another test," said Dr. Leibman. "Your preliminary tests show there may be some blockage. We need to do an angiogram just to make sure. This is surgery, but it's not major. I don't expect bad results from it, but it is necessary."

"This doesn't make me happy, Jesse."

"Believe me, this is a lot better than my having to tell you you need an emergency quadruple bypass," said Dr. Leibman. "I'm going to schedule you for five o'clock to-day."

"What!" said Philip. "Why so soon?"

"It's better to get this out of the way. Why don't you use my phone to call Honey and ask her to come over. Don't alarm her. That's not necessary."

Honey, thought Philip. She probably isn't home. She's never home. "I'll just stay in your office and make a few calls, if that's all right. Just let me know when you want me to go to the hospital," said Philip.

"I'll be back for you in thirty minutes," Dr. Leibman responded.

Philip called Powar first and tried calmly to tell her what was happening, reassuring his distressed daughter over and over again that he was going to be fine. Honey was next. Did he detect something in her voice? Was she already counting stock options? He hoped not.

Powar got to the hospital first and was at the point of hysteria. "I must see Dr. Leibman now. I'm Philip King's daughter." Tears were ready to flow, and she was shaking.

"Don't worry, Ms. King," said the receptionist. "Your father is going to be fine. I'll bring you into the doctor's office right away."

Powar flew through the door. Dr. Leibman was waiting for her and just held her.

"Please, Powar. Don't lose it. We're just doing tests. He has some chest pains, and we need to figure out why. He's not going to drop dead at your feet. Please get a hold of yourself so he doesn't see you're this frightened. We want him to be as calm as possible."

The thought of something being wrong with her father was too hard for Powar to take. She would never be prepared to lose him and was determined to pull him through this singlehandedly.

"Your father is being prepared for the test now, so the best thing you can do is go to the waiting room. It will take a couple of hours. What we are going to do is called an angiogram. It's where we shoot dye throughout the heart to see if everything is okay. No procedure is without risk, but I can tell your father is in excellent shape for the test. I'll come to you as soon as it's through, and then you can see him. I promise." Dr. Leibman smiled reassuringly at her, and she went to the waiting room.

After about fifteen minutes, Honey showed up completely relaxed, carrying a couple of issues of *Town & Country*. "Don't worry, Powar, he'll be fine. Your father is indestructible."

"No, Mother, he is not. You are the indestructible one. You are the one with the unrelenting schedule that could drive anyone into the ground. All Daddy ever cared about was the art of making movies. You did nothing but interfere his whole life. If anything happens to him, I'll hold you personally responsible."

"This is not a proper conversation to conduct in a public waiting room, young lady." Honey pulled her into the ladies' room. "Furthermore, you don't have a clue as to what I did or did not do. You merely reap the benefits. You don't have the slightest idea what my life has really been like or the choices I have been forced to make. Everything you have is because of what I've done, not your father. Don't you ever demean me again or you'll learn what it's like to have nothing!"

"I know you're implying more than what you're revealing at this moment, but I'm not going to take the bait, Mother. No matter who you claim to have control over or what strings you're pulling, there is no substitute for natural ability. That is something you gave me, whether you like it or not, and something you can never take away. We'll just see who controls whom. Right now I think you would do well to concentrate on Daddy's health. Call up God and pull his string, why don't you?"

They walked back to the waiting room and sat silently for what seemed forever. Eventually Dr. Leibman came out from the operating room. "Congratulations, ladies. He's going to be fine. There is no evidence of any heart damage. He seems to have a condition of involuntary spasms brought on by stress. This is not a typical heart condition that we treat with medication, but I will give him nitroglycerine pills in case of emergency. I don't anticipate problems if he can just slow down a bit. Have him rest for three days and then resume a limited schedule. I know you both will take very good care of him." He looked directly at Honey on that last part and walked away. Powar just glared at her mother and followed the doctor down the hall.

She couldn't see her father because he was still in recovery. She felt a little light-headed with all the excitement, and she knew she was near Dr. Melinkoff's office. She was sure he wouldn't mind if she went in to lie down for a moment. Sure enough, he was delighted to see her. She told him about her father and felt better just talking to him.

"I'm glad you stopped by. You haven't seen me in about a year. I think you've been neglecting yourself. You look a little rundown. And since you're here, why don't we do a brief physical?"

Powar agreed. She had been feeling less energetic lately and a little dizzy from time to time. "I've just been working too hard, and I need a vacation, but you're right. We may as well do this."

As soon as the physical was over Powar drove out to the

studio for the taping of "Neighbors." She didn't want to miss it, or Andy, though things had been a little strained between the two of them since he had returned from his honeymoon.

She went to Caroline Spencer's room to lie down in between tapings. Caroline was in a notes session with the producers before taping the air show, or the real one to be seen on TV, as opposed to a tape of the dress rehearsal. Powar turned on the TV and saw a doctor reporting on something, which reminded her that she hadn't called Dr. Melinkoff to hear her results. He'd said he'd be working late, so she dialed him. "Hi, doctor. Well, am I alive?" she said jokingly.

"You certainly are, my dear girl, very much alive. Something did come up, however," said Dr. Melinkoff.

"What do you mean? Am I okay?" she asked.

"Of course you are. I just need to tell you that you are going to have a baby." There was no response from Powar, so the doctor continued. "You are over two months pregnant. Congratulations."

Powar tried to find her voice. "Doctor, I need some time to think. This is not necessarily a pleasant surprise. It is very complicated."

"Powar, you must come talk to me in person. You are not alone. Please remember this."

She hung up. She couldn't face Andy now. She had to go home and be surrounded by her things. Whenever she was upset about something, she needed to be in her own bed. Feeling familiar things around her that made her feel secure was the only way she could come up with a plan. Unfortunately she didn't have a clue as to what it might be. She left a note for Caroline telling her she felt as though she were coming down with the flu.

* CHAPTER 15 *

owar really couldn't catch her breath for about an hour. This baby was inconvenient, to say the least. She was at the peak of her job, the father was newly married to someone else, and if word of this got around Hollywood, lives could be destroyed. Yet she kept seeing Andy's face as he told her he loved her. A baby is a gift from God, she thought. If He didn't want me to have it, He wouldn't have given it to me.

She got up and started to pack. She filled two suitcases and a carry-on, taking both light and heavy clothes, although she concentrated more on outerwear, realizing she would eventually have to get maternity clothes. She then sat down at her desk and wrote four notes and called a messenger to pick them up and deliver them in the morning. Her next call was to Air France for a ticket on the morning flight to Paris with a rental car waiting for her at the airport. Having done all that, she curled up on her bed and fell asleep out of sheer emotional exhaustion.

When Philip got to the studio the next morning, Powar's note was waiting for him. He thought it was unusual, and he rushed to open it.

Dear Daddy,

By the time you read this I will have left the country for a six-month retreat from this "charming" world you brought me into. Don't worry about me. I really am fine. I just needed some time away from the pressures. My job will be safe for me, and my health is fine. You always taught me to go with my instincts, Daddy, and that is what I'm doing. You will hear from me from time to time. Do not worry. Take care of your health, and tell Mother to remain calm.

Love, Powar

Philip was very anxious about what Powar was not saying. This was not like his daughter, no matter how fine she seemed to make everything.

Andy had a different reaction when he read his note. He had felt guilty about his relationship with Powar, and it was unbearable to see her every day. Although he felt sad that she had chosen to get away, he felt he was the cause of it. Maybe it would be better to put some distance between them. After a few minutes he came to respect her choice, and he would honor it. As Powar had said, "The shows are running smoothly, and I can take a break knowing they're in your capable hands. I just need to breathe some new air, and what I'm doing is something I'm doing for both of us. It's the most important thing I have ever done." Whatever it was, he had to trust her and try to get through the time that she was away.

Maria was absolutely panicked when she heard about Powar. "Dear Maria, be calm," said Powar's letter. "No one will know where I am going except you. I can trust you after all the years we have known each other. Even though you have chosen to not talk about whatever is bothering Jonna, I know that one day you will confide in me. I have never seen a mother as devoted as you are. The kind of sensitivity you have toward Jonna is what I would expect from a friend. I am going away for six months to rest. I will call you at least once a month. I have enclosed a sealed envelope with my whereabouts should an emergency occur. Please don't worry about me. I am fine. Believe me, I know what I'm doing, and soon you will know. Remember, I am talking to you as my friend, *not* a member of the press. Nothing should appear in your paper, and don't talk to anyone if they ask you questions.''

The only phone call Powar made was to Howard Pohlmann. She called him at home because his secretary, Diana Steere, was a busybody. There was no way she could leave the head of PBC a note and just vanish. That would be too unprofessional.

"A personal situation has come up, Howard, and I must have some time off from my job," said Powar.

"Are you all right, Powar?" asked Howard. "This is highly unusual."

"I know that, sir, and if I could handle this any other way, I would. I have great respect for you and the position I hold. I would not want to compromise the company in any way. I will need six months off, and if that's too much, I am prepared to resign." Powar waited for his response.

"Whatever it is, you are not a frivolous girl. I respect you as well, and we need you. I will wait for you. You can have a leave of absence," he said.

"Thank you. I am very grateful," said Powar. "I have very good department heads, and things are running smoothly. This is the slowest time of the year, and I don't foresee any problems. I will be calling you." And then she hung up.

Powar was terrified as the plane lifted off. Had she done the right thing? Was she going to lose the network and all that she had worked for? She put her hands on her stomach and knew the answer. Nothing was more important than the gift of life. But what kind of life was this child going to have? He or she couldn't go back to Hollywood with her. For the first time in her life she felt overwhelmed with thoughts. She was trying to solve everything at once, and as a result she just got more confused. She should just concentrate on each day as it came. She wanted a healthy baby above all.

When she landed in Paris she expected to get on the tram and go to her rental car; instead she was met by Genevieve. As soon as Powar saw her with her outstretched arms, she started to cry.

"Now, now, my child," said Genevieve as she stroked Powar's head. "Don't you worry. I'll take care of everything."

Powar felt so good with Genevieve. It hadn't taken her but a few visits as a child to figure out what was going on between her father and this beautiful woman, and she completely understood why her father wanted and needed her in his life.

By the next day there were headlines in the newspapers. THE MYSTERY OF THE DISAPPEARING VEEP was hot copy. The people who received letters did not release them to the press, but that didn't stop reporters from trailing Philip, Maria, and Honey. No one could figure out why someone so visibly successful would walk away from the spectacular job she was doing. Only Dr. Melinkoff smiled as he read the headlines. Good girl, he thought. He was very proud of Powar's choice.

There was one other person who was happy, and that was Honey. She didn't know why Powar had gone away, but with her gone she had more freedom to move and plan. Even Philip would see that this kind of irresponsible behavior would never do for the head of a studio.

"So, what are you going to do without your favorite person around all the time?" she said to Philip at breakfast the day after the notes arrived. They were having a new version of eggs Benedict, with prosciutto on a croissant with a peach Hollandaise sauce, prepared the way Wolfgang had taught her.

"That's unfair and you know it," said Philip. "She's our daughter, and we should be helping her. She probably didn't tell me anything because she didn't want me to be under pressure from you to tell."

"Powar doesn't hate me," said Honey. "She respects what I have taught her about the business and what I have done for the studio."

Philip took a sip of passion fruit juice and said, "You poor woman. If you weren't so greedy, I could have more easily accepted the help you have given me. But you were so obnoxious about it that I didn't want to deal with it."

Honey jumped up from the table. "Obnoxious! Did you ever think why I might be frustrated? That maybe I had talents other than planning parties and spying, and your silent, selfish, refusal to help my singing and acting might have driven me to this anger? I really had something, and you just threw it away!" She was angrier than he had ever seen her. "You dismissed me," Honey continued, "and that's the worst thing you can do to a person." She grabbed her breakfast plate, complete with unfinished eggs, and smashed it over Philip's head.

He was stunned and felt pain over his right eye. Honey was standing over him triumphantly. His hands reached up to her throat, and she was smiling.

She felt him loosen his grip a bit as her hands went to his zipper. "Aren't you going to throw me to the floor now, Philip?"

Philip looked at her for what seemed to be a long time. He realized that the moment had finally come. He knew he was responsible for this. Years ago, in a hotel room, he had somehow given her permission to treat him like this. He was taking away that permission now.

Honey could see the struggle on his face before he spoke. "No more." He got up and walked out of the room.

Honey knew that he had crossed some sort of threshold. It was the first time her sexual power over him hadn't worked. The fear that gripped her body was unthinkable to her, but here it was. To be out of control was frightening. She found herself slowly walking up the stairs. She entered their bedroom and walked straight to her dressing room area. It was dark, and she didn't turn on the lights. She didn't want to feel "bigness" around her. She looked around and saw her reflection in the faint light on the mirrored closet doors. Without hesitation she opened the doors and walked in the closet. She shut the doors behind her and crawled to the deepest corner, where she sat down, holding her knees in front of her. The devastating feeling of loneliness was overwhelming. The only way she could cope with the fear was to put herself in the one safe place that she ever remembered. The smells of her childhood came back to her now, and feeling slightly better, she curled up on the floor and waited for the dream of the forest to envelop her.

* CHAPTER 16 *

Powar was so anxious to get to Honfleur that she didn't even suggest tea at the Ritz to Genevieve. They did, however, go to Fauchon, the gourmet food store, to stock up on goodies. All the way to the Normandy countryside Powar was soothed by the pretty villages and scenery, happy that her baby was going to be born in a calm atmosphere.

"I'm not going to pry for details, Powar," said Genevieve. "I'm sure you gave this a lot of thought."

"Yes, I did. The father doesn't know, and the circumstances are such that it is not appropriate to tell him. I love him a great deal and want to have his baby."

Genevieve put Powar in the room where she used to stay as a child. The same wooden bed was there with the multicolored quilt, the pine armoire was awaiting her things. There were fresh flowers in the ceramic blue vase on the little table next to the window. The window seat still had that faded green seat cover on it. From her window Powar could see over the meadows to the town of Honfleur. It was an ancient city built around a harbor, and Powar had always thought it was the most beautiful place she had ever seen. Most of the boats were old fishing boats or sailboats with different colored sails that reflected in the water. At sunset the beauty of it was astonishing.

The first thing Genevieve did was introduce her to Dr. Vuillard, the kindly gentleman who took care of all the villagers. "This should be a simple pregnancy," he said. "If there are complications, we could always take you to Paris, but I don't think that will happen."

Genevieve had given up cinematography years earlier, but that did not mean she'd given up taking pictures. She gave Powar one of her cameras, and together each day they would traverse the countryside, shooting pictures. Genevieve showed her the different kinds of light and what different lenses would do.

"This is a really beautiful spot," said Powar as they stopped to picnic one day, looking at the perfect meadow surrounded by trees, with a château at one end.

"I'm glad you like it," answered Genevieve. "It was a favorite of your father's."

The two women smiled at each other.

"I miss him," said Powar. "It's hard being away from him. How did you do it all these years?"

"I knew when we met that our relationship didn't have rules attached to it. I also knew that we would always love each other, but the miles would eventually determine the intensity. We'll always be there for each other," said Genevieve.

As the weeks turned into months, the peace of the land engulfed her, and Powar found that she was missing the United States less and less. She was growing larger and larger and enjoying each moment. Mara Burson sent a packet of mail and memos from the network each week to a post office box in London registered to "Toni Chapman," and Genevieve saw to it that Powar got it each week. Powar stayed in touch with Maria every few weeks, and that made them both feel better, although Maria still knew nothing.

One night, eight months into her pregnancy, Powar heard

the rush of steps at her door and an urgent pounding. She opened the door to find a nervous Genevieve.

"Oh, Powar, such sad news. Your friend Maria's husband has just died of a heart attack. You must call her right away."

She picked up the phone and dialed. "May I speak to Maria, please? It's Powar King." Powar waited. "Maria, can you hear me? We have a bad connection. I'm so sorry. Is there anything I can do?"

"Yes," said Maria. "Come home."

Powar looked down at her now very large stomach. "I'm getting closer to where I can do that, Maria. I'm going to give you the phone number of where I am. Please don't give it to anyone. If you see Andy, tell him I'm fine and I'll write. I'm sorry for what you're going through, and I hope that Jonna is okay. And Maria, I think you and Jonna will be better off this way." Powar could feel Maria smile.

"I know what you mean, my friend," said Maria. "Don't worry about us. I'll talk to you very soon."

Maria hung up and went back to her guests. The house had filled up with many of Nathan's friends and some of his enemies. "That was a wonderful eulogy, Mrs. Goetz. I'm sure your father was looking down on you with pride," said Maria. Since Edith Goetz was a daughter of Louis B. Mayer of MGM and she had known Nathan very well, Maria felt it was fitting that she spoke at the service as a representative of all the original studio heads. The funeral had taken place at Hillside Memorial Park, a lavish Jewish cemetery south of Culver City, where Al Jolson had a tomb and monument the size of a small apartment. It was a real Hollywood cemetery, owned by the Groman family of Beverly Hills. Maria had long been familiar with the saying, "You aren't dead if a Groman hasn't buried you."

Maria looked around the room at people she thought looked more like they belonged in jail than her living room. They were attacking the buffet as if they were eating for twelve. Then she realized that she wasn't going to have to see them any more if she didn't want to. According to Nathan's will, which he'd written after Jonna's birth, Maria had inherited everything free and clear.

"Maria," said Honey, "we are terribly sorry about Nathan."

"Yes," said Philip. "He was very helpful to me in the beginning, and I'll always be grateful to him."

Honey was wearing a black suit with a black wide-brimmed hat and a red silk blouse, with her trademark Rita Hayworth hair. Her looks were still the talk of any gathering.

"Thank you very much," said Maria. "Have you heard anything from Powar?"

Philip's face turned sad. "No."

"Oh, don't worry, Philip," Honey piped up. "I'm sure she's fine."

Maria excused herself to take care of the other guests.

"We've spent enough time here, haven't we?" asked Honey.

"I think we should stay longer," Philip said.

"I think it's time to go," Honey retorted. "This event has peaked, and it's time to go."

"Then take the car and leave and send it back for me," said Philip.

Honey thought about it, and even though she would have liked to win this one, she thought it would be more important to stay by his side. She wouldn't want to give the impression to the guests that they weren't together. Besides, if he were up to something, her presence would thwart it.

Within a month after Nathan died, Powar woke up with labor pains. It was six o'clock in the morning, and she called for Genevieve.

When Genevieve walked in the room she was prepared. "I'm going to call the doctor and then I'll be with you. Don't worry. Just keep breathing and try to stay calm. Breathe through the pain."

Powar started to cry. She wasn't so brave after all. She

wanted to be in Cedars with Andy by her side, holding her hand. She wanted to see Dr. Melinkoff's reassuring face and know that her father was waiting just outside the door. She had never felt so frightened or so alone.

Soon the doctor was there, and he gave her something for the pain, and six hours later a little girl was born. Powar named her Jordan King. It was March 31, 1973, exactly one year after Powar had been on the cover of *Time*. Powar just held Jordan and started to cry. As she held the baby she made an oath with herself never to make Jordan feel the way Honey had made her feel. She wanted her daughter to know that she was wanted and loved. Powar always wanted to put Jordan first, above herself. She knew at that moment that there wasn't anything she wouldn't do for her. She also knew that there was no way she could just hop a flight back to the States in a couple of weeks. A mother and daughter should not be separated. She would stay another three months and then leave.

One of the first things Maria did after Nathan's funeral was call a decorator to redo their master bedroom; but she waited four months before she redecorated Nathan's office. She decided that was enough time. Maria loved the way the office looked now, a dusty pink with a deeper rose carpet, her couch a floral print with pinks and greens and purples. The furniture she'd chosen was natural blond wood. She redid the bathroom, too, with an oyster-shaped sink with Sherle Wagner fixtures.

She reveled in being in complete charge of the paper. She remembered her earlier days at the paper, where Nathan sat upstairs in his shrine with a direct phone line to the editor. Now, every time she called down to an editor, the entire city room jumped. Now she was the one upstairs with the special line. There wasn't an employee within fifty miles who didn't know that she was in charge. Before anything could be committed to print, Maria had to approve it. As a woman owner of a large publishing corporation, she began receiving honors from the mayor's office, Women in Business, and even the USC School of Journalism. She had a special fondness for USC and immediately set up a scholarship in her name and Nathan's.

As the publisher of the paper, Maria had to go out almost every night, but she always went home to see Jonna first. Gladys, Jonna's nurse/nanny, was now part of the family, and Maria had even moved her into her mother's old bungalow.

"Don't you worry, Jonna, I'm going to be back really soon," said Maria. "You'll know when I'm back because you'll feel my kisses in the night."

"She'll be fine, ma'am," said Gladys. "Don't you worry about that little upset stomach. She had a baked potato for dinner."

Maria also saved Wednesday afternoons and Saturday mornings to take Jonna to her gymnastics classes. She'd begun when she was an infant, and Jonna loved them so much, they'd become a part of her young life.

Maria was not happy about getting into western gear for the party at Paramount. Producer Joe Levine, a blowhard who got Italian financing to make a few hits, was throwing a flashy party for his company on Paramount's western street, and Maria was obligated to go because Joe spent a lot of money on advertising in her paper. It was the least she could do. She was wearing all black, which fit her mood—tight black jeans, boots, a shirt, and a cowboy hat like the bad guys wore in the Clint Eastwood westerns. She just wanted to stay for an hour or so and then get out. When she arrived at Paramount a valet took her car and showed her to the horse-drawn buggy to drive her to the back lot. Joe's sparing no expense, thought Maria.

When she got there she saw at least one thousand people milling around campfires. A huge barbecue setup a block long on either side of the main street was laden with ribs, chicken, corn, salads, and pies. There were tables everywhere with red-and-white-checkered tablecloths. Maria decided to go to the bar for a Coke, and she ran right into Falkner Cantwell.

"Maria, how nasty you look this evening," said he. "Black is my favorite color."

"So I've heard, Falk," countered Maria, who had long ago found out everything about him from Powar. He was not one of Maria's favorite people.

"How's our disappearing friend doing? Do you hear from her?" asked Falk.

"I certainly do," said Maria, "and she's doing very well. She'll be home soon."

"You'd better tell her to hurry," Falk retorted. "Howard Pohlmann isn't going to wait much longer. That's something I know firsthand." He smiled his best capped-teeth smile.

Maria paused before responding, looking him squarely in the eye. "You know, Falk, I'd be careful if I were you. You wouldn't want to read a story about a producer who gives special parties at his house wearing a dress with some cute little extras, would you?" Maria walked off and left him stunned, staring after her. She was having a better time than she thought she would. She spotted Suzanne Pleshette and decided to talk to her. She was always fun. After a few minutes of dishing other people at the party, they began to smell smoke.

"Do you think it could just be all the barbecue and the campfires?" asked Maria.

"I don't know," said Suzanne. "There's an awful lot of smoke." Everyone else around them started to talk about it, too, and then some men with bullhorns appeared.

"Everybody evacuate the area immediately. Walk quickly and calmly back to the front gate." They kept repeating the announcement as part of the walls of the town at the end of the street went up in flames.

"When Joe gives a hot party, he's not kidding," said Suzanne.

Maria took out her notebook and pen and started writing.

"Are you nuts?" Suzanne said. "We have to get out of here."

"You go ahead. I'm going to stay just a few more minutes and do an eyewitness account for the paper," said Maria. She was watching Hollywood history burn up before her very eyes. Although she didn't enjoy seeing it go, the reporter in her loved being at the scene. She ran to the gate just as a wall came tumbling down behind her, singeing her shirt.

Her heart was pounding as she raced back to her office. It was eight-thirty and the paper would be closed, but the print shop would still be operating. She slammed on the brakes when she hit her parking spot. Hurriedly she unlocked the door to the print shop. She was not expected, judging by the looks of surprise on the faces of the crew. "Get me the page one plate and proof right away, and stop the run," she ordered. "How many have you done so far?" she asked the foreman.

"About one thousand," he replied.

"Dump them," she said. "I'm pulling a story and adding a new one."

Moments like this got her journalist's blood going. There was nothing more exciting than being in on a story from the beginning, then racing to be the first to report it. That rush and desire is something that could not be taught in school. They could teach the construction of a story, but they couldn't get your heart going. This was what Maria lived for. When she picked up her paper the next morning to see the headline that beat out everybody else, it would put her on a high that would last for a couple of days. Conversely, if she or one of her reporters missed a big story, it would be very ugly around the office. If a reporter missed two big scoops in a row, he or she would be fired. Maria was going to see to it that her paper was number one, and that was that.

Powar just couldn't get over Jordan's hands and feet. They were so small and perfect. She loved to trace them with her own hands and feet and then kiss them all over. She was simply entranced with her and had never experienced anything like it. She didn't want to leave her. For a while she entertained the idea of coming home with her and saying she had adopted her in France, but she knew that wouldn't wash. She was just going to have to deal with living away from her for periods at a time.

She and Genevieve started taking Jordan with them wherever they went. People thought Jordan was gorgeous, and she responded in kind, a very happy, alert baby. Genevieve and Powar took hundreds of still photographs of her. Jordan seemed to love it, and she kept grabbing at the camera. Every Tuesday and Friday there was an outdoor market in Honfleur. The main street around the harbor would be lined with carts full of flowers, fruits, and vegetables. Genevieve, Jordan, and Powar went each time.

"Look," said Genevieve, "look how pretty this cabbage is, Jordan. See how each leaf is formed in its own way. And look how bright this carrot is. This is an orange-colored carrot."

Powar loved to see Genevieve teaching Jordan. It made her realize that Jordan was in a very safe place. As people were through shopping they stood around, turning it into a town meeting. People would go leisurely from cart to cart, taking a break to sit on the wall of the harbor. Sometimes they would go into a café for coffee and a croissant. Powar loved to do that, only if it was after eleven A.M. she would have a baguette with ham, cheese, and mustard. Nowhere in the world did a ham-and-cheese sandwich taste like this.

As they were driving back to the house, Genevieve could see how difficult the separation was going to be on Powar. "I have a wonderful idea, Powar. Why don't you try to come back in October for Deauville? We'll think of a way to keep your father in the States. That way you and Jordan will be together again for two weeks. The festival is only two months away. Then you can come for Christmas, which is only two months after Deauville. It will all work out," said Genevieve.

Powar pulled the car off the road and started to cry. "I

don't see how I can leave her at all. I just can't do it, I can't,'' she sobbed as Genevieve held her.

"Yes, you can. I love her and I'll take care of her. You know I'll devote my life to her. I'm sure as soon as you can you will figure out a way to take her to the States. You're doing the right thing for now. You're too public a figure, and you have too many responsibilities to yourself right now. Jordan is the delight of everyone here, and you know it. She'll be treated like a little princess. Now it's time for you to go home. You've been away too long already, and you know it.''

Powar knew Genevieve was right, but her feelings and priorities had shifted. She was wondering how she would feel about the network world when she went back. Was one share point really that important in the grand scheme of things? Powar knew she had to get out of there as fast as possible before she changed her mind.

Genevieve made plans to have Dr. Vuillard sit with Jordan while she drove Powar to Paris to make the night flight. Powar called Maria from the airport in Paris and asked her to pick her up in Los Angeles, making her swear to keep her arrival a secret.

All the way home on the plane Powar was filled with apprehension. She was going to have to face the press and her family and friends, and Howard Pohlmann. Being away for so long in a land so beautiful and free of the stress of Hollywood had Powar questioning all her choices. She really didn't know what she would do about anything . . . anything, that was, except Andy. There wasn't a day that she didn't miss him. They had spoken a couple of times, but the conversations had been strained, she not wanting to give too much information, he afraid to ask. She was going to have to fix that somehow.

Powar and Maria hugged each other for a good five minutes when she got off the plane.

"Just come with me,'' Maria said. Powar followed her out

to the curb and a black Lincoln limousine. A driver got out and opened the door for them. "Just give him your baggage tags and he'll bring them to us. Let's wait in the car," said Maria.

Powar looked at her and then looked at the car. "You're hilarious! What else has changed around here?"

Once inside, the two of them just looked at each other. "Okay," said Maria. "I've been a good scout. I have covered for you. I want to know what I was covering up." Tears welled up in Powar's eyes. Maria softened immediately. "Please tell me what happened. I want to help you."

Powar swallowed and then pressed the button to close off their section of the car from the chauffeur's. "I went away to have a baby, Maria. I have a beautiful little girl who is three months old." Powar looked so vulnerable.

"Oh, my God. I don't know what to say. I hope you're happy, and I hope she's healthy," said Maria, putting her arms around her. "Who's the father? I can't help it. I have to know."

"It's Andy," answered Powar. "And he doesn't know anything about it. If you tell anyone about any of this, I'll kill you."

"A double 'Oh, my God,' " said Maria. "It must be so painful for you. This is just awful. Where is your baby?"

"She's with Daddy's friend Genevieve in France. I can trust her."

"Yes, I remember what you told me about her in college," said Maria. "Wow! This is some situation. You know Andy deserves to know, don't you? And you deserve to have him. No one can stand Franny. She thinks she's going to overthrow your mother for the Hostess of Hollywood trophy. It's so obvious and disgusting."

Powar sat silently as the car headed up toward the Sunset Strip. "There's one thing missing from this confession time, old buddy, and that's yours," she said to Maria. "Don't give me that blank look. I don't know what it is, but ever since Jonna was born there was a change in you. It's tied to her, but I haven't figured out what it could be. Now's the time, Maria."

And then Maria told her the story about Jonna's "ambiguous genitalia." Powar was stunned by this revelation. "Well, aren't we the pair?" she said. She had never heard of the condition, but she offered to help Maria in any way that she could.

"You know," said Maria, "our kids are only a little less than four years apart. It would be wonderful if they could grow up together."

Powar looked down. "Maybe one day," she said.

When Powar was left alone in her house, the first thing she did was take out her photographs of Jordan, kiss each one, then lock them away in her wall safe. She sat down on the bed. It was as if she hadn't really been anywhere the past twelve months. All she had to do was pick out what she wanted to wear to work and go to bed as if nothing had ever happened. But, in fact, that wasn't really true, and she knew she didn't want to rush to the office. She didn't really know what she'd find. She really didn't know for sure whether or not she had a job. Yes, she was on a leave of absence, but it had been much longer than she anticipated. The network was also running smoothly without her.

No one knew she was in town yet, so she had the advantage of being back home and thinking things through in her own environment without being hounded by people . . . at least for a couple of days. The person she wanted to see most was her father. Andy was a high second on the list, but she needed to talk to Philip. It was a Friday morning, and she knew he'd be at the office. She dialed his private line so his secretary wouldn't be able to hear how close her voice sounded.

"Hello," said Philip.

"I'm back, Daddy," said Powar.

"Oh, thank God," said Philip. "I have missed you so much. Are you all right?"

"Don't worry, Daddy, I'm just fine. I feel great. It was exactly the right thing to do. I'd love to see you as soon as I can, but I don't want anybody to know I'm back. Can you come over here?"

"Of course I can. Let me bring some lunch and I'll see you at twelve-thirty."

Powar couldn't wait to see him. It killed her that she couldn't tell him he had a beautiful granddaughter. He would have been so happy. She showered and put on jeans and a T-shirt, not yet ready to get back into her mogul wardrobe.

Precisely at twelve-thirty her doorbell rang. She opened it to see her father holding hot dogs from Tail o' the Pup, the place they used to go to all the time when she was a little girl because it was across the street from Beverly Park, the amusement park at Beverly Boulevard and La Cienega that was right in the middle of the city. He was grinning from ear to ear because he knew she would be so delighted with his surprise. He knew exactly which hot dogs to get, too. He knew she loved the one with the barbecue sauce and the baked beans and the other with cheese, grilled onions, mustard, and relish. What made Tail o' the Pup so great, besides the fact that the building was shaped like a hot dog, was that they split the hot dogs down the middle and grilled them on both sides. No other stand in the city ever did that.

They hugged forever. It felt so good to Powar. They landed in her breakfast room, where she took out two bottles of Dr. Brown's cream soda and a bag of potato chips that she found, and they started to eat.

"What's been happening? How is everything? I'm dying to know," said Powar.

"Now hold on. I'll answer those questions in a minute," Philip said. "But you should go first. Just tell me where and why. I deserve to know."

Powar took a deep breath. "I was in Honfleur with Genevieve for part of the time."

"What!" exclaimed Philip. "How could that happen?"

"Oh, Daddy, I've known about her ever since I was a child."

Philip stopped and took a few seconds to swallow the cream

soda. "I should have realized that. It's always a mistake to underestimate the King women," he said with a smile. Then, turning serious, "Genevieve means a great deal to me."

If only you knew how much she means to *me*, thought Powar, clenching her teeth, hating that she couldn't really tell her father the truth.

"It's not that I haven't loved your mother," Philip continued. "I have tried to make things work. I've tried to compromise with her. It hasn't been easy. I'm sure you've noticed how our marriage deteriorated. It's just that she loves power and control so much. It's what she lives for. It became too much for me, but I tried to do the best for you."

"Since you know about King women, Dad, you would have to know that I already am aware of everything you're saying. Please don't feel bad about Mother. I know who she is, and I know who you are. I'm very lucky to have had a father like you."

"My God, even the hot dog's crying," Philip said to lighten the moment just a bit. "So what's going on with you? Why did you leave? It was very hard on me."

"I'm sorry, but I just had to go. You know you raised a smart kid. I know what I'm doing. I had just had it with the sniping and insincerity that goes on in this business. Some of the executives and producers I was dealing with on a daily basis were treacherous people. I'm in this business for the same reason you are. I love the art of it. I love to come up with product that entertains people . . . shows that make them laugh or move them. I just needed to get away to get some perspective on the world. I walked right into this zoo the day I got out of college. I never spent any time in my house. I had never traveled alone. I just needed to grow up a little bit more. I also recognized the chance I was taking by abdicating power even for just a little bit after I had risen so far, but it was right for me."

"And what did you learn, sweetheart?" asked Philip.

"I'm still thinking about it, but I know that I really do love this business, but you can't be a whole human being unless you take some time out to be a person. Even if it's just once a month, going away for a weekend where nobody knows you, or even going to Europe every eight weeks or so, it's a way of having a fuller life. That can't help but make one more creative and do better product."

"There is something else in the world that is as important as being a whole human being, and that is family. Our family," said Philip. "We aren't just ordinary people, as you know. Our name is synonymous with Hollywood history. We have an obligation to our industry and our own sense of history to continue our 'dynasty.' One day you will hopefully continue that with children of your own."

Powar had almost stopped breathing.

"But our family dynasty is intertwined with business, and that is something we can talk about today. It is time for me to step down as president of King Pictures. You must take over now. I will become chairman and chief executive officer, to whom you will report, but the day-to-day operations of running both the motion picture and the TV divisions should go to you. You worked hard at PBC and earned the respect of everyone in the industry. No one will say you're too young to take over the family business. Darling, it makes no sense for you to build up somebody else's company. You don't own PBC, and we all own King Pictures. That is where you belong. Please say yes."

Powar's heart was soaring. She realized now that another lesson she'd learned in Europe was that it was time to let go of the ugliness of the network. Even though she had mastered it, why did she need it in her daily life? A studio was no picnic, either, but it was her park, not somebody else's. "Daddy, I don't know what to say except that I am honored. But one question. How does Mother feel about this?"

Philip chuckled. "You always go right to it, don't you? She knew this day would come, and she's done everything to prevent it. But I always knew that when it came right down to it, she would rather let this happen against her will than publicly prevent it and present a divided family for this town and the press to write and talk about. As long as she feels she and I are holding the top corporate positions, which we would be doing, she'll be fine. The bottom line to Honey is whether or not we turn a profit, and she knows that you'll take care of that. She knows your friends are making the hits now, and business is business with her.''

They toasted each other with Dr. Brown's as Powar said, "Okay, then, *you* tell her!" They broke up laughing.

When her father left, Powar knew where she had to go next. Andy would be at the bungalow at the Beverly Hills Hotel, writing. Only she and Andy had keys, and she knew right where she had placed hers when she left. She put on a navy blue leather jacket that she'd bought in France and went to her garage, hoping that her assistant, Mara Burson, had done her job by running the T-Bird's engine and keeping the car in perfect shape while she was gone.

She had. The car started perfectly, and Powar was on her way to the hotel, wanting to fly there now that the moment had come. She parked on Crescent Drive by the side of the hotel, where she could walk through the grounds to get to the bungalow rather than go through the lobby, and soon she was standing at the door of number thirty-three. She put the key into the lock and opened the door to see Franny Stromberg sitting on the living room couch. Powar recovered first.

"Franny, how nice to see you."

Andy heard Powar's voice from the bedroom, and came running in as Franny was attempting to be polite. "Powar, you're back," he said. He kissed her chastely on the cheek while he held her hands. "Franny, look who's here."

"How are you, Powar?" asked Franny.

"Just fine. I feel very rested and renewed after my vacation," replied Powar.

"That was quite a vacation," Franny interjected.

"Yes, it was," said Powar.

"I came to pick Andy up over his objections. He wanted to keep working," said Franny. "We're going to Santa Barbara for the weekend for the Angels benefit."

"Yes," added Andy. "I was going to drive up tomorrow morning, but Franny insisted."

"Well, don't let me keep you, and you have a wonderful weekend," said Powar, exiting, knowing full well that the moment she was out of sight, Franny would be on the phone and her arrival back in town would be in Monday's papers.

Powar felt sick as she walked to the car. Andy did not belong in that situation. He wasn't meant to be an appendage to an Angel member. He should be free to write and live life on a different level. She was going to have to do something.

When Powar walked out the door Andy thought he was going to kill himself. He had missed her so much, and knowing she was back in town made his upcoming weekend with Franny seem like a death sentence. He didn't know how he was going to get through it. He knew he wasn't in love with his wife, but he didn't quite know what to do about it. She devoted herself to him and did everything she could to give him a wonderful life. He was always behind closed doors writing or in a studio producing. He had no time even to think of the social necessities, that he might like to go to a baseball game or a concert or have dinner with friends. Instead she made his life a perfect place to be. He never would have had clean clothes without her. All his clothes were taken care of and returned freshly cleaned or laundered to exactly where they were two days before. His drawers and closets were kept perfectly neat at all times. He would have had takeout food or frozen dinners if not for her. If he was working late at the studio, she would appear with a plate of his favorite chicken and deep-dish apple pie. On the weekends he frequently didn't know where he was going or what he was doing, he would just find a note on his bathroom mirror saying "Be back here and ready to go in black tie," or whatever was appropriate at whatever time they were supposed to leave. Sometimes he would find himself at Dodger Stadium with friends he enjoyed, sometimes he ended up at a charity dinner at the Beverly Hilton that he would rather not go to, but he knew she'd scheduled him there because it was right for his business. She would see to it that there were fresh flowers all around the house, and each day there would be a new one in a bud vase by his desk in the office in his house. He was taken care of like a prince, and over the past twelve months it had proved very seductive.

Seeing Powar immediately awakened his feelings again, and there was no way Franny couldn't have sensed that. As Franny was driving him to the Biltmore in Santa Barbara, he had to fight thinking about Powar. He had been devastated when she left, and now that she was back he realized he had to make some changes.

Franny pulled into the Biltmore, a beautiful Spanish-looking hotel right across the street from the ocean in the very wealthy city of Santa Barbara. It was a formal hotel where it wasn't proper to wear tennis shorts or any bathing attire inside the main building. They were famous for the charity balls in the grand ballroom and their beautiful tennis and pool area, and they even had a putting green in the middle of the grounds. Most people chose to stay in the bungalows rather than the main building because they preferred the privacy.

"Isn't this hotel divine?" said Franny. "I just love the layout, and the service is so wonderful. Maybe we should get a house up here so we can have a weekend place to entertain people. We could have our own Santa Barbara Biltmore."

"I'm sorry, Franny, what did you say?" said Andy.

"Never mind," said Franny, knowing full well how thrown Andy was by Powar's arrival. She was just going to wait and watch him.

He and Franny were shown to the Caballero bungalow, which was a one-bedroom suite decorated like a Spanish villa. The furniture was heavy, carved, dark brown wood upholstered in burgundy velvet. There was a fireplace and a bar in the living room, and in the bedroom was a giant four-poster bed with very thick carved columns. Andy longed for Powar to be there. He was lucky, in one respect. He knew that Franny did not expect much from him sexually. When the magic hadn't been there on the honeymoon, neither had complained. Franny was getting what she wanted by being married to Andy, and that was fine with her. Although the two of them never discussed it, they both knew that they had settled for some sort of arrangement very early on. And Franny knew that what she did for him and his life-style was somehow far more important for their marriage than prowess in the bedroom.

Since Franny was always the one who unpacked and made their nest ready, Andy felt free to leave the room. "I'm going for a walk around the grounds," he said as he left, and that seemed fine with Franny.

"Powar," Andy said warmly into the phone in the men's locker room in the tennis area of the hotel. He made sure that no one was around to hear the conversation.

"How's Santa Barbara?" asked Powar. She had been disappointed when she saw how well he had "adapted" to Franny's life-style. It was unnerving to her after spending so much time in Europe away from the hypocrisy of Hollywood.

"I don't like it here because you're not here," replied Andy. "I want to see you when I get back so we can talk."

"I would like that," said Powar.

"Where have you been?" asked Andy. "I couldn't stand it."

Powar thought before she answered. "I was on another continent trying to get a break. I feel much better now and am planning some changes that I'll tell you about when I see you. I'll meet you in the bungalow Monday at three. I presume you'll be alone."

"Yes," said Andy. "I'll make sure of it."

Andy finished his walk by crossing the street and walking along the beach. There was something in Powar's voice that was different. Something had changed in her, he just couldn't figure out what it was.

When he returned to the room, Franny had some caviar and champagne waiting for him and his tuxedo all laid out.

There was a fire in the fireplace, and she was wearing a silk turquoise dressing gown. He hoped this was not going to be one of the rare times when he would have to perform.

"Shall we have some goodies before we get ready?" asked Franny, handing him a toast point filled with beluga. Andy accepted it and sat down next to the champagne. "Didn't you think it was strange that Powar just appeared out of nowhere?" asked Franny.

"Yes," said Andy.

"I wonder why she disappeared," Franny continued. "There's no way she just needed to get away. You don't do that when you're in the career position she's in. There has to be something more to it, don't you think, dear?"

"I really don't know, Franny. Powar has always been different from most people in this town."

"Well, I'm going to do my best to find out what's happening," Franny said emphatically.

Andy got up and went to take a long shower so he didn't have to get involved.

Franny was in her glory at the benefit. She had on a brand-new St. Laurent black-and-gold gown, and she had set up her table perfectly. She was now the recording secretary for the Angels, a job no one wanted except Franny; but she'd do anything to get in closer with the ladies. Honey was now president emeritus. It was something that Franny wanted one day, but she knew she'd have to work hard for many years to achieve it. That was fine with her. Whatever it took.

Honey's table was closer to the stage than hers, but that was accepted. There was a generational dividing line between the old and new guard of Hollywood. Franny understood that, too. Honey and Philip were the king and queen. Seated at their table were Lew and Edie Wasserman from Universal, actor Carroll O'Connor and his wife, Nancy. O'Connor's show "All in the Family" was so hot, it made him the most sought-after man in Hollywood at the moment. Also seated there were Gloria and Jimmy Stewart; Ellen and her agent husband, Jack Elliot, who had just sold their agency to a New York conglomerate for $50 million; and movie star Richard Callaway, who at sixty was turning out to be as big for King Pictures as Clark Gable was for MGM in his day. For just one second Franny wondered if Callaway and Honey ever were an item, because everybody knew about Philip's mistress in Europe.

Honey looked over to Franny and waved, which Franny responded to, and then Honey nodded to the guests at Franny and Andy's table. Honey was impressed to see Burt Reynolds and Dinah Shore; the star cast of Andy's hit TV series "Neighbors"; the beautiful new star Lynda Carter, who had been in town less than two years and was just named, at twenty-one, one of the ten most beautiful women in the world by *Vogue* magazine; Howard Pohlmann and his wife, Ruth; Blair Lawson; and everybody's favorite hairdresser, Monsieur Max.

Franny had sought Blair out at Angel meetings, wanting to become her friend. As a young girl living just south of Beverly Hills and not having any of the benefits, but being able to see them up close, Franny soon realized that the pretty, WASPy blonde women were the lucky ones. Just by virtue of their looks they got better tables in restaurants, they won Homecoming Queen, they had better men, they were asked to join all the right organizations . . . in short, they were privileged without having to do a thing. Franny wanted desperately to be one of them, but she knew she couldn't, not even with the help of a plastic surgeon. The next best thing was to bask in their glow and let a little bit rub off on her. Because she was Mrs. Andy Stromberg she was privileged, too, but it never was because of who *she* was as a person. And so she was drawn to Blair, who looked just like Grace Kelly. If Franny could win Blair over, maybe she'd feel a little like Grace Kelly herself. Tonight Blair had on a winter white strapless chiffon gown, and she looked like a vanilla ice-cream cone. The vision was startling. She hadn't come with her lawyer husband, John, because they were getting a divorce. It was friendly, but Franny knew that Blair felt more comfortable tonight with Max. Everybody loved Max. He was French Moroccan with black hair pulled back into a ponytail, and he had great cheekbones. He had a fabulous sense of humor, and everybody went to him, knowing he could transform almost anyone into a beauty in about forty-five minutes.

"Check out Norman Meyer's wife, will you?" Max said, nodding to the table to his right. "She looks like she got off her plastic surgeon's table this afternoon, she's so tight."

"Oh, Max, we can always count on you to brighten things up," said Blair, who definitely did not live or die for Angels events.

"There's something I have to do," Franny said. "I'll be right back."

She walked over to the Kings' table and stood between Honey and Philip.

Honey looked up at her and said politely, "Good evening, Franny. Are you and Andy having a good time?"

"Oh, yes, we certainly are. This is a wonderful party. By the way, isn't it great that Powar's back?"

Honey tried to keep her eyes from falling out of her head. Amid cries of "What!" "When?" from the guests, Philip said forcefully, "Yes, I'm delighted. We saw her yesterday, and she seems very happy. Wherever she was, she came back rested and healthy." Philip looked at Honey and smiled. While he had saved her from total embarrassment in front of her friends, he knew that she would be wild with him when they finally were alone tonight because he hadn't told her.

Franny, pleased with starting the rumor ball rolling, wished everyone a happy dinner and went to another table to spread the news. Andy was watching her but didn't have a clue as to what she was doing. She made her way back to the table. "Isn't this fun? Everybody's talking about how Powar King came back to town today. Did you know that, Howard?" said Franny, trying to hide her smugness at being the one "in the know."

"Yes, I did. As a matter of fact, we have a meeting scheduled for Monday at ten," said Howard.

With that Franny sat down and kept her mouth shut for a while. In between dinner and dessert, Blair rose to go to the ladies' room, and Franny followed her. "I'm organizing a few people to go riding tomorrow at the San Ysidro Guest Ranch," said Franny. "I would love it if you and Max would join us."

"Max can't because he has to be in his shop on Saturday, but I'd love to. I think it would be great fun."

Franny was thrilled. "Why don't we all meet there at ten, and I'll arrange for a picnic to be set up along the way around one in the afternoon. The Biltmore will pack baskets for us, and we can make a day of it."

"Sounds good to me," said Blair. "I love how you organize everything. I don't know what I'd do without my staff. I just have no interest in planning things. I just want it taken care of. I admire your ability to do that."

That was the clue that Franny needed to make herself indispensable to Blair. Just as she was getting ready to return to her table, Honey walked in.

"Oh, hello, Franny dear," said Honey, relishing the opportunity. "How did you know Powar was back? She wanted it to be a secret."

"I know," said Franny, "but I ran into her when she dropped in on Andy as we were leaving to come here."

"Really?" Honey said provocatively. "That's very interesting, don't you think? You should think about that visit."

Their eyes locked.

The screams coming from Philip and Honey's room were reverberating through the trees surrounding the bungalows. Franny immediately stopped what she was doing to try to make out what was going on. She could tell it had something to do with Powar, but every time Honey got to what it was, Franny could hear Philip trying to quiet her.

"Do you know what would happen if people heard about this now?" Philip yelled. "Keep your voice down and . . ."

That was all Franny could hear. It was quiet for a few minutes, and then she heard Honey scream, "Over my dead body! You can't do this without my approval!"

Again there were muffled words from Philip, and it was quiet. Franny was dying to go out into the night and sit under the window of their bungalow, but even she thought that was too drastic. She would have to put her Angel spies on it on Monday.

Powar had a miserable weekend. She missed Jordan terribly and telephoned her every day. She was really too little to understand what it meant when Genevieve held the phone to her ear, but it made Powar feel better that she was attempting to communicate. Because she had been out of the country so long, she decided to take a day and walk around Westwood, where all the movie theaters were. She saw a couple of movies and then went over to Maria's house to play with Jonna. Maria had a jungle gym in the backyard, and all three of them got in it.

"Jonna, look at Mommy," said Maria as she started to swing from rung to rung.

"Me, me," Jonna yelled.

"I have an idea," said Powar. "I'm going to lift you up and hold you as you go. That way you won't fall. Okay, Mom?"

Maria laughed while Powar held Jonna up and put her hands on a rung. With that Jonna swung herself to the next one before Powar knew it.

"She's really strong, isn't she?" said Powar. "I've never seen anything like it." Then tears started to well up in her eyes. Playing with Jonna made her miss Jordan more. The only thing that sustained her was the knowledge that she was about to take her rightful place in her family's business. It was time to do it. She would do it for her father, for herself, and for her daughter, the next King in line whether her father knew it or not.

Precisely at nine forty-five A.M. on Monday, Powar walked back into PBC. Her office and Mara were waiting for her. It felt good to be back in the sanctity of her office, and for one second she was concerned about the choice she was making. But then it all went away. Now she wouldn't be restricted by working in just one medium. She could do movies, television, and even back theatrical productions if she wanted. It was an incredible opportunity. The phone was ringing as she arrived, since the *L.A. Times* and all the newscasts had devoted time to her return. Powar realized she was public property, and she would simply deal with it.

At ten A.M. she walked into Howard Pohlmann's office. She wasn't sure what to expect. To be technically correct, Powar had breached her contract when she went away, and she could have been sued. Her contract now had only six months to go. If worse came to worst, she would offer to buy it out herself. King Pictures had the money to do it.

Howard Pohlmann was dressed all in gray except for his starched white shirt and charcoal shoes. "Powar, nice to see you back." His greeting was almost warm. "Won't you sit down?" he said as he showed her to the couch. "Are you feeling better?"

"Yes, I am, Howard. Going away was very good for me. It cleared my mind, and I think it will sustain me for a long time. How is everything around here?" asked Powar. "I went over the ratings this morning, and it looks like everything is fine."

They both were fencing to see who would reveal what was actually going on first. "I am aware, Howard, that I took a chance by doing what I did. It was not necessarily the best thing to do for my career, but it was right for my health. I hope I didn't inconvenience you."

Howard took a sip of his tea before answering. "You did make life difficult. We were on our way to climbing new plateaus, and it was difficult to lose our quarterback so abruptly. Fortunately you did have good executives backing you up, so we did not suffer. I'll never know how much better we could have done had you been here." Powar was just looking at him calmly. "We both are faced with choices now, Powar. I have the right to fire you or hold you to your contract. What do you think I should do?" This was not the tactic Powar expected, but the unexpected was what made Howard the leader he was in broadcasting.

Powar smiled. "I think we should keep it friendly. We both recognize that unhappy people, on either side, don't do good work. I think we should realize that no matter where I work, whether it's here or someplace else, I will do a good job because that's what I do. It would benefit both of us to remain happy. I, too, have choices. I could sit here for the next six months and supervise work well, but not come up with particularly powerhouse ideas until after my contract is over. Or I could just go on another extended sick leave. The insurance company would recognize that. I don't think any of this is necessary. You gave me a chance when I needed to prove something, and I will always be grateful to you. I appreciate your recognition that it was crucial for me to leave when I did. I love this company very much. Together you and I made PBC a real contender. I have set you up with a team to continue to do that. The time away has made me realize that I would like more entrepreneurial opportunities. I will always take care of PBC in my heart and make sure you get good product no matter where I am. Why don't we just keep working together in the spirit in which we always have? I just would like us to shake hands and terminate my contract together. There's no need to fire me because you would have to give me a lot of money from my severance clause. Let's stop my salary right now, and when I announce what I am doing next, your graciousness in the handling of this situation will be duly noted by me in the press."

Once again Powar King amazed Howard. He realized it would always be in his best interest to have her on his side.

"Aloha, Powar," said Howard with a smile as he shook her hand. They both laughed uproariously at the Hawaiian reference.

"Andy," said Powar, "meet me at the Franklin Canyon gate in thirty minutes, okay?"

"You got it!"

Powar went to Greenblatt's Deli to get two turkey, ham, and Swiss with coleslaw and Russian dressing sandwiches on rye to go. She also bought some ruggelach cookies and two Dr. Brown's cream sodas. She and Andy arrived at exactly the same time. When they both got out of their cars and saw each other in a place that meant so much to them, the good feelings came flooding back, and they clung to each other and kissed like high school kids.

"Oh, Powar, I was so worried about you. This has been the longest twelve months of my life."

"And you have no idea how much I needed you, Andy. It has been very difficult. Everything about you and me is difficult right now because of your situation. I'm not sure how either one of us will handle it," said Powar.

"Let's just go for a walk and eat and talk about this slowly," said Andy. They sat under the tree where he'd carved their initials over a year ago.

Powar told him she'd been in Europe in the countryside of France, staying with Genevieve. She had told him of Genevieve's existence earlier, so it didn't seem unusual. He bought her story about "burnout."

"I'm in a dilemma about my marriage, Powar. You have to know that. I never should have married Franny out of fear of not wanting to hurt her feelings. I could kick myself for not pursuing you earlier. Now I'm getting in deeper with both of you. Deeper in love with you and deeper into a comfortable situation with her. She's devoted to me. Now I'm consumed with guilt. How can I leave her as we celebrate our first anniversary?"

Instead of pushing him, which was not her style, Powar

wanted him to come up with his own solution. She didn't want him if he didn't want her badly enough, and obviously he just didn't get it yet. It made her a little angry, so she changed the subject and told him about her move to King Pictures. This would, of course, bring them together every day since he was under contract to the studio. He kissed her again to congratulate her on King Pictures, but he really wanted more with that kiss.

"I need to get back to my office," she said, pulling away. But she needed to think, and she hoped he would, too.

Andy looked crestfallen. He wanted to make love to her so badly.

"This is a confusing time, my darling. Let's be careful and think about what we're going to do. I feel that everything is in transition and we both need to make some decisions." She took his hand and led him to the car.

Honey was still so angry about Powar and Philip that she refused to have a family press conference. The "dynasty" story would be eaten up by the media, but it was something she simply wouldn't allow. She still had control of the stock, but she wasn't a stupid woman. She realized that at this point in time it would be better for Powar to work for her father. Philip was not as young as he used to be, and it would be dreadful to have someone who wasn't a family member get into that position, even though Honey would always have the control. Powar was talented and would bring the studio to new levels of accomplishment, but it just galled Honey that she'd spent a lifetime never getting any of the real credit, and now Powar was going to take it.

Instead of a press conference, the studio publicity department released a story to everyone simultaneously about Philip becoming chairman and CEO and Powar becoming president of motion picture and TV production. A woman getting this kind of position was gigantic news, even if her birthright had something to do with it. Powar had enough respect on her own after PBC to get by the nepotism cracks, which were very few indeed. Within forty-eight hours she was on the

"Today" show, the evening news on all four networks, and "Good Morning America," and "60 Minutes" wanted to profile her. In each interview she thanked Howard Pohlmann and promoted the cause of advancement for women. She was having a great time.

Just as she was getting ready to leave her house for her first day at the studio, her phone rang. "Powar?" said Honey. "I thought it would be proper to wish you well as you leave today."

"Thank you, Mother," said Powar. "I certainly didn't expect this call. You have never wanted me to be involved in the studio, nor have you ever voluntarily 'wished me well,' to use your words. What do you really want?"

"You're a tough girl, Powar, but you're my daughter, so what else could I expect? You're quick to judge, and you don't really know the history of anything."

"Since you never wanted to give it, what else do you expect?" said Powar, once again turning Honey's words back at her.

"I'll tell you what I expect. I expect you to see to it that King Pictures remains the most respected, successful studio in the business, and I'll be right there to see that you do," said Honey.

"I have no doubt of that, Mother. Now I'm going to be late. Thanks for your generous thoughts," said Powar as she placed the phone on the hook.

The first morning that she drove on the lot in her new position, she saw that her father had had her "Powar King" parking space moved directly in front of the executive office building. Powar met Philip at his office, as he had asked her to.

"Powar, I've been waiting for this moment all my life." He held out his hand, and she put hers in it. "Come with me."

He led her back into the hall and walked her next door. The large nursery that had been hers, next to her father's office, had been turned overnight into a new office by the studio set decorating department. Philip knew that his daughter would appreciate that he had chosen that spot for her. The office was equal to his and featured a private bathroom and a large reception room and office for her assistant, Mara, who had followed her from PBC to the studio.

The first thing Powar noticed was Mara busily putting her things away in the reception area. This area had always been painted eggshell with Oriental rugs in blues and burgundies. Powar noticed that there was a fresh coat of paint. The reception room was round with crown moldings painted white. In the center was a large Sheraton table with a huge floral display on it.

"Go in your office alone, Powar," said Philip.

Powar walked into her favorite fantasy. She had always loved deep powder blue, white, and navy blue with traditional furniture like the Federal houses back east. She found herself standing in a room painted the perfect blue with the crown molding in white, standing on a rich navy blue carpet. The furniture was all Sheraton mahogany. The desk really did look as if George Washington should be sitting behind it. On the walls were American Impressionist paintings. The ceiling-to-floor drapes behind the desk were pulled back with gold ties, and the valances had gold trim. There was even a Federal mirror in a gold frame over a magnificent subtle print blue-and-white couch. In front of the couch was a coffee table with an inlaid military seal.

Powar walked over to the desk and sat down on the brown leather chair to match the wood. She touched her hands to the desk and looked up to see her father staring at her from the doorway. Tears silently crawled down their cheeks. Never had either of them had a moment so filled with love and pride.

"At last," said Philip as he walked toward her to hug the future.

JORDAN

* CHAPTER 17 *

The first four years of Powar's reign as head of King Pictures were phenomenal. She took Andy's play, *Traffic Stop*, a drama about personal forks in the road, and turned it into an Oscar-winning picture. Everybody told her it was too introspective to make, considering the blockbuster action pictures that were hits at the box office, but Powar insisted. She got Czechoslovakian director Milans Kral to make his English-language debut, and she filled her cast with a combination of New York stage actors and stars like Jack Nicholson and Paul Newman. She tried to have at least one picture entered at Deauville each year so she could visit Jordan then, as well as at Christmas and in the spring.

Not being with Jordan was heartbreaking for her in the beginning; her tearful phone calls to Genevieve were nonstop. Then, as she got more and more involved in her work, the calls were more infrequent. Her life had once again taken on a pattern of meetings and more meetings, her desire for a more balanced life pushed into the background. She had two major weekly meetings at the studio with her staff, one with the motion picture area and the other with the television side. They were held in the boardroom at nine A.M., movies on

317

Tuesday and television on Thursday. Powar saw to it that Nate 'n' Al's Deli sent over bagels, lox, and cream cheese for everyone.

She had set up her staff the same way she had at PBC, with two production vice-presidents on the motion picture side, and she divided their responsibilities equally. Each person listened to pitches for films and then, if they liked them, they had to come to her to get approval to have a script written. Or sometimes a full script was submitted, and if they read it and liked it, they would have to give it to her to approve. Along the way of each production from script to film, these executives supervised everything and reported it to her. The same thing happened in television, only she had three executives there. One was for comedy series, one for drama series, and one for movies and specials. Nothing was approved by them unless Powar approved of it first. There wasn't a project that went forward at King without her approval. There was also an arrangement as to which writers, producers, and directors could pitch to which executive. Agencies chose among their clients as to which would go to which executive, and that was fine with Powar. Naturally they chose people they got along with, and Powar felt that was as it should be. There was no point in being in an adversarial position. She wanted her executives to be liked so she would get the best projects brought to her first.

"Now remember," said Powar in a meeting with Leslie Pallas and Andrew Frank, her division vice presidents, "it's up to you, Andrew, to get closer to Coppola. He brings all his projects to Paramount, and I want us to have a chance."

"I have him under control, Powar. He goes to Matteo's every Sunday night, and I've been there the past three in a row. We're getting along great. I also took a meeting with his agent, who wants us to sign a lesser-known writer. The new guy isn't bad, and if we do it for a price, the agent will be grateful and then we can zero in on Coppola."

"Very good," said Powar. "We'll play the game for now. Leslie, you know that NBC's contract with 'Savages' expires in June. If they don't give us the license fee we want, we can shop it around, and I think that CBS will buy it. The show probably has two years to go before the ratings drop significantly, and CBS could use it. Investigate and report back to me.''

Philip was quite happy with the new arrangement. He would occasionally sit in on the meetings, but he knew Powar had everything under control. He was spending more time at Hillcrest Country Club and the Friars Club with his buddies. He used those places to get away from Honey, who was driving him crazy. His trips to Europe had dwindled to almost nothing, something Honey noticed. She never asked what happened to Genevieve. She just presumed that, like most things, time had taken care of it.

"Did you bring home the minutes, Philip?'' Honey asked as she was trying on a Marie Antoinette costume.

"I told you that I'd bring them home every Friday,'' Philip said testily. "It isn't necessary for you to ask me for them every day. Your obsession with the studio has gone beyond anything that is tolerable, and since Powar took over you've been worse than ever.''

"Maybe it's because I'm the one who should have taken over,'' snapped Honey. "I'm the one who earned that right, and that's something you'll never see.'' Philip turned to go out of the room. "Wait a minute,'' Honey shouted. "You're not disappearing tonight. It's the Parisian Ball for Muscular Dystrophy. Your costume is in your closet.''

"You have been dragging me to these affairs for twenty-five years, and I won't be missed at this one. I'm sick of pretending,'' Philip yelled. "You have become completely intolerable.''

Honey really didn't care, knowing it was hopeless arguing about this particular party. It didn't matter to her what happened inside their house, as long as everyone outside believed in the Kings. In the meantime, she'd continue living the role of the grande dame to the hilt. When she walked into a room it was as if Hollywood royalty had arrived. As for King

Pictures, there was no way she was going to relinquish control over the proceedings. She was just biding her time. She had a definite plan for the future.

Andy's bungalow at the Beverly Hills Hotel had given way to a building at King Pictures. He was such a successful writer-producer that his TV shows and movies were earning him in excess of $175,000 a week. The building was in the back of the lot, something he had requested. It could have been along "Main Street," a studio street where a lot of movies were shot, but Andy wanted peace and quiet. He also wanted a building large enough to be a house for him. His was a two-story building that looked as if it belonged in a New England town, and whenever a show needed a New England exterior, they used his building. On the first floor there was a reception area and powder room in the front. Down a hall and to the back was Andy's office, with a big bay window overlooking the back lot of trees. His office was paneled all in walnut, with green plaid sofas on a hunter green carpet. He also had his own small bathroom, which he entered through the door on the side of the bookcase. On the other side of the bookcase was another doorway that led to a staircase. Only Andy, and whoever he designated, could use it. Upstairs was a bedroom, another large bathroom with a steam shower and sauna room, and a playroom that served as a screening room and a gym. It also had the latest sound equipment for music and was full of overstuffed couches. Andy let Franny do all the decorating. He thought it would keep her busy and make her feel needed. Powar understood, but since it was a sanctuary for her and Andy, she had difficulty overcoming the feeling that Franny was watching them all the time.

"I think we should give it to Natalie Wood," said Powar. She and Andy were presiding over a casting meeting on his new movie, as yet untitled, which was a comedy written directly for the screen, the adventures of a group of people traveling on their own in Europe.

"I don't know if she'll take it," said the casting director, a woman named Barbara Boyd, who seemed to not have a chip on her shoulder, a rarity for that profession. "It's an ensemble piece, and she normally prefers a starring vehicle."

"That's true," said Powar, "but I think we have something special going on here. This is Andy's directing debut. He's already one of our most respected writers, and his friends love to work with him. Why don't we try to go for really big stars in each role and ask them to all work for the same lowered salary and then give them each a very small percentage of the profits? I think they'll go for it."

"Powar, that's genius," said Andy. "Let's make a list of the perfect actor for each part without thought to price and just go after them. If Barbara has a problem dealing with their agents, we'll just go to them directly."

"You know how agents hate that, Andy," said Barbara.

"Yes, he does," said Powar, answering for him, "but we only have one goal in mind, and that's to make the best movie we can. Believe me, the agents aren't going to say a word if I call. They don't want to make me mad."

Barbara nodded her head and left the room.

"Powar," said Andy, leaning back in his chair, smiling, "you never cease to amaze me. Let's go upstairs. That's enough work for today. There's an album I'd like to play for you."

They landed on the center sofa in the playroom as sounds of Earth, Wind and Fire filled the room. "Aren't they incredible?" asked Andy. "They're a new group on Columbia that combines rhythm and blues with jazz and Latin. I just love them."

"This is a great album," said Powar. "I love it. Do you think they could score a film? It might be interesting to think about them for this one."

Andy was gently pushing her down on the couch and putting his face closer and closer to hers. "You know, someone is going to have to scout locations for the movie. You and I could go to Europe together and go to all the places in France and Italy that you've told me so much about. We could deliberately pick locations for where we want to play," said Andy.

Powar got very nervous. She didn't want him anywhere near France, yet she longed to make that trip with him.

"You know that Franny won't want to go if it doesn't involve lunch and shopping, but it's something you and I should do. The Deauville Festival is coming up soon. You always go. Unfortunately I'm sure Franny would like to go for some of the parties, but then she'll go home and we could stay. The timing is perfect to do the scouting because it gives us enough time to shoot for the spring. The weather is good then, and there are fewer tourists. Everything is perfect."

Not exactly, thought Powar as she felt his mouth on the inside of her elbow. He knew that was a favorite area. Powar was very conflicted. She loved him a great deal, and they were fabulous together. But she couldn't understand his hesitation in getting rid of Franny. She was beginning to feel used sexually, yet he was so sweet and sincere. She felt his talented tongue inching its way toward her neck. As far as she was concerned it could go wherever it wanted on her for hours on end, the moist warm tickling effect driving her up the wall. He was able to undress her and himself without ever taking his tongue away from her. The steady movement on her neck now was driving her crazy. She wanted him so badly that she didn't care whether her clothes were on or off, and he knew it. He deliberately slowed down the process by just taking off his clothes first and was completely nude pressing up against her, pushing to get inside. She started to pull her own pants down, and he stopped her. Instead he put her hands on him to feel him pulsate. She was raising and lowering her hips now in anticipation. His tongue was solidly in her mouth, simulating what would happen down below. She wrenched her hands away and placed them on his rear end, grabbing him to her. With a quick stroke her pants went down to her ankles and he was charging to her rhythm. She felt as if she were on a fast motorcycle racing up a hill until she floated off into blissful nothingness, that rosy glow that took over after you've conquered the mountain. Her arms and legs were wrapped around him like a vise, and even after the glow she wouldn't release him, not for a very long time.

Franny loved walking into the Palais at Deauville as Mr. and Mrs. Andy Stromberg, thrilled to have their picture taken, hearing that whisper among the crowds as they were recognized. The gambling casino in Deauville looked like a Louis XIV ballroom with gold molding, crystal windows, and velvet furniture. Even Andy seemed to be excited by it. Franny resented it when Powar King entered the room, to the flash of cameras, but she was so happy to be there that it almost didn't matter. Max had come over to do Lauren Bacall's hair, and at the last minute Blair had decided to join him. It was Franny's dream come true. With friends there by her side she didn't seem to be afraid of being swallowed up by a foreign land. Powar, on the other hand, was the queen of the festival, greeted warmly by many people there who had known her since she'd come as a little girl with her father.

Powar checked into the Normandy Hotel, one of the two great beachfront hotels in Deauville. They looked as if they were right out of the movie *Gigi*, and it was a joy to be there and go for some tea in the morning and then walk along the boardwalk. Powar took the same suite that she and her father had always taken, one that overlooked the town rather than the sea. That way they could see who was arriving and keep an eye on the action at all times. It had a balcony that ran the length of the hotel, and every time Powar went outside she saw cameras trained on her. It was fun, but it was also very difficult to sneak away. She had alerted Genevieve to the fact that she was going to have to be very careful with Andy and everyone else around, leaving for Honfleur very early in the morning or late at night. Sometimes she'd show up at a cocktail party and then excuse herself and drive out to stay over night. She and Jordan could not go to Fèrme St. Simon or any of their usual hangouts because Powar would be recognized immediately by the Americans in town for the festival.

"Mommy, why can't you just stay here all the time?" asked Jordan.

The question killed Powar. She hugged the beautiful blonde-haired, blue-eyed child to her. Jordan was a very precocious five-year-old who was beginning to ask a lot of questions. "Remember when I told you that France was a very pretty place to live and that Mommy just worked in the United States, which is why she had to spend a lot of time there?"

"Yes," said Jordan, "but I don't like it. Why can't I have a mommy and a daddy like everybody else?"

"Sometimes little children are chosen to be special, and you are one of them, darling. God knew that you could be strong for me and take care of me because your daddy went away. God sent you to me to help me. He also made me special, too, and gave me a very special job to make movies and TV shows to make people happy. I don't like to be away from you, either, and as soon as I can work it out we will be together, I promise, little one."

Genevieve was standing behind Jordan, looking at Powar. This was a difficult situation for all of them. Jordan had started school in Honfleur, and Genevieve had registered her using her own last name rather than King. When the little girl had asked her why, she'd told her it was better if she had the same last name as her *maman*, which is what Jordan called her.

Andy and Powar were participants in a panel discussion on the future of American cinema at a luncheon the next day. It was held in the courtyard just below Powar's suite and was televised nationally throughout France. Sitting right in the front row was Franny, looking at her husband adoringly. It made Powar uncomfortable. She knew it was being done for the press, but it turned her stomach. According to Andy, he hardly ever touched her, and that was fine with her. She was enjoying the conversation and listening to George Roy Hill talk about *The Sting*, but she really wanted to go to Jordan.

As soon as the luncheon ended she bowed out quickly. Rather than use the car and driver at her disposal, she went to a rented car that she had parked at the Royale, the hotel next door. She loved driving through the countryside and really felt as though she had two homes. She took the long way around, past Fèrme St. Simon. She was going to have dinner there tonight with some French distributors of King Pictures in Europe, not with Jordan, unfortunately. She realized that the older Jordan got, the more difficult it would be to hide her from the press. She was going to have to give that careful consideration.

When Powar arrived at Honfleur, Genevieve had everything set up for the three of them to go painting. There was a wonderful château about two miles away that had a beautiful garden with flowers and bridges. Genevieve had arranged it so they could go in and just do some watercolor work. Jordan, at the normal age for fingerpainting, took up the brush with ease. Her work was crude, of course, but her balance, perspective, distance judgment, and use of color were very advanced. It did not go unnoticed by the two women.

"Maybe we should see if there is a special art school for gifted children nearby," said Powar. "Would you like to play with the painting more, Jordan?" she asked.

"I like this, Mommy. Come paint with me," said Jordan, taking her hand.

When Powar touched that little hand she felt a sense of well-being that was unmatched by anything else in her life, and it was harder and harder for her to leave this joyful time. She was missing her child's best years and was instead listening to script changes and agent pitches. When she was in France, she never wanted to leave. But when she came back to the studio, the magic was overwhelming, and Powar truly felt that by being there she was doing what she'd been put on earth to do.

Andy had to stay in Europe for three weeks scouting locations with his producer and cinematographer. Powar knew he was hoping it would be with her, but he had accepted her story that she needed to go back for important meetings. Franny went home on the same plane with Blair and Max.

Powar was having a lazy Sunday and, for a change, allowed herself some time for breakfast. She decided to make herself a poached egg on roast beef hash with just the right amount of ketchup on the side, then ate it while watching the Sunday morning news shows. She saw in the TV section of the paper that a Sherlock Holmes movie starring Basil Rathbone was coming on at eleven, and she was waiting for it. She could watch old movies over and over again and hoped that some of the movies she made might turn out to be classics. Just as Moriarty was about to discover that Sherlock Holmes was masquerading as Dr. Tobell, and once again he would be foiled in his attempt to get the bomb site, Powar's phone rang. She did not want to be disturbed and hesitated answering it. She finally picked it up and heard her mother's cold, mechanical voice.

"Powar, your father has had a heart attack."

"Well, is he all right?" Powar asked anxiously.

"I don't know," said Honey.

"What kind of an answer is that? Are the paramedics there?" Powar screamed. "What do you mean they're having trouble reviving him? Tell them not to stop trying and take him to Cedars Emergency. Tell them I'm on my way."

Powar slammed the phone down, picked up her purse and keys, and ran out to her car. She couldn't see or hear, she was so blinded by the fear of what she was going to find. She was only eight minutes from Cedars, and she made it in record time, parking her car askew in the red zone and running into the lobby.

"Where's my father? I'm Powar King. Where is he? He should have been here about two minutes ago."

The attendant behind the desk, a young overweight black man, had seen this scene before and was used to it. He said calmly, "I need his name, and I'll check in the computer to see what's happening."

"His name is Philip King and the paramedics are bringing him here. He should have been here by now. Get me your supervisor immediately." The look on the attendant's face revealed he realized this was not going to be routine.

Honey looked at her husband lying on the living room couch. He still looked handsome to her. He had very little gray in his hair for a man of his age. His eyes were closed and his shirt was torn open where the paramedics continued to work on him. She walked over to the men and said, "Obviously this is not working. Just leave him here and I'll take care of everything. Thank you very much for your efforts."

The two men looked at each other. Honey sounded as though she were thanking a secretary for trying to get her the right bottle of perfume and failing. When they left it was just Philip and Honey. She'd always known it would end up like this. There were no stars around, no Genevieves, and most of all, no Powar. That was the way Honey wanted it.

There was no hope for Philip before she even called Powar. Honey didn't care that Powar was going to go to Cedars and find nothing. This was Honey's time. Together she and Philip had put together a glittering fiefdom that she wanted never to share . . . not with Philip or anybody else. She had loved him. And she loved him more now, because in death his greatest gift was that of giving her full, unobstructed control of the studio. She had been waiting a long time. She put her hand on his cheek, which was still warm, and said, "Thank you, Philip," and then she kissed him lightly on the mouth.

By the time Powar realized that her father was never coming to Cedars, she was wild. It did not surprise her as she drove to her parents' house to see that the lawn was already occupied with reporters and there were cars and people everywhere. As soon as she got out of her car she was hit with lights and cameras, and she just waved them off and ran into the house. The first person she saw was Don Bryson, head of King Pictures publicity. He had been with the company only ten years, so he was not one of her father's old cronies. He was a smart, efficient, controller of the press, and that's what they all needed right now.

She just looked at him and said, "Please handle everything right now. I know you'll do your best." She was fighting back tears, but she was so angry at having gone to Cedars on a wild goose chase that she didn't know what she'd do when she saw her mother. There were already too many people in the house looking at her, so she tried to remain as composed as she could. Familiar faces were just a blur because she was in so much pain. She suddenly spotted her mother, who was playing the perfect hostess. Powar stood and watched her for about thirty seconds, amazed by the graciousness, the tender touch, as she comforted people who were trying to comfort her. She heard her ask one of the help to call Chasen's and order a buffet for about one hundred people brought up as soon as possible. And then Powar could stand it no longer. She walked up to her mother. The friends backed away for the private moment between mother and daughter.

"Would you excuse us, please? We need to have a moment alone," said Powar as she grabbed her mother's elbow strongly and guided her to the butler's pantry. For a second the two women were alone staring at each other. Powar looked her mother straight in the eye and smashed her across the mouth with her fist. Honey was stunned by the blow, but she kept herself from falling by holding on to the countertop. "Who appointed you coroner, Mother?" Powar seethed. "Since when are you the one who decides medical treatment?" The women were shoulder to shoulder.

Honey raised her body up to the tallest it could be and said, "Your father was dead, Powar. Dead is dead, whether it's on Bedford Drive or at Cedars. Now let's get out there and do our job." She turned to go back into the living room. She looked back at Powar and said, "Your father's in the downstairs guest bedroom."

Powar saw the body of her father on the bed, awaiting the pickup by the mortuary. Philip looked asleep and peaceful. Powar imagined any minute now he was going to wake up and ask her to go to Tail o' the Pup to get their favorite hot dog. That kept her from crying immediately. But that lasted for only a minute or two. When she thought about his dying without ever knowing Jordan, she was devastated with guilt and self-loathing. They would have loved each other so. She sat on the bed holding her father's hand and sobbing.

Powar went into seclusion for the next forty-eight hours preceding her father's funeral. Don Bryson was turning down all requests from the press to interview her. Honey, on the other hand, was on almost every channel. She always wore a different black ensemble and should have gotten the Oscar for her performance. Powar spoke only to Andy, Maria, and Genevieve on the phone.

"How are you doing?" Powar asked softly.

"I feel like a part of me died," said Genevieve. "He was so good, so sweet, and he loved you very much."

Powar started to cry. "The funeral is this morning. Would you like me to put that beautiful handkerchief you gave me in the casket?"

Now Genevieve was crying. "Thank you," she said during muffled sobs.

"What will you be doing for the next three hours?" asked Powar.

"I will light a candle and put on all of our records and try to dance with him one more time. Jordan is at the Vuillards', and she doesn't know anything."

"I love you," said Powar. "I'll call you tomorrow."

Powar thought that Genevieve was handling it as well as could be expected. She was more concerned that Jordan not figure anything out. Andy wanted to come see her, but she needed just to be alone. Immediately after her father died she stayed in bed, under the covers, for two days. She awoke only to stave off hunger pangs by eating avocados or macaroni and cheese. Powar and Honey did have one discussion about the funeral. Powar knew her father would have wanted a private, dignified ceremony for family only and a few close friends. He would want either a memorial service at home or a short service by the graveside at Hillside Memorial Park, the cemetery owned by the Groman family.

Honey agreed to a memorial service at home, and that was fine with Powar.

Powar invited Andy and Franny and Maria and Jonna and the gate guard at the studio who had been there for thirty years, plus her father's secretary. Her mother invited the rest of the people. The night before the service, Honey called Powar's answering service and asked Powar to wear all beige clothes and tennis shoes for the service. She asked Powar to call the few people she had invited to do the same. Powar was starting to do a slow burn. What kind of theme was her mother dreaming up now? Since when were guests color-coordinated to funerals, unless the color was black? Maybe her mother just wanted muted colors but no black to make her a little cheerier. Powar wasn't sure, but she was uneasy about the whole thing. She also refused to wear tennis shoes. That made no sense at all, but she would have them with her just in case. In case of what, she didn't know.

Honey called the event for seven A.M. to throw off the press, and that did make sense to Powar. At seven A.M. that morning, all the guests gathered in the living room. It looked like a sea of beige, so bland-looking that the only thing that distinguished people was hair color. Her mother kept everyone waiting fifteen minutes. There was a silver coffee service set up laden with croissants and sweet rolls and a black-tie waiter to serve. Honey entered, wearing beige, of course, and said hello to everyone.

"Powar, whatever you do, don't look in the corner," said Honey.

Naturally Powar and everyone else immediately looked in the corner. Sitting atop the Louis XIV table was a wooden box that looked a little larger than a cigar box. It was brand new, and immediately Powar got a sick feeling in her stomach. Something just told her that her father was in there. This was not part of the plan. She looked back at Honey, who reveled in Powar's shock.

Andy walked over to Powar and whispered, "Hold on. I'll be by you today no matter what. I wonder why we're just standing here. Where's the rabbi?"

The doorbell rang, and the butler went to answer it. He came back into the living room and announced, "Mrs. King, the officers are here."

"Please show them in," said Honey.

"What officers, Mother?" Powar asked agitatedly.

"The navy," replied Honey.

"Navy? What on earth would they be doing here? My father didn't have any connection with the navy."

"Oh, Powar, dear, you know how much your father loved those old submarine movies"—Powar knew of no such "love"—"and besides, my father was a navy man, and I thought this would be nice. Now just entertain the officers and I'll be right back down, and then we can leave for the ship."

The mourners were stunned into silence as twelve navy men in full-dress uniforms carrying rifles walked into the room, accompanied by a military chaplain. If Powar wasn't so shocked and upset, she would have laughed. Her father would have laughed. She could just hear him saying, "What on earth does a Jew boy do with a chaplain and a gun?" The chaplain walked over to Powar and expressed his sympathies.

Powar was polite to them and offered them some refreshments. What else could she do? She didn't have a clue as to what was going to happen next, she only knew that when this was all over she would see to it that her mother's body was in the same shape as her father's. No one was speaking. Finally Franny said, "Does anybody have any Dramamine?"

Honey's footsteps were heard on the stairs. Everyone turned to see her enter the room. "Anchors aweigh, everybody," she said, dressed in red, white, and blue from head to toe, including a nautical hat. In her arms were dozens of red, white, and blue carnations with gold glitter on them. "I thought these were festive, and they matched my outfit. We'll all throw them when the time comes. Let's go!"

Powar thought she was going mad. If anyone had written this scene into a movie script, it would have been taken out because nobody would believe it. Outside the house was a row of limousines lined up behind a military transport. Her mother's oldest friends, Ellen and Kate, both widows themselves now, went in the limo with Honey. Powar rode in the second limo with Maria and Jonna.

The funeral party made its way from Bedford Drive to San Pedro Harbor in forty-five minutes, where a gigantic ship was waiting at the dock. At least fifty white-uniformed men were at attention along the railings, waiting for the group. A Chasen's catering truck was parked at the dock. As the party walked up the gangplank a military band played "Anchors Aweigh." Powar noticed that her mother had put the box containing her father's ashes in a Gucci bag. He hated Gucci, she thought. Once everyone was in the main salon, the ship headed out to sea. It was illegal to throw ashes into a harbor; you had to be out from the jetty a certain number of miles.

"Help yourselves, everyone," Honey said as she was circulating.

Chasen's had been working overtime. There were scrambled eggs with chives, smoked salmon, O'Brien potatoes, cinnamon toast, bagels, fresh fruit, and mimosa cocktails. Powar was not hungry at all, but she had to admit it was a beautiful buffet. She was surprised her mother had allowed the bagels, though. She was also just so crazed at what her mother had done, she couldn't concentrate on anything else. Suddenly the chaplain was at her side.

"I just love all the TV shows you do," he said.

"Thank you," answered Powar.

"You know," the chaplain continued, "my niece wants to be an actress, and I'd just love it if she could send you a picture and a résumé and maybe you could talk to her."

Shocked by his tastelessness, Powar held back her true response and just said, "Excuse me, I need to talk to my friend," and walked over to Maria. "Do you believe all this?" she asked.

"Of course I do," said Maria, "and you do, too. Do you know that your mother just asked me if I was going to write this up for the paper? She's really something. I'm going to do a beautiful editorial on your father, though. He was a wonderful man." Jonna, age nine, looked sweet in a beige running suit and tennis shoes. "She's the only one who looks right on this ship," said Powar, hugging her. "I'm so glad you're here, Jonna. You make me feel better." And when she hugged her, both Powar and Maria knew she was really talking to Jordan.

Finally the ship reached its destination and shut off its engines. The slapping of the waves against the hull made it seem almost peaceful as the group gathered on the deck. The chaplain said, "Please gather 'round, folks." He then proceeded to say a few words about a man he had never met. With all the fantastic people whose lives had been touched by her father, Powar couldn't believe this man was giving his eulogy. At that moment she wanted to interrupt him and take over, but she thought better of it. She was already involved in a circus. They were then led in the Lord's Prayer. Powar saw the twelve rifles assume their firing position. They fired twenty-one shots while everyone stood with their heads bowed. With the sounds of gunshots ringing in their ears, Powar barely heard her mother say, "Cue the band!" The chaplain nodded to the leader, and the band started to play "Feelings." Philip hated that song, and Honey knew it. Powar just glared at her mother.

It was time for the contents of the Gucci bag. Honey took

out the wooden box and handed it to the chaplain. As she did that, the ship lurched, and the plastic bag with his ashes started to fly out. Powar grabbed it and held it, not believing her father had been reduced to gray dust in a Baggie. She felt as though she were going to pass out. Honey looked at Powar holding the ashes, and Powar knew she wanted them back. For one second she thought about keeping them, but she was not prepared for what her mother might do.

"Here, Mother," said Powar, handing Honey the ashes. "I'm sure you have a plan for these, too."

Honey took the ashes while juggling all the carnations as well. She handed the carnations out to the guests and started to open the plastic bag and release the ashes out to sea. Just as the bag opened and the ashes started to go, a gust of wind came up and blew them all over the chaplain. Powar walked over and started brushing his suit with her hands.

"Here, let me get my father off of you, he would appreciate it."

"Thank you," said the chaplain. "Oh, by the way," he said as Powar continued to brush, "could you get me an autographed picture of Farrah Fawcett?" Powar was sure she heard Philip laughing himself silly.

Powar, Maria, and Jonna got out of there as fast as they could. Powar didn't even want to go back to her mother's house to get her car, but she had to. They slipped the limo driver a twenty-dollar bill to beat everybody there by a good ten minutes. Powar didn't say a word in the car. Maria and Jonna just let her be. When the limo pulled up she hugged and kissed them and told them she had to go.

"Where are you going?" asked Maria.

"The only place I know of," said Powar, and then she jumped into her T-bird and took off.

Maria thought of following her, but then she thought better of it.

Powar gunned the car and went south on Bedford down to Pico. She had to get to the studio. It was the only way she could feel her father around her. She needed to sit on his chair and feel the curve of his body. She wanted to smell his cologne. She wanted to hold his pen and make his desk set hers. She would never let go of it so he would be with her always when she sat at her desk. She would get his guidance as she used his pen to write. She might even sleep there tonight or every night for a while. She didn't know. She just knew she had to get there. She drove up to the studio entrance and looked at the sign, "King Pictures," and held back her tears. She didn't want Scotty, the guard, to see her that way. King Pictures, like all studios, had a guardhouse at the gate. There were two sides of the gate, one for the visitors and one for the employees. Each employee had a sticker on his or her car, and the guard just pushed the button to open the gate when he saw a sticker. Through the years the guards got to know who was working there, and the gate was flying up constantly. For the executives, a special key was made so they could open any gate in the studio because some didn't have twenty-four-hour guards.

Powar drove up and saw an unfamiliar guard.

"Where's Scotty?" she asked.

"I'm sorry, I don't know him. This is my first day," said the guard.

That's peculiar, thought Powar. "I'm Powar King. Will you please open the gate?"

"I'm very sorry, but Mrs. King has changed the locks and we're under orders not to open it for you or we'll get fired."

Powar went wild. "Are you out of your mind? I'm president of this studio. You open this gate or I'll ram it down."

He looked at her and said, "This isn't my battle, Ms. King," and then he opened the gate.

Powar drove as fast as she could to her office. She pulled into her parking space next to her father's and noticed that both their signs had been painted over to read "Mrs. Philip King." Her grief turned to rage, and she went running to her office. There she found three empty rooms that used to be her reception room, office, and private bath-dressing room. She ran in a state of blinding shock to her father's office. Everything about it had changed. Her mother's name was on the door. The English office had been turned into a Country French spring boudoir. She walked into her father's bathroom, which was now ceiling-to-floor mirrors, a sunken marble tub, and a special makeup and hair area like the one in the makeup and hair department at the studio. There was no trace of her father anywhere. She screamed, ''No!'' from deep inside her as she turned away. She couldn't stop her hysteria. It had taken her over completely, and she was hitting the walls with both fists as she repeatedly called, ''Daddy!''

When she calmed down, she decided to go home to strategize. She had only a few hours before this news would hit the street. When she pulled up to her house she saw a moving van putting all her office belongings in front of her garage. Instead of screaming at them, she had enough presence of mind to recognize that they were just doing a job they had been hired for. She instructed them to put everything in the garage. When they were through, she went inside and called her lawyer, Neil Burkhardt, and her father's lawyer, Paul Schreibman. Honey had no idea that Paul Schreibman existed. Philip had explained a long time ago to Powar that he wanted to have a separate personal attorney for private matters. Honey would always think that their attorney, Charles Ziffinham, was the only attorney. Powar was quite certain that Ziffinham was in the clutches of her mother.

Within two hours Schreibman and Burkhardt were at Powar's house. By that time the word had gotten out, and her phone was ringing off the hook. She was not answering it. When the one-ring code came, she knew it was Maria and picked up.

''I know, I know,'' Powar said instead of hello. ''Listen, I know you have to print what happened, but just know that you will get an exclusive that will rip this town apart. I'll arrange everything for you to be somewhere at exactly the right time, and I want you to bring a photographer. Just quote me now as saying I have no comment. And Maria, don't worry. I've learned things from *both* parents that will be useful.''

"Powar," said Burkhardt, "I suggest that you not have any contact with Honey whatsoever and let us do the talking through letters. There isn't a court in the world that wouldn't make her pay up on your contract, so let's make that our first letter.''

"That's fine with me, but I think we had better watch her next move after that. We know what we have. Let's wait before we let everyone meet Mr. Schreibman," said Powar.

When Powar got up the next morning she turned on the news to find herself staring at the face of Charles Ziffinham, who was holding a live press conference on Honey's behalf.

"According to the laws of the state of California, because Philip King died without a will, all his assets go to his wife, Honey King. Mrs. King wishes to express her appreciation for the calls and flowers coming in. She is devastated by the death of her husband and will have a difficult time ahead. Thank you,'' said Ziffinham.

Powar's phone started ringing immediately. She didn't pick it up. On the other line she called Schreibman and then Burkhardt on a conference line. "Forget the simple letter about my contract. I want you to send the killer one,'' she said.

When she hung up she knew she couldn't stay around the house. She considered packing a small bag and going to France, but she couldn't leave while things were unresolved. She got dressed in jeans, a sweater and dark glasses and went to the back door. She ran to her car, but when she started the engine she heard the sound of footsteps from the reporters and cameramen in the driveway. She floored it in reverse and just drove as fast as she could. She had to get away.

Honey turned off the television set and practically purred. Ziffinham was perfect, she thought. She stretched her body to its longest length, feeling the satin of the sheets rub against her nightgown. She wanted desperately to get up and go to the studio. She had waited so long to be in complete control. But she knew it would not be in good taste. She would wait forty-eight hours and then claim that "working would make her feel better." She had a day and a half to kill. She knew the Angels were coming for tea, and that would kill time. She didn't mind wearing black for a while, it was one of her good colors, but she hated suppressing her cheeriness. She decided to book a massage and a hair and makeup appointment at the house.

Gina Furth was just finishing Honey's hair when her houseman announced that a messenger was there with a registered letter. "Just sign for it and bring it to me," she said, dismissing him. He was back in two minutes and handed it to her. "Thank you. That will be all," she said. She put the letter on the dressing table without looking at it and went back to her hair. Through the corner of her eye she saw the engraved return address, which looked like a legal office. Her curiosity got to her, and she reached for the envelope and opened it.

The letter went as follows:

> *Dear Mrs. King:*
>
> *My name is Paul Schreibman, and I have been Philip King's private, personal attorney for the past twenty-five years. Enclosed you will find a copy of his complete, legal will. You will see that he has divided his shares of King Pictures equally between yourself and your daughter. I have many legal documents of Mr. King's through the years, and the veracity of this will may be proven easily. If you or your lawyers have any questions, please feel free to call me.*
>
> *As for Powar King, you are legally bound to pay her for the extent of her contract, as you have illegally terminated her. We expect a check in forty-eight hours.*
>
>

Cordially,
Paul Schreibman

"Ahhhhh!" screamed Honey. "Get away from me! Leave me alone!" With a one-handed sweep she threw everything off her dressing table as the hair and makeup people ran for cover. Her photograph of Philip fell to the floor, and she stepped on it as she ran to the phone to talk to Ziffinham.

Powar had already calculated that Honey's share collecting throughout the years would allow her to retain the position of CEO of the studio because she had more than Powar. Even if Powar counted the shares she'd received when she was eighteen, it was not enough to gain control of the company. She knew that together, Schreibman and Burkhardt would put enough pressure on Honey's attorney to get them to pay off Powar's contract. It was a legal document, and there was no reason to go to court over it. Powar was going to be quiet for a while. She knew her mother was absolutely furious over the new will. She had caught Honey at her own game, and she was just going to savor it. She was offered everything in the world. She could go back to a network. Four other studios offered her very rich independent-producing deals. But she realized she didn't have to take a job anywhere. She was quite wealthy, and the only thing she wanted was to take over King Pictures again. She was going to do it for herself and for her father.

"I think it's important that we don't meet in off hours for a while," said Powar. She and Andy were having dinner at Powar's beautiful house in Holmby Hills above Sunset Blvd. Powar had bought it about five years earlier when she'd wanted something more than her bachelor pad above the Strip. It looked like a Spanish hacienda, with a fountain in the courtyard, beautiful gardens around the pool, and a lavish guest house. "People are following me, and I don't want to give my mother any ammunition."

"I really hate this," said Andy.

Powar had been looking forward to seeing him. She'd made a special dinner of pan-fried chicken in country gravy, mashed potatoes, and a string bean casserole. Over dinner, Powar realized as she looked into Andy's face that his love, romantic though it still was, was also going to help her over the loss of the comfortable love of her father. Andy was her playmate the way her father was. He liked to go to the hot dog stand, too, or the park, or on restaurant binges. She realized she wasn't alone. Of course with Jordan she never was alone in the world, either, but she couldn't see her that much. She was hoping that the time off from the studio would allow her to go to Europe for an extended period. But the planning it was going to take to pull off what she had in mind would allow her only a very short trip.

"Let's talk about business first, because I think it's all related," said Andy. "Your mother is courting me practically every day. She realized my contract is about to expire. She is also aware of the 'key man' clauses you put into the contracts of all the actors, writers, directors, and producers you signed at the studio. She knows that they can invoke that at any time and leave. She's panicked, but trying to act calm. I'm sure you realize that you can go to each person under contract and get them to sign a letter of intent to follow you, and then you can take those letters to any financial institution in the world and get the backing for your own studio."

"Of course I know that," said Powar. "That's not good enough for me. There will be only one King Pictures, and I'm going to run it."

Andy smiled. "That's what I thought your response would be. No doubt you have a plan."

"Andy, there's something I want you to do for me. Because you are on the lot you can keep a better eye on whose contract is up. I want you to quietly and confidentially spread the word that I want all my people to remain in place on the lot. Tell them they are not to sign renewals, but just let their contract lapse and work without an agreement. My mother will be so desperate to have them, she'll take them any way she can get them. In six months we have our annual board meeting.

Just tell them that in six months everything will be back to normal.''

"You're not going to tell me what the plan is, are you," Andy said.

"If you believe that I loved my father, and that I love you and what our future could be, I don't need to tell you any more," said Powar. "Let's just play it cool."

Andy pushed back his chair from the table and knelt down in front of Powar. "From the moment I saw you I have loved you with all my heart. I promise you that more than just the studio will change in six months. I know we'll be together the way we've always wanted to be. I really promise you that." He held her face in his hands and kissed her so tenderly that she started to cry. "I love you, my little one," he said as he lay back on the floor and pulled her on top of him. He rubbed her back in a circle to soothe her, feeling this was the first time she had really let out the pain of losing her father and the studio. His shirt was wet with her tears, and he began rocking her just as he would a baby. The slow, gentle rocking calmed her, but now the rocking was becoming arousing. Neither one had realized how long it had been since they'd had each other. Too many business and personal problems had come between them, and they hadn't protected their private time.

Their passion was just like the first time. They couldn't get enough of each other's bodies, and they couldn't stop kissing and crying. It was as if they had discovered each other again and would never let go. Somehow Powar knew that she was going to have to make everything work. She had lost her father and her studio, her love was still married, and her child was overseas, but if she had to die trying, she would do all she could to right the wrongs.

* CHAPTER 18 *

Honey was sitting on the seat where she had wanted to be for more years than she cared to remember. She was fifty-seven years old, and as far as she was concerned it had been too long a wait. She knew the town was now very divided. There were those who supported her and knew of her unsung involvement through the years. To others she was the greedy mother who'd dumped her daughter. She didn't care what either side thought. She was the winner, and she would sign only winners.

The first thing she did was to fire Philip's secretary and hire away Miss Hobson from Falkner Cantwell. Falk had been very happy over at Columbia for the past several years, and although Honey thought it would be amusing to have him around at King, she decided against it. It would be more valuable to have Miss Hobson, who would help her know exactly who at that studio was unhappy so she could lure them to King. She was aware that Powar was not just sitting at home. Powar was making herself very visible, having lunch at Le Dome on the Sunset Strip twice a week, once with a star and once with a producer or director. When either Powar or Honey booked Chasen's, each made it clear to the maître d' that the other was not to be there. Powar had started going to Imperial Gardens, a sushi bar on Sunset frequented by young Hollywood. She always knew where the new talent was coming from. Powar and Steven Spielberg loved California roll. That was a problem with Honey. Her age kept her within a certain circle of friends and associates. In order to control the future you had to hang out with it. Honey would rather have dinner with Mrs. Jules Stein than Jaclyn Smith, and Jaclyn would rather be with Powar. Honey was obviously not a fool, and she assumed that Powar would make some sort of play at the board meeting in January.

"Get me Peter Guber, please," Honey said through the intercom to Miss Hobson. Peter Guber had just come out of Harvard, and he was the youngest studio vice-president in the business. Honey was intrigued with him because she knew she needed youth on her side in order to compete. She was thinking of having a drink with him just to see whether or not she wanted to offer him a job at King Pictures. Part of her was afraid, though, because the word around town was that he was very ambitious and smart, and she was worried that once he was at King, he would try to usurp her power. Guber's response to the invitation was polite, and a date was set.

Honey ordered some tea and waited for her next appointment. Yesterday she'd screened the latest movie from Ericson Drake, one of the newer directors under contract to the studio. It was something Powar had agreed to put into production, and Honey was horrified by it. She didn't want to release it, but if she didn't, the studio would lose money on it.

"Mr. Drake is here," said Miss Hobson.

Ericson Drake had long blond hair and was wearing an Indian jacket and jeans.

"Please sit down, Ericson. As you may or may not know, your movie was made before I was in this position. But I now have to make the decision as to whether it is to be released—"

"What do you mean?" he cut her off sharply.

"I feel King Pictures has a certain standard to uphold. We

don't like to do rebellious pictures that agitate people,'' Honey continued.

"Now just a minute! Powar loved this script, and she wanted to make movies that make people think,'' said Ericson.

"Powar isn't here anymore,'' Honey said coldly. "Now we do have a solution here.''

"What exactly might that be?'' he said equally coldly.

"We'll work together to cut the picture. I just saw the first cut, and I think there's too much bad language and suggestive sex,'' said Honey.

"This is a movie about soldiers, and it's very realistic, and besides, my contract also says the director's cut is final.''

"Yes, it does,'' said Honey. "But as president and owner of King Pictures, I can decide to release something or not. The end result will be your choice, Mr. Drake. Just a few minor adjustments will see your movie released, or it can stay in the can and be released to television years from now. Please let me know your answer by Friday.''

When Sam Lewis's parents died in the early 1970s, their stock had been inherited by Sam Jr. Sam knew that Honey had been responsible for his banishment to Europe, and although he ultimately preferred living there, and reveled in his knowledge of Philip and Genevieve, he couldn't wait to jack up the price of his stock and sell it to her. The money was worth more to him than the control. He hated the King family because of what they'd done to his family.

"Sam, darling, how are you?'' said Honey.

"You know exactly how I am and how much stock I have,'' said Sam. "I may be in France, but we hear everything.'' He was actually surprised that Honey had been the first one to call him. He and Honey hated each other, and Powar knew of his stock. He thought that was very odd.

"What's your bid, Honey? And remember, there's already one on the table.'' Sam enjoyed playing this role. It was the first time he'd had her over a barrel.

"Don't play games with me," said Honey. "Just tell me what you want and I'll send you a cashier's check. I don't have time for this nonsense."

"Okay," said Sam. "I want two hundred and fifty thousand dollars for it."

"What!" exclaimed Honey. "That's more than seventy-five thousand dollars over what it's worth."

"Fine. If you don't want it, I know someone who will."

"Wait," said Honey. "I'll have the documents drawn up and sent to you by courier tomorrow." And then she hung up.

Sam actually let out a cheer. He had made a fortune, even though his parents' shares were greatly reduced when the Kings took over.

As far as Honey was concerned, the minute she got Sam's shares the fight was won. There wasn't anywhere else for Powar to go. The other people on the board held so few shares that their votes would not matter, even if they all went for Powar. Honey just carried on with her life, living it the way she had always dreamed it would be.

Powar . . . thought Honey, sitting at her desk. She just sat there and thought for a few minutes. There was something bothering her, like a pecking at the back of her head. She knew she hadn't thought of everything yet, and she couldn't afford to make any mistakes. What was it about Powar's life? The pattern was the same, thought Honey . . . work and France, work and France. France? What was it about France and the Kings?

Honey sat bolt upright when it hit her. Genevieve! Could it be? And why? Honey's body was almost vibrating. It was like a truth barometer. She could always rely on it to guide her. She opened the bottom drawer of her desk and pulled out a small file box. After opening it with a key taped to the inside of the top drawer, she pulled out a card with a high-lighted stripe on it and dialed the number of private detective Roger Martin.

"This is Mrs. King," she said in her usual authoritative

manner. "I have a job for you. Be on the next plane for Paris, rent a car, and get a hotel room in the town of Honfleur, about a thirty-minute drive from Deauville. Check out a woman named Genevieve LeJeune. I want to know if my daughter is with her and exactly what is going on. Report to me every day."

"That'll be easy," she heard him say. "Your daughter is easy to spot. No problem."

Powar finally made it to Honfleur by Christmas. By this time Jordan was old enough to notice her mother's absences, and she was a little distant. "No, thank you," she said quietly as Powar passed her the potatoes.

"But, Jordan," said Powar, "you love them."

"I'm not very hungry. *Maman,* may I be excused?"

Genevieve said that she could. "I know you've noticed a difference," she said when she and Powar were alone. "Jordan is very bright and is asking a lot of questions. She knows who you are. She saw you in a magazine. You can't go on telling so many lies. If her trust is lost now, it will be very difficult to get it back."

Powar was quiet. "I know I'm making mistakes here. I need your help to figure out what to do," she said.

Genevieve thought carefully before responding. "You tell her the truth about who you are and why you can't be here. She hasn't yet asked why she can't live with you, but that won't be for long."

Powar was worried. "I just can't have her know about her father yet. It's too dangerous. I'm not ready to have her come to the States. It's just too tricky. I can tell her something truthful to keep her calm, but that's all I can do at this point." She got up from the dinner table and went to Genevieve and embraced her. "I don't know what I would have done without you. I know so well why my father loved you. You are more a part of my family than my mother ever could be." The next morning Powar went into Jordan's room just as she awoke and looked at her. "Aren't you going to hug Mommy?" she asked.

"I thought I couldn't call you that," said Jordan.

"Jordan, darling! Of course you can call me that. Oh, Jordan," said Powar, sitting down on her bed. "Listen to me. I love you very much. You are a very special girl who has a famous mommy. I do work in the movies, and that takes me away from you a lot. Sometimes I don't like other people knowing about things I do, or where I go, or people I know. It's a very hard business and sometimes it's necessary to keep secrets. Right now it's important for me that you're my special secret. One day, and I hope it can be soon, we can tell everybody, and, my darling, I want that more than anything. You must always know that. As soon as we can do that I'll tell you. Do you understand?"

"Yes, Mommy," Jordan replied without much enthusiasm.

Powar felt it and tried harder, realizing Jordan was not a little girl any longer. "What do you say we all drive to Paris and go to the Louvre? And then we can go get some wonderful ice cream." Jordan smiled, and so did Powar, hugging her. Things were going to be okay after all, she hoped.

By now Powar's close friends just accepted the fact that she disappeared at Christmas. She did call Andy and wish him a Merry Christmas, and she had a special surprise for Genevieve and Jordan. Maria and Jonna arrived on Christmas Eve. They were going to stay through New Year's, and then everyone would go back together. It was the first time Genevieve and Maria had met, although they had talked on the phone and knew of one another throughout the years. Powar and Maria were particularly eager to have Jonna and Jordan get to know one another. They were both special in their own way, and even though Jonna was a few years older, they thought they would get along very well.

Genevieve's house was decorated like the North Pole, and

the girls loved it. In every room there was something Christmasy. The tree was a fresh one, cut in the countryside and brought to the house. With Genevieve's eye for style and composition, the house could have been photographed from every angle. On the tree were ornaments she had made over the years, and now Jordan and Powar had been adding to that tradition. The first thing Maria and Jonna did when they sat down was make two ornaments to go on the tree.

One night as they were stringing popcorn after the girls went to bed, Maria said, "I know something's up. You've been too quiet, and the board meeting is on January tenth. What's up?"

Powar smiled. "Just hold page one open for the eleventh. You'll fill it."

"That's it?" asked Maria. "You won't tell me any more?"

"I can't," Powar said. "Everything is riding on my plan. I do trust you, but this time I can't say anything. Please understand." And that was all she ever discussed with Maria.

Powar seemed very calm, and Maria didn't get it. Powar's whole future was riding on that meeting, and all she wanted to do was make snowmen and go for walks.

Honey was used to Powar's disappearances around the holidays. She'd never given them a second thought. But this time, thanks to Roger's early reports, she knew he had located Genevieve, and she hoped it would only be a matter of time before some valuable information would be revealed. Actually, this year she decided to enjoy having the town to herself and was busy calling up each member of the board to triple-check their votes. She wasn't going to leave anything to chance. She had several meetings with her lawyers, she had copies of the will ready . . . she had thought of everything. Powar, as a shareholder, had as much right to a seat on the board as anyone else, Honey just wanted to be sure that she remained sitting at the head of the table.

When January 10 came Honey thought the charcoal-and-gray herringbone suit would be nice, with the white crepe

Bergdorf blouse. She put on very sheer black hose and her black suede Joseph pumps. In the past few months Honey had changed the look of the public areas of the studio and, of course, Philip and Powar's office. She did not change the boardroom at all. She had always wanted it to look the same way it had many years ago when she and Philip took control from the Lewises. She always had the paint color freshened and the furniture recovered and the tables and chairs polished, but the paint color never changed, and the fabric was just replaced with the same pattern. She knew one day she would be seated at the head of the table, and she wanted the room to look the same.

It was January 10, 1978. She and her attorney, Charles Ziffinham, were ready. They met at 8:30 A.M. in Honey's office to go over everything again. Precisely at 9:45 they walked into the boardroom. It was down the hall from the main office. Honey had had it totally freshened for the occasion. The walls were a gleaming yellow. The furniture was very heavy Gothic carved wood on a green, yellow, black, and brown Oriental rug. The seats of the chairs were covered in green leather. Honey ordered fresh roses for the center of the table. Since there were only four board members left, she could order the roses to be high because the people could all be seated at one end of the table, which could seat twelve.

Honey was seated at the head of the table, with Charles at her right, when David Alpert and Barry Pressman walked in. They said hello to Honey like the friendly allies they were and sat down on her left. At 10:00 A.M. Powar walked into the room with Paul Schreibman and Neil Burkhardt. She had on Calvin Klein jeans, western boots, a white T-shirt, and a blue blazer. She had no intention of playing her mother's clothes game, plus she wanted to point up the differences in their generations. Without saying a word, Powar walked to the center of the table and took the roses off and placed them on a side table. She then sat down opposite her mother at the other head of the table. Schreibman and Burkhardt flanked her. No one from her side said a word as the normal corporate agenda was addressed by Honey and the year-end report was read.

When it got to new business, Powar spoke for the first time. "It is no surprise to any of you that I am here this morning. You are all familiar with my family's public struggles, something of which I thoroughly disapprove. I don't believe in public displays, but I have been forced into that position." Her eyes narrowed just a bit as she looked at her mother. "I have formed a company called PhilPow Inc., which is prepared to take over the ownership of this studio. I believe we have the necessary shares to do this. As soon as it is accomplished, I will call for the resignation of Honey King. Any of you who support her will also be asked to resign. I call for a vote."

"Powar, dear," Honey said condescendingly, "this is unnecessary. It is impossible for you to have more stock than I do. We both know I am aware of the gift that your father gave to you when you were eighteen, and that, coupled with the shares he left you upon his death, still cannot give you control. The numbers just don't add up. With Mr. Alpert and Mr. Pressman I go over the top. There's no reason to even take a vote."

Powar smiled at her mother's arrogance, and she looked at Burkhardt and gave a nod. "I have a reason, Mother." With that, Burkhardt opened the door and Genevieve entered. The gasps that came from such a small group were still considerable. Genevieve looked gorgeous. She was younger than Honey, and she was dressed in a camel Chanel suit straight from Paris.

Honey's face was distorted by the anger created by Genevieve's presence. The anger that she had been keeping in all these years was about to escape. "Well, well," said Honey. "I thought you were disposed of years ago when Philip got tired of you."

Genevieve smiled politely and replied, "The saying still holds that the wife is always the last to know." With that she sat down at Powar's end of the table.

Powar then spoke. "Genevieve LeJeune is the sole owner of Chateau Normandie Inc., a holding company in the LeJeune Family Trust, of which she is the sole heir. Mr. Schreibman arranged each year for the transfer of a small number of my father's shares in King Pictures. The number was so small that it was not necessary to file it with SEC. Through the years, though, the number has grown and is now considerable, and my new corporation, PhilPow Inc., has just acquired these shares. I am now the majority stockholder in King Pictures."

A deafening silence ensued. Honey looked at Ziffinham as though he were a dead man.

"Mother, you have until three o'clock today to vacate these premises. That's more time than you gave me. You may take Mr. Alpert and Mr. Pressman with you. My staff, which is waiting outside in the hall, will escort you to your office and supervise your move. Now if you'll excuse me, I have some more business to take care of with my lawyers and Ms. LeJeune. Good day." Genevieve and Powar laughed out loud as they heard Honey's screams in the hall.

As Franny clutched the copy of *Town & Country* to her bosom, she couldn't believe she'd finally made it on the cover as the "Hollywood Hostess of the Future." She had been so envious when Powar King got a *Time* magazine cover ten years earlier when she took over King Pictures. Franny had waited a long time for equal time. She knew all about Andy and Powar, and while she was jealous when she first found out, she soon realized that she could use it to her advantage. She could get precisely what she needed out of Andy in a marriage that suited her exact needs. Honey King might be the "grande dame," something that Franny accepted, but for Franny's generation, she was number one. During her rise she was always very careful to be deferential to Honey. She admired her and learned from her. Honey knew and was flattered by it. Franny lived for parties and, in fact, had set up a really special one for tonight. When she learned the publication date for the *Town & Country* issue, she asked Andy to throw a party in her honor. She knew he couldn't refuse, and she was right. At 7:30 tonight, 150 of the most important people in Hollywood were coming through her door. She originally couldn't decide whether or not she wanted an intimate power dinner for fifty or the big blowout. Obviously her ego won. One of her friends, Seth Baker, the handsome publisher of the prestigious newspaper *Beverly Hills 213*, was sending a photographer and doing a whole page of pictures on the party. George Christy of the *Hollywood Reporter* was doing the same thing. The *Los Angeles Times* would cover it but not give it a full page, and *Town & Country* was sending its own set of photographers to shoot. At 5:00 P.M. she met with the caterers from Great Presentations, who were beginning to set up. Regal Rents in conjunction with Flower Fashions had designed the huge tent that covered the tennis court. Rather than having a serious black tie event, Franny thought she would pull a switch and have everyone wear white. It was the beginning of summer, and one of the lessons she'd learned so well from Honey was that a party should have a cohesive theme. She was the star of the night, of course, and she thought for a second about having blow-ups of her cover displayed in the tent. But then she realized someone might think it was tacky. Instead she decided to have Harry Finley make a centerpiece for each table that incorporated a copy of the cover at the base of the arrangement. It was a little more subtle. She then decided to name this a "Grazing Gastronomique Adventure." Each guest was told on the invitation that he or she could go region by region, eating "local food." She had the caterers set up separate buffets, each decorated with the appropriate objects for the region. The Texas area had a cowboy theme and served ribs, beans, coleslaw, and corn. For the Northeast area she served Maryland crabcakes and had a "sea" theme. In the South she had magnolias and twinkle lights and waitresses in hoop skirts serving black-eyed peas, catfish, hushpuppies, chicken-fried steak, grits, and dirty rice. The California section had a Mexican theme, with tacos, enchiladas, rice, and beans. The Northwest had fresh salmon and caviar, while the Midwest had a baked potato bar where you could add any number of toppings you wanted. She had hired different bands for different times of the evening, from a Mariachi band to a country-western one. Franny wanted people to be talking about this party for a long time to come.

Franny's dressing area was her pride and joy. It really consisted of three very large spaces, a closet, dressing area, and bath area, and it encompassed approximately two thousand square feet. The closet area was three full wall racks, both upper and lower rows, with all her clothes color-coordinated. There was a section for each type of clothing: blouses, slacks, pants, and skirts. The shoes took up the fourth wall, and they were on shelves with glass cabinet doors. Each shoe was wrapped in a plastic bag, and the matching purse was next to it, also wrapped in a bag. Franny had read a biography of Joan Crawford once and remembered that was how Joan had stored things. The dressing area consisted of wall-to-wall mirrors and lights with a section that included a professional makeup table and mirror and a shampoo bowl. All of the colors of this area were light pink, with white clouds painted on the ceiling. In the bath area the white clouds were on the pink ceiling and the walls. All the fixtures were pink porcelain, and the handles were pink-and-white Wedgwood. In one wall was a big TV set and a VCR. The floor was pink Carrara marble, as was the tub, which would have held at least half a football team. In front of the TV was a pink satin chaise and reading table. Under the sink there was a little refrigerator. Franny actually never had to go out into the world ever again. She could just live in her bathroom. Even though it was on the second floor of the house, a set of stairs led to the tennis court off the balcony.

There was a vault behind a mirrored panel that no one knew about except for Andy. Franny had an extraordinary jewelry collection of "ensembles" of diamonds and rubies, diamonds and sapphires, diamonds and emeralds, or just plain diamonds. She secretly knew they were Andy's guilt gifts, but she didn't care. She loved to go into the vault and try them all on. She felt positively "royal." She would usually go in wearing a pink satin robe to match the room. Once inside, she would take it off and stand there completely nude. She would place on her body, one item at a time, a necklace, ring, earring, and whatever belonged, feeling the coldness of their beauty. She would turn and look at her reflection in the full-length mirror in the vault and see the jewels shining against her skin. It gave her a thrill that was beyond description. Whenever she was depressed in any way, all she had to do was go in the vault and repeat her ritual. Some days it was all diamonds, or some days she felt like she needed a color. Whatever it was, it worked for her every time. When she sat in the vault for long periods of time, her mind began to drift off to moments in her life that were very special. Franny was glad that Blair would be here tonight to celebrate with her. Their friendship meant a great deal to her, and they had become inseparable during the years of Franny's marriage. From the moment she first saw her she knew they would be good friends. Blair had everything that Franny always wanted for herself, especially those Grace Kelly looks.

That first time Franny arrived at the Paul Williams–designed house on St. Pierre Road in Bel Air, she was greeted by a butler who said, "Miss Blair will be about twenty minutes late this afternoon for tea. She suggested I give you a tour."

Franny was excited. Her eyes could not believe the carved wood ceiling in the halls and foyer, the painted ceiling in the living room, the statues around the atrium, and the ballroom downstairs complete with a stage for an orchestra. She was not taken to the private quarters upstairs, of course.

"Now I'd like to show you the grounds," said the butler. "Please follow me."

Franny went outside into what seemed like a rain forest with trails that led to a bridge to the shallow end of the pool.

"This house was built for Marion Davies by William Randolph Hearst," the butler explained. "The pool is three hundred and fifty feet long, as you will see."

There in the pool were two gondolas. The pool was so long that it looked like a never-ending river.

"I will walk you through," said the butler. They went along a path by the pool that curved around to include a sandy beach. "Mr. Hearst brought in the sand for Miss Davies, and we have kept it exactly the way it was."

Franny noted you could dive from the beach into the pool. There were three bridges crossing the pool at various times along its whole length. In another area there were caves built into the rock foundation under the house. All of this led to a gazebo and guest house. Her breath was literally taken away. She went to the den to wait for Blair. Passing the grand piano in the living room, she saw the photos in silver frames inscribed to Blair from the Eisenhowers, Nixons, Fords, Jack and Robert Kennedy, and Frank Sinatra. Upon entering the den, she saw a silver tea service all set up. She was browsing through the book titles when Blair appeared. She was wearing tan slacks, a cream-colored silk shirt, and tan espadrilles. Her blunt-cut blonde hair was classically parted on the side.

"Do you remember the movie *High Society?*" asked Franny.

"How did you know?" Blair exclaimed.

"Well," said Franny, "I'm looking right at Tracy Samantha Lord in the opening scene."

"How positively 'yar,' " Blair replied in a line from the movie. The two of them laughed at the same time.

Franny had seen *High Society* eighteen times as a child, and now here she was having tea with her own "Grace Kelly."

"Today we are going to celebrate," said Blair. "I am no longer going to be the ex-Mrs. So and So. Something fantastic has happened. I'm going to write a book. I told a friend about my idea for a novel, and they brought it to Random House in New York and they bought it. I'm so excited!"

Franny was thrilled for her and also thought Andy could produce it if it was right. "What's it about?" she asked.

"It's about what happens to members of a women's consciousness-raising group in different decades," answered Blair. "Would you like to hear a little bit of what I've written?"

Franny was honored. She already felt close to Blair, as though they had known each other for years. Blair poured the tea, pointed to the sandwiches, and started to read. The novel was written in diary form, and the part Blair was reading dealt with a fantasy one of the women in the group was having. It took a while for Franny to catch on that the fantasy was about another woman in the group. Blair's writing was really sensual and well paced. Her sentences deliberately left breathing room for the excitement to build for the reader. Franny had stopped drinking and eating. She was transfixed. She felt a tingling feeling come over her that was completely unfamiliar, felt her breathing start to change, too. She kept staring at that one long lock of Blair's hair that almost covered her right eye. Blair had finished reading.

"How did you like it?" she asked.

"I think you are a beautiful writer," said Franny, "but how could you think up all those things? You must have a great imagination."

Blair smiled and said, "Thank you." She patted Franny on the hand. "I'll be right back." She went to an area behind the bar in the den and pulled out a little bottle. "There's a lot you don't know about," Blair said. "You really should experience more of life. You'd be a lot happier."

Franny was nailed to the couch as her heart started a strange beating.

"Shut your eyes and hold out your hand," said Blair.

Franny did as she was told. "I promise I won't hurt you. It will be totally pleasurable," said Blair.

All of a sudden Franny felt Blair's hand covering hers with a cool silky liquid. She felt Blair's fingers swirling around in her palm.

Franny opened her eyes wide. "What is that liquid?" she asked incredulously.

"Astroglide," said Blair. "It's incredible, isn't it?" Blair let Franny take all this in before she asked her next question. "How do you feel about brushes?"

"What?" exclaimed Franny.

"I'll be right back," Blair said. She was back in a second. "Now shut your eyes again and don't worry. This is just a face brush from a Dior powder kit."

Franny again closed her eyes, and this time she felt the velvety-soft touch of the brush on her face. It was caressing, not brushing. She felt it on her eyelids, her lips, her neck. . . . It was exquisite. She began to imagine what it would be like to feel that all over her body. Franny opened her eyes and looked at Blair. "You're amazing," she said. A few too many seconds went by as their eyes locked.

Finally Blair answered, "So are you."

In a moment of sudden panic, Franny jumped up and said, "I've got to go now," and walked very quickly to the front door and out to her car. The feelings that were stirred up in her frightened and excited her at the same time. She had never felt anything like this with Andy. She looked back at Blair, who was standing in the doorway smiling at her.

Two hours later Franny found herself standing at Blair's front door. The butler answered the bell.

"Is Mrs. Lawson expecting you?" he asked.

"Not really," Franny said timidly.

"I'll tell her you're here."

Blair came bounding into the den, a smile reaching from ear to ear. She kissed Franny on the cheek and whispered, "I'm so glad you came back. Let's go to the upstairs den."

Franny followed her upstairs. Blair's den was a special room that you could get to only by going through her dressing room area. It was a totally round room done all in beige, with a big bay window overlooking the pool. All the way around the room there was a beige couch with pillows. In the middle of the room was a round English drum desk. There was a cabinet on the wall that held a TV and a stereo.

"Do you like Dusty Springfield?" asked Blair.

"Oh, yes," Franny said.

Blair put on an album that started with "The Look of Love."

"I've never seen a room that's all one color before," explained Franny. "It has an unusual effect. It's almost like one is floating inside a fluffy pillow."

"Come sit by me," Blair urged.

Franny walked slowly toward her. Her heart was beating overtime. She sat down and felt Blair's hand on her face.

"We're going to have a very special relationship, aren't we?" Blair said softly.

All Franny could do was nod in silence. Blair's face came closer and closer. She started to kiss Franny on her cheek, just barely letting her lips touch her. As the lips got closer to her mouth, Franny's body was tingling. She was so excited. It was a feeling she had never felt before. Blair's lips were on hers now, and it was like a lightning bolt hit her. She thought she was actually hearing whistles. Andy never gave her these feelings, and she had never felt such intensity just from a kiss!

Blair reached under the couch and pulled out something that looked like a wooden door covered in tufted beige satin. In each corner was a metal eye with a beige silk cord attached.

"What's that?" Franny asked breathlessly.

"It's a pleasure board," said Blair. "It's for both of us." Blair kissed her again and started to take off Franny's clothes. For every article of Franny's she removed, she took off one of her own. Totally nude now, Blair gently pushed Franny onto the board.

"This is so soft," said Franny.

"You're going to love this," Blair whispered in her ear as she started tying each of Franny's limbs with the beige cords. "Now shut your eyes."

Franny felt the brush that Blair had showed her earlier start to stroke her forehead. The bristles felt like velvet. It was over her eyes, then her mouth. It went languidly down her neck to her right nipple. She let out a little gasp and moved involuntarily. The brush was just touching the tip over and over again. She felt her left breast ache for it. Finally Blair moved the brush to answer Franny's soft moans. As soon as the lower half of her body began to move, Franny felt the brush go down her stomach and land on her inner thigh. It was going from her knee all the way up to her special spot. She was getting wet now as the brush landed exactly between her legs, gently exploring every crevice. It was driving her crazy. Then she felt Blair's hand replace the brush. Her fingers were probing inside her with a pulsating action. Franny tried to pull her legs out of the ropes. She wanted to put them around Blair so badly that she could scream. Blair's thumb was outside on her pleasure spot now, while her fingers remained inside. She felt the climax starting from her toes. It was intensely hot and crawled up her body with ferocity. Her scream of joy shocked her. It was involuntary and penetrating. She looked up at Blair and started to cry.

Blair immediately loosened Franny's arms and feet so they could cradle each other.

Franny knew she had found the most special person in her life. She finally felt accepted and safe and hung on to Blair for dear life.

Honey King couldn't help but watch her reflection in the glass covering the towering King Pictures' movie posters lining the walls on the way to her office. She knew her home looked like a shrine, but she didn't care. Her blonde Rita Hayworth—styled hair cascaded over her shoulders to the exact point where the front wave swooped to end right where the collar of her pink Chanel suit began. Honey had always pretended that she didn't know how "hot" she was . . . that the sophistication of Chanel suited her. In fact, she loved Chanel because of the visual contrast, knowing it was a combination that deliberately knocked any quarry senseless.

"Good evening, Mrs. King," said her assistant, Miss Williams, looking up as Honey walked through her outer office door and kept going. Miss Williams got up and followed her, notebook in hand.

"What's my schedule tomorrow, Judith?" asked Honey, sitting behind her Louis XIV desk.

"You're all set for Mr. and Mrs. Stromberg's party tonight at eight, Mrs. King. At nine A.M. tomorrow morning, Mrs. Gallery and Mrs. Fields will be here to go over the decorations for the Angels' cocktail party. At one P.M. you and Mrs. Begelman will be at the Bistro. Three-thirty back at the house I booked Carl, that new masseur you liked, and then at five your hair and makeup people arrive. Saks is delivering your gown, and Mr. Diller is picking you up at seven-fifteen. The concert at the Music Center starts at eight. For tonight, I told Lupe to take out the navy blue St. Laurent and the short, black Chanel dress in case you wish to wear either one of them this evening."

"Thank you, Judith, I'll see you in the morning."

Honey watched her close the double French doors and then glanced at her desk. The thought of reading more mail annoyed her, and reluctantly she opened the thick correspondence folder. She looked quickly through the usual engraved invitations and then noticed an unopened airmail letter marked "Confidential." Her fingers quickly released the contents. As she read, her eyes focused more intently, then eagerly, devouring the information. A huge, almost frightening smile broke out on her face. She sat back in her chair triumphantly. "Well, well, my daughter," she whispered half-aloud. "You've managed to keep the secret for years. But now I have it, and now I will use it to destroy you."

Maria decided she was going to take Jonna as her date to Andy and Franny's party. Instead of asking one of her press agent friends or some actor who wanted to get his name in print, she was going to take her daughter. Jonna was eighteen now, and although she'd been raised around Hollywood parties, she really wasn't that interested in them. But Maria felt it was time for her to make her "debut."

All Jonna was interested in was her music and dancing. When she was around twelve, her interest in gymnastics switched to jazz dancing and then broadened itself to highly choreographed rock 'n' roll street dancing. She loved Michael Jackson and really wanted to be him, spending hours in the mirror lip-synching to his records and trying to imitate his dance moves. Maria had used her influence to get tickets to all his concerts, plus those of Jonna's other favorite stars. Jonna was very much a loner, just like Jackson. Maria would ordinarily think that Jonna was imitating his behavior, but that's how she had been her whole life. She wanted to distance herself from people as soon as they got too close. She never wanted anyone to know the truth about her. Even when she saw therapists, they couldn't make any headway. Maria, who had been around stars for years now, saw in Jonna the same thing that she saw in many stars. They wanted to be loved, but only from a distance. On the stage they were vulnerable, but offstage you couldn't get near them. She could see why Jonna was being drawn to that life. Jonna did not really want to go to Franny's party. She would much rather go to the China Club and sit in the back listening to a group, but that was not to be tonight.

Maria was stunned when she saw Jonna walk down the stairs. She had on white jeans, a white silk cowboy shirt with fringe and rhinestones, white cowboy boots, and a white cowboy hat. Jonna was six feet one and definitely Nathan's daughter. Her jet black thick straight hair and wide-set eyes came from Maria. It was quite a combination. She really did have everything to make it as a star. Maria was in a soft white diaphanous dress with a white slip underneath and white sandals. They looked more like sisters than mother and daughter.

"I'm not happy about this, Mother," said Jonna as the valet was taking their car at the party.

"Jonna, every kid in America would kill to trade places

with you tonight. You don't need to be uncomfortable in this crowd. You are the daughter of Nathan Blumenthal and heir to the most powerful trade paper in the business. Just relax. People will come to you."

And come they did. By the time Jonna went from "Texas" to "California" she was overwhelmed by family friends and young men. Maria could see she was happy to see some of them, but the men unnerved her. Maria could understand what triggered it. If you thought that God played a cruel trick on you and made you half man–half woman, you would have a difficult time accepting yourself and relating to the opposite sex. Maria had tried over and over to explain to Jonna that she was a girl. She would have been tall anyway because of Nathan's size. Maria felt that Jonna did relate as a girl but just was insecure when anything more intimate might happen.

"Jonna, I'm so happy to see you. You look great," said Powar as she cornered her by the tacos.

Powar was alone so Jonna asked, "How is Jordan? I miss not seeing her as much as I used to."

"She's doing very well in school and loves living in Switzerland. I'm going to try really hard to put together a trip so we all can get together again. I'd love it," said Powar. Just then Andy came up, so Powar quickly changed the subject. "How is your music coming along? Maria tells me you have a very powerful voice. I'd like to hear it sometime."

"You will one day, I hope," said Jonna as she headed in another direction.

Powar turned to Andy and asked, "How do you like your party?" knowing full well that he hadn't had anything to do with it except financially.

Catching her sarcasm, he replied, "It's my strong suit. I just love them, don't you?"

Powar paused for a moment. "You're beginning to remind me of my father, and that's not necessarily a good sign. He genuinely loved parties, as you know, but he was sorry he settled in his personal life."

Powar just walked off with a wink and a slight shake of her head, creating a gentle flowing of her dark hair. She was not rude to Andy. She loved him. She just felt it was time he knew she was getting upset. Powar began to realize that she, too, had settled in her personal life. She put business ahead of everything, and it was beginning to take its toll. She had come early to the party because she knew her mother would come very late and make an entrance. She figured she had another twenty minutes to visit people and then she would leave. She would never let her mother think that her presence would be the reason Powar would leave a party. Being with Franny and Andy was not Powar's idea of a good time.

* CHAPTER 19 *

Fifteen-year-old Jordan King looked in the mirror and was fairly pleased. Her mother always told her she looked like Candy Bergen, and that was fine with her. She was more than pleased with her looks, having been quite aware at an early age that she was more beautiful than most. She was constantly being stopped on the street by strangers and had been ever since she was a baby. With her mother being so dark, Jordan couldn't figure out how she turned out to be so blonde. She sometimes stared at her mother and got a strange feeling.

It had all come to a head last Christmas. Powar, Jordan, and Genevieve were sitting around the tree exhausted. All of the presents had been opened except one.

"I wanted you to save this one for last," Powar said to Jordan. She handed her a very large, heavy box wrapped all in pink.

"This must really be something, Mother," said Jordan. She ripped through the wrapping very quickly and reached inside. "Oh, my God," she said as she pulled out a blond mink coat.

"I just had to do it for you, Jordan. I knew with your hair

color and coloring it would be impossible for you not to have this."

Jordan jumped up and started modeling it. "Oh, Mother, I love it!"

Genevieve and Powar smiled at each other. It was a breakthrough, the first time Jordan had been enthusiastic over something Powar had given her.

"Let's go look at it in the mirror," Powar suggested.

Jordan went to a full-length mirror and stood there with Genevieve and Powar behind her.

"You are absolutely dazzling," said Powar. "Your hair is the exact same color as the coat."

"Mother," said Jordan, "exactly how did I get this hair? I don't have your coloring. Do I look like my father? Are you sure you don't have a picture of him?" Jordan knew this line of questioning would not be well received, but she didn't care. She was tired of being lied to. She wanted to know who she was.

"All right," Powar said very slowly and tensely. "You look like your grandmother."

"On whose side?" asked Jordan.

"Mine," Powar said quickly.

"Why do I get the feeling there's a problem here, Mother? I know who our family is. My grandmother is a very famous Hollywood lady, yet you never talk about her? What is it?"

Powar glanced at Genevieve before she answered. "Your grandmother is a difficult woman with very strong opinions."

"Gee," said Jordan, breaking into a smile. "It sounds like you're describing one of the magazine stories about you."

"That's not necessary, Jordan. I don't deserve that. Until you have all the facts you shouldn't form opinions."

Jordan jumped for glee. "Exactly!" she said. "So what are they?"

"It's still not appropriate for us to have this discussion, darling. It will be one day, I promise you." Powar felt trapped, realizing her answers were unfair to Jordan.

"Do you mean I still have to sneak off to the library in

Paris and continue to read press clippings about King Pictures and stock transactions?" said Jordan. "I'm no longer a little girl. I don't deserve this."

"Oh, Jordan," said Powar, turning her beautiful daughter to face her. "Soon you'll have all the answers to all your questions. And remember . . . I love you."

Jordan's curiosity about her birth and her heritage had changed from just curiosity to anger through the years as her mother's visits became less frequent. Jordan was a very bright young lady and read everything about the Kings. She knew she was being given the best life in Europe that money could buy, and she loved Genevieve as her real mother. But part of her resented missing out on what America and her family had to offer. When you grow up as a secret, you have a hard time feeling that good about yourself. Jordan was bright enough to realize that and fight the feelings whenever they tried to take her over, and she was determined to be successful at whatever she tried. Even though she had been sent away two years ago, she was still trying to deal with life at Des Alpes Vaudoises, the private girls' school in Vevey, Switzerland.

Des Alpes was very beautiful. It looked like a giant château where a king lived. It had stupendous bright green rolling lawns and gardens, stables where the girls kept their own horses, and its own stream and forest. When Jordan was taken here by Genevieve she tried to put up a brave front. She could tell Genevieve didn't really want her to go, so it was very hard on both of them. Upon arrival they were greeted by the headmistress, Miss Elizabeth Plowforth, a humorless, birdlike woman who looked pinched-in everywhere. She was in her sixties and obviously had never been out on a date in her life.

"My dear young lady," said Miss Plowforth, "Jordan is such an unusual name. How do you get it?"

Jordan noticed that when Miss Plowforth asked a question it was like an interrogation, where her brow lowered itself even more and all her features moved into the center of her face, making her even more birdlike. "I don't have the slightest idea," Jordan answered.

"Please follow me," said Miss Plowforth. "You have already seen the grounds, but I'd like to show you the inside. To our right as we walk along there is the parlor, where we allow young men to come visit on Saturday afternoon. They are never allowed to cross this line that we are standing on now. Des Alpes prides itself on its sterling reputation, and we intend to keep it that way. All our young women here are ladies with excellent manners and backgrounds. We enforce a very strict curriculum and only allow outside activities that will make them more well-rounded people like glee club, table setting, menu planning, and sewing."

Jordan and Genevieve looked at each other in silent horror. Neither one of them wanted her to go to this school, but Powar had insisted on it.

"You've seen the chapel outside, but we have a smaller one here, just in case any of our young ladies likes to pray more than once a week. We definitely encourage stopping in here as frequently as possible. On your left you see the dining room. It is really quite beautiful," said Miss Plowforth.

For once, Jordan and Genevieve had to agree with her. "This is truly magnificent," said Genevieve. "I really appreciate the carving and the moldings, but the murals are even more special."

They were eventually shown to Jordan's room on the third floor of the château. There were no elevators, and it was quite a climb up the steep steps. For a second Jordan was sorry she had brought all her camera equipment; it was really weighing her down. But it had become her salvation. The Super 8 camera she got two years ago for Christmas from Genevieve went everywhere with her. She loved shooting anything and everything. She was particularly interested in shooting people in close-ups, and she wished she had enough hands or cameras to run two at once. She wanted one camera just for close-ups and the other for a master. Genevieve had instilled her love of the camera in Jordan. When Genevieve had seen Jordan's ability, she'd called Powar and Powar had sent over another camera and some editing equipment. Jordan would spend hours in her "lab," selecting shots, editing, and making little films, and Genevieve happily encouraged her, hoping Powar would come to France soon so she could see some of them. . They were only one or two minutes long, but Jordan definitely had something. Instead they were now at this boarding school.

"Here it is," said Miss Plowforth. "We call it our Princess Room."

The room was painted white and had white organza curtains covering the French doors that led to a balcony. There was a set of twin beds covered in matching white bedspreads. The only color in the room came from the floral carpet. On the wall was a picture of Miss Plowforth, which apparently was standard in every room.

Jordan thought it looked like a hospital room but didn't want to say it. Into this moment of silence strode thirteen-year-old Princess Arianne of Yugoslavia, with three servants carrying her bags and a guitar after her.

"Who are you?" she demanded in her perfect English accent.

"Who are *you*?" demanded Jordan with matched intensity.

"Girls, girls," said Miss Plowforth. "Let me introduce you. Your Highness Princess Arianne, I'd like you to meet Jordan LeJeune, your new roommate."

The girls shook hands very skeptically, each already staking out territory for herself in the room. "You both are going to have a wonderful time here and get a good education. Now come along, Ms. LeJeune," said Miss Plowforth, "let's let them get on with it."

Genevieve hugged Jordan tightly and then left. It was impossible for them to speak with Miss Plowforth and the princess staring at them. "Call me all the time," Genevieve said as she left.

Jordan and Arianne sized each other up. They looked like sisters in blonde-dom. Arianne's hair was much longer than

Jordan's. It was down to her waist and made her look like a princess from those fairy-tale books. Jordan noticed that her mouth formed a perfect cupid's bow and that the distance from her upper lip to the tip of her nose was just perfect. In fact, everything about her was picture perfect. She even had those round blue saucer eyes like all the models. She was very slight and fragile-looking, and Jordan wanted to hate her because of all this perfection.

What Jordan didn't know was that Arianne thought Jordan was the one with the perfect looks. Arianne had always felt she was too thin. She wanted to be more athletic-looking, like Jordan.

"Shall we just get on with it then," said Arianne. It was a statement, not a question.

"Of course," said Jordan, and both girls began to unpack.

"Are you a righty or a lefty?" asked Arianne without waiting for an answer. "I'm a lefty, so I hope that's all right with you. In every school I have ever been in I've been on the left. It's sort of a tradition with me."

"How many schools have you been in?" asked Jordan.

"Six," Arianne said.

"But how could that be? You're only thirteen," said Jordan.

"So are you, and you're here," said Arianne. In terms of deciding who had what in their room, there was no problem. Everything in the room was very equal. The ease with which they worked together to set up the room surprised them. Quickly they assessed that they would be better working together than apart.

During the weeks of adjusting to classes and figuring out their individual relationships with the rest of the girls, they became closer. They developed a pattern of going for a walk on the grounds each night after dinner.

"So you mean you don't know who your father is?" asked Arianne as they were sitting by the well in the moonlight.

"No," said Jordan.

"Don't feel bad," Arianne said. "My mother has been married eight times. I have too many fathers. Maybe I could loan one to you."

Jordan laughed aloud for the first time in a long while.

A mutual trust developed over the next two years. Arianne and Jordan figured out that each had been deprived of something important growing up. Jordan didn't have a father, and Arianne didn't have a country. The monarchy had been thrown out with her grandfather, and she'd been born in London. It was "have title, will travel," but Arianne soon realized that as long as she had Jordan she would never be alone again.

"I hate green beans, don't you?" said Jordan as they were walking in the damp night air once again.

"Not really," Arianne said. "They remind me of my mother. She told me when she was a little girl that she had a private garden inside the palace walls and she decided to grow beans. Even though she had many servants, she said she was most proud of the night that her own beans were served to everyone for dinner. She was only eight, and she felt so accomplished," said Arianne. "I would have loved to live there in the palace and feel that history around me. It must have really been amazing."

They were at the stables, and Jordan stopped and looked at her. "I would have loved to have spent enough time with my mother to even have a memory of a green bean story," she said matter-of-factly.

"Hey, silly," said Arianne, trying to get things on a lighter note. "Why don't we try to have more fun now? We're both dumped off here and forgotten. What do you say?"

"Okay," said Jordan without much enthusiasm. Arianne was much more frivolous than she was. Jordan was very serious most of the time and lived through her cameras.

"All right, then," said Arianne. "I'm planning something for Saturday."

Sure enough, Arianne was up early. Jordan felt her pushing

her shoulder. "Okay, kid, let's go!" she said. She always called Jordan "kid" because she was three months younger.

Jordan opened her eyes and saw Arianne wearing beige jodhpurs, a black silk blouse, and black riding boots. She meant business.

Jordan got up and went into the bathroom. A few minutes later she emerged, looking much more awake. She went to her closet and put on blue jeans, a man's white shirt, brown boots, and a Pendleton wool jacket. The outfits defined each girl's persona very well. Jordan picked up her camera and said, "I'm ready now."

"If you're going to insist upon lugging that thing, then I'm taking something, too," said Arianne, and she went to the closet and pulled out her guitar. She had played only one song for Jordan in all this time, but Jordan had liked her voice.

"That's a good idea," said Jordan.

"Now, I have a plan."

Their horses were saddled and ready for them when they arrived at the stables. Jordan's was all black, and she had named him Whirlaway. Arianne's looked just like her. It was a golden palomino named Catherine, after her mother.

It was a gorgeous day for riding. The sky was very pale blue, and the light was almost filtered on the countryside. Jordan's eye worked like a camera, so as she passed flower beds and ancient stone walls she was constantly photographing them in her mind. Arianne had something else on her mind. A few weeks ago while they were riding they'd come across a group of young men from a nearby school. The girls at Vaudoises were allowed to meet boys only in chaperoned mixers, and Arianne had recognized them from one early on in the term. One of them in particular caught her eye. His name was Clive Herndon, and she remembered him as being charming and funny. Arianne had not stopped talking about him, so it didn't surprise Jordan what their Saturday activity was.

"Look! Here's my surprise," shouted Arianne.

Jordan looked at Clive. He had sandy hair and a ruddy complexion, with a decent build and almost a blank face. It was a look she hated because it was nondescript and would certainly photograph that way. He was "pink" all over, and Jordan hated "pink" people. It was her opinion that people were either pink or beige, and she personally could only tolerate beige. Pink almost made her nauseated. Pink people were puffy and soft with no guts. Arianne galloped over to Clive.

"Hello, there," she said. "What are you doing over here?"

"We were going hunting," said Clive, "and I guess we've succeeded very well."

Arianne giggled as Jordan rode up. "You remember Jordan, don't you?" she said.

"I think so," Clive said in a slightly disinterested manner. "Meet the guys," he said as he looked around at the three pasty-faced boys on horseback to his right.

Jordan was concerned about Arianne's seemingly empty-headed nature when she got around boys. She was too trusting and inexperienced. Jordan had no experience, either, but she'd been "born old." She just always seemed to have knowledge and experience. It was a gift and she accepted it, but it frequently meant that she kept everything inside. She wasn't free with her emotions. It was as if she carried the weight of the world and everybody else's problems with her wherever she went.

"Hello, Clive," said Jordan as nicely as she could.

"It's nice to see you out for this ride. Are you going to shoot pictures today?" he asked.

"An idea is forming in my mind about it," said Jordan.

"I hope you don't mind, but I'm going to abscond with your leading lady for a while. There's a special place that I want her to see."

Before Jordan could answer, Arianne said, "You don't mind, do you? I just love surprises," she said, giggling again.

"Of course not," said Jordan. "Have a good time. I have plans for these three anyway," she looked at Clive's pals. "Have you guys ever seen the Three Stooges or Laurel and Hardy?" she asked.

Everybody laughed as Arianne and Clive waved good-bye. Jordan heard him say, "C'mon, Princess, I'm going to show you your new kingdom." She felt very uneasy.

Arianne looked back at Jordan, wishing she would participate in things more. She kept trying to teach her how to have fun, but Jordan was interested only in her own kind of fun—shooting pictures. Perhaps later this afternoon she might mention something to Clive about fixing her up with someone. As they rode along, Clive pointed out different flowers. Arianne had never been this far away from the stables before. Clive seemed so stately on his horse. She found his strength exciting. When they got to a patch of very thick trees, he stopped and got off his horse.

"This is it, Princess. We walk from here."

As Arianne got down she noticed how beautiful the sun was through the trees. The shadows were playful and charming. They had been riding uphill, and it was cooler than she had expected. A wind was blowing as well.

"Give me your hand and shut your eyes," said Clive. "Don't worry. I won't hurt you. You will love what you are about to see."

She gave him her hand and they walked through the trees very slowly. Within a few minutes she felt much more light and wind on her face. She knew they had changed environments somehow.

"Open your eyes," said Clive.

Arianne was startled by the beauty she was now taking in. They were on top of a mountain that overlooked a lake and village that appeared to be lifted from the picture page of a children's fairy-tale book. The colors of blue and green were vivid, even from that height. Arianne noticed that the clearing they were in was enclosed by a crudely made stone fence that formed a semicircle on the grass. The open part of the semicircle became a window to the lake. You could sit down on the grass and not be seen by anyone unless they came around to the opening in front.

"This is the most magical place I've ever seen," said Arianne. "I think I shall pretend that I'm looking down from the window of my castle."

"It is your kingdom, Your Highness," said Clive. "You may rule from here for all time."

She noticed that his smile went from ear to ear. He was very endearing and eager to please. When the sunlight hit his reddish hair it looked almost golden from where Arianne was sitting.

"And now some royal snacks," said Clive. He knelt down and reached into his knapsack. Out came apples, cheese, a bottle of red wine, and a couple of very small brown paper bags.

"What's in those?" asked Arianne.

"An appetizer," Clive replied. He opened the first bag and took out two white pills. "In England we call this Mandrax. It's called Quaalude in the U.S.," he explained.

Arianne had heard of it. She had never participated in things like that, but she was not ignorant. Clive could see that her curiosity was piqued. "I can't tell you how incredible it is to take this and then just sit here. You are already on top of the world, and this pill lets you float even higher. It's very gentle." He popped one in his mouth and washed it down with the wine. He put the other pill in Arianne's hand and looked at her sweetly. She hesitated for a moment and then put it in her mouth. Maybe it was time for her to do some living.

They started to eat the apples and the cheese. "Look down there," said Clive. "Can you see it?"

"What?" said Arianne.

"The children playing down there."

"You must have very good vision," she answered. "To me they look like little specks. They're even sort of fuzzy."

She looked at Clive and he looked a little fuzzy, too. For

the first time he also looked pink. There might be something to Jordan's pink-beige theory after all, she thought. She felt a warm glow and looked into his eyes.

Clive knew when to strike, and he leaned over and kissed her. She felt as if his lips were melting into hers, and her whole body started to respond. If this was what she was saving herself for, it was time to stop saving and start experiencing. He was reading her mind because his hands started carefully unbuttoning her blouse one button at a time. She just felt so relaxed and loving, she would let him do anything he wanted.

After the second open button, her breasts were exposed. Before he went to the next button he started caressing both breasts in his hands. He kissed her very deeply. Arianne felt herself lean back, caught up in feelings she had never felt. When Clive got to the last button he let his hand drift down between her legs. She began to moan. He quickly took off her boots and pulled down her jodhpurs, leaving her underpants on. He reached for the wine bottle and filled his mouth with wine. He got on top of her and placed his mouth over hers and let the wine trickle from his mouth. She felt as though she were six feet off the ground as she opened her mouth wider to catch the flow. She could feel him next to her underpants. She was confused because she didn't understand why her pants were still on. She had confidence in him, but that technique certainly wasn't in any of the books she'd read.

He reached between her legs, and she felt his fingers move the center part of her pants to one side. The fingers dallied at her opening, and she spread her legs involuntarily. She felt the glow of the pill from head to toe. It was as if her whole body were melting and floating at the same time. Now she felt something bigger and harder probing at her. Clive had to have known she was a virgin because he was taking care not to hurt her.

He waited until she started to move with him, her body begging for it, and then he let her have exactly what she wanted. She gasped and he felt her nails in his back. He knew she was experiencing her true calling at this very moment by the way she reacted.

She couldn't get enough.

He knew it and increased his speed even more. He knew her scream meant that she'd gone over the top. He pulled out quickly, not joining her ecstasy deliberately. Her eyes were shut as she lay, spent, on the grass. He just held her for a while without speaking.

She opened her eyes and reached for his face, smothering it with kisses. She didn't know what came over her, but she knew she hadn't had enough. She was kissing him harder now, almost chewing his mouth off. This time he practically threw her to the ground. The rougher he was, the more she liked it. He was even harder than he was before, which was his plan. He knew when it was right to save up. He ripped off her underpants at the same time that she wrapped her legs around him. She felt him ram himself into her until he almost came out the other side. It was a feeling she loved instantly. This time was completely different from the way it was a little while ago and totally right for the second time. She put her hands around his neck and he pulled her up until she was sitting on top of him, gyrating. He could finally hold it no longer, and she felt a volcano burst inside her. As they both lay back, she knew she still wanted more. Clive had unleashed something in Arianne. Arianne now knew what she had been missing, and if she couldn't have her kingdom, she could certainly have her king.

The moment Arianne came back to the room Jordan knew something was different. She came in about sixty miles an hour and was talking nonstop. She told her everything about Clive and was still excited beyond belief. Jordan didn't like Clive, and she tried to change the subject.

"Look what I got today from my mother," she said. "It's fabulous! It's a Beaulieu sixteen-millimeter camera with sound. Can you imagine what I'd like to do with that?"

"No," said Arianne, who was very disinterested in it.

"Listen to me," Jordan insisted. "You know that song that you wrote called 'Silver Needles'? I'd like to shoot you singing it."

"You're kidding," said Arianne, finally focusing on her. "Do you know what Clive's father does?"

"No, and I don't care," said Jordan. "Let's just talk about something for us to do and leave him out of it."

"But wait," Arianne said insistently. "His father owns ATV."

Jordan knew that ATV was the MTV of England, but it didn't impress her. She was trying to get Arianne's mind off Clive, not more involved.

"Don't you see?" said Arianne, pressing her case. "It'll be great. You'll shoot a video of my song, and Clive will get his father to play it on TV. We'll be famous."

"Calm down, Ari," said Jordan. "I just want to play a bit."

For the next week Arianne talked about nothing other than shooting the video and Clive. Jordan agreed to do it on the weekend just to keep her quiet. However, a thought had taken hold in the back of her head. Wouldn't it be amusing if she did make a name for herself in the industry without ever using "King" or King Pictures? She could show her family. If then they didn't want her, she never needed them in the first place. She'd have to keep a big eye on Arianne, but it might be worth it. She thought to ask Clive and his friends to hold the reflectors for the light. She was going to use natural light in the film to give it a Swedish look, which was perfect for Arianne's hair and coloring. Genevieve had shown her a film a few years back called *Elvira Madigan*, which used the technique of lighting to make a statement. Jordan noticed that most of the videos on ATV were harsh. She thought she would go the other way, and that would get her videos noticed.

Word got out at the school that Jordan and Arianne were shooting, and many of the girls wanted to come. At first Jordan thought it would be a bad idea, but then she thought it might be very interesting if they all showed up in their uniforms and she shot them. She would place them on a hill, just swaying to Arianne's song, and then in the lab she would intercut that with Arianne, sometimes dissolving and sometimes superimposing. All the while they were shooting they felt something special was happening. She saw Clive take Ari for a walk on the first break.

"Ari, where are you going? I need you to check the lights," said Jordan, trying to keep her attention on the work.

"I'll be right back," Ari shouted. "Don't worry."

She was only gone about ten minutes, and Jordan was ready to shoot. Ari's song "Silver Needles" was about the pain of childhood, with lyrics everyone could relate to.

Ari looked like a young Marianne Faithfull with her long, thick blonde hair and her wistful eyes. Jordan was sure it was a look that would make the camera melt. Clive was as crazy about Ari as she was about him, and Jordan knew he'd go running to his father with the video. If she had to be subjected to him and his low-life habits, she might as well make him and his contacts work for her.

When Jordan started assembling the film in the lab, she could tell right away that she was right about Ari. She had the magic. A couple of weeks into the editing, around midnight Jordan heard a knock at the door. She hated to be disturbed, but when she heard it was Ari, she let her in.

"How's Fellini doing tonight?" Ari said.

"This really takes concentration," said Jordan. "There are so many ways to put it together and so many shots to choose from that the process is amazing. I could stay in here for a year!"

"Try not to do that," said Ari. "I'm dying to see it."

"I promise you will, but not now. I really need to work alone. Just know that you're absolutely fantastic," said Jordan.

Ari left and Jordan buried herself in editing. As soon as she was finished Jordan transferred the film to videocassette and ran it for the whole school. She wouldn't let Clive or Ari see any of it beforehand. She set up a showing right after dinner one night and ran it for the whole school. This was the first time an audience was looking at her work, and she was nervous.

As Jordan turned off the lights and pressed "play," she stopped breathing. It was only a three-minute film, but there was pandemonium when it was over. The girls were cheering and calling for Jordan and Ari to come up front and take a bow. In the joy of the moment they hugged each other and went to the front of the room.

"This is really great," said Jordan. "I can't possibly tell you how good it makes me feel. And thank you, Ari, for your beautiful presence and your fantastic song." She stood aside and clapped for Ari along with everyone else.

Ari just stood and loved it. She finally felt as though she belonged somewhere.

And Jordan was hoping that that was what might help her feel good about herself.

She whispered to Ari, "Take all of this in and keep it in your heart. All you need is your talent."

Jordan took Arianne home to Honfleur for the holidays because she didn't have anywhere else to go. Genevieve welcomed her generously, and the three of them were having a wonderful time playing together. One night at dinner the phone rang, and it was Clive calling for Ari.

When she returned to the table she was bubbling. "I'm not sure what's happening, but he's planning some sort of surprise for us. Something is happening this Saturday night, and he told me to be by the phone. I can't wait. I just know it'll be good."

Ari was sitting by the phone on Saturday as Clive requested. Jordan was reading up in her room. They had no idea that at that moment Clive was sneaking into ATV Studios. He knew that on the weekends the videos that were played were programmed in by computer. That way there was no technician on hand, and it was cheaper to run. Clive had the key to the back door copied, and he let himself in. He went right to the dubbing room and transferred a copy of Arianne's video "Silver Needles" to the tape on the main computer. That done, all he had to do was sit at the computer and program in when he wanted the video to go out over ATV. He programmed it to be played once an hour for twenty-four hours starting Saturday night at eight P.M. He never thought he would be able to get away with it for a full twenty-four hours, but even if it aired two or three times before he got caught, he'd be the winner.

He picked up the phone and called Jordan's house. "I did it," he said when he heard Ari's voice.

"Did what?" she asked.

"Turn on your satellite to 'Moves' tonight at eight," he explained. "From eight to midnight every Saturday night, 'Moves' in Switzerland picks up the ATV feed from England. So do Germany, Italy, and France. I'm going to call you back at eight-thirty. Just watch it." And then he hung up.

Precisely at 8:00 P.M. Jordan, Genevieve, and Ari were in front of the TV. Then at 8:17 P.M. they both saw "Silver Needles" start and they screamed.

"Oh, my God!" said Ari. "How did he do it?"

"I don't know," said Jordan, "but I think he's going to be in trouble again."

At 8:30 the phone rang, and Ari answered it. She could not believe it when he told her how many times "Silver Needles" was going to run. By 9:30, after the video had run two times, the ATV switchboard was flooded with requests for it. Everybody wanted to know who Ari was. By the next morning when Clive's father was looking like a hero for this discovery, Clive told him what really happened. Always wanting to ride a winner, Mr. Herndon was not angry. He knew he had something big on his hands.

"Ari, guess what?" Clive shouted when he phoned Honfleur. "My father wants to put you and Jordan under contract. He's going to manage you and get you a record deal. Jordan can direct all your videos. Isn't that incredible?"

"I can't believe it," said Ari. "Let me go tell Jordan and we'll call you back."

Jordan and Genevieve were in the room by that time, beginning to comprehend what was happening. "I think this could be wonderful for you both," said Genevieve, "but I must caution you about show business. It is brutal. You are too young for this. The most important thing that both of you can do now is finish school. I know that everybody will start talking about this video, but your talent will always be there. It's not going anywhere for two years, and then you can both go to work."

"I can do anything I want," said Ari. "My mother doesn't care about anything."

"That may be true," said Genevieve, "but I care. Somebody must protect you. Jordan will tell you that I have never given her bad advice." Genevieve looked at Jordan, who had not yet spoken. "And you, Jordan, have a mother. We must call her and give her an opportunity to discuss this."

"I don't want to do that. I'd love to quit school and go to London to work," said Jordan.

"London will also still be there when you graduate," Genevieve chided as gently as she could. "I'm going to call Powar in the morning. Now let's all just think about things until then."

At breakfast the next morning the girls eagerly rushed down to hear from Genevieve. They didn't even bother to start buttering their toast.

"Well, I spoke to Powar, and she agrees with me. It is much too early for you to consider leaving school."

Jordan was not happy. "I don't think it's right for her to make decisions on my future since she hardly ever sees me," she snapped.

Genevieve placed her hand over Jordan's. "I know you've grown up in unusual circumstances, but your mother loves you very much. In fact, she asked me to send her a copy of your video, and she's going to come here in five days."

"I don't want her to have the video," said Jordan in a slightly raised tone. "That work is mine. It has nothing to do with her. She just breezes through here for her own conscience and then goes back to running the world. She has no right to share in my work."

Genevieve felt very sad. These were the harshest words that Jordan had ever spoken about Powar. She knew so well the hard choices that Powar had made, yet her heart went out to Jordan. She was very torn. "My darling, I can only tell you that genes are very important, and your talent comes from your family. It doesn't matter whether you see them every day or not. It is in your blood. You have no choice. The genes make up the future. Please remember what I say."

Jordan just looked up at her and felt trapped.

Jordan's mood did not improve when she returned to Des Alpes. "I just hate it here," she said to Arianne as she was vigorously brushing her thick, shoulder-length blonde hair.

"You don't look like you're unhappy," said Arianne. "You look like you're about to be shot for the cover of *Vogue*."

Jordan had an innate sense of style. She was somebody who could put on a man's oversize shirt and a pair of jeans and boots and just knock your socks off. Today she had on cream-colored jeans with a powder blue work shirt and a light blue, cream, and navy print scarf just thrown around her shoulders in one of the "brilliant accidents" that most women never figure out how to pull off.

"So what do I do about Mrs. Lord?" asked Jordan, holding the handwritten note mysteriously delivered to her at school by the concierge of Beau Rivage, the most exclusive hotel in the area. "Look at this," she continued. "It's written on her own personal stationery. What kind of woman would travel with that attention to detail, and why would she want to see me? I don't know any Mrs. Lord. And how could she have seen my video?"

"Look," said Arianne. "We both know your curiosity is

killing you and that you're going to meet her for tea. Do you want me to go with you?''

"No, I'm going to do this alone."

As Jordan walked into Beau Rivage she looked up to the ceiling. Every time she came here she loved to study it. It was a gigantic dome in gold and glass that formed concentric circles. She could get dizzy if she looked at it for a long time. At certain hours of the day the light swirled around the lobby, creating a dazzling effect. Jordan had wanted to capture it on film for some time. She was nervous as she asked the maître d' to show her to Mrs. Lord's table. She saw an older blonde woman staring at her from a table in a corner. Jordan immediately sensed that she was the one.

"Mrs. Lord, your guest is here," said the maître d' when he arrived at the corner table. He bowed and left. Jordan remained standing. Mrs. Lord looked up at her warmly and said, "Jordan, I'm your grandmother, Honey King."

Jordan broke out into a huge smile. "Well, well, the truth lives."

"We're *both* looking at it, dear," said Honey. "Please sit down. I have already ordered for both of us."

Jordan was instantly comfortable. There was a feeling about this that was so right. Maybe it was because looking at Honey was like looking at a mirror image of herself. Suddenly all the mysteries were coming together. She knew life was about to make sense.

"We have so much to talk about, my dear," said Honey. "The watercress sandwiches are lovely here. Please help yourself as you tell me about school. Do you like it?"

"I love learning, but I don't like being isolated and deposited somewhere. Did you really see my video?" asked Jordan.

"Yes, and you're very talented. Having virtually made King Pictures successful by myself, I ought to know what I'm talking about."

"Yes, I've read as much as I could find about the Kings, but I'd love to know more. Powar has never told me anything," Jordan explained.

"There's so much I can tell you. Our family is part of Hollywood history, and it's a shame you haven't yet experienced it firsthand. How would you like to come to Beverly Hills and live with me?"

Jordan was astonished. She had never thought something like this would happen. "I'd love to," she said quickly. "Don't worry, I can sign myself out for the weekend, and when we get to L.A. we can call the school and Genevieve. I know she'll be mad, and I hate to upset her, but there's no way I could miss this!"

"That's wonderful, dear. I'll get the tickets, and you should meet me at the hotel tomorrow morning at nine. Our driver will get us to the airport in plenty of time," said Honey.

Jordan jumped up. "I've got to pack! This is great!" She looked at Honey for a second, and their eyes really locked. It was the first time that Jordan had ever really felt a family connection. "Thanks. I better get back to school," she said excitedly.

Honey watched her as she raced to the hotel entrance. Slowly a smile came over her face. It had been easier than she'd expected.

* CHAPTER 20 *

I don't know how much longer I can stand this," said Andy. "Our whole relationship is spent with my leaving you to go to some dinner party with Franny. I don't know why I keep living this way, but I know if I leave her, she'll kill herself. She has nothing else in her life."

Andy sat up on his side of the bed as Powar propped up her pillows for the discussion she'd been waiting for. She finally had her opening. After seventeen years, what started out as a romantic encounter one spectacular night had turned into a comfortable pattern. Both she and Andy were so caught up with their work, and their love of their work, that they hardly noticed the years go by. Powar's last film for the studio had won five Academy Awards. How could she notice that she and Andy were going nowhere? She was too caught up in the present. They never planned for the future. They never really grew up. For all Powar knew, Jordan was more mature than she was. Powar felt that if she told Andy about his daughter, he would certainly do something about Franny, but for a long time she hadn't really wanted that disturbed. She had things to do, and their part-time relationship suited her perfectly. But over the past year or so she'd come to realize she really had no life. She had no family. Work was work, it wasn't a life. She was missing out on Jordan's growing up. She never spoke to her own mother. What did she have to show for the years she had put in? Plenty of material things—the house, the cars, the enviable life-style, the respect of her profession. It was time she paid as much attention to her personal life as her work.

She pushed her hair out of her eyes and looked at Andy. "How do you know Franny has nothing else in her life? I've heard rumors for years. What does she do every day?"

"You know, I haven't really thought about it. My secretary hands me our social schedule, which is planned by Franny, and I know to be home at a certain time and to wear certain clothes, and she's always there ready to go."

"That's at night," said Powar. "Where does she go during the day?"

"Well," replied Andy, "she goes to lunch a lot. And then there's shopping. If she's decorating, she has a lot of meetings, and then there's the charities. They take up most of her time."

Powar said very casually, "Why don't you find out for sure?"

"Just what are you suggesting?" asked Andy. "You never say anything unless there's a point to it." He paused. "Do you want me to have her followed?"

Powar placed her chin in her hand and said, "Maybe. You might find it amusing."

"This isn't like you," said Andy. "You never paid any attention to her."

"Maybe it's time we both started," said Powar as she jumped up to take a shower.

Andy was a little unnerved as she left. When Powar came out of the shower there was no mention of the previous conversation, and it was business as usual. But he knew Powar was too bright to bring something up if she hadn't thought it through. He was going to think about it seriously.

* * *

Franny woke up early Saturday morning. She loved Saturdays. It was a casual day, and you could just go around doing anything you wanted. The phones were quieter and the pressure was off, unless of course she was giving a party on that night. She looked at Andy, who was still sleeping, and wondered why he had been looking at her strangely all week. He just kept staring at her in a way she had never seen before. Oh, well, she thought, I just can't worry about it. At some point in the day she was going to end up at Max's shop to get her hair done. She had a great time there. It was like a sorority meeting where everyone talked about the news of the day. News to Franny, of course, was who bought the first Adolfo suit off the line at Saks. Before her Max appointment she was going to Aida Grey for a facial and a massage, but before any of that she was on her way to Blair's. They were going to have an Angels meeting, and when they got together it gave new meaning to the word *meeting*.

Franny put on her new Andrea Carrano ballet flats, jeans, and a close-fitting T-shirt. She drove immediately to Blair's house. As usual, the butler answered, and he showed her to the study, the room where she and Blair had had their very first "tea" years ago. A few moments later Blair came in wearing a one-piece, shiny black bathing suit. Franny jumped up and they hugged.

"I've missed you," said Franny.

"Don't give it another thought," Blair said, smiling. "Just follow me." She led Franny around the back to the path that took them to the pool.

Franny loved the three waterfalls on different levels of the path. The sound of rushing water immediately transported her to another zone. A bright red, carved gondola floated in the shallow end. "Oh, my God! You really never cease to amaze me with the ideas you come up with," said Franny, gazing deep into Blair's eyes. "You never fail to thrill me."

"If it was good enough for Marian Davies and William Randolph Hearst, it's good enough for us!" She helped

Franny into the boat. "Just stay in the back, like they do in Venice, and I'll do the rest," she said. She put on a gondolier's cap and pressed the button on a cassette player. Connie Francis's rendition of "Al di La" from *Rome Adventure* filled the air. Franny and Blair got hysterical.

"You're too much," said Franny. "How did you know that was one of my favorite movies?"

"I know everything about you," Blair said softly. She then took the gondolier's pole in her hands and proceeded to push the boat along the pool. Since the pool was 350 feet long, one really could escape and pretend to be anywhere. The foliage changed, and you went under a couple of bridges. It really was an adventure. After about fifteen minutes they reached "the Grotto."

"I know how much you love this area, and we haven't been here in a while," said Blair. "I thought it would be a nice change from the beach."

She tied up the boat and helped Franny out. They walked up the stone steps. "This is so spectacular," said Franny. Blair just smiled.

When they entered the cave there was a reflecting pool that took up half the floor space. There was the smell of dampness inside, and it was humid. Franny's clothes started to get sticky. The sides of the cave were chiseled out to make landings for sun mattresses to rest on as a break from swimming.

"We're going on a Treasure Hunt today," Blair explained.

"What does that mean?" Franny asked excitedly.

"You'll see, sweetheart. First let's start right here." Blair gently pulled off Franny's top and then unbuttoned her jeans. Franny helped her slip them down to the floor and off her ankles. Blair knelt down, kissing Franny's stomach, and slowly pulled off her bikini pants. She then stood up very slowly, letting her tongue rest underneath Franny's bra. With her teeth she quickly undid the front clasp. She took Franny's hand and led her to the mattress, which was covered with a burgundy velour terry cloth. On the landing was a crystal bowl filled with red grapes, Franny's favorites. Blair sat down beside her. "Take off my suit, darling," she said.

Franny did it immediately. Blair then lay down. Franny got a rush seeing that beautiful blonde hair against the burgundy.

Blair pulled Franny on top of her. With her other hand she took a grape and put it in her mouth but didn't chew it. "Eat it," she said to Franny as she began to move slowly underneath her.

Franny opened her mouth and bit down on the grape, leaving half for Blair. Franny felt Blair's hands caressing her back.

"It's treasure hunt time, darling," said Blair. "Start at my feet."

Franny was already throbbing at the thought. She loved Blair's feet. She didn't know why feet excited her, but sometimes she would rather have seen a naked foot than any other part of the body. Blair had particularly fabulous feet. They were size 4½ B, and they looked like baby feet. Her toes were perfectly formed little ice-cream cones in Franny's mind. She started stroking the bottom of Blair's left foot with her tongue and then moved to the instep. She could have done this for hours. She kissed each toe very carefully, one at a time. With her hand she started caressing the other foot at the same time. She could hear Blair's breathing change. They both were loving every minute of this. Now Franny grabbed both feet and started on the two big toes at once. She was taking little bites. She moved her tongue to the ankle and then the calf. From this position, if she just raised her hand above her head, it would find the pleasure spot between Blair's legs. She used her thumb on top of the outside, just the way Blair did it to her.

Blair moaned, "Come closer."

Franny knew what that meant. Her mouth was supposed to find the V. She couldn't wait to taste more of her. This was always her most exciting moment. She loved Blair so much. Her mouth began to inch its way up the thigh. It arrived at its destination and started kissing. First they were little baby kisses, but her passion could no longer contain itself and the kisses became very deep. She dug deeper and deeper with her tongue. Blair raised her knees and grabbed Franny's head, pushing her more inside. Blair's derriere was off the ground now. Suddenly Franny's tongue felt something it had never felt before. She felt something hard surrounded by the softness. It startled her and she looked up at Blair.

"Don't be afraid," she said. "Go after it!"

Franny let her tongue go wild. She hooked it around the hard object and pulled it toward her. Into her mouth passed the juiciest grape she had ever tasted. She was laughing with abandon.

"Go back and get the rest of them, darling," Blair said as she arched her back.

One by one they all came out, and they were devoured by Franny. She took the last one and scooted up to Blair's mouth and gave it to her. They were wet with sweat and excitement, and they meshed their bodies together and undulated to oblivion, their screams of joy echoing off the walls of the cave. Neither one of them heard the sound of the camera clicking.

Andy was sitting in his office when his secretary buzzed him. "Mr. Johnson is here."

"Send him right in," said Andy. Johnson had called him a couple of days earlier and said that he "had something." Andy's door opened and in came a man who looked like a shy accountant. He was holding a manila envelope. Andy had a funny feeling in his stomach. He didn't like himself very much for hiring a detective, but he knew it was something he was supposed to do.

"Good morning, Mr. Stromberg. I'd rather you looked at this in private," said Johnson. "I believe it will be useful information. Good luck, Mr. Stromberg. You know where I can be reached." He was out the door quickly.

Andy just stared at the envelope, then slipped his finger under the flap and pulled out the pictures. He was holding a picture of Franny kissing Blair Lawson on the mouth while

Blair was fondling her breasts. He gasped for air as he felt his stomach start to go. He ran to his bathroom and slammed the door, breaking out in a cold sweat. How many people knew about this and were laughing at him behind his back? He wanted to get rid of Franny, but he'd never had any idea that this would be the way. He was going to have to think about the best way to make this work.

Powar heard the screening room door open behind her. "Now what is it?" she said testily, turning off the video she'd been watching over and over for an hour. She was in no mood to talk to anyone.

"That's a nice greeting," Andy said.

She looked at him, and pain filled her chest. Seeing him at this moment was agonizing. How she ached to be able to discuss his daughter with him. It was almost unbearable. But she never wanted to use Jordan to get what she wanted.

Andy came rushing toward her, and she noticed he looked a little odd. One point of his shirt collar was sticking out of his sweater, which was something that he normally would have noticed.

"I told your office not to disturb us," he said. "I need to talk to you."

"What is it?" said Powar. "You don't look well."

Andy sat down on the plush velvet reclining seat next to Powar's and started to talk. "Remember when we talked about Franny last weekend? Well, I started thinking about how unhappy I've been. I was too young when we got married to realize that I had choices. I just don't like to hurt people." Tears started forming in his eyes. "I hurt you by never really turning what we have into a real relationship. I wrote about them in my movies all the time, but I didn't even notice what I was doing in my own life. I hurt Franny because I virtually ignored her all these years. I haven't been any good to anyone."

Powar held his hand, knowing not to interrupt him.

"I'm not proud of what I've done in the past, and I'm

certainly not proud of what I did this week. I had Franny followed. I . . . got results I never suspected, but it has freed me. I need to talk everything through with you.''

Powar was at instant attention.

He touched her cheek and held it for a moment before putting down his hand. ''You are my life, Powar. I want us to get married and be together forever, just like the vows say.''

Powar now was crying softly with him. ''Andy, what have we both done with our lives? You have no idea the mistakes that I have made, too.''

''I have to tell you what I found out, Powar. We will be free now if I just handle this the right way.''

She took Andy's face in her hands. ''I think I've loved you since that first day at Nathan's house when I was in college and you looked like Ned from the Nancy Drew books. I probably have always been waiting for you to pick me up in your roadster and take me away.'' The two of them started laughing.

''Here. Look . . .'' He handed her the envelope, and she took out the pictures.

As she raced through each one of them, her eyes got wider and wider. ''Well, well, Andy, you may have been ignoring her, but someone was paying attention.'' She put the pictures back in the envelope. ''Do you want me to make some suggestions?'' she asked.

''That's exactly what I want,'' he replied.

''The first thing you need to do is lock the negatives in a safe. Then I think you should go to your lawyer and draw up a very fair divorce settlement. Do not tell him anything about the pictures. It is more important that they never are seen. Be generous with Franny—not to a fault, however, but just enough for you to come out looking like the wonderful person you are. When you and Franny are home alone, after you have the settlement agreement in your hands, present her with the pictures and the agreement for her to sign right then and there. Offer her no time and no options. She desperately wants to be Mrs. Andy Stromberg, but she will see it's better to be the *first* Mrs. Stromberg and keep her reputation intact. You will always be able to handle her since you have the pictures, and then we will have our life,'' Powar said with a confident smile.

"No wonder you're running the studio," Andy said as they kissed the best kiss since his wedding night.

The lawyer got the agreement together in two weeks. Andy was waiting in the den for Franny to get back from her six-thirty appointment or whatever it was she was doing. He was wearing a gray suit and tie and had come home early from the office. She had to pass by his den to get to her office, where her social secretary was waiting. They met at the end of each day to go over each other's schedules and plan for the evening. It was not unusual for Andy to be seated at his desk when she came in.

"Hi, how's everything?" Franny said. She was wearing a camel, brown, and red Adolfo suit with red pumps and a matching bag.

Andy was surprised that his first thought was to notice how nice she looked. "Were you at the Bistro Garden today?" he asked.

"Why, yes," Franny answered. "Blair was giving a luncheon for her cousin."

"Sit down for a minute before you go into your office," said Andy, his tone betraying nothing.

"I can only stay for just a minute because I must do a couple of things in my office before we leave for the Mirisches'."

"I'm not going tonight, Franny," Andy said extremely seriously.

Franny sat down. "What do you mean, darling?"

"Franny . . . we are going to get a divorce, and you are going to behave rationally and calmly."

"What!" said Franny. "Don't be ridiculous. We're perfect together. Everybody loves us as a couple. We have a wonderful life, and you know it."

"No, Franny, you're the one with the wonderful life. You have it all . . . the marriage, the parties, the money, the respectability, and someone who loves you. I'm the one who pays for it all and gets very little."

"Andy, please don't do this," Franny pleaded. "If I've upset you, or failed you, I'll fix it. I've been good for you. I've helped your career enormously."

"I need more, Franny, and we both know you can't give it to me," said Andy, placing his hands on the two manila envelopes in front of him.

"Right," Franny snapped, "and I suppose Powar can?" She jumped out of her seat.

"That's enough," Andy said angrily. "Sit down here and look at these two envelopes. I'm going out now. Look at the one marked 'A' first, and then open 'B' and sign the documents in it. I want to find it completed on my desk when I get back."

"You can't leave here like that," said Franny, still shouting.

"Yes, I can," Andy answered very quietly.

And then she heard the door shut. She stared at the envelopes before her and started to shake. She had never seen Andy like this. As she reached for the first one she noticed how perfect her new "tipped" nails looked. Whatever this is, I know I can handle it, she thought.

She ripped into the envelope and took out the picture of her and Blair, and a bloodcurdling scream came out of her mouth. Her secretary came running in immediately. Franny saw her and clutched the pictures to her chest.

"Go away. Leave me alone. Leave the house!" she screamed.

She opened the second envelope and saw the divorce settlement. She put her head down on the desk and was sobbing and gasping for air. She was panicking, and she knew she had to stop and catch her breath. She tried holding her breath to keep from gasping. Slowly she began to calm down. She spent a few minutes reading the settlement. As she went through the pages she began to realize that Andy was being extremely generous. Whether she was married to him or not, she was still going to be Mrs. Andy Stromberg. She still had all the financial benefits and none of the responsibilities.

"Oh, my God, Blair!" Franny thought. She was suddenly terrified that Blair would find out about the pictures. Franny was frightened that Blair might not want to see her anymore. She realized now that most of her freak-out was, deep down, about Blair. She loved her so much, she couldn't live without her. She ripped up the pictures, knowing full well that Andy had the negatives. She was going to talk to him about that. Frankly, she doubted that he would want those pictures floating around any more than she would. She was going to have to tell Blair the divorce was her idea. She was going to have the whole town believe that—and she would.

She took a deep breath and signed the papers, then went to change her clothes for the Mirisches' dinner party.

She would say that Andy was taken ill at the last minute. That would work for now.

Powar was literally sitting by the phone waiting for it to ring. She hoped that her life was finally going to start coming together. The doorbell rang instead of the phone, and Powar jumped. She wondered who it could be as she walked to the door. She heard Andy call her and she raced to open it.

"It's done!" he said. "We're finally free." They grabbed each other and held so tight that they could barely breathe. "I should have done this years ago," Andy said. "I'm so sorry, Powar. I love you."

"I love you, too," said Powar. "I feel like we're just going into the playhouse for the first time."

Andy picked her up and carried her into the bedroom,

taking off articles of her clothing along the way. He was swallowing her with his mouth. His lips and tongue were savoring her all over as if she were a rare delicacy.

"Wait," said Powar. "I want to go to get something."

Andy resisted letting her go.

"Believe me," said Powar, "you're going to want this." She was back in a few seconds, holding a silver-and-bronze jar. "Remember this?" she asked. "I got it in France for us."

"I certainly do," said Andy. "I love it, but I can't remember what you called it."

"It's honey dust," she answered.

"It certainly is," said Andy as he pulled her down to him and put his fingers in the jar.

"No, not that way," Powar purred. "Take this brush."

A quick study, Andy said, "It's time for my favorite dessert," as he slowly brushed it over her back and hips. He dipped in for more and ran the brush right up between her legs, generously covering that precious area from behind. When he got down to her feet he gently rolled her over and with a feather touch "dusted" all around the front, paying particular attention to the nipples.

"My turn," said Powar. She turned him over and swished gobs of the glistening white powder over his body at approximately four-inch intervals. She then lay directly on top of him, and with her body she swirled around and around, letting the heat from their bodies melt the dust into sticky honey.

Andy started to moan. He clutched her to him. She knew just when to land and then move again. It was driving him crazy. In a desperate move he managed to pull her over and slide on top of her. He slid down and spread her legs for a taste test.

Now it was Powar's turn to moan for him. She couldn't get enough. She grabbed his head for more, but he slid through her grasp and floated up toward her face. She wrapped her legs around him to consume his passion. They both were so wet and creamy that she had to grab hold of his member with her inner muscles and squeeze. They both were in a frenzy to reach the highest heights of their lives. On this very special night, free for the first time, it felt better than it ever had before.

It happened to them at exactly the same time.

"Marry me, marry me," Andy moaned.

"Yes!" screamed Powar in ecstasy, feeling that finally her life had begun.

They decided afterward to go to Chasen's to celebrate. Many of their peers went to Spago, but Andy and Powar wanted to go to a place filled with memories of when they first met. Julius, the maître d', seated them right at booth number one.

"You both look so happy tonight," Julius said. "What show are we celebrating?"

"None right now," said Andy, "but you'll be hearing about something soon."

Julius didn't get it, so he just sent over their usual drinks.

Then Tommy, the captain, brought them some cheese toast and took their order.

"I'll have a Caesar salad and filet of sole Veronique with asparagus," said Powar.

"Hobo steak and creamed spinach, and save a huge piece of banana shortcake for dessert," said Andy.

After a few minutes, Powar brought the conversation around to something she had wanted to discuss for seventeen years. "Darling, there's something I'd love for us to do."

"What is it?" asked Andy.

"You know a hiatus is coming up soon. I would love to go to Europe with you for a couple of weeks. There are some very special friends of mine that I'd like you to meet in Honfleur."

Andy beamed. "I'd love to go away with you. You know how much I have wanted that. I'll go anywhere you want."

"That's great," said Powar. "May I make all the arrangements? I want it to be a special surprise. I'll work things out when the time comes."

"I'll be ready," he said.

Powar looked at him and thought to herself, I hope you are, my darling, I hope you are.

Within a few days Andy had moved to his old bungalow at the Beverly Hills Hotel. The minute that happened, it was unofficial confirmation of the rumors that had been flying. Andy allowed Franny to announce the divorce. His lawyer would arrange for a Mexican "quickie" done by proxy. With the settlement already signed there was no problem.

The realities of the divorce and the upcoming "surprise" were taking its toll on Powar, as she realized she would soon have to deal with the going public of it all. It would be scandalous, but she felt they could get through it. She was used to being a public person.

Franny hadn't been sure how Blair would take the divorce news. She was in Blair's kitchen, making her favorite pancakes, working up to telling her.

"What shall we do today?" asked Blair as she swept in wearing a butterscotch satin robe with big shoulders and wide lapels. Franny would never get over the sight of her. Blair took her breath away constantly.

"I'm not sure," Franny said. "We could take a drive to Idyllwild and have lunch. I love going to the mountains."

"That's a possibility," said Blair. "What time do you have to be home tonight?"

"I don't have to go home at all," replied Franny, pouring hot maple syrup onto the thin, crisp cakes.

"What do you mean?" Blair said.

"I have some good news," said Franny. "Andy and I are getting a divorce, and now you and I can spend as much time together as we want. Isn't that great?"

"What do you mean?" said Blair. "Why would you do a thing like that?"

Franny was thrown a bit by Blair's reaction.

"Well, I just thought that it would be better all the way

around. You know about Andy and Powar, anyway. Who cares anymore? I think it's time I learned to be myself. I love you very much, Blair.''

"And I love you, too, dear, but I wish you had discussed it with me first.''

Franny was frightened now and didn't want to be too pushy. "I didn't want to upset you. I'm sorry we didn't discuss it. I won't do that again.''

"Would you get me the blueberry syrup, please?" said Blair. "I'm in the mood for that now. You know, Franny, I hope you don't take this the wrong way, but I suddenly feel the need to drive alone today. I feel like Lake Arrowhead. I hope you understand. I'll call you when I get back tonight.''

Franny put on a brave front. "Of course. I'll just finish up breakfast and go do some chores. I think it's important to give people time to themselves.''

"I knew you would understand,'' said Blair.

But Franny didn't. She wanted to spend every waking and sleeping hour with Blair, and she didn't know how she was going to make it through the day.

"So what do you make of it?" Powar said to Maria. They were spending one of their typical Saturdays playing tennis at Maria's house. "Let me see that again.''

Powar handed her a handwritten note.

> Dear Powar,
>
> Although our differences are great, we both believe that nothing is more important than the King name. To this end I am going to establish a Philip King Motion Picture Museum with the majority of the proceeds going to charity. I believe you would want me to hear your input. Please be at my house Monday night at 7:30. I will expect you.

"It certainly seems like an appropriate note,'' said Maria, "but then it's *your* mother, isn't it.''

"That's right," Powar agreed. "And with her, nothing is what it appears to be on the surface."

"What are you going to do?"

"I'm going, but I don't have a good feeling. It's been years since I've been in that house, and I'm not sure how I'm going to feel."

They were sitting in the shade in the bleachers in Maria's court. She'd had them built after Nathan died because she wanted to hold tournaments at the house.

Powar sipped her lemonade and looked at Maria. "Can you imagine what my mother might do when she finds out she has a granddaughter?" she asked, changing the subject.

"She'll be too busy with her charities to notice," said Maria. "You know very well that since she stopped running the studio her days and nights are too full being the 'grande dame' of Hollywood."

"She may be busy, but that news would really hit her," said Powar.

"Don't worry about it," Maria said. "Your mother hates children."

"That's right," said Powar, "I almost forgot." And the two of them giggled as if they were back at USC.

Powar decided to park in the street in front of her parents' house rather than in the driveway. She didn't want to get familiar again with these surroundings. As she walked up to the front door, she shook away a chill despite the fact that she was dressed warmly in pants and a sweater.

"Miss Powar, I'm so happy to see you!" exclaimed Lupe at the door.

"I'm so sorry I haven't seen much of you," said Powar, hugging her. She looked up midembrace and saw Honey, a vision in hunter green—like a healthy tree without the Christmas ornaments.

"Hello, Powar. I'm glad you decided to come."

"Anything with my father's name interests me. You know

that," Powar said, noting that Honey had made no move to get closer to her.

"Would you like a glass of wine?" said Honey, turning toward the living room without expecting a response.

Powar noted that the room was strangely absent of hors d'oeuvres and flowers, as would normally be there for one of Honey's meetings. "Where is everybody?" Powar asked as Honey handed her a glass of white wine.

"Only one other will be joining us."

"I've never heard of one of your charity committees with only three members," Powar said.

"This one only needs three. Let's go right to the dining room. Follow me."

"I know where it is, Mother."

Powar thought her brain was going to explode when she saw Jordan seated at the table.

"Hello," Jordan said tentatively.

"What are you doing here? I don't understand this at all," Powar shouted. Quickly getting her control back, she looked at her mother and said, "Ah, yes. Honey stings again."

"I'm sorry you're shocked, but I kept asking you about the family and you would never answer me. You just never got it," said Jordan.

"Powar, please sit down," Honey said. "We're all here now, so let's just get on with it."

Get on with what? thought Powar, suddenly panicking that Andy had never been told anything. Her mind was racing with images.

Just then the first course of consommé with julienne of carrots appeared. Powar thought she might throw up. She had to stay calm.

"I'd really like to live in the States, Mother. There's so much I've missed. I want to learn everything and see everything. Grandma has already taken me to see Grauman's Chinese Theatre and Musso's and all the movie stars' houses on Sunset." Jordan was bubbling with happiness and excitement.

"Yes, she just loved those flannel cakes," said Honey, patting Jordan's hand. "And she's still talking about Rudolph Valentino's grave."

"That was great, Grandma, but I really loved sitting on Tyrone Power's bench."

Watching Honey and Jordan talk to each other was like being on the sidelines at a tennis match. Powar's eyes kept darting from person to person, all the while feeling that she was definitely not in on the action. For tonight, at least, she would continue to be an observer until she came up with a proper course of action. What could she do? She'd have to tell Andy right away. Her mind kept racing, trying to keep up with her feelings.

"Mother," said Jordan, "I'd like to live at Grandma's."

Powar put down her spoon. "Darling, you must understand that I haven't had time to comprehend all of this. None of this is as simple as it may appear to you."

"I'd love Jordan to live here," said Honey, touching Jordan's hand possessively. "It would make me so happy."

Powar looked first to Honey and then to Jordan. "I think that we need to talk about this day after tomorrow. My first reaction is that if Jordan lives here at all, it should be with her own mother."

"But you just left me in Europe. Without Grandma I might never have gotten here," said Jordan, getting more and more upset.

"Jordan, please, let's all try to calm down. I think the best thing is for you to stay overnight here and just remain in the house. I'll call you tomorrow night."

Powar turned her gaze toward Honey. "Do you understand what I'm saying, Mother?"

Honey smiled.

Powar knew she had to tell Andy immediately. Implicit in Honey's letting her know that she could find Jordan was the message that she also knew about Andy. There had been rumors of their affair for years.

Powar got home and invited Andy for a midnight hot fudge sundae. She had extended that kind of invitation before, and Andy loved it. He was at her door in thirty minutes, and she knew he was filled with anticipation. But this time his treat would really be unexpected.

Andy sensed it immediately and put his arm around her.

She was having a difficult time. I didn't know it was going to be this hard, she thought.

They both sat down in front of the display of sweets. Powar was trying to be light and fix their sundaes. As he was about to take his first bite, Powar gently put her hand on his and said, "Wait."

Andy put the food down.

"I need to talk to you about something," Powar said.

"What is it? You sound concerned," said Andy.

"Don't worry, I'm fine," said Powar, "there's just something I want to share with you. I want you to know that all the years we've shared together up until now were a mixed blessing for me. It was much harder for me seeing you with Franny than I ever let you know."

"But that's all over with now," Andy interrupted. "There's nothing to be upset about anymore."

Powar took both of his hands now and continued. "I'm not upset, I just need you to listen to me very carefully, and know that as I talk to you, I love you more at this moment than I ever have. I need you to know that I deliberately never wanted to interfere with you and Franny. You had just married her, and I felt that no matter what happened between us, I owed it to you to give you a chance with her."

"I know that, Powar, and one of the many reasons why I love you is your sense of honor," said Andy. "You don't have to say any of this now. I love you more than life itself, and that will never change no matter what happens."

Powar swallowed and tried to continue. She knew this moment would be difficult. Her heart was expanding in her chest with fear. How on earth is he going to handle this betrayal? she asked herself. She so wanted him to be all right about it. "Remember back to your wedding reception at my parents' house?"

"Of course I do," answered Andy. "How could I ever forget it?"

"Well, I never really told you the impact that had on me, but my so-called disappearance shortly after that had a lot to do with it." The food was melting, but neither of them cared.

"I was so guilty that I did what we did to Franny, that at that point I was trying to forget it, even though I knew that it was probably the most important thing that had ever happened in my life," said Andy.

"And I knew you were terribly upset and trying to honor a commitment, and I made the best choice for both of us at that time," said Powar.

"Choice about what?" Andy asked innocently.

Powar squeezed both his hands harder. "Something happened back then to me, something that I had to face alone, and I really hope that you think I did the right thing. I got pregnant that night, Andy, and I decided to have the baby. That's why I went away. We have a beautiful fifteen-year-old girl named Jordan who has been living in France. I have not told her about you, either. Keeping this secret from everyone has been the hardest thing I've ever had to do."

"Powar, my God," said Andy, crying and hugging her at the same time. "A daughter . . . why didn't you tell me? I would have done everything to help you. You never would have had to go through this alone."

"I told you," cried Powar, "I didn't want to burden you."

"You never would have done that. I love you, I would have made it work. I know I would have."

"Then you're not angry with me?" asked Powar.

"I'm not angry. I don't know what I feel. I'm still in shock," said Andy. "I do know I'm very sorry you didn't tell me, and I wish I could have known my daughter growing up, but I understand what you did. I'm just so grateful now to have you." They just held each other by the fire for a long time without saying anything. Then he said, "When am I going to see her?"

"Tomorrow," answered Powar.

Genevieve was on the plane two hours after receiving Powar's call. Des Alpes did not find out until Monday that Jordan was missing. Powar's call reached Genevieve just as she was about to call her. Genevieve was as shocked as Powar that Jordan was at Honey's, and Powar didn't even have to ask her to be there when Andy met Jordan. It was a difficult situation under normal circumstances, but the thought of Honey being there terrified Genevieve. She wished the plane were a missile so she could get there faster.

* CHAPTER 21 *

B y the time she was eighteen Jonna had gone through seven years of therapists. She had always sensed something about herself that was different. She always had too much of everything as a child. There were too many toys and too much attention. If she showed an interest in cooking, her mother arrived with a small kitchen. If a car interested her, a pedal-driven sports car appeared. She discovered through talking about it in therapy that she'd always felt something was not right. She wasn't being given the presents because her mother had a lot of money. She sensed that she was given things to compensate for something. When she and her mother went to a department store, she loved to buy clothes from the boys' department. She was always bigger and stronger than kids her own age, and she felt more comfortable in jeans and T-shirts or khakis and a sweater. She hated frilly things. She found herself having more fun playing football with the boys, and they really wanted her because she could throw farther than anyone else.

By the time she was thirteen, she was five feet eight and very striking. She had straight long black hair and wide-set American eyes. She always looked older than she was, and if she ever went out alone, people were attracted to her immediately. It made her very uncomfortable because she didn't know what they wanted. She was the happiest when she was in her room listening to music. She loved her mother's old records of Little Richard, James Brown, and Elvis Presley. She wanted desperately to be Elvis, and when she was ten her mother had bought her a guitar and arranged for lessons.

Jonna and the guitar were a match made in heaven. When she was twelve she began to develop crushes on boys, even though she still had many more male friends than female ones. She had heard about "menstruation" and began to wait for it to happen. She played and sang like Elvis but was raised to be a girl. It was a unique situation. As time went by and one by one her friends started their periods, she became increasingly anxious. By the time she turned fourteen and it still hadn't happened, she started going to school once a month wearing a sanitary napkin under her pants for gym class. She allowed this to go on for six months until she just had to go to her mother. She loved her mother very much. She felt like a sister to her because they spent so much time together playing. If Maria had to go away for a weekend, she would take off a half day at work to spend with Jonna.

"Mom, there's something I just don't understand," said Jonna.

Maria had come home unusually late from a premiere, and she was exhausted. She had been working since seven A.M. "Jonna, what are you doing up? What's wrong? This isn't like you to be up at this hour."

"I can't sleep, Mom. I have a real problem," said Jonna, sitting down on Maria's bed.

A little alarm went off inside Maria's head.

"I don't understand why I haven't gotten my period yet. It doesn't make sense to me, and all the other girls have theirs already," Jonna continued.

Maria looked into those beautiful, innocent eyes, and her heart broke. She was going to have to tell her everything.

"Come sit closer to me, sweetheart. You are a very special child, and I want to talk to you about something."

"What is it, Mom? You're scaring me," said Jonna.

Maria took a deep breath. "There's nothing to be frightened about. There's something that happens to a few special babies that are born each year. And you are one of those babies. You're not unhealthy or sick, your body just formed in an unusual way."

"I . . . I don't understand." Tears started to roll down Jonna's cheeks.

"Please don't cry," Maria said tenderly as she wiped away the tears. "You're just fine. You're going to live a long life."

"But what's wrong with me?" Jonna asked meekly.

"Sometimes babies are born with both sets of genitals. They have an equal amount of male and female genes. The genitals are infant-size, and in most cases the doctors decide by watching for the first six weeks of development to see which side grows more. In most cases the babies turn out to be girls, just like you did. They do a small operation to remove the penis and testicles, and the baby develops normally. The only thing that happens is frequently, the ovaries, if there are any, don't function, and the girl can't menstruate and is unable to have children because she has no uterus."

"And that's me?" Jonna gasped.

"Yes," said Maria.

"But I don't want to be different. I don't want to be a freak," said Jonna.

"You aren't a freak. You are a very special girl who has many talents. You're actually lucky, but you don't realize it yet. It's a lot of trouble having a period. It affects every aspect of your life. You never have to worry about it. Turn it into a blessing. You can always adopt a child if you want one. Celebrate the fact that you are a special, unique person. I thank God every day for giving you to me."

"Did Daddy know this?" asked Jonna.

"Yes," Maria replied.

"What did he think?" Jonna continued.

"He loved you very much."

"Are you sure? I'm getting a funny feeling," said Jonna.

"That's nonsense. Your father adored you."

"Well, maybe he did, but he'll probably be the only man who will!" Jonna wailed as the tears started to flow.

Maria tried to put her arms around her, but she jumped up.

"Don't do that. I'm a freak. I'm horrible!" she screamed as she ran out of the room crying.

Maria followed her to her room, devastated at Jonna's reaction. "I promise you that everything is going to be all right, sweetheart. You must believe that," she said to Jonna's curled-up body on the bed. It killed Maria to see her daughter in pain. She was going to do everything she could to make her life better.

Jonna threw herself completely into her music. She would practice playing and moving for hours in front of the mirror. She soon branched out into writing her own songs, and the only thing she ever asked of Maria was to take her to rock and roll concerts. For her high school graduation, Jonna wanted to see Little Richard in concert at the Universal Amphitheatre and then go backstage to meet him. Maria loved him, too, and really wanted to go. She ordered a limousine to take them. When the car arrived she told Jonna to get in first. Jonna was looking hot that night. She dressed all in black—jeans, shirt, and boots and a gold vest in honor of Little Richard. The driver opened the door for her, and when she got in she let out a scream.

"I can't believe it! Oh, forgive me for acting this way."

"Happy graduation, Jonna," said Rick Nelson. "I understand you play guitar, too."

"Mom! You did this for me? This is great," said Jonna. "This is amazing."

Maria joined them on the backseat, and they drove to the theater. On a table in the middle of the floor in the back of the limo there was caviar and champagne, and in special hidden compartments in either door there were sodas and juice. In a console in between the windows there was a machine that had buttons on it labeled "V," "B," "S," "G," and "W." If you put a glass under the spout and pressed "V," you got vodka. Bourbon, Scotch, gin, and water were also available. They opened the champagne.

"I've known Rick for years," Maria explained. "He always used to sit with me because we were the two youngest people at the party. I also thought he was the handsomest man in the room."

Rick just smiled.

Jonna thought he was the shyest person she had ever seen, but she went one up from her mother. She thought Rick was beyond handsome. He was absolutely beautiful.

"Mr. Nelson?" said Jonna.

"Please call me Rick. My dad was Mr. Nelson," said Rick.

"Would you mind if I played some of my music for you sometime? I know you're more acoustic than I am, that . . . that you really pioneered country rock, but I'd love it if you'd hear some of my songs."

"I have an idea," said Maria, "Why don't I have Rick and his daughter Tracy, who is your age, come to lunch one Sunday and everybody can play?"

"Wow, that'd be terrific," said Jonna.

"I'd really like that," Rick added.

When they pulled up to the Universal Amphitheatre and Rick got out of the limo, he was greeted by screams and cheers. Jonna was completely caught up in the rock and roll atmosphere. She loved the groupies, the crazy clothes, and the weirdness of it all. Rick, Maria, and Jonna were taken to front-row seats. When Little Richard came out wearing gold lamé from head to toe, the audience went wild. An hour and a half later the audience was standing on chairs, screaming for more.

Then Little Richard said from the stage, "Tonight, ladies and gentlemen, we are blessed because my Man is here. He's the prettiest man. I just love him and I love his music. Ricky Nelson, Ricky Nelson, come up here!"

The audience screamed even louder. Rick looked at Jonna and shrugged his shoulders, and then he got up and went on stage. From the wings, the Jordanaires, Elvis Presley's backup singers and now Rick's, walked out carrying Rick's guitar. Jonna absolutely went berserk when she saw the Jordanaires. She was jumping up and down on her seat, grabbing Maria's arm. "Oh, man! Oh, man!" was all she could say.

Rick and the Jordanaires did "Lonesome Town" and then joined Richard on the finale of "Rip It Up." When it was all over Maria took Jonna backstage to see Richard and Rick. Up close she could see Richard's face and eye makeup. His mascara was running, and his hair had so much gel on it, it didn't move. It made no difference to her.

"Thank you for having me back here, I can't tell you what this has meant to me," said Jonna.

"Rick tells me you are a soul sister," said Richard. "You play the guitar."

"That's right," said Jonna.

"Hey, Rick, hand me that guitar over there," said Richard. He handed it to Jonna, and she froze. "C'mon, girl. Give it to me," he said.

Jonna turned on the guitar and just wailed. Four bars into it Richard's drummer got onto his practice set in the dressing room and Richard went right to the piano. A crowd gathered immediately. Jonna started to sing, and Maria's mouth dropped open. Jonna never let her see anything that she was practicing, so Maria was seeing her daughter for the first time along with the crowd. She almost forgot that Jonna was her daughter. There was no question in Maria's mind that Jonna had enormous talent and could be a very big star. She could think of no young woman who could do men's real rock and roll. She knew she had something very special in her hands, and she must treat it carefully and not let the Hollywood sleaze people to try to take control. Word was going to get around about this impromptu session, and the "sharks" were going to try to get to Jonna. Maria could hold them at bay, however, until she thought Jonna could handle it.

* * *

Andy stayed overnight at Powar's where they were up for hours. Powar had told him about Honfleur, Genevieve, Des Alpes, and everything she could remember. A limousine delivered Genevieve to their door at seven A.M. Opening it, Andy saw an elegant-looking woman in her seventies emerge. She hugged and kissed Powar as if she were her mother. Andy liked her immediately.

Genevieve turned to him and embraced him. "I have waited so long for this moment."

"Thank you," said Andy. "I've only recently heard how wonderful you have been to Jordan, and I am very grateful to you."

The limousine returned one hour later with Jordan. Andy jumped at the sound of the doorbell.

Sensing his anxiousness, Genevieve said, "What we're going to do here today won't be easy, but I'll be here to help you. Jordan is a bright, complex young woman who does not keep her opinions to herself."

Andy laughed. "Gee, I wonder where she got that from?"

"She's really talented, Andy," said Powar. "Wait until you see her work."

"Do you have any here?" he asked.

"Yes."

And then Powar opened the door. Jordan was all in black and feisty as ever.

"Jordan, this is your father, Andy Stromberg," said Powar.

"This has been some week," Jordan said, checking him out.

"Maybe a week for you, but only a day for me," said Andy.

"Aren't you the writer?"

"Yes, I am," replied Andy.

"I've seen some of your things. You're very good."

Andy looked at Powar and beamed.

"Genevieve!" screamed Jordan with delight, and then, remembering that she'd run away, "Oh, Genevieve . . . I'm sorry."

"Oh, Jordan, my darling, I'm mad at you, but I love you," said Genevieve, holding her close. "Please try to have an open mind," Genevieve whispered. "This is hard for everybody."

"Jordan, will you please sit down, I want to talk to you," said Powar.

"Okay."

"I need to tell you how I feel about certain things. I'm really sorry that I haven't done this sooner. First I want you to know that I am very proud of your directing. I think you have great talent."

"Thank you," said Jordan, wondering what this was leading up to.

"I also want you to know that I regret very much that we haven't spent more time together. I really feel terrible that we have not been together as much as I have wanted."

"Have you been in therapy or something?" Jordan asked a little sarcastically.

"We all know you have a right to carry some anger with you," said Genevieve, "but please try to listen just now."

Powar saw that Jordan was sitting stiffly, on the edge of her chair, ready to bolt out the door on a moment's notice. "Sometimes things happen to you in your life that cause you to make decisions that are right at that time. Years ago I found myself in that position. I was not ever legally married to your father because he was married to someone else. We loved each other very much then, and we do now. I couldn't tell either one of you until now because he was married. Not giving you that information made your growing up easier, too. We are very well-known people in this world, and I wanted to shield you from prying eyes."

Jordan and Andy were staring at each other as though they were ghosts. Jordan couldn't take her eyes off him during the last part of her mother's talk. "How could you keep this from me?" she asked, feeling even more betrayed and hurt. "I had a right to know that I had a father, that I wasn't some secret that you stashed away because it was convenient. What gave you the right to make that decision? You've ruined my whole life!" She got up and ran out the front door.

Genevieve, Powar, and Andy looked at each other, not knowing what to do.

"Hurry, Andy," said Genevieve. "I think you should be the one to go after her."

He found her standing by a tree in the front yard. "I know exactly how you feel," said Andy. "I only found out yesterday that you existed." Jordan wouldn't look at him. "I hope you won't be mad at me. I'm as new at this as you. I'd like to think that we can help each other through it."

Jordan looked at him for a second.

"You know, when Powar told me about you, I was mad, too, but it only lasted for a second. I'm older than you, so I obviously have learned a little more about life. Time is such a precious thing, and it's something that Powar, in her attempt to do what she thought was right for both of us, actually ended up stealing from us. But she didn't do it deliberately, and I knew when she told me that if I stayed mad, I would be the one taking time away now. We have to turn this thing around and be grateful that we found each other now before it is too late. I love her very much." Andy persevered, "Anyway, if you're my daughter, you have a sense of humor. It's in the genes. I always tend to see the funny side of any situation. Can you imagine how this is going to go over in Hollywood? I have an ex-wife who will go crazy. I rather like that."

Jordan laughed.

"There, you see? I knew you'd get it," said Andy. "Let me really look at you," he continued. He studied her face for a good moment.

"I have your eyes," said Jordan.

"And you also have my heart," said Andy, kissing her on

the cheek. "Come back in the house. We'll spend the day together, and maybe we'll all even stay over tonight. Let's just see."

The next morning Jordan woke up with tremendous anxiety. She felt a little better going to sleep after her talk with Andy, but she didn't wake up that way. Too many things were happening. There were too many unanswered questions. As a little girl she used to fantasize about what it would be like to have a real family. Now that one had appeared, she didn't know what to do with it. She really didn't know her mother well, and nice though he seemed to be, Jordan didn't quite know what to make of Andy. There was a knock at her door. "Come in."

Andy and Powar entered.

"Good morning," said Jordan.

"How are you feeling today?" asked Powar.

"I haven't been awake long enough to tell," was Jordan's answer.

"Andy and I have been up almost all night discussing possible plans for all of us. We have missed so much that we want to start being a family right away."

This was exactly what Jordan was afraid of. She held on to her own arm under the covers.

"We'd like you to live with us and spend the summer at the studio. Andy and I want to get married right away."

"But what about Grandma? She wants me to live with her."

"There must be a way to come up with a solution here," said Powar.

"After what I've read about you and Grandma, I don't think compromise is in your vocabulary," Jordan retorted. "How about this? I stay in your guest house. That way Grandma won't get as upset. I'm sort of separate from the house. I'll spend the weekends with her. Okay?"

Powar and Andy looked at each other. It was obviously the only way to go.

"Fine," said Jordan. "I'll tell Grandma today when I get some of my things."

"Jordan, you're going to love it here. I meant it when I said I loved your video. I can tell that you can direct. You have real story sense as well as composition. Unfortunately you haven't had the opportunity to absorb firsthand the knowledge that your family could have given you. But things can be different now. You can be an apprentice through an entire movie every summer."

"I say that you sound like you're in a board meeting, that's what," said Jordan. "You have hurt me, and you can't just fix it with a routine Hollywood speech. You sound like Faye Dunaway in *Network*."

Andy laughed.

"This isn't funny, Andy," said Powar.

"No, but Jordan really has a sense of humor, and I think I know where she got it from." He winked to her, trying to lighten things up. "Please consider what your mother said, Jordan."

Powar had the King Pictures press department notify journalists on Friday that a major press conference would be held at the studio on Monday. "It's a big story," she said. "We may as well let them have it and give them the week to let them run with it. No more hiding." Then they told Jordan.

"I have called a press conference for Tuesday morning at ten. I'm going to make an announcement, telling the truth, introducing you and Andy. Then I'll take a few questions, and that's it. Don't worry, you don't have to say anything."

"No," said Jordan. Both Powar and Andy looked at her and wondered what was next. "I've been in the background long enough. If anybody has any questions of me, they can ask me directly. That's the only way I'll agree to this."

Andy laughed. "See, Powar?" he said. "What did I tell you about the apple and the tree? Let's take her for a drive and have some fun."

"Look, Jordan, see that house set back from the gates? Sonny and Cher live there, and Tony Curtis used to live there before them," Powar explained. "And you see that pink house on the corner with the glitter in the paint? That was Jayne Mansfield's house. Now Engelbert Humperdinck lives there."

"Really?" said Jordan. "This is cool."

For the first time Powar could sense some genuine interest and appreciation. "Before we get back to our house we'll pass where Elvis Presley lived when he died, and Barbra Streisand's house." Jordan seemed to be having a good time. Powar wanted it to be that way.

Andy thought it would be a good idea to take Jordan to Disneyland on Sunday. He and Powar couldn't really be seen around town with her, and it would be a good place to go with a lot of distractions. On Monday they prepared for the press conference. There were wardrobe fittings and discussions, followed by hair and makeup rehearsals. It was a new experience for Jordan to be the object of attention. She usually was shooting those people. Powar introduced her only as "Jordan" to whoever arrived as part of the process. Jordan did not meet the press agents from the studio. Powar merely called them Monday morning and asked them to set up the press conference in the main theater at the studio. She asked for lights, a podium, and a mike. When they questioned her about the reason, she brushed them aside.

Tuesday came quickly. Jordan had become instantly fascinated by American TV, and except for the day at Disneyland, she spent her time watching it. Powar left for the studio at seven to coordinate things and have her hair and makeup done.

"A car will pick up you and Andy at nine-thirty. You both will get ready here," explained Powar.

"Doesn't anybody drive themselves in America?" Jordan asked.

Andy laughed. "Of course they do, just not on special days . . . at least in Hollywood."

It was decided that Jordan would wear the beige Calvin Klein suit and a cream silk blouse, as planned. Andy would wear a gray glen plaid suit, and Powar would wear a purple Saint-Laurent suit with a skirt.

"I know this is a very big day for all of us," said Powar, placing her hands on Andy and Powar like a quarterback leading a huddle. "Our family has always been strong and honorable, and together we will uphold the tradition today. I love you both very much." She kissed them and left.

"Is she always so intense?" asked Jordan.

"Only sometimes," Andy said. "There's a lot you need to learn about who your family is and what they stand for. You are carrying on a dynasty, and you'll soon learn that. Be very proud."

Precisely at nine forty-five Andy and Jordan went up the back stairs to Powar's office. It was far enough away from the theater so they wouldn't be seen. Powar's staff did not see them enter, and they were surprised when she invited them to the press conference. She had never done anything like that before.

"Please go on ahead of me," she said. "I'll see you there at ten." And then she and Andy and Jordan waited for Don Bryson to come get them. He came up at 10:02, and they started their walk. Powar patted Jordan on her back and squeezed Andy's hand.

"Let me go in ahead of you two," said Powar. "Wait five seconds and then let yourselves in and stand by the door."

When Powar walked in all heads turned to her and cameras started clicking automatically. She went to the podium and saw about one hundred faces and as many cameras, both still and videotape. She saw some people in the crowd whom she had seen her whole life and had become friendly with, and she also saw people there who'd always hated her. She felt the lights on her face and knew instinctively that the lighting was correct.

"Good morning, everyone. It's nice to see so many of you here on such short notice. Thank you very much for coming.

Today I have some personal news to discuss. It has absolutely nothing to do with King Pictures."

A murmur of voices in the crowd began to build. Powar waited for them to settle down.

"I'd like Andy Stromberg to join me up here, please. You all know him," she said matter-of-factly. "We are very happy to announce that we are getting married within the week at a private ceremony. We met each other a number of years ago and fell in love, but circumstances were such that it was inappropriate for us to marry at that time." The reporters were spellbound. "We are making this unusual public announcement because we want you to know that fifteen years ago we had a child—"

Loud gasps interrupted Powar's speech. "If you would wait, please, and let me go on. . . . Thank you. She is here in America for the first time. We are very proud of her, and we are proud of our efforts to become a family before your very eyes. I'd like you to meet Jordan King." People started looking around frantically until the spotlight picked Jordan up against the door.

"Please come up here, Jordan," said Powar.

The lights nearly blinded Jordan as she walked to the podium. She looked at the crowd and managed a smile. As she got up there she began to get a sense of what it was like to be a King and live your life in the Hollywood spotlight. By the time she reached Andy and Powar, she realized that all of this was her birthright, something she had been cheated out of, and now she really believed she deserved it, and she was going to have it. She looked out confidently at the crowd. Every camera in the room was on overtime.

"Thank you very much for coming," Powar said as the room exploded into questions. "No, we won't tell you where and when we're getting married," answered Powar. "Mr. Stromberg concurred fully with me at all times about this arrangement, yes."

"Miss King?" said a reporter. "I'd like to know where you've been all these years."

Jordan stepped to the mike. "To answer you, I grew up in France and I didn't meet my father until two days ago."

There was another explosion of questions, and Powar stepped in. "That's all we have to say now, thank you." Powar could still hear the reporters screaming questions as she rushed Andy and Jordan out of the room.

* CHAPTER 22 *

W e're going into shark-infested waters, Jordan," explained Powar, "but it's the only way to handle things." They were being seated at the Bistro Garden for lunch, and there was a specific reason why Powar wanted to take Jordan there, and it wasn't just for the apple pancake.

"This is the place where all the 'wives of' or 'wanna be wives of' go to eat. They don't care about the food. They just want to gossip and be seen," continued Powar. "I thought it was important to bring you here today, Jordan, because we are on page one of most of the newspapers in the world, and it's important for us to go right out and face everyone and be proud of who we are."

"Why are you proud of us?" asked Jordan.

"Because we are finally being who we really are," said Powar, "and that's particularly hard to do in Hollywood. Just take a look around this restaurant. You see that blonde woman in the navy suit over there? The one with the huge diamond ring? That's her third face job. She gets one from each husband. She doesn't know it, but the guy she's having an affair with, who just happens to be president of a bank in Beverly

Hills, is never going to leave his wife. She thinks the wife doesn't know what's going on, but she actually sanctions it so she doesn't have to sleep with him.''

"This place is outrageous," said Jordan. "I have never seen so many coiffed, plastic people in one place, and they seem to be just pretending to have a good time."

"This is actually a microcosm of this town," continued Powar. "There are some nice, genuine people here, some successful producers and executives, some hookers, some doctors who'll prescribe anything you want, and some people who are praying that their lunch partner picks up the check."

"No wonder everybody stopped talking when we walked in here," said Jordan.

Just as the Dutch apple pancake and lobster salad were served, Powar's eyes went to the four women entering the room. Mrs. Marvin Davis, wife of a billionaire businessman, and Wendy Goldberg, wife of producer Leonard, were accompanied by Franny and Blair.

"Here it comes," said Powar.

"What?" asked Jordan.

"I thought something like this would happen, and I sort of wanted it to. It's better to get everything over with all at once. Andy's ex-wife is over there, the one in the red. Brace yourself.''

In seconds Franny was standing at their table. Not a utensil was being moved by anyone in the restaurant. "My, my," said Franny, aware that everyone was listening, "if it isn't my husband's mistress and her illegitimate child."

Powar completely ignored the viciousness and in a very ladylike manner said, "Jordan, I'd like you to meet Franny Stromberg."

Taking her mother's cue, Jordan got up, extended her hand, and said, "It's nice to meet you. Would you care to join us for a drink to celebrate?"

"No, thank you," Franny said icily. "I don't care to associate with people like you."

"Really?" said Powar, tilting her head slightly in Blair's direction so Franny got the point and the rest of the crowd missed it. Franny turned on her heel and went back to her table in a grand huff.

"Way to go!" said Jordan as she laughed as discreetly as she could. They started to eat their meal, and about five minutes later Barbara Walters came over.

"This certainly is quite a day," said Powar. "Jordan, this is Barbara Walters, she's a very successful newsperson here in the States."

"I think what you both did yesterday was very courageous. I'd really like to interview your whole family next week on '20/20.' We should even get Honey King on and have a reunion. I think it would be a great story," said Barbara.

"I'll think about it," said Powar, "but I doubt that we'll say yes, at least at this moment."

"Please call me at ABC in New York either way. Jordan, my dear, it's a pleasure to meet you," said Barbara, exiting.

"Look," said Jordan, "she's going over to Franny's table now and talking to her."

"There's no question that this would be a good story," said Powar, "but I think we've told enough, don't you?"

"I think we've told enough to the public, but I want to know more about my grandmother and grandfather. Was it really as bad as what I read in the newspapers in Europe?"

"It certainly was, and I want to tell you all of it," said Powar. "You'd better order dessert because it will take a while."

The day after the press conference Honey woke up on fire. Normally Lupe's soft knock on the bedroom door would awaken her gently, and Honey would begin to stir as her drapes were opened. Just as she was getting ready to buzz, Lupe came in carrying breakfast and newspapers on a white wicker bed tray.

"Hurry up, Lupe," snarled Honey. "Forget the drapes. I need to see the papers. Just leave the tea and remove the egg and toast. Not this morning, please. I'm sorry, this just isn't a good day. Thank you."

Lupe did as she asked and left the room.

Honey picked up the *L.A. Times* and glanced at the front page. A picture of Andy, Powar, and Jordan was front and center. For a second she started to throw the paper across the room, but then she threw back her head and sighed. She paused for only a moment, taking it all in, and then she started to laugh. Her plan to destroy Powar had backfired! She had to give it to Powar—she'd risen to the occasion and turned everything into a positive media event! And now there was going to be a wedding. . . . No, she really shouldn't be there; after all, business was business. She was just going to go on with her day.

At three-thirty that afternoon Honey heard Jordan and Lupe at the front door. Her heart jumped.

"Look, Grandma!" said Jordan, bounding into her office with all the papers. "My picture . . . isn't that wild?" she said, giving Honey a hug and a kiss.

"Yes, it is, and you look wonderful today. Welcome to Hollywood! How would you like to go shopping with me right now?"

"*Absolutement, Grand-mère,*" Jordan said, giggling.

At 7:30 A.M. on Friday morning, Andy woke up in his bungalow. He had one hour to get dressed before he was to meet Powar and Jordan at the tennis court entrance on Beverly Green Road on the other side of the hotel. Precisely at 8:25 A.M. he left his bungalow dressed in a navy blue Polo blazer, gray slacks, a white shirt, and a burgundy-and-navy club tie. On his feet were navy Brioni loafers. He checked to see that the key he'd gotten from the tennis pro was in his pocket. The door was double-locked for security reasons. He got to the door at exactly 8:30, opened it, and laid eyes on his bride and his daughter.

"I never thought I could be this happy," he said, kissing both of them.

Powar wore a cream satin Isaac Mizrahi double-breasted suit, cream stockings and heels, and she was holding a nose-gay of white carnations. "Quick, let's get to the room," she said. "Nobody saw us leave the house!"

Once inside, she pinned a boutonniere on Andy. "Thank you for loving me," she said. They were kissing when Jordan came out of the bedroom. She had changed into a gray silk suit, and she looked beautiful. The doorbell rang. "Check and see who it is before you open it," Powar cautioned Andy.

"It's safe," said Andy as he let in Maria and Jonna, Joan Wimberley, and his best man, producer David Thompson. Jordan was going to be Powar's maid of honor.

"We'd better go," said Andy. "Let's go around the out-side and go in through the kitchen entrance to the Crystal Room." They made it without a hitch.

"Wait here just a second," said Maria. "I want to see if everything's ready. I'll be right back."

Powar looked at Andy. "How are you feeling? Are you nervous?" she asked.

"A little. How about you?" he said.

"I feel fantastic. I just know that everything is going to be perfect."

"I'm so glad we're all together today," said Joan. "It's very special to me. I want you to wear this blue garter. Now you have something new, borrowed, and blue."

"That's so sweet of you," said Powar, "but what's old?"

"I am," said Andy.

"Okay," said Maria. "Follow me, everyone. Andy and Powar go first."

When Powar stepped into the ballroom she couldn't believe her eyes. It was lit and decorated as if it were a Saturday night. A piano player was playing "The Shadow of Your Smile." There was a long center table right in the middle of the dance floor covered with a white linen tablecloth and a huge centerpiece of white carnations. Along the front of the raised green velvet stage there was a strip of more carnations. Standing on the stage was Judge Ronald George, who was married to a classmate of Powar and Maria's at USC. There was a red carpet leading from the table to the stage for the wedding party to walk on, with baskets of white carnations on either side.

"This is too much, isn't it," said Jordan to Jonna, who was dressed in an Elvis Presley dinner jacket.

"I think this wedding idea is really cool," said Jonna.

"I guess so," Jordan said. "I like that jacket."

"Thanks. Elvis is my hero," said Jonna. "I'm glad you're here. It's too bad we couldn't see each other as much as we wanted when we were growing up."

"Well, I'm here for a while," answered Jordan.

"Okay, everybody, let's take our places," said Judge George. "Since we are a small group, I'd like all of you to stand together behind Andy while Powar walks down the aisle. When she reaches him, just close ranks behind them."

Powar walked to the head of the carpet, and the piano player started "Here Comes the Bride." When Powar heard the music she had to fight back the tears because her father wasn't standing alongside her. He would have been so proud.

She looked up at Andy's smiling face as she started her walk. They were going to be so happy together. She looked at Jordan's quizzical face. How much could she expect, having thrown her daughter into this whirlwind? She took Andy's hand.

"Dearly beloved," said the judge. The ceremony was over in less then ten minutes. Finally Powar and Andy Stromberg were one. A cheer went up from the guests as they made their way back down to the table. Immediately the waiters brought Louis Roederer Cristal champagne and individual smoked salmon appetizers. That was followed by Cobb salads and eggs Benedict with berry croissants.

Andy rose from his seat. "I'd like to make a toast. To my beautiful wife and daughter. I am the happiest man on earth today, and I know it will last a lifetime."

Powar kissed him as the piano player started "The Way You Look Tonight."

"May I have this dance, Mrs. S?" said Andy. They danced completely alone on the big dance floor.

Jordan leaned over to Jonna. "Do you want to get out of here and go over to Tower Records?"

"Deal," said Jonna. "As soon as this dance is over."

"And now we have one more thing to do," announced Powar as the dance ended. "All my life I have loved Hansen's Cakes. When I was a little girl I saw a wedding cake in the window that had three tiers and bridges connecting them to smaller cakes on the side. I'd like to thank Maria for organizing all of this today, and now for the best of all . . . the cake I have been waiting for my whole life." She gestured toward the kitchen door as four waitresses pushed the gigantic cake to the center of the room.

"You two hold the knife now and cut it," said Maria as she spontaneously sang "The Bride Cuts the Cake."

Andy and Powar made a wish, cut the cake, and toasted each other with champagne. Then, turning to their guests, he said, "Powar and I want to thank you from the bottom of our hearts for being here today and sharing in our love and supporting our new family. We love you all."

Within two weeks Jordan and Jonna had rekindled their friendship as if they never had been separated. Both Powar and Maria were happy they had found each other. "How do you feel about them going to those clubs every night?" asked Maria during one of her almost daily phone calls to Powar.

"It sounds a little dangerous to me, but I guess I have to remember when we liked to go out. Our parents were probably just as nervous."

"Do you know that Jordan is also spending a lot of time with Jonna when she rehearses? I think they're up to something," said Maria.

"It wouldn't surprise me," said Powar. "Never mind that, though, I need to ask your opinion on something. Paulette Wilde, a star my father developed in the fifties, is desperate to do a supporting part in a great new script we got from

Horton Foote. The picture doesn't rest on the part, but it is significant. I'd rather offer it to Jessica Tandy because she's a known commodity and Paulette hasn't acted in years. I hate to ask her to come in and read, that's too much of an insult to her. What do you think I should do?"

Without hesitation Maria gave her an answer. "If you've seen her lately and she looks okay, you should give her the part. Her working again will be an event. You can get a lot of press on it. If she can't cut it, you know what to do."

"Fire her," said Powar.

"Right," Maria said. "That will get you press, too. Either way you win."

"I was hoping that's what you'd say," said Powar. "I'll call her right now. Thanks, Maria."

"There's no question about it, I have to put you on video," said Jordan. "Nobody has ever seen any girl like you before. You move like a guy."

"What do you mean by that?" Jonna asked defensively. "Do you think I'm a guy or something?"

"Calm down," said Jordan. "All I'm saying is that most women on stage are a little wimpy. That's not really rock and roll. You will blow people away. Play that song again."

They were in the soundproof studio that once was a guest house on Nathan's property. It was where Jonna spent her happiest moments. Jonna did a song that she wrote called "Papa Ain't Home."

Jordan was glued to everything—her performance, the lyrics, and the music. "Okay," she said. "This is serious business. The music is terrific and so are you. I don't think the lyrics have the right hook. You have room for four syllables in the title. What would happen if we changed it to 'Rock and Roll Home'?"

"I like it, and it's more commercial," said Jonna, "but we'd have to change the rest of the lyrics."

"Then let's do it now," said Jordan.

* * *

"I'm so glad that Jordan is having Jonna over for brunch with us," said Powar. "It's the first real gesture she's made toward joining us as a family. I want everything to go well."

"I'm sure it will, darling," said Andy. "You bought out Nate 'n' Al's. What could go wrong?"

"There it is," said Powar. "You answer the door and I'll buzz Jordan to come in."

Andy welcomed Jonna in and noted that she looked particularly good in her black jeans and shirt. "That's sort of a uniform with you, isn't it?"

"Yes," replied Jonna. "I feel comfortable in it, and I don't have a problem choosing what to wear all the time."

"Jordan and Powar are in the breakfast room." They walked past a den that held two Oscars and three Emmys.

"That must be amazing to live with those awards every day," said Jonna.

"It really is. Not a day goes by that I don't look at all of them, as does Powar, and feel awed."

The table looked gorgeous. Even though it was all takeout deli, the items were either on silver platters or crystal dishes.

"I'm so glad you could join us, Jonna," said Powar. "Please sit down."

Powar and Andy sat at opposite ends of the table while Jordan and Jonna sat opposite each other the other way.

"I'd like to show you both something that my father showed me a long time ago. You take a bagel that has been cut in half and toasted. You put a layer of chopped liver on it and then you put a layer of coleslaw on top of that. The coleslaw sticks to the liver so it doesn't fall off. Then you put a layer of smoked salmon on top of that. It is an incredible thing to eat."

"I remember when you told me about that," said Andy. "We were in our twenties." Powar's eyes met his, and they both smiled.

Jonna copied everything that Powar was doing, but Jordan

preferred cream cheese and lox. "Have you spoken to Genevieve lately?" asked Jordan.

"I talked to her yesterday. She's getting over a cold, but she's fine. I told her everything was fine over here, too."

"I really miss her," said Jordan.

Near the end of the meal, after the polite conversation had been exhausted, Jordan spoke up. "There's something Jonna and I need to talk to you about."

"Of course," said Andy.

"Jonna has written a great song, and I've shot a demo video on a home camera so we can show it to you. I couldn't edit it, of course, but you can get the feeling. We think it's really special. Can we run it for you now?"

"Absolutely," said Andy. "Just leave everything on the table, Powar, and we'll go into the screening room."

They all settled onto the plush chairs and watched the three-minute cassette. It was a very, very hot number. Jordan was very aware of Jonna's androgynous quality. She knew that Jonna thought of herself as a female Presley, but she really was more like the androgynous Jagger. When the lights came up Andy and Powar applauded.

"That was just great," said Andy. "I predict big things for both of you."

"Good," said Jordan, "because we can use your help. We'd like to borrow twenty-five thousand dollars from you to make a real video. This isn't London, and I don't have my sources."

"Well," said Andy, "I'm very impressed with both of you and—" He was cut off by Powar.

"And we both wish you well," she continued. "Twenty-five thousand dollars is a lot of money. You've only made one video, and although it was fantastic, it's not a good investment."

Andy was stunned, but he knew better than to interfere with Powar and Jordan. Everything was too new for him to start coming between them and taking sides, even though he would have given Jordan the money in a second.

But Jordan was furious. "You've ignored me for almost sixteen years, separated me from a father I never knew existed, and paraded me in front of the press as some trophy. You *owe* me this! What happened to all this talk about the family supporting one another? You really don't care about me. You just wanted a neat little ending to the script you wrote in your head."

"That's not true, Jordan," said Powar. "I owe you love and respect, and that you will get, but I will not buy you."

Andy was dying inside. Keeping his mouth shut was very difficult.

Jordan got up and motioned to Jonna. She got the cassette from the machine and said, "Let's go, Jonna. We're obviously not welcome here."

When they got in the car Jonna was shaking. "I'm really sorry, Jordan. I didn't want to cause a fight like this."

"You didn't have anything to do with it. It's been coming for years," said Jordan, calming down. "Don't worry. I have an idea. I think I know exactly where we can get the money, and we don't have to go to England. Watch this." She started the car and drove a few blocks to a phone booth. "Just wait right here," she said to Jonna. "I'm going to make a call."

"Who are you calling?" Jonna asked.

"You'll see, if it all works out." Jordan picked up the phone, deposited money, and dialed a number from memory.

After a few seconds Jonna heard her say, "Hello, Grandma. It's Jordan. May I bring my friend Jonna over? We need to talk to you. . . . Thanks."

Jordan hung up the phone and got back in the car. "So far, so good," she said, smiling broadly.

"Do you know that your grandmother threw your mother out of the studio years ago and then your mother fought her for control and won?"

"Oh, yes. I read about all of that in the papers. So far, I can see why my grandmother did what she did."

Jordan's short time in Hollywood had given her a better understanding of what her family meant. When she and Jonna drove up to the house on Bedford this time, a sense of history enveloped her all over again. Perhaps it was because the house was so regal and evoked another time.

"Hi, Grandma. You remember Jonna?"

"Yes, of course, dear. Please come in."

Honey led them to the living room and sat them on the couch in front of the coffee table with a scrapbook on it entitled "King Pictures: The First Decade."

"Wow. May I see this?" asked Jordan.

"Of course you may," Honey said, pleased. "Take your time and look at all the pictures and stories. If you want, I can go over page by page and answer any questions." Before any of them knew it an hour and a half had gone by.

"I can't believe you managed to steal Clark Gable away from Louis B. Mayer!" said Jordan.

"It was only for one picture, but your grandfather made a great deal for him. The picture cost two hundred thousand dollars and grossed three million."

"This is just amazing," said Jordan. "I never could have learned all this just by reading the press clippings in Paris."

"Any time you want me to teach you about your family, I would be delighted," said Honey. "You know that. I missed you last weekend, but I know you are busy. I hope you'll be here this coming one."

"Grandma? There's something that Jonna and I want to talk to you about. I think it's a good investment."

Honey listened while Jordan talked about the video and asked for the $25,000. As soon as the figure was out of her mouth Honey was relieved that that was all it was going to cost her to get Jordan over to her side.

"And your mother won't help you?" asked Honey in as incredulous and sympathetic a manner as she could muster. "Jordan, you are a King. You are strong and talented. It is in your blood to fight for what you believe in. Powar is strong, too, but she takes after her father. You, I can tell, take after me. My darling, I want you to move in here. You can have the money and we will work closely together to see that your career gets going," said Honey.

"Can Jonna move in with me?" asked Jordan.

"Of course she can. You both are very welcome here," said Honey.

"There's one more question I have," Jordan said. "If I accept the money, and your career guidance, I need you to know that as far as what I shoot, I make those choices alone."

"I understand and accept your terms," said Honey, laughing out loud. "You are definitely my granddaughter."

Jonna knew Maria was out at a party that afternoon, so she and Jordan went over to her house to pack. Jonna left her mother the following note: "Dear Mother, I have decided to move in with Jordan so we can work closely together. I'm not leaving home for good. You haven't done anything wrong. This is just something I need to do for now. I'll call you tomorrow. Love, Jonna."

Maria called Powar as soon as she found the note. "Do you know where they might have gone?" she asked.

"I hope it isn't where I'm thinking," said Powar.

"Where's that?" asked Maria.

"My mother's."

"Oh, God," said Maria. "She can be very charming when she wants something."

"Well, we both know what she wants," Powar continued. "I'm just sorry that Jonna got caught up in it. It's probably partially my fault because of the money." She then told Maria what happened.

"That was a tough decision," said Maria, "but twenty-five thousand dollars is a lot of money. We both will help them in other ways."

"What if she won't talk to me if she's at my mother's? I can't deal with losing her so soon after she got here."

"Don't be ridiculous. She'll see through Honey. Everything will work out."

* * *

Jordan had been thinking about the theme for the video for a couple of weeks. It was in the back of her head subliminally from the time she drove up to Honey's house, and it hit her one afternoon as she and Honey were swimming.

"Look, Grandma," said Jordan, standing in the shallow end. "Come back here and stand with me. Look at the columns. Look at that veranda. You know, in England the thing that made my videos stand out was that I used contrasting images to the lyrics I was shooting. In Jonna's song 'Rock and Roll Home,' we wrote lyrics about a funky shack in the woods. You said you wanted to be involved in some way with what I'm doing, and I think I have it. I want to shoot the video right here in this house, using both the inside and outside. It'll be outrageous. What do you say?"

"I say I'm locking up my antiques and breakables," said Honey.

Within a week Jordan was calling "Action." She had done her storyboards and was ready to go. No sets had to be built, and Jonna was hot to shoot. Honey had the best hair and makeup people booked. Chasen's did the catering, and she paid for Bob Mackie to custom-make a black beaded pants and shirt outfit. Di Fabrizio did custom boots. They shot for two days, and the playback was so noisy that the neighbors called the police and restricted the shooting to 9 A.M. to 5 P.M.

Honey was having the time of her life. To her it was another party, only this time it was a rock and roll theme. She called in some members of the press, and Jordan, Honey, and Jonna were on the news. When Jordan told Honey she wanted the video to air on MTV, Honey got the names of all the board members of the parent company. She knew she would know a wife somewhere. A couple of well-placed phone calls and Jordan found herself sitting in the office of the president of MTV.

"I appreciate your seeing me," said Jordan. "I know this came about through unusual circumstances."

"Frankly, Jordan," said Mr. Merritt, "I am seeing you

because I have seen the video you did in London. That's the only reason you're here. We are pressured twenty-four hours a day by innumerable people with angles. I don't care who they are. I only care about the talent. Leave your new video with me. If I like it, I'll put it on Shannon O'Neal's show, 'Rock-O-Rama.' "

"Thank you very much for giving us the chance," said Jordan.

Within forty-eight hours "Rock and Roll Home" aired on O'Neal's show. The same crazy phone response that happened in London with Arianne happened again. The requests were so intense that Merritt called and asked Jordan and Jonna to appear live on the next show. The plan was to run Jonna's video and do an interview with her and then run Arianne's video and bring Jordan on. Jordan met with O'Neal the day before to coordinate everything, and she was struck by how much he looked like Jonna in person. It was eerie how they had the same jet black hair and wide eyes. It was as if they were twins.

The night before the show, after Honey finished coaching Jonna on how to give an interview, Jordan had to go lie down. She hadn't told anyone, but she had been feeling a pain in her stomach for some time. She thought it was because she rarely ate during shooting and editing. It had happened before, and it had always gone away. It was more severe this time, so she took a lot of Pepto-Bismol. Just as she was feeling a little better, the phone rang.

"Jordan, I think this has gone on long enough." It was Powar. "I want you to come home."

"Why should I?" asked Jordan. "Grandma brought me home. Now she's made me feel welcome. She believes in me more than you because she backed me."

"Jordan, she is famous for using her money to get whatever she wants. With all the good values that Genevieve taught you, you must realize that you shouldn't be for sale. She's just using you to hurt me."

"Genevieve taught me many things," said Jordan. "But

the most important thing that she said over and over again was that genes are stronger than anything. I am a product of both of you. I want success, just like each of you has wanted and gotten it, and like you both, I will take my opportunities where they come. I'm sorry. I have to go now." And then she hung up. The pain in her stomach was back, and she disguised it when Jonna came into the room.

"Shannon O'Neal, I'd like you to meet Jonna." Jordan had never seen a look quite like the one Shannon gave Jonna. It was as if he'd been hit with a stun gun.

"I love your record. I'm going to make it a hit," he said, looking straight at Jonna. It was as if Jordan weren't even in the room.

"Thank you. I'm a little nervous. I've never been on TV before," said Jonna.

"Don't worry. Just pretend you're talking to me and don't even think about the camera. I have to go start the show now, but you'll be out really soon."

Jonna looked as though she'd been shot with the same gun.

"Cute, isn't he?" said Jordan. "I hear he's nice, too." She waited for a response and got nothing. "Jonna? Can you hear me?"

"I'm sorry. I feel funny," she said.

"You'll be fine. Just go out there and answer the questions honestly." A production assistant came to get her and take her to the stage. "Have fun!" Jordan called out.

After the video ran, Shannon and Jonna were on camera. She looked beautiful. The more he talked to her, the more she came out of her shell and blossomed. Jordan thought, watching, that they were acting as though they were on a first date. It was sweet. Jonna had never really discussed boys or anything personal with her, and it was good to see her having fun. Jonna clearly looked like a star, and with the heat the video was generating, it would be no time at all before she would get a record deal and Jordan's career would be launched as well.

After the show was over Shannon congratulated both of them on a good job. "Jonna, would you like to go have coffee with me? Jordan, you don't mind, do you?"

"No, I'm actually looking forward to going home and lying down. You two go right ahead." Jonna gave her a funny look, and Jordan couldn't figure out what it meant, but she'd just caught it in passing and decided maybe it wasn't anything.

She was asleep when Jonna got home. She felt a hand on her shoulder, and it was Jonna's.

"Hi, how'd it go?" asked Jordan.

"It was incredible. We went to a coffee house named Java, and when I walked in people applauded. I couldn't believe it."

"That's great!" said Jordan. "How is Shannon?"

"He's great, too, but I need to talk to you about something. I'm not used to the kind of feelings that he's stirring up in me. I never wanted to feel them, ever. It terrifies me."

"Why?" asked Jordan. "It's wonderful."

Jonna broke down and cried wrenching tears.

"What's wrong? What can I do to help?" asked Jordan, terribly concerned.

"I'm a freak, that's what's wrong," said Jonna.

"What? You're beautiful. What are you talking about?" said Jordan.

"I hate what I am. It's going to ruin everything."

Jordan held her gently and said, "I'm sorry, I don't understand. Please tell me what's the matter."

Jonna then very haltingly whispered about her "secret" surgery as a baby.

Jordan was totally shocked but didn't show it. "When I don't know something I go to an expert. It seems to me that you should go to a gynecologist and straighten this out. From what you've told me, everything was fixed when you were six weeks old. I bet you're fine. We'll find out someone to call. I'll even go with you."

"No! I want to go by myself. I'm just so frightened. What if I don't look like other girls 'down there'? What if Shannon or whoever I love finds me repulsive? I can't stand it," she said, sobbing again.

"I promise you we'll get an answer and everything will be fine. You must believe that everything will be okay. You have your whole life ahead of you."

"I just don't know what to do," Powar said to Andy. They were sitting in her office, having a quiet lunch. "I thought that everything would be fine with Jordan here. I thought our love would rub off on her and we could take her to premieres, and restaurants, and Santa Barbara. I so wanted us to be a family."

"I know you did, but it's something that you have to put effort into. You can't just resume your normal schedule and expect her to tag along," said Andy.

"I've disappointed you, haven't I?" asked Powar.

"I love you and you know that," said Andy. "I might have handled some things differently, but you never consulted me. Being in a marriage with someone is not like the way we were before when we were two separate individuals who loved each other and got together when we could. You've never lived with anybody before and you haven't really adjusted or made accommodations to it yet. Regardless of how my marriage was with Franny, I did have the experience of sharing a life with someone."

Before Powar could speak, her secretary buzzed her. "Leslie is on line two."

"I have to get this, Andy," said Powar.

"Do you?" he commented.

"Leslie, what can I do for you?" said Powar. "I know. I feel terrible about that. The script has been sitting here for two weeks. I promise I'll do it tonight and give you an answer in the morning.

"Now look at what's happening," Powar said to Andy as she hung up. "I'm so distracted worrying about you, Jordan, and my mother, that I'm not doing a good job here, either. Something has got to change."

"I don't know how you can read that script tonight," said Andy. "We're supposed to go to the Angels party."

"Oh, no," said Powar. "That's right. This is the lucky night when we get to face everybody."

"If you would look to me more to help you, things might be easier," said Andy. "For instance, when Jordan asked for the twenty-five thousand dollars I was about to answer her by asking her to let you and me talk it over and let her know the next day. That would have given us time to think it through carefully, but more important it would have let Jordan know that she was important to us and we wouldn't just dismiss her with an instant 'no.' "

"So now you're blaming me, too," said Powar, starting to cry.

"Of course not," said Andy. "I'm just trying to help you make things better. Come here. Let me hold you. It will get better, I promise. Let's just try to have some fun tonight."

Powar finished putting on her lipstick, ran a comb through her hair, and looked at herself in the mirror. She was wearing a powder blue cowgirl outfit from head to toe. She did not think that black would be appropriate this year. She knew Andy would be wearing white, and she didn't want to look like the bad guy.

"Ready to go?" said Andy, sticking his head in the door. He had on a white hat with a black jeweled band, a white shirt, white kid trousers, and black boots.

"You look fabulous!" said Powar.

"So do you," said Andy as he took her in his arms and messed up her lipstick.

"Do that one more time and we won't go to the party," Powar said seductively.

"I'd like nothing better," said Andy, "but you know we have to do this."

They went into the garage through the door in the kitchen and got into Andy's navy Mercedes. "I'm glad we didn't take a limo tonight," he said. "It's almost more fun this way."

When they pulled up in front of the Santa Monica Civic Auditorium, the paparazzi were ready for them. As the flash bulbs were going, one of the photographers shouted, "Where's Jordan?" Powar pretended to ignore it and tried to move along as fast as possible.

The Santa Monica Civic had a gigantic foyer with bars at either end. Tonight, the Angels had turned the foyer into an Old West amusement park like Knott's Berry Farm, a real park south of Los Angeles. Everywhere you looked there were games to play, like water balloons, a shooting gallery, a ring toss, a baseball throw. The booths looked like cabins, and the people who manned them looked as if they were dressed for square dancing, wearing red-and-white-checked shirts and blue-jean pants and skirts.

"Let's go shoot the balloons," said Andy.

The doors opened up on cue, and the people entering walked in to the orchestra playing "Home on the Range." All the tables set up on the floor of the auditorium had a centerpiece of a covered wagon surrounded by flowers and sagebrush. There was a small sign under each that read "For Sale: $500." The Angels were always looking for a way to make money for their charity.

Powar and Andy were seated at a table that Powar's PR man had put together for her. Two of her production VPs were there, as well as Norman Brokaw of William Morris, who had brought Maria as his date, and Joan Wimberley and her date, Tom Selleck. On top of each guest's place setting there was a blue box from Tiffany as a favor. Considering its shape, it had to be a pen.

"Well, we all have them already," said Joan, "but I can always use another one, particularly since it's free. How resourceful of the Angels to get Tiffany to donate all of these. That's quite a coup."

The dinner was catered by Great Presentations, the best in the business. In keeping with the western theme there was cornbread soufflé, a chuck-wagon stew, and a salad of lime-stone lettuce, walnuts, and pears. "I'm so tired of filet mignon, peas, and two roasted potatoes," said Powar. "This is a pleasure."

While coffee and dessert were being served, Sandy Alpert, the current president of the Angels, took the mike to welcome everyone.

"Good evening, and welcome to the twenty-seventh annual Angels extravaganza. As you know, before we do our auction, every year we award that one outstanding Angel member with the Angel of the Year award." A hush fell over the crowd. "This year the award goes to a very special woman who has had a difficult year. Even as she was facing a personal crisis, she never once let us down, and worked harder than she ever has before. She even talked Tiffany into giving us favors for the first time ever. This year's award goes to Franny Stromberg."

A cheer rang out from the opposite side of the room as Franny stood up to make her way to the stage. Powar and Andy were frozen to their chairs. They knew that people were looking right at them, and they applauded right along with everyone else. No one at Powar's table stood up, and it seemed an eternity before Franny got to the stage.

"What on earth is she going to say?" Powar whispered to Andy.

"Just pray she always remembers the pictures," he said.

And then she was speaking. Fighting back tears, she said, "You don't know what this award and this organization means to me. You have become my family and given me the strength to go on. Thank you."

"I want to go home," said Powar. "This is nauseating. What a crock."

"Try to keep your voice down," whispered Andy. "We can't leave now. It would make things more horrendous than they already are."

"Hello, ladies and gentlemen, I'm Joey Bishop. Tonight's auction features trips all over the world, cars, and fabulous jewelry. Don't be shy now, don't hang on to your money. It's for a good cause." Fortunately, everyone was now concentrating on Bishop. "Our first auction item is this diamond bracelet from Tiffany's. You saw it on display earlier this evening, and now you can have it. It's worth twenty-five thousand dollars. Who will start the bidding?"

Powar leaned over to Andy and said, "Get it no matter what it costs. It's an important statement for us to make right now. We can't sit in the shadows tonight."

"Five thousand," said Andy.

"I hear five thousand from Mr. Stromberg. Do I hear seventy-five hundred? . . . Good. How about eight, do I hear eight?" said Bishop.

Two other people were bidding now. Andy jumped in with $10,000. He wanted to get this over with.

"I have a bid of ten thousand. Do I hear twelve? C'mon, ladies and gentlemen, do it for the kids. Let's hear twelve." There was silence. "Okay," continued Bishop. "I have ten thousand once, ten thousand twice—"

"Twenty thousand," said a voice about six tables away from Powar's. She turned and saw Blair smiling at Bishop and then nodding to Franny. The crowd gasped and turned to Andy. Powar grabbed his arm to hold on for the ride.

"Twenty-two five," said Andy.

Before Bishop could even repeat it, Blair said $25,000.

"I have twenty-five thousand," said Bishop. "Do I hear twenty-six?" Everyone looked at Andy.

"Thirty thousand dollars," Andy said evenly. He could see Blair hesitate and then choose to pass.

"Sold to Andy Stromberg for thirty thousand dollars," said Bishop.

The crowd burst into spontaneous applause. Andy walked up to the stage, got the bracelet, and then went back to the table and placed it on Powar's wrist for all to see. As he was doing it he couldn't help but wonder whether Blair had really wanted to buy the bracelet or had just driven up the price to annoy him. If the latter, she had succeeded.

At six A.M. the next morning Powar woke up Andy. "I've got it!" she said.

"What could you possibly have at this hour of the morning?" said a sleepy Andy.

"The way to fix the Jordan situation. She made a great video with Jonna and I made a terrible mistake not helping her for many reasons. I need to show her I believe in her, and I've found a way."

"What is it?" asked Andy.

"Remember that script that Leslie was pushing me to read? Well, I got up at four A.M. to do it. Leslie was right, it's a smash, and I want Jordan to direct it."

"You're going to put an entire movie into the hands of an eighteen-year-old? I know she's talented, but isn't that risky for the studio?" said Andy.

"This is perfect for her. It's like one long music video. The script is by an unknown, so it will cost nothing. It's about a ballet troupe struggling to make ends meet. They decide to change their style to rock and do a touring live show like a video. There's tons of music. Maybe we could even find a part for Jonna. That would work, too. I don't see how Jordan could turn me down. Not only is it the correct artistic choice, but it will help me win her back. I'll just hire the best line producer in the business and the best assistants. She won't get into trouble. We'll use all unknown actors, too. It's called *Smashpoint*, and that's exactly what it's going to be."

"It really does sound wonderful," said Andy.

"I'm going to call her right now at Mother's. I don't care what I have to do," said Powar.

Jordan answered the phone herself because Honey was still asleep. She heard her mother's idea, and while initially she loved the sound of it, she was suspicious. "Why are you doing this? First you won't give me any money and now you're putting a one-million-dollar movie in my hands. And you accuse Grandma of trying to buy me? I'm beginning to feel like a Ping-Pong ball."

"Jordan, please. I was wrong in the way I handled the

video with you. And I do want to help you. But I'm not an idiot, either. This is a low-budget film by today's standards, but it's totally acceptable. I happen to know that the first studio that manages to make a feature like a music video will have a hit. I'm not doing this just for you, although I'd rather not have to go to Al Magnoli or Peter Jensen to direct. I'd rather give you the shot. But this is a movie I'm going to make. I just wanted you to have the first chance. I'll send the script over right away, and I'm sure you'll see a spot in it for Jonna, too. Try to call me by five today. If you like it, you tell me who to call to make a deal. Everything will be by the book. What do you say?"

"I'll be waiting for it," said Jordan.

When the announcement hit the trades two days later that Jordan was directing a movie for King Pictures, it made page one.

"Look, Grandma, it's about the movie," said Jordan over breakfast.

"I know that, Jordan. I'm glad you asked me to read the script, and I think it's a good career move. But it's very difficult for me to see you going to that studio after what your mother did to me." Honey had decided to adopt a good attitude with Jordan until she could regroup and plan her next move. She also thought that Jordan would indirectly report her "good behavior" to Powar, and it would lull Powar into a sense of false security.

"You know, in Europe the family means everything," said Jordan. "Even though Genevieve and I were only two people, there wasn't anything we wouldn't do for one another. There are so many people in the world who try to divide you, because they know strength comes out of unity. I think it's sad that after all the history and good deeds of this family, there really isn't a family at all."

When Jordan moved onto the lot for preproduction, Powar saw to it that she had a nice office in the director's building, but she didn't want to go overboard and alienate other people she had under contract.

"So what do you think of it?" Jordan asked.

"I think it's fabulous," answered Jonna. "I can't believe any of this is happening. I can't believe I'm going to be able to play and sing my songs in a movie."

"Well, you have six weeks to prepare," said Jordan.

"What I don't have is any more time to prepare for Shannon," said Jonna.

"I see," said Jordan. "But you have nothing to worry about. You know what the gynecologist said."

"I know, but it's an emotional hurdle I have to get over," said Jonna.

"Lighten up and have a good time," said Jordan. "You have everything going for you, and Shannon's great."

"I know, but he wants me to meet him at his apartment tonight to play some new songs, and I know where that's going to lead. I don't know if I can handle it," explained Jonna.

"How does he make you feel when you kiss him now?" asked Jordan. "Are you comfortable with it?"

"More so, now," said Jonna. "When I can forget about myself I really love it."

"You have to let yourself go, you deserve it. Take the day off and go to Aida Grey. Get a massage, a manicure, a facial, whatever makes you feel good about yourself, and then go to his apartment," said Jordan.

"I'll try," said Jonna.

At eight P.M. Jonna was knocking on Shannon's door. She had on a navy suit with pinstripes, a white shirt, and boots. When Shannon opened the door wearing a white T-shirt and jeans, she thought immediately of James Dean and the movies her mother used to run for her. Shannon's apartment was one of rented furniture. It was clean and serviceable, but he hadn't really settled down yet.

"Let me show you my prized possession," he said. "Here is the top-of-the-line Nakamichi audio equipment. I even have four speakers, just like a recording studio. Here, listen." He sat her on the couch and put on Led Zeppelin. "There's nothing like a Jimmy Page solo to test speakers.'' Sounds of what seemed like fifty guitars filled the room.

"Wow, that's sensational. I'll never play live in this room," said Jonna, patting her guitar case.

"Oh, yes, you will," said Shannon. "You said you have some songs you want me to hear."

She just loved how his black hair fell down over one eye.

"I have some wine chilling for us. I just tried a chardonnay and really liked it. Usually I have Chablis, but this is something new for me. I'll go get it."

A shiver went through Jonna when he left the room. He was so adorable, she had never felt as she did right now. He was back with two glasses.

"I even chilled the glasses," he said.

Jonna tasted the wine and thought it was delicious.

"I want to hear the new song," Shannon said.

"I'm not sure now that I want to play it," said Jonna.

"Please do it for me," said Shannon.

"It's called 'Baby Blue Eyes,' and I wrote it for you," said Jonna. "It's not a rocker," she continued. "It's more like Elvis's 'Are You Lonesome Tonight?' "

"Just sing it, already!" Shannon teased.

Jonna sang the song tentatively at first, but then she let the mood of it carry her away. She was open and vulnerable for the first time.

"That was so beautiful, Jonna. And you are beautiful," said Shannon, reaching over and taking her guitar and placing it on the floor. Then he took off her coat and boots and gently pushed her back on the couch so he and Jonna were lying side by side. There was an urgency in his touch that she had not felt before, and she knew what was coming.

"Would you turn out the lights, please?" said Jonna.

"But you're so beautiful, I want to see you," urged Shannon.

"Please," said Jonna.

Shannon complied, and her heart rested a little bit. They were in total darkness now except for a small streak of light coming from the bedroom. He began kissing her very lightly. She was entranced by how sweet he was. As his tongue grew more insistent she tried to relax and let him in. She felt herself getting moist between her legs, and she jumped a bit.

"This is new for you, isn't it," said Shannon.

"Please don't tell anybody," Jonna whispered.

"There's nothing wrong with just starting out with something. It will be fun for both of us," said Shannon. "Don't worry. I'll take care of you." He took off his clothes as quickly as he could without frightening her, and then he started to undress her. She was shaking, and he thought that maybe it was anticipation rather than fear.

Jonna knew differently. He started to pull off her underpants, and she stopped him. "Wait?" she said.

"Why?" said Shannon. "Haven't we both waited long enough? I know you are beautiful everywhere. Let me kiss you awake."

As he moved his head lower on her body, she thought she was going to die of fright. It never occurred to her that he might actually look in there. Her underpants were off now, and he was gently pushing her legs apart. Jonna was praying for this nightmare to be over, and then she felt his tongue and it was the most exciting thing she had ever experienced. He was in there and he didn't seem to be noticing anything weird. She spread her legs more willingly now, and he went in deeper.

"Amazing," he said as he lifted up his head.

"What's the matter?" Jonna practically shouted. "What is it?" She was afraid that her worst fears were about to come true.

"I'm not sure how exactly to say this," said Shannon, "but you have the biggest pleasure button I've ever seen."

Jonna was starting to cry.

"No, no, don't cry. Are you kidding? You are the luckiest girl in the world. You're the best." And he went back to his explorations. "Boy, are you going to be a happy girl."

His praise of her made Jonna feel special for the first time and allowed her to start to relax.

His tongue was now stroking her button. He was tickling it and then sucking smoothly. She was breathing heavily, and he knew it was time to enter, but as he attempted it, he noticed she was totally dry. The only juice was what was left over from him. He reached under the couch and pulled out a tube of K-Y jelly and put it all over the two of them. Jonna had no idea that this wasn't always the way things happened. He was on top of her now, grabbing her shoulders.

"Put your legs around me and relax," he said.

Jonna did as she was told and couldn't believe the feeling as he slipped inside her. She could feel every inch of him, and with every move he made she felt herself swell within. They were getting tighter and tighter with each thrust until she thought she was going to burst. And when it happened it was as if stars were shooting out from in between her legs. She screamed out loud, and so did he. He looked into her eyes and saw tears, which he thought were tears of happiness. Jonna, on the other hand, was overwhelmed that after all these years of being terrorized, she was finally free.

The next two months flew by as Jordan and Jonna devoted themselves to *Smashpoint*. Powar saw to it that Jonna had a good dressing room and that they both had reserved parking places. Every day after shooting was completed, Jordan and the crew would sit and look at dailies. Frequently both Powar and Andy joined her, but they kept their mouths shut on which takes to choose unless Jordan was about to make a mistake. As head of the studio Powar had a right to make comments, but she kept them to a minimum. Jordan, rather than get involved in a personal discussion with her mother or Honey, tried to stay to herself. The strain of finishing the movie on time and fielding the "affection" of both Honey and Powar was almost more than she could bear. Her stomach never really recovered from the demo video, and she hadn't had time to go to a doctor. She would just keep sneaking into her trailer and drinking Pepto or Maalox.

"Oh, Jordan," said Honey one evening when she returned

from work, "I really would love it if I could come to the set to see you work."

"You know that won't work, Grandma," she explained. "We're on the lot, not on location. If Powar saw you there, it would be terrible."

Honey sipped on her martini before answering. "My dear child, I'm almost seventy-five years old. How many more opportunities am I going to get to see you work?"

"I'll do my best, Grandma, really I will," answered Jordan. By this time she was suspicious that both Honey and Powar were trying to use her to get information to each other. It was not a position she enjoyed. Even Andy was dropping by the set now just to visit, claiming he wanted his own time with her. She was under terrible tension trying to finish the movie. She felt as if she were being pulled apart.

From the time of the first shot, through the editing and scoring, *Smashpoint* was able to make its Easter release. Powar wanted it for Easter vacation. She knew it was a kids' movie, and she didn't want to go head to head with the summer blockbusters. On the basis of advance screenings, Jonna had four record offers and Jordan had a stack of scripts to read for possible directing jobs, having signed with William Morris at Honey's urging.

Honey was beside herself watching all the action around Jordan. She was sure that soon she would be so successful that she would be taken away from her again. Before the picture was about to open, Honey finally came up with her plan.

"Jordan, I'd like you to think about something for me," said Honey one night as Jordan was going to bed. "I think you might be wrong to stay at King. There may be some other studios that will give you more money. Why don't you let me make some phone calls?"

"I'd like to think about it," answered Jordan. "Powar has given me a very good offer. She gave me the opportunity to make the movie, so I must give her consideration, purely on a business level."

"But I was the one who got you started here with the video money," said Honey. "Doesn't that count for something?"

Jordan thought Honey was becoming pathetic. Both Powar and Honey were transparent to her now, and she just needed a rest from all of it.

"Of course it does, and you know it. I'm very grateful to you, but I'd like to go lie down and talk about this in a few days," said Jordan.

Jordan lay on her bed and looked at the ceiling. She was still in slight pain, but she had a clear head. She knew that other studios would want her. She was also certain that whatever offers were made, her mother would match or better them. Ever since she'd come to Hollywood she'd experienced its tension and not its joy. Honfleur, that's what I need right now, she thought. She had spoken to Genevieve only two weeks ago, and she really missed her. She knew Genevieve wanted her to try to make a go of it in the States, but right now all Jordan wanted to do was get on a plane and go "home" for a couple of weeks. She had some time. The premiere of *Smashpoint* was on the twenty-second. It could all work.

She called Air France and booked a flight for the next day. She would just pack in the morning and leave. She debated calling Genevieve or surprising her, but she thought she should call in case Genevieve wasn't going to be there. It was the middle of the night in France, so Jordan went to sleep dreaming of the countryside. She would call in the morning.

She woke up with the sun and decided to call right away. She was even more excited than the night before at the thought of leaving.

"Hello, is Genevieve there? This is Jordan. Who's this? Dr. Clement? What are you doing there? Is Genevieve all right?"

"How strange that you would call now, Jordan. I was just getting ready to call you," he said. "I'm afraid I have bad news for you. Genevieve had a heart attack early this morning. I'm afraid we've lost her."

"No! That can't be," she wailed. "No!" Jordan's body ached with a heaviness and a pain that she had never known. She felt faint, as if life were ebbing out of her, too. Genevieve was the only mother she had ever known, the only family she'd truly loved.

"Jordan! Jordan!" She could faintly hear the doctor's voice coming from the receiver on the floor. She picked up the phone again and continued to sob.

"Please try not to cry. Genevieve regained consciousness briefly, and she wanted me to tell you that she loved you and she doesn't want you to grieve. She told me that if anything happened, she wanted to be buried here immediately under the tree by the swing. She asked me to tell you not to come back until you were happier. My wife and I will take care of the house. It is now yours, of course. The last thing she told me was to tell you she believed in you and you would know what to do now. She said it was in your genes."

With that Jordan doubled over in pain and started throwing up blood.

After about a minute or so she managed to hang up the phone and hit the page button that ran throughout the house. It was very early in the morning, but she hoped her voice would be heard.

"Help, Grandma, help me." She was very weak, but she spoke as loudly as she could and then she collapsed on the floor in her own blood.

Honey came running in and saw her. "Oh, my baby!" she said as she felt her pulse and called 911. "This is Honey King. Please send an ambulance to 607 North Bedford. My granddaughter has collapsed and is bleeding from the mouth." She grabbed a towel and put it under Jordan's head. Although she couldn't imagine why, she dialed Powar's number. "This is your mother calling. Jordan is very sick and I have called an ambulance. We are going to Cedars."

"Oh, no, not you and Cedars again," snapped Powar. "I've never forgiven you for Daddy. What kind of trick is this?"

"Your own daughter is bleeding on the floor. This isn't a trick, you stupid girl. I hear the siren now." Honey hung up.

By now Andy was up listening to everything. Before the conversation was over he was already half-dressed.

"Oh, my God, Jordan. You just can't live with that woman without disaster befalling you," said Powar, rushing to put on sweat clothes.

In two minutes they were in the car and on the way to Cedars. In the fifteen minutes it took them to make it, Andy kept reassuring her. "Jordan is young and healthy. Whatever it is, I'm sure the doctors will take care of it."

"Oh, Andy," cried Powar. "I can't lose her now. I should have done more to help her. I'm going to kill my mother if she's responsible for this."

Andy left the car in the emergency zone, and they went running into the waiting room. Honey was waiting for them inside the door. "The emergency crew is working on her now," she said. "I still don't know what's wrong."

"What did you do to her?" said Powar.

"Knock it off, kid," Honey said.

"Let's just all try to calm down until we talk to a doctor," said Andy. "I'm going to find one." He turned and saw one coming toward them.

"Are you Jordan King's family?"

"Yes," they all answered.

"She has a bleeding ulcer that has ruptured, and it must be stopped before the internal bleeding gets out of hand and it's too late."

"My God," said Powar. "You mean she might die?"

"Let's just say that it's critical that we get her into surgery right away," he answered. "She's being taken now to fourth-floor surgery. Go to the waiting room there, and I'll come talk to you. The surgery could take two to three hours. She apparently has been ill for some time."

"How could you not notice?" Powar snapped at Honey. "She lives with you."

"And she works with you," retorted Honey, "and you didn't notice, either."

The wait on the fourth floor seemed interminable. From time to time Powar and Honey would just glare at each other and then go to their solitary thoughts. Andy was trying to smooth things over. "I'm going to the coffee shop to get some coffee and bagels. May I bring some for anyone?"

"I'm too nervous to eat, thank you," said Honey.

"She probably doesn't remember, but I eat when I'm nervous," said Powar. "Bring a doughnut and a bagel."

"I remember," Honey said quietly.

"Hurry back, Andy," said Powar.

He was back in fifteen minutes. They had just finished their snack when the doctor appeared. They all stood up at once.

"She's all right. Another thirty minutes and she might not have made it. We've removed the ulcerated area and sewn her back up. The next forty-eight hours will be critical because we don't want any surprise eruptions. I don't expect any, but we have to keep a close watch. You can't see her now. I suggest you all go home and get some sleep and come back tomorrow morning. There's nothing you can do."

"Nothing!" said Honey and Powar in unison. It was hard for women like Honey and Powar to do "nothing." They could fix anything.

"Thank you, doctor," said Andy. "We'll do as you suggest. C'mon, ladies."

Powar woke up at two A.M. It was impossible for her to sleep. She was so frightened for Jordan. She looked over at Andy and thought about waking him up, but then she thought better of it. Instead she looked at him and silently thanked him for being such an understanding person. She felt he needed his rest. It hadn't exactly been smooth sailing since their marriage. She got up quietly and went into her dressing room. She lay down on the chaise to read a script, but her mind kept going back to Jordan. How could she let her be there alone any longer? It just wasn't right. She put on jeans and tennis shoes and a sweater. She put a note on her nightstand saying where she was, and she crept out of the room.

The doctor said Jordan would be in room 302, and as Powar walked quietly down the carpeted hallway, she took care not to disturb the other patients. As she opened Jordan's door, so softly that it didn't make a sound, she saw Honey sitting there in the dark holding Jordan's hand, comforting the still unconscious girl, and she remembered how her mother had held her hand every night when she went to bed. For the first time in forty years she remembered the feel of her mother's touch. She was very surprised to see her mother. In this light, away from all the posturing of Hollywood, she saw a slight, gray-haired woman, who looked very much alone. The larger-than-life woman whom Powar remembered in costume after costume, sweeping across dance floors on the cover of *Vogue* magazine, was really alone in life. Whether justified or not, Honey's entire family had left her.

Powar took a step toward the bed, and Honey turned at the sound. She looked ashamed and embarrassed at being caught in such a vulnerable state. Without saying a word, Powar sat down on the opposite side of the bed and took Jordan's other hand. They stayed that way for a long time, enjoying the silent comfort of being on the same side for the first time. Jordan began to stir. Powar and Honey looked at each other hopefully.

Jordan's eyes were not open, but she felt as though she were floating on a cloud. As she became more conscious, her eyes opened and began to focus. She hazily saw Powar and Honey, and just before she drifted off again, she took each of their hands and brought them together over her heart and smiled.